Genevieve Ly ... Dublin, where ... actress. She be ... and was one o. ... Theatre. Ms Lyons gave up her acting career to bring up her daughter Michele, and has also spent time teaching drama and writing original plays for schoolchildren.

She lives in London, but spends much of the year travelling abroad.

Also be Genevieve Lyons

SUMMER IN DRANMORE

Genevieve Lyons

WARNER BOOKS

A *Warner* Book

First published in Great Britain in 1992
by Little, Brown and Company

Copyright © Genevieve Lyons 1992

This edition published by Warner Books in 1994

The moral right of the author has been asserted.

A CIP catalogue record for this book
is available from the British Library.

ISBN 0 7515 0381 9

Printed in England by Clays Ltd, St Ives plc

Warner Books
A Division of
Little, Brown and Company (UK) Limited
Brettenham House
Lancaster Place
London WC2E 7EN

*This book is for my sister Maria
and my brother Oliver,
and for Michele, with love.*

PART I

Chapter One

'You're useless, Briana, do you hear?' Miss Marshall's voice was cold. She stared at the girl standing behind her desk, head drooping, chin on chest. 'Sacred Heart, you're utterly useless!'

Briana's hair was heavy and dark. Her head seemed weighed down by it, and the teacher's diatribe. It sank lower and lower as Miss Marshall upbraided her.

'What shall I do with you? Can you tell me that? Hum?' Her voice squeaked. 'What in the name of the good God shall I do wi' you?'

Briana did not know the answer. She stared at the scratched top of the desk. Each scratch and groove was a familiar map, often perused yet mysterious and incomprehensible, the hieroglyphics of other, past pupils, grown up, gone, their dreams frozen in time, carved in the desk lid. Initials abounded: some flamboyant, some miniature, apologetic; some tentative, some neat. There was an arrow through a heart. A love-sick girl mooning over a fellow a long time ago. Where were they now? Briana wondered. Had their love been as strong as hers for Iain or light and fleeting, blown like smoke through the air?

She traced the etched curve at the side of the heart with her index finger. There was a lump near her nail. It was, her mother said, a result of pressure; the finger against the pen. Briana clutched her pen very tightly when she wrote. It was tension, her mother said. Well, how could she help

3

being tense when all she could think about night and day was Iain? Why would any girl of seventeen want to bother about mathematics when her mind was full of questions?

Did her cousin love her? What did those feather-light touches of hand on hand, finger against finger, mean? As much to him as they did to her? If he did love her, then was his love as grand as hers? Would Auntie Colista and Uncle Eddie forbid them to see each other if they found out? Who could care about mathematics with all that on their mind, for Pete's sake?

Briana sucked in her cheeks and veiled her eyes. She looked as if she were trying to disappear.

The sun blazed outside and a bluebottle flung itself relentlessly against the window pane, then gave up and rubbed its back legs together. A girl at the back sniffed and Tansy Quin giggled. She always giggled when there was silence. Tansy couldn't bear silence and got into a lot of trouble about her persistent sniggering.

'Tansy Quin, stop that at once or I'll have to ask you to leave the room,' Miss Marshall said severely. 'You are *not* stupid, Briana,' she continued, 'but you behave as if you were. You don't seem present half the time.' She has a point there, Briana thought, but her expression did not change. 'And you sit there, a daft look on your face, and don't listen to what I say!'

Briana examined her nail and saw it was torn and split. It would catch in her lisle stockings when she took them off. Her lisle stockings wouldn't ladder like the gossamer silk her mother wore for best. You only had to look at them, her mother said, and they disintegrated. Which was why she hardly ever wore them. She kept them for weddings and funerals and Christmas. They were too precious to be worn.

The ragged nail would catch the lisle stocking with an unendurable roughness that made Briana shiver thinking about it, then get angry. She hated ragged nails. She tried

4

not to listen to the voice that droned on and on, dripping like water into her head. Drip, drip, drip. Do boring thoughts, complaints and criticism, leave a rusty residue like a leaking tap on a bath? A brown line? Briana wondered, and smiled at her thought. A rusty brain would be like a walnut and not the milky colour they showed you in biology. Biology in the convent was mainly about the head and neck, arms and legs. She knew all the nerves and tissue and names of bones in those areas, but nowhere else. It was considered immodest for girls to learn about sex, so the torso was given a wide berth.

Exasperated, Miss Marshall said, 'Take that smile off your face, Briana O'Shea! Sometimes you behave like a second-former.'

Would she never stop? Briana kept her head lowered. Miss Marshall had a brown wart with three hairs sprouting from its centre at the side of her mouth. Her mouth would be turned down in a sarcastic twist. She was not really bad-looking, only the wart and the sarcastic droop to her mouth took away warmth.

Miss Marshall was her form teacher. She took the top class for maths and geometry, trigonometry and Latin. They were all subjects Briana had no aptitude for. No, she amended, she was stupid at these subjects, really thick. She was sadly lacking in logic. It was never obvious to her that if so-and-so equalled so-and-so, then so-and-so was the clear deduction. Everyone else saw at once what Miss Marshall was driving at. Some even pre-empted her occasionally by shouting out an answer, before she'd finished the question, but never Briana. She would sit stupidly trying to come to grips with what they were talking about and drive Miss Marshall mad with her inability to understand what was, after all, quite simple to everyone else. Briana was aware that Miss Marshall thought she did it deliberately. But she didn't. In those subjects she was obtuse.

5

One of the reasons Miss Marshall ranted at her so much was because Mother Felix who taught her English and history, and Sister Rose who taught her R.E., found her brighter than normal; a brilliant student, in fact. It was as if, Miss Marshall often reflected, they discussed two different girls.

'I'll have to speak to the Reverend Mother about you, Briana O'Shea, if you don't improve,' she said now to the bowed head.

The bell rang. That'll be Mourna, Briana thought. Mourna was her elder sister and also head girl, so she got to ring the final bell at four o'clock on Friday.

Both Miss Marshall and Briana sighed deeply with relief as the enthusiastic clanging pierced the air of the warm, sleepy classroom. Miss Marshall kept the windows closed which induced an alarmingly soporific atmosphere. She was afraid of draughts. Her little sister, whom she had adored, had caught a cold from sitting in a draught and the cold had turned to pneumonia and the pneumonia had carried her away, leaving a terrible hollowness within the teacher that nothing had been able to fill.

'God'n she hates you,' Tansy Quin whispered to Briana as desk-tops slammed and pencil and pencases rattled and satchels were filled.

Miss Marshall's back was turned. She was cleaning down the blackboard. White chalk-dust fell in a cloud on her navy blue cardigan. She had heard the remark and its unfairness hurt her. 'Never say that, Tansy Quin,' she said, turning and waving the buff at them. A spill of chalk-dust cascaded from the cleaner into the front row and caused Mary Brady to sneeze. Mary had asthma and Miss Marshall knew that. Mary Brady looked at her teacher reproachfully.

'I don't hate anyone,' Miss Marshall said. 'How could I go to Mass of a Sunday and receive the Holy Body of Christ if I hated Briana O'Shea, tell me that?'

6

The girls had all stopped their packing. They stood or sat, frozen by the teacher's voice, surprised by the emotion; obedient to authority addressing them, but indifferent to what she was saying, anxious for her to finish. It was, after all, last class Friday.

'I said Briana O'Shea was impossible and useless in these classes. I did *not* say I hated her. Is that clear?'

'Yes, Miss Marshall,' the class chanted in unison, eager to escape, longing to leave the stuffy classroom, aching for the liberating freedom of the weekend, away from the discipline of school.

'All right then. You may go,' Miss Marshall dismissed them.

Tansy Quin rolled her eyes at Briana and grimaced, and the two girls filled their satchels with homework and empty tuck-boxes.

'Janey, she's in a rare old mood today,' Tansy whispered. Then, 'God, we've got so much homework.'

'Well, I'm not going to worry about it.' Briana shrugged philosophically. 'We've that lovely dissertation on Japan Mother Felix gave us, and 'the quality of mercy' to learn and an essay about today – "What life is like in the fifties". Miss Marshall thinks I'm useless so useless I'll be. No use disappointing her!'

'Oh, Bri, you're awful!'

Briana gave a defiant snort. 'Well, she asked for it,' she said.

They walked down the wide corridor together. The passage smelled of wax and was lined with framed prints of great masterpieces, representations of the Virgin and Child by Murillo, Leonardo, Lippi and Raphael.

Half-way down the corridor another classroom door opened, and further down yet another, and pupils erupted into the corridor; fat girls, thin girls, tall and short girls, pretty and plain, all in their brown uniforms with brown and silver striped ties and cream shirts, chattering

7

like birds released from cages, unable to suppress their excited anticipation at the weekend before them.

'Girls, girls!' Mother Felix popped her head out of a classroom door. 'You are supposed to walk, not run. And talk quietly, not shout.'

'Yes, Mother Felix,' again in unison, and they were stilled, subdued, but only for moments. It was a useless command. The cacophony rose almost immediately, soaring higher and higher. At the end of the corridor they turned and ran down the stairs, a river now, a tide of children coming from all sides, running to freedom.

'Girls, keep your crocodiles, please.'

'Yes, Sister Rose.' Stemmed again, restrained, channelled obediently, slowing the pace, the impetus. But only temporarily.

Tansy and Briana walked side by side to the cloakroom. 'Doin' anythin' excitin'?' Tansy asked.

She had a moonface and was a favourite with the teachers because she looked gormless and their expectations of her were low. But she always did extremely well and they fancied the credit was theirs. 'Tansy uses her brain,' they said. 'Don't be fooled by her face.' Which, Tansy said, was a back-handed class of a compliment.

Briana pulled her blazer out of her locker. It was brown, worn at the lapels and elbows. It had the silver crest of the school stitched to the right-hand breast pocket and had once belonged to her sister Mourna.

'Oh, it's going to be great, Tansy,' she said, cheeks flushing in excitement. 'We have visitors tonight, it's my auntie's birthday, and tomorrow we go to Wicklow.'

'Oh, it's well for some!' Tansy said automatically in a hoity-toity voice. 'What you wearin' to the dance?'

'You going to the hop Sunday?'

'Yeah, but I can't wear my pink again. I wore it last week an' the week before an' they'll know it by heart, that bloody dress. But me mam won't buy me a new one. She says I

8

have to wait until I get a job, an' then I'll have as many dresses as I can afford. D'ye ever hear the likes of that?'

'Well, it's got a bow at the front, hasn't it?' Briana asked.

Tansy nodded. 'What's that got to do wi' it?'

'Well, tell your mother to take off the bow and put something else there – a flower or some lace.'

'Oh, *your* mam can do things like that, Bri, not mine. My mam would make a muck of it, never fear. Jasus, you shoulda seen what she did to my sister's First Communion dress. It 'ud break your heart. It was a tragedy.'

'Listen, Tansy, the lads in the tennis club like you. It doesn't matter what you wear. You're never short of a partner.'

'That's true!' Tansy looked pleased.

It was true, Briana thought, as they slammed and turned the key in their locker doors and she followed her friend out to the bicycle shed. Tansy was popular with the boys. She had a natural acceptance of people, a bounteous good nature. She was the most uncomplicated person Briana knew. The boys accepted Tansy and she accepted them in a way that was beyond Briana's scope. Shy and bold by turns, Briana always took refuge in games. She tried and failed to be honest with the opposite sex. Except with Iain. Iain was different. But he wouldn't be at the hop.

They unchained their bikes and pushed them past the tennis courts to the back gates of the school. Briana turned her face to the sun, squinting in its pale glow. She saw Mourna serving to that snobby Patty O'Brien-Moynihan. Her sister's long legs were the colour of milky tea and her tennis skirt was shorter than regulation allowed. Sister Benedict, the house mistress, was always writing letters to Mr and Mrs O'Shea about it but Briana's mother was proud of her eldest daughter's legs.

'Let her show them off,' she'd say. 'You never know where they'll take her.'

Mrs O'Shea was an optimist and visualised a great future for her brood.

Mourna had left school. She was two years older than Briana who was seventeen and doing her finals, but the nuns had asked the O'Sheas to allow Mourna to be head girl and help out with the younger girls in the lower classes in the convent in this year of her 'coming out', and Mourna, who was nothing if not amiable, happily agreed.

Her mother, tight-lipped, said: 'Typical of the nuns! Getting unpaid slave labour!' But Mourna only laughed.

Briana sighed as usual when she came upon her sister. She was always bowled over by Mourna's beauty. Who is that lovely creature? she would ask herself, then realise a second later, it was her sister. Then came an immediate twinge of jealousy, then guilt and shame.

I am a terrible person, she would tell herself. I must be the only person in the world who feels like this about my own sister. It wasn't as if Mourna was ever nasty to her. She was kind and nice. But it was easy to be nice when you were beautiful, Briana thought, when God had given you long legs and eyelashes, fine skin and clouds of curls and eyes the colour of cornflowers or violets, depending on what she wore.

'She's gorgeous, your sister,' Tansy said now, staring at Mourna as she raised her racquet aloft and hit a ball.

'Yeah, I know,' Briana said tersely. Then she cheered up. 'I'll see Iain,' she said.

'Your cousin?'

'Yeah.' Briana plucked a daisy from the grassy verge beside the tennis court. She sat on the saddle of her bike, tiptoes on the ground to balance, and picked off the petals, one by one. 'He loves me, he loves me not, he loves me, he loves ...' She dropped the daisy, looking suddenly dejected. 'But I think he loves Mourna.'

'He'd be mad if he didn't,' Tansy said tactlessly. Her voice had that awestruck tone people used when they spoke of Mourna. Briana shrugged despondently and Tansy giggled. 'Oh, come on, Bri, quit kidding and let's go home. I'm starving.'

They wheeled their bikes out of the school gates. Tansy lived up the street from the O'Sheas so the girls rode home together, standing on the pedals to get under speed and up an incline, then taking their feet off, sticking them out in front as the incline dipped and they sped down the road, the wind tearing their hair. Briana's was damp at her ears and the breeze through it was wonderfully cooling. She gave an exuberant yell as they pedalled along Dorset Street and over the Dargle Bridge and past the Archbishop's Palace.

John Charles McQuaid himself, Archbishop of Dublin, nipper of pleasure in the bud, a prelate devoted to gloom and doom and above all guilt. Best not to ask what you were *not* allowed to do, it was easier to ask what you *could* do. He was the real ruler of the city, a dictator of the morals and sexual behaviour of his flock; he was the third party in every bedroom in Dublin.

But Briana was not thinking of John Charles McQuaid as she passed his palatial mansion. She was brimming with a happiness that threatened to bubble over. Life was out there; she could feel it, touch it. Wonderful things were going to happen, she knew, and Iain would be there with her. She let out another yell, stuck her legs out stiffly in front of her, took her hands off the handlebars and went careering down the hill before the steep climb to Griffith Avenue.

'Yaa ... hoo ... eee!'

'Janey Mac, do you want to get killed?' Tansy shouted, but her words were caught by the wind and blown away. 'Briana O'Shea, what's up wi' ye?' she asked herself as she pedalled furiously to catch up with her friend's flying figure, legs pumping, hair blowing, cheeks tingling, yelling at the top of her voice like a Red Indian.

She didn't manage it until they were nearly home.

11

Chapter Two

Mrs Oonagh O'Shea was in the kitchen when Briana arrived home. Briana shouted, 'See ya!' at the gate, and Tansy, who was puffing with the effort of keeping up with her friend, said nothing, just waved and got off her bike, pushing it down the Avenue to her own house.

Briana walked her bike down the short path and around the side of the semi-detached. She unlatched the bockity, waist-high gate and wheeled the bike down the garden path to the tool shed at the bottom.

Her mother waved at her through the kitchen window. The sight of her face gave Briana another jolt of emotion, a tide of love so overwhelming that she charged into the kitchen and, when she reached her mother, twined her arms around her and buried her face in the soft flesh of her neck.

'Oh, Mummy, I'm so ... so ...' She couldn't think of a word and her mother laughed softly, gave her a hug and continued making pastry. Oonagh turned to Auntie Molly who was licking some fresh whipped cream off her fingers.

'She's a terrible child, is Briana,' she said gently, her voice full of love.

'She is that,' Auntie Molly replied, nodding and smiling at her niece. 'Aren't I going to get a kiss at all?'

'Oh, yes,' Briana said ardently, and smacked her lips damply on her aunt's cheek.

'You think the sun, moon and stars shines outa these kids,' Auntie Molly said.

Molly Moran was married to Oonagh's brother Tom. She was dark and exotic – like Linda Darnell, Briana thought – and her past gave her a glamour that fascinated her nieces. For Molly had been married twice, and that was a rare thing in Holy Catholic Ireland. However, her two marriages were perfectly acceptable to the Church because Sean O'Rourke, her first husband, had died, leaving Molly a widow with a small son, Banan, to take care of. But Briana, Emer and Mourna could only contemplate with awe the fact that two men had desired her and wed her. They always stared at Auntie Molly and wondered about that.

Auntie Molly was pretty, that was true, but she was not exceptional. She had a firm, strong body, a radiant skin, and wild dark hair. She was temperamental – a fire-cracker, Tom Moran said. Unpredictable. Advantage taken of any underdog filled her with righteous indignation, and, as life was terribly unfair, she was often in a state. 'Fit to be tied!' Briana's mother said.

'Your Auntie Molly gets easily worked up,' Briana's father, Gabriel, would say, and nod his head.

But the girl's attempts to copy her were nipped in the bud by their mother.

'There'll be no temperament in *this* house!' Oonagh O'Shea was very firm on that point.

Now Molly shook her head and said, 'I'm going down there on Monday and setting them free. I don't care if I have to go to jail.' Her eyes were snapping, Briana saw, and she looked at her mother for enlightenment.

'It's the birds in Fogarty's,' Oonagh said in explanation. Briana still didn't understand. She looked from one to the other.

'There's a shop, Briana love, called Fogarty's, down the Quays,' Molly said. 'He's selling birds. Poor little things!

13

Linnets and starlings, half a crown each. Larks, even. All caged. Singing their hearts out. Trapped, they are. It's an outrage, a disgrace! It's got to be stopped and I'll do it if no one else will.'

It was something Molly often did; acted when others merely tutted. Briana's father said, with something like admiration, that Molly had the courage of her convictions.

'But then, it runs in that family,' he said.

Auntie Molly's family had been in the old Irish Republican Army and had all been heavily involved in Ireland's struggle for independence. Molly had been a courier when she was a little girl and had proudly 'done her bit for Ireland's freedom'. She rarely talked about it, and when Briana asked her would close one eye and put her finger to her lips and say nothing at all.

Molly had a pool hall in Abbey Street. It had been her inheritance from her first husband who had died so tragically when Molly was expecting their first baby.

Briana found everything about Auntie Molly romantic and Irish and sad. She reminded her of the great Gaelic heroines, Maeve and Deirdre; beautiful, brave women, going forth to fight for their freedom or their lovers.

Oonagh O'Shea was as unlike her sister-in-law as she could possibly be. A plump faded blonde, her body and face were soft and shapeless, but to her family hers was the most beloved female form on the face of the earth. Her eyes were cornflower blue, set in laughter creases. Hers was a plain and kindly face and body.

'Briana, take your paws off that cake,' she said now, severely, as she caught a glimpse of her daughter's furtive fingers scooping out some of the jam and cream from the sandwich sponge cake.

'Here.' Auntie Molly held out the bowl she had whipped the cream in and Briana took it and commenced cleaning it with her finger.

'It's not good for you,' her mother said, bustling about

14

the kitchen. 'Here, Molly, do these for me, will you?'

She handed Molly a tray of sausage rolls, a little brush and a bowl of melted butter. Molly dipped the brush in the primrose liquid and painted the uncooked pastry that covered the sausage meat.

'What time's the others coming?' Molly asked, her thick eyebrows drawn together in concentration.

'About seven,' Oonagh said, arranging sliced apples on pastry cases glazed with apricot jam. 'Do you think two tarts will be enough?' she asked her sister-in-law, and Molly dissolved into giggles.

'Oh, an' I'm sure two tarts's enough for anyone!' she laughed.

'Enough of that, Molly. Pull yourself together, for God's sake! Remember the children.' Her mother didn't look at Briana.

Molly winked at the girl and said soberly, 'Oh, surely 'twill be enough. You've got the sponge sandwich and the bowls of strawberries.'

'Briana, eat an apple,' her mother commanded.

'Oh, Ma, can't I have something else?' Briana looked with greedy eyes at the goodies on the long wooden table. The delectable feast made her mouth water.

'No, not yet. You can eat as much as you like later, when the others come.' Her mother was adamant. 'Now, darling, get out from under our feet, and don't go messing the drawing room. You can skip practice today.'

The piano was in the drawing room.

'Peggy's in there now fixing everything,' Oonagh added.

Peggy was the maid-of-all-work, the only help Mrs O'Shea had. She had been part of the family since Briana could remember. She had been midwife and babysitter, cook, cleaner and housekeeper for the O'Sheas since they were married. However Peggy was never treated as an inferior and they divided the work between them, the mistress doing an equal share to the maid.

15

Their days were never-ending. Oonagh and Gabriel O'Shea had six children and she was expecting the seventh, a fact that was still a secret from her husband. Mourna the beautiful, born of their passion, was the eldest. Nineteen years old! Oonagh couldn't believe it when she thought about it. Mourna, finished already, her leaving certificate done, head girl, enjoying her status and freedom, poised on the threshold of great things. Then came Ardel, eighteen, Briana, seventeen, Laughlin, sixteen, Emer, fifteen, and Emmett, thirteen. Now, suddenly, most unexpectedly, she was pregnant again.

She had not told her husband yet because she could not be sure how he would react. She looked at Molly as Briana left the kitchen. 'Oonagh, what is it?' Molly glanced at her sister-in-law shrewdly. 'Something's up an' you might as well tell me as nurse it to yourself.'

'I'm pregnant again, Molly, an' I don't know what Gabriel is going to say when he finds out,' Oonagh said, her eyes clouded with worry.

'Doesn't he know then?' Molly asked. 'There's not much Gabriel misses.'

'No, he doesn't know. Oh God, Molly, I can't bring myself to tell him. He's so content at the moment. He feels we're nearly done, with the debts, the bills, the mortgage. And they've promised him a raise and a promotion, think of that! It'll destroy him when he finds out.'

Gabriel O'Shea worked in Barnet's, the big fashionable store in Henry Street. Barnet's paid well for, they said, they liked to employ a nice class of person so that the gentry felt at ease.

'Ye can't have our customers trying to understand the Dub-be-lin accent,' Mr Wilmot, the Managing Director was fond of saying. 'In this store all our staff are expected to sound posh.'

'Mind you,' Oonagh continued, working all the while, popping the tarts and the sausage rolls into the oven, 'we're stretched. Fully stretched,' she added, tightening her lips and sighing. 'Money's tight and how we'll manage another …' She shook her head. She had little circular curls held firmly by brown slides. One of them fell out and the the curl came loose and hung down beside her cheek in a corkscrew. Oonagh felt it and picked up the clip. 'Rosie's heavy on the perm,' she muttered. 'She doesn't know when to stop and always goes too far. It'd be a ball of frizz if I didn't put these in.' She held out the clip, then re-anchored the corkscrew of faded blonde hair deftly and looked at Molly.

'You're lucky,' she added, 'being naturally curly. My hair doesn't do what I tell it. It's a disaster to manage.'

'Now, Oonagh, you always look lovely, so you do. Your hair's always gorgeous,' Molly lied. She didn't mean what she said. She deplored poor Oonagh's hair but the family didn't believe in telling the truth when it was hurtful. They always encouraged and admired each other. It made everyone feel better.

'Anyhow, he'll guess pretty soon,' Molly said. Oonagh knew she was talking about her pregnancy.

'He will, God knows.'

'He has only to look at you an' you get caught,' Molly said.

'Ah now, that's not fair, Molly. Isn't it fourteen years since Emmett was born.'

'Yes, well …' They both knew that Molly was thinking of the last three pregnancies that had ended in miscarriage.

Oonagh sighed again. 'God, ye know Molly, every time we get straight something banjaxes it.'

'Well, isn't that life!' Molly said with equanimity.

'Is Tom driving your lot over?' Oonagh asked. Molly nodded but didn't reply. She was staring out of the kitchen window into the back garden. Mourna sat on the swing. She seemed to be having an intense conversation with her brother Laughlin.

'She's so very beautiful, Oonagh,' Molly remarked, staring at Oonagh's eldest with something like awe.

'I know. I'll never understand how me'n Gabriel managed it.'

She joined her sister-in-law at the window, watching the couple in the garden under the apple trees.

'I wonder what they're talking about?' Oonagh said anxiously. 'They look so serious. I hope nothing is wrong.'

'And what could there be?' Molly asked. 'Ah, kids! They get themselves into such states over nothing. They don't know the half of it, do they?'

'Deed'n they don't. Still, I wonder …'

'Leave them, Oonagh love, leave them,' Molly said, and let the little lace curtain fall as she drew her sister-in-law back to the cooking.

Chapter Three

Out under the apple trees Mourna pushed her foot into the hollow that the children had worn away over years of prodding the swing into motion.

'I'll tell Daddy. Don't you worry about it any more,' she said to Laughlin.

She stared at her brother's thin face. He was small for his sixteen years. Mourna looked at him tenderly. There was something very vulnerable about him, defeated almost, at his age, disillusioned before his life properly began. Mourna's strong maternal feelings ached to soothe and comfort him. He's like a fawn, she thought, wary, frightened, apprehensive.

'We'll fix it for you, never fear.'

He didn't look convinced. 'Will Da believe you?' he

asked doubtfully. 'It's so weird.'

'Oh, he'll believe me all right. And it's not weird, Laughlin. Only the people who do it to little boys are weird.'

'I'm sixteen!'

'Yes, I know. But you're too young to have that anxiety. To find out about ...' she waved her hand '... that sort of thing.'

The breeze cooled her cheeks and sent shivering fingers through her cloud of dark hair. It felt lovely. She shook her head to enable the air to circulate.

'It makes me feel sick,' he said, shaking, fear snaking through him. 'I hate it.'

She took his hand, feeling the fine tremors course through his body.

'Well, forget it now. It's Auntie Dot's birthday and I can see Mummy and Auntie Molly in the kitchen, so there'll be lots of lovely food and fun. So forget it now and enjoy this evening.'

'I don't think I can.' Laughlin stared up into the trees, the nerves in his face atremor.

'Yes, you can, if you make up your mind to,' Mourna said firmly, 'There's Auntie Molly waving. Let's go in. I'll talk to Da.'

'No, I'll stay here. You go.'

'All right, Laughlin. See you later.'

She left the swing and walked up the garden path to the kitchen. At the door she turned.

'Don't worry,' she called.

'It's all very well for you,' Laughlin muttered. 'Nothing gruesome ever happens to *you*.'

Mourna waved again and sighed. She hadn't really understood what he was talking about. A Christian Brother didn't do that sort of thing, did he? A Christian Brother was almost a priest.

Almost, but not quite. A priest had standing in the

19

community, a Christian Brother had none. A priest was welcome in the golf and country clubs, but not a Christian Brother. You had to be humble to be a Christian Brother, or you got bitter and resentful about your second-class status. Christian Brothers only became Christian Brothers because for some reason they failed to become priests. Weren't clever enough. Didn't have their leaving certificate. Were illegitimate. The clergy rejected bastards. Unless you were born in wedlock, you couldn't be a priest in Ireland.

Laughin had been happy in Belvedere with the Jesuits. Oh, it was supposed to be an awful place, according to James Joyce, an intellectual if ever there was one, but it suited Laughlin down to the ground.

But last year Gabriel O'Shea had found himself short of money. He could not meet expenses and cuts would have to be made. He talked it all over with Oonagh, showing her the figures, agitating over where they could make a saving. There was the mortgage, electricity, coal, gas and food bills. They both decided they were being as frugal and as economical as possible in those departments. That left education, the crippling expense of the school fees. Either the girls would have to be taken out of the convent or the boys from Belvedere. There was no question that one should have a better education than another. *All* the girls would have to go to a National (God forbid) school, or the boys, *all* of them, would go to the Christian Brothers. It was a terrible choice, but one that had to be made.

'I'm not sending the girls to a National school, an' that's final,' Oonagh said firmly. She plumped, as she always did, in favour of the girls. She was convinced that boys needed a less refined education. Girls grew up to be wives. They made the home, created the atmosphere in which their children grew up. A man needn't know all that much apart from his work. It was the wife who should know about Beethoven, Shakespeare, Rembrandt. Men went to football

20

matches, played tennis, fell asleep during the second act of the opera. As long as they had a comprehensive grounding in grammar, maths and logic they could carve a career for themselves, no trouble.

Girls were different. A girl with taste and style and knowledge could catch a husband in a higher social or economic bracket. She could get her man promotion. She could make a different to a husband's progress through life. And above all she had control of her children and could guide and direct them to the top.

None of the relations or friends could understand Oonagh's reasoning. Their daughters' academic progress interested most people far less than their sons'. They tut-tutted at Oonagh, but she stuck to her guns.

'But Laughlin, Ardel and Emmett will be the bread-winners,' they'd say. Oonagh stubbornly shook her head.

'Laughlin, Ardel and Emmett can only go as far as their capacity allows,' she would insist. 'Their wives can push them further. Mourna, Briana and Emer can aim very high if they are educated, erudite and polished.' There was no shifting her. 'It's all decided,' she'd say. 'Gabriel can get Laughlin into the bank. He's just what they want.'

Like Barnet's, the Bank of Ireland wanted well-spoken employees. Mr Wilmot, Barnet's Managing Director would give Laughlin a grand reference, and he would pass the exam easily. Unlike Briana he was good at maths, Laughlin was. Yes, he'd be a first-class bank clerk.

Ardel would go into business. He was canny and already made a profit returning jam-jars, swopping and selling second-hand comics. Oonagh was not sure how exactly he earned all the money he had and shied away from finding out. Sometimes Ardel's spiv-like qualities alarmed his mother but she calmed her fears with the thought that even if he bent the rules a little, he was far too quick-witted to be caught.

Emmet would be a priest, that seemed sure. He was a boy

21

of ardent faith and had already told Oonagh that he wanted to be a missionary.

'I want to go to Africa, Mammy, and convert the little black babies,' he said, eyes shining.

Oonagh didn't want him to be a missionary. That was excessive in her opinion. Africa was too far away. She planned more on a parish in Galway or Cork, somewhere they could go on holidays, to visit him. Then a parish of his own, somewhere poor in Dublin, Cabra or Drimnagh, where she would have easy access to him and could look after him. Oh, not obviously, but she could ask him home for dinner, feed him well ('My mother's the best cook in Ireland' – this to his colleagues, a throw-away line, she could imagine it), give him presents of knitwear, that sort of thing. Then, eventually, Bishop. The rewards of service. Position. Power. She was too superstitious to go much further than that, but in the deepest recesses of her mind she did not draw the line at allowing a wisp of a thought to drift through: First Irish Pope!

Yes, the boys' paths seemed clear-cut. When it came to the girls, Oonagh was certain of one thing: she wanted them to make good marriages. Boys could not transcend their social and economic background in the way that girls could. It was possible for Emer and Briana to marry into a profession. The thought made her shiver with excitement. A rising young barrister, solicitor or doctor. Even Des Keogh, the chemist's son, who was expected to follow in his father's footsteps and inherit the shop in Baggot Street one day, caused a speculative gleam to appear in Oonagh's eyes. Whereas Laughlin, Ardel and Emmett, having no precedent, would hardly be likely to aspire to doctoring or the law. No, the girls could aim high and it was unlikely, Oonagh argued, that with the good convent education they were receiving they would be satisfied with yokels.

And Mourna was the jewel. With her beauty, grace and charm the world was her oyster. Oonagh didn't want to

22

spoil her chances by any lack of educational polish.

So the boys had been taken out of the relatively academic Belvedere and sent to the more rough-and-tumble Christian Brothers. It had been a difficult choice.

The youngest and the eldest had thrived on the change. Emmett became even more religiously (rather than spiritually) fervent. Ardel's entrepreneurial flair flourished. The Brothers lacked the Jesuits' acumen and were more easily duped by Ardel's sharp practices.

However, sensitive Laughlin did not find the transition easy. He found the cloddish Brother Seamus indifferent to finer feelings and incapable of understanding his love of culture, his natural inclination towards poetry, painting and music rather than football, hurling or gym. In fact the Brother teased him unmercifully about his preferences, loudly and often.

Brother Nathan was completely different and initially Laughlin stuck close to him, finding in him a sympathetic and understanding audience.

Little by little, however, Brother Nathan's friendship and attention took on an alarming furtiveness and tactile familiarity and Laughlin, too gauche to object, far too nervous of authority to report what was happening, grew scared of the Christian Brother's wandering hands. Sometimes he thought he imagined it; the light touches, the fleeting pressure in areas that both horrified him and gave him a sick thrill of terrible pleasure, but gradually logic told him there was method and accuracy in these seemingly random caresses.

For a month now Laughlin had been preoccupied with his problem, ill with guilt and worry, frightened and perplexed by turns. At last, driven by the cancer-like anxiety that gnawed at him, he told his sister. He had always been close to Mourna. She had sensed his unease and had asked him on several occasions what ailed him, but he had found himself incapable of actually putting his problem into words.

This evening in the welcome shade of the apple trees he had blurted it out and had been reassured by her response. Not completely, though. His father might not believe him; might think he had invented his bizarre accusation. After all, in Laughlin's mind there was something foul and disgusting in what had been happening to him and his father might chastise him, or else despise him merely for suggesting that such things happened.

But he was not afraid of his father and knew that Gabriel would be fair. He was glad Mourna was going to speak to him because he was sure he could not. The very idea of trying to get the words out appalled him. It had been difficult enough with Mourna, to whom he could say anything. But Da? Jasus!

He looked upwards at the lattice of branches scattering the last of the white blossom on the grass beneath.

What was that other feeling? The one beneath the anxiety and fear? It lurked there like slime at the bottom of a pond, threatening sometimes to engulf him. He shook his head. He could not bear to think it through, it shamed him so.

He sighed. Mother and Auntie Molly were waving at him. They were looking out of the window again. He shook off his gloom. Mourna was right. Forget it for tonight. Tonight there would be good food and cousins around, great crack and laughs. Tonight he would put all thoughts of Brother Nathan aside and try to enjoy himself, as he had once done – oh, ages ago.

Chapter Four

'Let's have a cup of tea,' Oonagh said to Molly in the kitchen.

'That'd be lovely, Oonagh. And how is the family? We've not talked about them at all except to say how gorgeous Mourna is.'

'Isn't she though?' Oonagh O'Shea's heart soared with excited pride.

'She can have anyone she sets her mind to,' Molly said. Oonagh's mind flicked lightly over visions of Mourna in a house in Blackrock, married to a doctor; in a detached Georgian home on Adelaide Road, married to a lawyer.

'She can indeed, no doubt of that,' she said to her sister-in-law.

'And Laughlin? He seems a bit down in the dumps out there,' Molly said. She glanced out of the window where Laughlin mooched under the trees. There was a dejected droop to his body, an anxious nervousness about his movements as he pushed the swing or pulled a blossom-laden branch, that revealed an inner tension even at this distance.

'Oh, he'll be fine,' Oonagh said briskly, putting tea in the scalded pot.

'Roac's to do the Bank exam next year,' Molly said. Roac was her son by her second marriage to Oonagh's brother Tom.

'Won't that be smashing for him?' Oonagh said warmly.

'Laughlin will be taking it too. They might be together. Wouldn't that be grand? And how's Mena?' Mena was Roac's sister.

Molly didn't reply. 'Here comes Mourna,' she said, and at that moment Mourna came into the kitchen. She kissed her mother and her aunt.

'Get out of your tennis clothes, Mourna, and put on something real nice,' her mother said. 'Uncle Eddie and Auntie Colista are coming and I want them to be impressed.'

'An' how could they help it?' Molly twinkled at Mourna, giving her an affectionate hug.

'Oh, Ma!' Mourna laughed.

'Mummy! Call me Mummy,' Oonagh insisted.

Eddie and Colista were the rich members of the family. The Bensons lived on the fashionable South side, had a Bentley, and belonged to Kilcrony, the most exclusive country club in Ireland. They played golf, had a boat, and were members of the R.D.S. and Arts Club. Colista, who was Oonagh's sister, had one boy, Iain. She had always longed for a girl and Oonagh had pushed Mourna towards her in the hope that Colista would 'take the girl up' and introduce her to the 'right sort of people'.

'Wear your best,' Oonah said and gently shoved her daughter out of the kitchen.

Briana heard Mourna's footsteps on the stairs. As always her heart plummeted and she was overwhelmed by a feeling of depression. It was not that she did not love her sister. Truth to tell she adored Mourna and would cheerfully die for her. In her fantasies she was sometimes Mourna's willing slave – and therein lay the problem. Mourna made her feel inferior in every way. She did not mean to, she would not even understand what Briana was talking about if she had answered truthfully when Mourna asked, 'What is the matter with you, Bri? Why must you

26

always be so sullen?' If Briana had said, 'You make me feel so inferior, fat and ugly and gross,' her sister would not have known what she meant.

Briana was not fat or ugly or gross but Mourna made her *feel* that way. Mourna's natural beauty was a reproach to other girls, as if there was some laziness in them, something they neglected to do to make themselves as beautiful as she. Beside her Briana felt inadequate.

She turned her face to the wall as Mourna came into the room.

'You okay?'

'Hurrumph,' Briana grunted in reply and shook her book, indicating that she was engrossed and did not want to talk.

'Oh, okay, be like that. Anyhow, that's *my* book, Bri, that you're reading, and I'll thank you to give it back when you're finished.'

Briana had forgotten that she had pinched it without asking, and the rule was if you wanted to borrow you had to ask permission. It was *Anna Karenina* and Mourna was reading it herself. Her reasonableness only aggravated Briana the more.

'And,' Mourna continued, 'I *was* going to be considerate and ask what time you'd like the bathroom, but now I won't. I'm going in there first.'

Briana couldn't argue. She was always getting herself into situations she hated, all through her own silly fault. She bit her lip in vexation and tried to read, but the words ran together meaninglessly and she lost the thread.

'Oh!' she yelled, turned around and threw the book at her sister. 'You beast! Oh, you are horrible.'

'What have I done?' Mourna looked at her wide-eyed, ducking the book expertly. 'Janey Mac, I think you're mad, Bri.'

She opened the wardrobe and rummaged around at her end. One of the infuriating things about Mourna was that she rarely lost her temper. It was difficult to get her riled. Adults were always saying she was sweet-tempered.

I'd be sweet-tempered too if I was that beautiful, Briana thought when she heard their remarks. It seemed to her that if she had her sister's beauty she would indeed be perfect.

Mourna took out a blue dress with a sweetheart neckline that Briana had coveted.

'I'll wear the green, Bri, if you'd like this,' she said.

'Keep it,' Briana snapped ungraciously, hating herself with all her heart, infuriated with herself that she could not accept the dress that she would dearly love to wear.

'Okay, okay.' Mourna put the blue dress back in the closet and closed it firmly. She picked up her toilet bag and moments later Briana heard her banging on the bathroom door.

'Come on, Emer, out. I gotta go *now*. I can't wait.'

Briana knew it was an idle threat but it always worked. No one wanted to take the chance of calling someone's bluff and finding out they'd told the truth.

Emer spent ages in the bathroom anyway. She was expecting to get her first period and spent hours on the toilet waiting for it to arrive. Briana, lying on the bed, was overcome with remorse. She could hear her mother's voice saying, 'Little birds in their nests,' and she shivered and went into the corridor. Suppose Mourna died? Suppose something awful happened and those were the last words she had spoken to her sister? Suppose she had to live with the fact that she had been totally unreasonable to poor Mourna who had only offered her one of her best frocks?

'Mourna, Mourna, I'm sorry. I'm so sorry,' Briana cried.

'That's okay,' Mourna said serenely, then rolled her eyes. 'She's certain she's going to bleed to death when it comes,' she giggled.

Mourna and Briana had been having their monthlies for ages and felt infinitely superior and terribly sorry for Emer.

28

'She'd spend all day on the john if she was let,' Briana said.

'I heard ye! I heard ye! Shut up, y'hear me, or I'll tell Ma!' Emer yelled from inside the bathroom.

'Well, prove it then. Come outa there or I'll burst.'

Mourna and Briana collapsed on the floor laughing. There was a frenzied squeal from the other side of the door.

'You're beasts, so you are. I'll tell Ma, so I will, then you'll be sorry.'

'Oh, Emer, quit it and come on out. Mam told me to get dressed. She'll be up in a moment with Auntie Molly, an' I'll tell them you wouldn't leave your favourite place. I'll tell them to have your sandwiches sent up to you. I'll tell them ...'

Emer opened the door. She stood trying to look dignified in the face of Briana and Mourna's mirth.

'You are horrible, and I'll tell *Da*, so I will.'

She flounced away leaving Mourna and Briana looking after her.

'She's nuts,' Mourna said.

'Can I have the blue, Mourna? Please?' Briana asked.

'Sure, Bri,' Mourna said, and went into the bathroom.

'Don't bang the doors, girls,' Oonagh shouted from below.

Molly said suddenly, 'I'm tired of Tom's little floozies, Oonagh. I'm so tired of it all.'

Oonagh didn't want to hear about Tom's infidelities. Such confidences made her acutely uncomfortable. She wanted everyone to play the game according to the rules. She hated people suddenly revealing unpleasant aspects of their lives to her. It was unexpected and it alarmed her. They all knew that Joe drank and that Rita was broke. No one minded discussing that. But when people who appeared happy together suddenly showed another side to their relationship and expected you to be helpful and sympathetic, it annoyed her. It was as if they had been cheating, pretending they were all right. And it was scary, it showed unpleasant things just beneath the surface. What Tom was doing, Gabriel could be doing too. Oh, she knew he was not, but it shook her.

She wished Molly would shut up and did her utmost to change the conversation. And, after all, it was Oonagh's brother Molly was criticizing. It would be disloyal of Oonagh to get into such a discussion, and anyway she simply didn't want to know about such things even if they were true. So she asked her sister-in-law where she had purchased her lovely red frock.

'That colour suits you, Moll, it really does. You're lucky. So few people can wear such a strong colour.'

'I got it in Switzer's,' Molly said, giving her a funny look.

'Well, you should have gone to Barnet's. Gabriel would have got you family percentage off.'

'Really? How very nice.'

She glanced at her sister-in-law. Was Molly being sarcastic? Oonagh couldn't think why.

'Is Joe coming tonight?' Molly asked, and Oonagh raised her eyes to heaven. Joe was the black sheep of the Moran family. He did not live in a proper house and had an allotment in Finglas. His wife was common, Oonagh said. Masie Moran was a lazy cow who didn't seem to care what people thought of her. She stayed on the outskirts of the family, never getting too close. She did not allow the niceties of what Oonagh considered 'their sort' to trouble her in the least. But then, as Gabriel said, she had a lot to contend with. Joe's drinking was getting worse.

'Yes, he is. With that woman. She's a disgrace.' Oonagh shook her head. 'No shame. She has no shame at all. She's always letting the side down.'

Molly smiled to herself. She was not a Moran by blood and she sometimes found their rules and regulations about what was 'done' and 'not done' a trifle amusing. It

30

was not as if they were gentry. But the Morans had a sense of their own importance that was far greater than, in Molly's opinion, the rest of the world accorded them. Still, they were a warm and loving family and she was grateful to be part of it. If only Tom would keep his eyes and his hands to himself.

'Joe still lives in that …?' she began.

'Yes, yes,' Oonagh cut her off swiftly.

Joe and Maisie lived in a caravan. Oonagh deplored the fact. It brought the family down. It was a blot on their name.

'Like tinkers,' she said with scorn. The other members of the family reacted each in his or her own way.

'A caravan's no good unless you have a car to attach it to!' Granny O'Shea said.

'I'd love to live in a caravan. I'd park it on the end of Dun Laoghaire pier and watch the waves and read *Dracula*,' Briana said.

'Poor Uncle Joe. It seems terrible he can't afford a house. I wish he could get work,' Mourna said.

'You could be a saint livin' in a caravan, makin' sacrifices,' Emmett said.

'Bloody stupid fool,' Ardel muttered. 'He could turn it into an ice-cream van or sell sausages offa it outside football matches and make a mint, if only he had the brains.'

'Maybe he *likes* it,' Emer said.

Tom Moran shook his head. 'Opportunities squandered,' he said.

'He drinks too much.' Oonagh, his sister, used her most judgemental tone. 'It'll be the finish of him yet, you mark my words.'

Molly followed her into the drawing room. It was a rather grand term for what was really a room kept for 'best'; a parlour.

They would sit around the fire there in winter and talk. There would be no fire tonight, not in late June and the

31

weather glorious, so Oonagh had arranged a Japanese screen across the empty fireplace. They would sit around it anyhow.

Oonagh checked the sherry and the whiskey and gin, then went next door to the dining room.

The long mahogany table had been pushed to the wall and was laden with plates of sandwiches; sliced white pan neatly quartered and containing ham, tomato, tinned salmon and cucumber. Peggy had put her heart into them.

'The sandwiches are lovely, Peggy,' Oonagh said to the plump porridge-faced woman who stood beside the table. She wore a slide in her grey hair, holding its iron waves down, a black dress and a large white apron tied at the back. She watched Oonagh's mouth as she spoke, frowning in concentration, lip-reading. She was a little hard of hearing. Her face broke into a broad, grateful grin at Oonagh's words, revealing gaps in her teeth.

'Oh, tank ye, Mrs O'Shea. Tank ye. Yis, they're works of art, if I say so meself. Each one done carefully.'

They were both looking with some complacency at the sandwiches when Molly shrieked, 'Linen napkins? Oonagh, are you mad? They'll be destroyed! Peggy, get paper ones.'

'But the Bensons are coming,' Oonagh cried.

Molly looked at her sister-in-law. 'God'n you're a terrible snob,' she remarked. Oonagh coloured.

'How dare you! I am not.'

Peggy was looking questioningly at Oonagh who nodded reluctantly at her. She did not want to be thought a snob.

'Oh, all right. The paper ones are in the top drawer, Peggy, with the coasters.' She indicated the sideboard at the other side of the room.

'As if I didn't know that!' Peggy tutted as she gathered up the linen pile and scuttled over to exchange them now she was sure Mrs O'Shea wanted her to.

32

'I hope you're right about them, Molly. I just want the guests to have the best,' Oonagh said piously.

Molly hooted. 'Ye just want to show off your style to the Bensons,' she said. 'Tell me now, if they weren't coming, and it was just us an' Joe an' Dot, would ye have them out then? The good ones, would ye?'

Oonagh blushed, but had to admit Molly was right. She hated to be seen through but made the best of her discomfiture. She would always admit it if she was wrong.

She went into the hall, looked up the stairs and called, 'Laughlin, are Emer and Ardel home?'

His voice was sharp. 'Why don't you ask them yourself?'

Oonagh looked at Molly, who had followed her. 'Good question,' she said, then shouted up the stairs, 'Laughlin, don't be cheeky or I'll tell your da.'

'I don't know about Emer,' Laughlin shouted back, 'Ardel's not up here. Bri is in her room and Mourna's in the bathroom, so it's no use telling me to get a move on, I'll have to wait till she's finished. An' that might take a year!'

Oonagh grimaced at Molly. 'I'd die for another bathroom in this house.' Then, 'Get a move on, Mourna,' she yelled.

'Okay, Mummy.' Mourna's voice sounded muffled.

Oonagh smiled softly. 'Ah, that one,' she said, leaning on the banister. There was a world of affection in her tone.

Chapter Five

Ardel could hear the whole conversation from the kitchen. He had slipped in as soon as he saw his mother and Aunt Molly leave it to check the dining and drawing rooms.

He looked around, sniffed the cooking smells of apple and sausage, opened the Aga door, snitched a sausage roll, blowing on his fingers as he did so. He palmed a layer of sandwiches off the top of a plate, got some greaseproof paper and wrapped his loot up, putting the packet in his pocket.

'Now where …?' He looked around the kitchen. 'Ah, there they are.' His eye fell on a stack of empty jam-jars. His mother or Peggy put them in different places (like an alcoholic's booze, he thought) each week, knowing he would try to find them, hoping he wouldn't. They didn't want him to have them but they couldn't be angry with him when he took them.

'These jars are not for your sole benefit, Ardel,' his mother would say, and give him some scratched or discoloured ones. He only got a penny for those. The man in O'Shaughnessy's gave him a penny ha'penny for a good jar, half pound size, and threepence for a one pound size in good condition.

Ardel whistled through his teeth – 'A Soldier's Song', the National Anthem. It was in his head because they had been playing it in band practice this afternoon, last lesson before he came home. He played flute and there was a smashing triddle-diddle-ah solo he had just at the end. He loved that bit and emphasized it now as he sang and whistled.

> 'For Erin's cause come woe or weil,
> We'll sing you a song (triddle-diddle-ah), a so-o-o-jer's
>   so … o …ng,
> Yes, we'll sing you a soldier's song.'

He filled his pockets with the jam-jars as he sang, selecting the best, got a string bag from behind the door and filled that. He was stacking five slightly damaged jars beside the gas cooker when Peggy came in. He put his finger to his lips and winked at her. He knew she couldn't resist him.

34

She went over and grabbed a fistful of his thick, black, curly hair and pulled his head back. He looked at her with his bright blue eyes guileless and innocent.

'Ouch, Peggy!'

'Put back a couple a dacent wans,' she hissed at him.

'Ouch, Peggy, leave off!'

'Do as I say or I'll tell yer ma.' She jerked his head back further. 'An I'll lave ye bald!'

'All right, all right, all right.'

He took one out from his inside pocket, put it on the floor, started to remove another from his hip pocket, and as Peggy relinquished her hold on his hair, dodged around the table and was gone from the room.

'Was that Ardel I heard?' Oonagh asked, coming back into the kitchen.

'Yes'm. An' he's taken the jars.'

Oonagh, however, had more important things on her mind this evening.

'Molly, I'll have to change,' she said. 'Look, it's getting late an' me in my curlers an' not dressed.'

'The Bensons would be shocked now if they saw you like that, Oonagh,' Molly said teasingly, her eyes twinkling.

'Well, they would. I'm sure Colista wouldn't be caught dead looking like this.'

'Nonsense, love. Colista puts her hair in curlers, just like the rest of us.'

Oonagh sighed. 'She has a bathroom of her own! Can you imagine the luxury of that?'

'Ah, Oonagh love, you'll have your own some day,' Molly said placatingly.

'I wish you were right, Moll,' Oonagh said wistfully. 'Only the way things are now, an' the state I'm in, it seems very remote.'

At that moment they heard Gabriel's key in the door.

'Oh lord, Molly, there's Gabriel. Go and have a sherry with him, would you? A sherry or a gin. I'll take only a moment to put some powder on.'

'Don't rush, Oonagh love. There's no hurry.'

Molly untied the apron Oonagh had lent her and hung it on the back of the door. She gave a little shove to Oonagh who left the kitchen and arrived in the hall as Gabriel O'Shea shut the front door behind him.

'Hello, love,' he said, kissing his wife's cheek. 'Molly!' He smiled at his sister-in-law. 'I suppose there's great goings on with the family expected?'

'Well, Gabriel, what'd you expect?'

'Keep you hair on, Oonagh love, I just asked.' He smiled fondly at his wife who shook her head.

'Now keep out from under my feet, Gabriel. Go with Molly to the drawing room and have a drink, the both of you. Only one, mind,' she warned. 'I want enough for the others.'

Gabriel and Molly exchanged glances. He took her into the drawing room and was pouring a whiskey when his wife put her head around the door,

'Mind the cushions. Don't lean on them.'

'I thought that's what they were meant for,' Gabriel said mildly.

'You know what I mean ... until later. I don't want visitors coming and finding them all squashed.'

'Visitors? Your sisters and brothers!'

'The Bensons,' Molly murmured. 'It's the Bensons she's thinking of.'

'Your Mother, Gabriel. Tom's collecting her.'

'That's nice of him, Molly.'

'Ah, he's a dacent sort.' Molly laughed, and there was a slight acidity in the sound. Oonagh gave a little hoot before she could check herself. She looked at Molly and then turned away and left quickly.

'What'll you have, Molly?' Gabriel asked.

'Whiskey, please, Gabriel. There's nothing to beat a Paddy.'

36

Gabriel laughed. 'Don't let Oonagh hear you saying that. She thinks Paddy is unladylike.'

'Ah, sure, Gabriel, I don't lay claim to being a lady,' Molly said, laughing.

'Has the place been in an uproar?' he asked.

'Not really. It's been *uncomfortable*; not being able to sit down, having to keep our hands off the food. But, no, Gabriel. It has not been in an uproar.'

'Do'ye know, Molly? I dread these blasted gatherings. Oonagh takes it all so seriously. You'd think she was on trial for her life.'

'Well, and we'll sit here in the quiet and relax, Gabriel.'

'Yes. And have a last bit of peace before the savages arrive.'

And they sipped their drinks, laughing as they did.

Chapter Six

Emer sat in the curve of the stairs. She didn't want to go upstairs and she didn't want to go down. She felt separate from the family – from everyone. She felt she lived in a glass bubble. Invisible glass. No one could see it was there. It removed her emotionally and physically from everyone, kept her remote, apart. So far as she was concerned her life was already planned but she couldn't seem to get it through to anyone else that there was no need for her to do certain things, no need for them to worry about her.

She was going to be a star. She could see her path directly in front of her and she took a small step forward each day, building a stairway to success. No one had told her how to go about it. She *knew*. She concentrated on her dancing and deportment lessons, on music and fencing. She worked at English and adored Shakespeare. She read a page every day – and if she did not understand it, well, that didn't matter too much. The words sounded lovely. She tended her skin, and her bright red hair. She walked with her back straight. She practised voice exercises. She was in no hurry. It would come.

She wished, though, this damn period would come. It was time, and she didn't like to be kept waiting. She had worked out when Briana and Mourna had started theirs and added a couple of months. But that span had passed and she was, by now, nearly a year behind them both. God, would it never happen? She wished she was anyone but Emer O'Shea waiting for her first period to arrive. She hated Mourna's sympathy, Briana's superiority. Even Ardel, who knew nothing about women's periods, kept making remarks.

She was retarded, that was it. She was backward. She'd never grow up, never have babies. But who wanted babies anyhow? Horrid little squirming things that squalled, dribbled milky messes and wet themselves. People always thought you wanted to hold them. Parents thought they were doing you a favour if they gave you their precious infant to carry, and all the little bundle did was pee on you or throw up all over your shoulder. Betty Lynch, Emer's best friend, had a sister with a new baby and every time she went to Betty's house she was given the child to hold, like it was a big compliment or something. Well, she *hated* it. She didn't want babies, ever, but she wanted her period. Then she could start being grown-up. She wondered how you could stop yourself having babies. How you could prevent them. She wanted to end up in the arms of someone like Tyrone Power and she wanted to experience whatever excitement was available in the love department, but she did not want to get pregnant.

38

She puzzled over it on the stairs. Betty Lynch said her sister wasn't having another. She said she practised rhythm. Betty Lynch had swung her curls out around her like a fan, twirling and singing:

> 'I got rhythm,
> I got music,
> I got my girl,
> Who could ask for anything more?'

Who could indeed? But Emer didn't believe it. It couldn't be that simple. Ellie Shaugnessy in the corner shop said that her mam had said that if you wore Tampax you couldn't get pregnant and that seemed more likely, but Emer wasn't sure about that either.

Emer thought about films. She planned to go into films. She did not want to go on the stage. She did not want to get involved with Chekhov or Ibsen. No, she wanted to be more like Doris Day. She wanted to spend a lot of time being recognized, mobbed, pursued, idolized, photographed, being the person everyone looked at. And you couldn't be that with babies. They took up all your time – look at Mam! You never saw Joan Crawford or Doris Day in those pin-up pictures with babies.

There was no doubt in her mind that she would succeed. The material was not promising. She did not have Mourna's beauty or Briana's subtle charm or Ardel's devastating if shallow good looks. But she had an energy, a vitality, that made up for what she lacked.

Her mother rounded the corner, startling her.

'Emer – what are you doing, darling?'

'Waiting for the bathroom.'

'But you've just come out.' Oonagh sat beside her daughter on the stairs.

'I know, Ma, it's just that I ... well, you see ...'

'Darling, if you forget all about this period, it'll likely arrive,' Oonagh said gently.

'In a gush! All over me! In front of everyone!' All Emer's fears burst out of her, hot tears cascading down her face like a tap suddenly turned on.

'Darling, no. It won't come like that. You'll get a warning; pains down your legs, cramps. Then you'll know it's on its way.'

'Really, Mummy?' Emer looked at her mother hopefully.

'Really, darling. Now I tell you what I'm going to do ...' She stood, took Emer's hands and raised her to her feet. 'You're going to come into my bedroom with me and I'm going to give you some proper sanitary towels to wear. I bought you a belt today. It's got lace on. I think it might be a good idea for you to wear it and a sanitary towel, so when the period comes you'll be prepared.'

Emer felt as if a great weight had been lifted from her. It was such a simple solution and she had never thought of it. She felt light and airy. She leaned her cheek on her mother's sleeve.

'Oh, thank you, Mam,' she said.

'Mummy,' Oonagh remonstrated. 'Mam is what working-class people call their mothers. And we're not working-class!'

Emer rubbed her mother's sleeve with her cheek.

'All right Ma ... Mummy.'

Chapter Seven

Emmett knelt on the floor beside his bed and dreamed of Africa. It would be hot there, almost too hot to breathe. He would wear a white robe, like a nightshirt, like his altar-boy garb, and sweat a lot. The black babies, gorgeous little creatures who would hang out of him, clutch on to his priest's garments and swing out of his arms, were waiting there to be converted. They knew nothing yet of the Lord Jesus and Heaven and how beautiful early Mass could be and how good it felt to be close to God.

There was a crucifix at the head of his bed but he did not look at that. It made him feel uncomfortable. Brother Francis said that Emmett's sins had helped nail Jesus to that cross; that every time Emmett broke God's law – or rather, more exactly, the laws of the Holy Roman Catholic Church in Ireland – he, Emmett, drove the nails that pinioned Our Saviour to his cross, deeper and deeper into His frail body. Emmett couldn't bear to think of doing that; the thought appalled him. So he averted his eyes from the crucifix and stared instead at the framed picture of Christ the King which hung on the wall. It showed a much more cheerful Jesus, a young Jesus, about the same age as Emmett himself. The Child was smiling and giving His blessing. Emmett liked it and found it easy to talk to the precocious and highly coloured face. The picture gave him a feeling of companionship with Jesus, a warm feeling that they were contemporaries and friends.

Emmett didn't enjoy family parties and hoped he could get out of tonight's celebration early and escape back here to his little bedroom and be peacefully alone. Or else spend the evening with Granny O'Shea.

His bedroom and Emer's on the other side were attics really. Little sloped rooms under the roof. Gabriel had had the loft made habitable as his family increased. Ardel and Laughlin shared a room, and Mourna and Briana, and of course his mother and father had the big, front master bedroom over the drawing room, but Emmett didn't envy them. He loved his little attic room and thanked God he did not have to share with anyone else. He valued his privacy, and when he shut the door on the world he felt at peace.

41

He looked now out of the high, sloped window on to the street. Denis Cowley was practising on his new skates. He kept bumping into trees and practically knocking himself out. He'd go, wham, into a tree, fall down, pick himself up and begin again. Denis was clumsy. He was famous in the district for his awkwardness. Emmett had seen him fall off a bus once, hanging on to the bar, then losing his grip and ending up in the gutter.

'You'd think he'd learn,' Emmett muttered to himself. Emmett never played in the street with Denis even though he was a friend. Emmett didn't like Griffith Avenue. He didn't like school, except for R.E. And he didn't like his relations. Auntie Molly and Uncle Tom, Auntie Dorothy and Uncle Ben, Auntie Colista and Uncle Edward, Auntie Rita with her sad face, and worst of all Uncle Joe and Maisie.

He refused to call her Auntie. She was a bad woman, a sluttish, careless female. And Uncle Joe got drunk and disgraced himself. It made Emmett hot and embarrassed to think of Uncle Joe. The other aunts and uncles merely pried into his thoughts, his dreams, his life. They wanted to *know*. They asked him things he had not even worked out for himself. Even when he answered 'What are you going to be when you grow up?' with 'A missionary', they felt free to smile in a superior way or, worse, become patronizing.

'Oho, you'll change your mind,' they said. 'Wait till you discover girls,' they tittered. They were so *certain*. He hated having to endure their invasion of his privacy, having to be polite. But however their intrusion rankled, it was nothing compared to the emotions his alcoholic Uncle Joe aroused in him.

The sight of Uncle Joe unsteadily raising his glass to his lips made Emmett shiver with fear and loathing. His father laughed indulgently at Joe's behaviour under the influence of Guinness or Paddy or both, but Emmett saw only a man rendered incapable and unpredictable and therefore dangerous. He also saw a man bereft of dignity.

He had come across Uncle Joe relieving himself against the wall of the house and the sight revolted him so much that he took the pledge.

Emmett's mother said that at least Joe had caused some good, but Emmett refused to acknowledge that.

'I'd a done it anyhow,' he told her.

He saw the Ford drive up the Avenue now. Uncle Tom drove slowly, and parked carefully. Denis Cowley stopped his self-destructive battering of the tree and stared at the car. He had told Emmett that after he'd cracked how to manage the skates he wanted a bike and after the bike he wanted a car. He adored cars. Emmett thought he'd have to improve considerably before he would be allowed to drive anything at all. Even a pram was not safe with him. Emmett wondered briefly if Denis Cowley needed glasses.

Uncle Tom stepped out of the Ford and nipped around to the front passenger seat. He opened the door and commenced prising and pulling, tugging and encouraging Granny O'Shea out of her seat. Behind her the three young passengers were pressed together like sardines, waiting until they too could unbend and escape.

'Look at him, tryin' to extricate her,' Molly said to Gabriel with a smile.

They had heard the car and were leaning over the sofa, peering through the lace curtains.

'Those lads must be creased,' Gabriel said. 'They're big lads too.'

Molly's two sons and her daughter had followed Granny O'Shea, quick as a flash. They stood now on the pavement, stretching and stamping their feet as Tom Moran guided the old lady up the path to the front door.

Gabriel, looking out of the window, couldn't hear Granny O'Shea, but Uncle Tom's face was flushed and the faces of the young ones behind looked angry. Only Banan seemed indifferent. Granny O'Shea was not known for pulling her punches.

Emmett heard the front door opening and Molly's high voice calling: 'That you, Tom? Granny O'Shea? Come in, come in. Oonagh sent me to welcome you. She'll be down in a minute. She's putting on a face.'

'Yerra, sure she doesn't need one!' Granny O'Shea cried. 'Isn't she lovely as nature intended? I don't hold, meself, with cosmetics. They were never intended for respectable women. Only whoors and tarts.'

Roac and Mena giggled.

'Granny O'Shea, *please*.'

Oonagh had arrived downstairs in a pale grey skirt and a neat little silk blouse with embroidery on the collar. Over it she was wearing her grey angora cardigan that Gabriel had got for her in Maurice O'Brien's, the most exclusive shop for jumpers in Dublin. Her hair was brushed out and she had a touch of rouge on her cheeks, a dusting of powder on her nose and a smidgeon of lipstick on her lips.

'The children'll hear,' she said, taking Granny O'Shea's black double-breasted coat and her hat. 'They don't understand words like that.'

'What'd'ye bet they don't!?' Granny O'Shea's small black eyes glimmered in the deep folds of flesh that surrounded them. Her hair was fine and sparse, rationed across her skull, her skin tissue-soft and crushed in a thousand crinkles. She had a few stiff hairs on her upper lip and she smelled of mothballs. She exasperated Oonagh, who couldn't understand why Emmett adored her.

'I lost the soap in the bath this morning,' she said, her mouth quivering. ''Twas cronic! Janey Mac, Gabriel, I was flounderin' around, lookin' for it fer ages. Nearly lost my balance. I was scared.' She stared up at her son, lips trembling, vulnerable as a baby. 'I coulda drowned! I was slippin' an' slidin'. 'Twas comic, Gabriel, so 'twas.'

'Don't worry, Ma. I'll fix you those little handles at the

44

side of the bath. The inside, you know, help you to get up.'

Granny O'Shea looked relieved. Everyone was standing around her in the hall. She waved her hand.

'That'ud be grand, Gabriel, grand. Now lead me to the booze!'

She pushed away helpful hands and left Oonagh holding her coat as she followed Tom Moran into the drawing room. She chose the biggest and most comfortable armchair to sit in.

'What'll you have, Ma?'

'A large Paddy, my son,' she cried. 'And don't stint yourself.'

'No, Ma, I won't,' Gabriel laughed, then turned to his wife. 'Oonagh love, what'll you have?'

She compressed her lips. Some people didn't do what was right, refusing to behave, in her opinion, as they ought, and it irritated her. Women should ask for a dry sherry or a gin, not whiskey. That was for the men. Yet Granny O'Shea and Molly, who should know better, drank their Paddy without batting an eyelid. It simply was not nice. But then, after all, Oonagh reflected, Molly was the proprietress of a pool hall, a fact that could not be overlooked. It accounted, in Oonagh's opinion, for her appalling breaches of etiquette. How could one retain a ladylike demeanour in a pool hall?

Oonagh sighed. What would the Bensons think? They were, after all, top drawer. She hoped they would not notice what the others were drinking. At least Granny was drinking whiskey. Last time she had been at a party at the O'Sheas' she had insisted on drinking Guiness – and nothing, in Oonagh's opinion, looked more common than a lady drinking Guinness.

Emmett came into the room and stood shyly at the door, waves of colour staining his cheeks, then receding and leaving him pale and worried-looking. He had Brylcreemed his hair and flattened it down, but it stuck up straight at the back and gave him a comical look.

45

'Emmett lamb, come here to yer granny.'

He moved towards the old lady but was waylaid by his Uncle Tom. A jovial, rotund sort of a man with furtive eyes, Molly's husband was the proverbial fool who rushed in where angels feared to tread.

'Well, Emmett, an' you have grown. You'll be leavin' school next. What do you plan to do then?'

He was silent, his head drooping. Tom persisted.

'Well, answer me, boy. What do you plan to do then?'

'Be a missionary, Uncle Tom.' Emmett muttered it reluctantly.

'Ach, now! Ye don't want to be botherin' with religion, boy. That's all right for women, but a man's got better things to do with himself, eh, Gabriel?' He nudged his brother-in-law and Emmett seethed. 'Takin' vows of celibacy and chastity, God's name! That's for old maids, isn't it? Ah, now, you wait a few years until ye grow up a wee bit more, then ye'll discover the good things of this world an' ye'll never look back. Am I right, Gabriel?'

'Well now, Tom, his mother seems to think this might be the genuine article. A real vocation.'

'Ah, sure, God help him then.' Tom shook his head at the tragic thought. 'To enjoy the pleasures of the flesh is a gorgeous thing, an' for anyone to give it all up for life is beyond me. Beyond me. It is, Gabriel, an anathema.' He looked up to see his wife staring at him, and moved away and began to talk to Oonagh.

Bastards, bastards, bastards! Emmett's thoughts were in turmoil. He had promised himself he would allow none of them to ruffle his calm, but here he was after a few words from Uncle Tom, in a state, fit to be tied. How would he endure torture? How would he stand inquisition if this was how easily he lost composure? How dare Uncle Tom? What did he know about it anyway? Emmett simmered, but kept his face smooth and expressionless, which was at least some small victory. Talking as if he was not there!

46

Treating his feelings with all the sensitivity of an elephant! Had he no tact? No diplomacy? No. The trouble was, to people like Uncle Tom, young people didn't count. Adults thought they didn't understand basic English. They behaved as if young people were deaf or stupid, and their own careless words had no impact. Well, they were wrong.

He caught Granny O'Shea's bright stare. She beckoned him over. 'You come here, *alanna*. Stand by me,' she said, and he made his way over to her. 'They pry, don't they?' she whispered to him. 'Nothing's sacred. Some men have the tact of a flea. Think they have the right to comment on anything. Think they know it all.' She smiled at him knowingly. 'Yerra, you got to keep your sense of humour, Emmett. What do they know?' She glanced over at Tom who was now talking to Gabriel. They were laughing hugely and judging by the sound it was a ribald joke. 'I'll tell you, Emmett. Nothing! Now you make yourself useful and plump up my cushions and top up my drink every time my glass looks even slightly depleted.'

He was glad to oblige. He said nothing and she did not expect him to.

Banan, Roac and Mena stood near the window, talking and drinking Aunt Oonagh's apple cider. It was tingly and fizzy and made their heads hum.

'Now mix, you lot,' Tom instructed, but they paid no attention and talked only to each other.

Mourna came into the room and all heads turned and remained fixed, staring at her as she made her entrance. It was unconscious but she stayed still in the doorway just that moment longer, allowing her appearance to register. She stood there in her full-skirted apple green dress, smiling at everybody.

'Ah, so the belle of the ball's arrived,' Tom said, and whistled. 'God, ye've turned into a lovely woman, Mourna.'

'Ye don't have te tell her, she knows,' Granny O'Shea said.

47

Oonagh thought, she could be a film star like Maureen O'Hara. Take the world by storm. Although, on reflection, that would involve hard work on Mourna's part, and what Oonagh visualized ideally was a man providing the wherewithal to keep her daughter Mourna in the luxury her beauty entitled her to, without any effort on her part.

'What'll ye have, pet?' her father asked.

'She'll have a dry sherry, Gabriel,' Oonagh said firmly.

'Where's Laughlin and Ardel? And Emer? And Briana?' Granny O'Shea sounded petulant.

'They're on their way.' Oonagh went out to hustle the rest of her family downstairs. The drawing room would be full soon. She'd have to encourage Tom and Gabriel to take the rest of the adults next door to the food. Maybe she should get Peggy to open the French windows into the back garden. Oonagh would have to see that the Bensons didn't actually go out. If they did they'd see the drains and the waste pipes and the bins against the back wall. But if they sat near the French windows *inside* the dining room, they would have a lovely view of the rose bushes, the square of lawn, then the apple trees at the back.

'Laughlin! Ardel! Emer!' she called. Then, 'Oh, Emer,' as her daughter came downstairs, 'can you run up and send the others down quickly?'

'I'll do what I can, Mam. Laughlin is in the bathroom, and Bri is sulking, and God knows *where* Ardel is. He went out ages back.'

'That boy!' Oonagh frowned. 'How can he go out when we're expecting visitors? He'll be the death of me, so he will. Anyhow, Emer, go upstairs and tell Laughlin and Briana to come down this minute.'

Emer looked at her mother. An icy look had come over her face. 'Oh-oh!' Emer exclaimed. 'Okay, Ma, I'll tell them.'

'Mummy. Call me Mummy, darling.'

Emer raced back up the stairs, eager to deliver the

ultimatum. 'Mother is getting *very* angry, Bri,' she shouted righteously. 'Laughlin, she's *furious*. She said *at once*! Or else.' She delivered the message with relish then the doorbell rang and she ran down to open it. She nearly collided with Banan in the hall. Her tall brooding cousin caught her arm, making her feel uneasy, 'Oops! Hello, Emer. Your da sent me to let them in ... whoever it is.'

He always made her feel stupid. He had a curiously offputting manner and a lack of humour that made the quips that rose easily to Emer's lips, wither on them unuttered.

She opened the door and he sloped off down the hall.

'Hello, Auntie Rita,' Emer said with false enthusiasm. Auntie Rita was another person who put out the light of cheer with her air of depressed melancholy.

The oldest Moran sister was a sad-faced, penniless widow who apologised for herself constantly. She had brought up her two children on her own and how she managed no one even hazarded a guess. They all felt that they ought to admire her yet couldn't quite bring themselves to because of her attitude, which was martyred. However, they harboured a guilty sense of responsibility towards her and surreptitiously sent her cast-off clothes and handouts at Christmas and Easter, and felt embarrassed by her poverty. It made them uncomfortable, as if somehow it was their fault.

'Are we too early? Oh, I'm sure we're early, Emer. Hello. Brigid, say hello to your cousin.' Emer and Brigid, who were great friends, fell on each other, loudly squeaking. 'Des, say hello. Where is everyone? Don't say we're the first.'

'Oh no, Auntie Rita, indeed'n you're not.' Emer remembered her manners and ushered her aunt into the drawing room.

Rita greeted everyone then sank down with a sigh of relief on the sofa, sticking out her ankles which were swollen, contemplating their unappetizing appearance and shaking her head regretfully,

'God'n it's good to sit down,' she said, smiling deprecatingly, a little-girl grin which sat oddly on her drooping mouth and eyes. 'I bin on them all day. Never sat down once, since seven.'

'Why doesn't she keep it to herself?' Molly asked Oonagh *sotto voce*.

'So have I, been on my feet since seven, I mean,' Oonagh whispered back, 'but I don't go on about it. Oh, Molly, we are awful!'

Molly nodded. She liked Rita, admired her even, but deplored her relentless implied criticism of their comparative comfort.

When Gabriel gave her a drink Oonagh saw with relief she was sipping a gin. But then, she reflected, Rita nearly always did the right thing, the thing you hoped she'd do. She never caused offence. She knew which side her bread was buttered on, Oonagh thought unkindly. But her dress looked so shabby, well past its prime. Oonagh immediately felt guilty as she always did when she mentally criticized her eldest sister.

'Wouldn't you think she'd *do* something?' Oonagh asked Molly in a sibilant whisper.

'But what, Oonagh? Rita is no Joan Crawford who can go out and snaffle herself a William Powell, because he can see clear as day that under that drab make-up she's a star! This is real life and she's an exhausted and penniless mother-of-two whose main consideration is somehow to get through the day.'

Oonagh glanced at Molly's flushed face. 'I suppose,' she said doubtfully.

The rest of the family were arriving in a steady stream. Voices were raised in greetings, the conversational level rose. Emmett shrank against the bookcase and wished he was a hundred miles away.

Ardel breezed in. He hadn't changed his clothes but was so full of charm that even his mother forgave him. He was taller than his brothers and joined in the male innuendo easily, flirting with all his female relations from Granny O'Shea down.

'Granny O'Shea, God bless us, I thought you were Bette Davis in person come to visit us! Isn't it younger you get not older!'

Granny O'Shea was delighted. 'Silly old fool, I think she believes him,' Tom said to Gabriel.

'Ah, sure, why not? 'Twon't hurt anyone, will it?' he replied.

Ardel also counteracted the slight awkwardness of Uncle Joe's arrival. When he walked into the room a hush fell like a blanket, and everyone looked at him, trying to assess his state, but Ardel greeted him with such *savoir-faire* that the sticky moment passed. Joe was not drunk so the company relaxed and continued their conversation.

Smoke from cigarettes curled up into clouds over their heads, shrouding the room in a blue haze. Gabriel refilled glasses as they emptied and the hard edge went off everybody. Only Joe seemed strained. He was pale and he shivered, his face beaded with sweat. This, Oonagh knew from experience, meant he had been holding on without a drink until he got to the party. He desperately needed one now. You could see him staring at the drinks tray while he greeted his relations with false fervour. His eyes were softly bloodshot, blurred in his face as if put in their sockets by uncertain fingers, and when Gabriel gave him a whiskey he took it in both shaking hands, tossed it off then poured himself another larger measure as his brother-in-law watched him with something like pity in his eyes.

Maisie, Joe's wife, didn't look at him but kept her eyes averted. Her hair was dyed red and it didn't match her complexion. She wore bright lipstick and drew her brows in half-moons over her eyes with a black pencil, without thought or consideration for the natural line. She looked as if she wore a mask. Molly said she had a heavy hand with the make-up.

Ardel felt sorry for her. She was such a mess but she didn't know why. She had been born without a sense of colour or style and her pink nylon blouse clashed horribly with an emerald green skirt that was far too short and revealed bony knees like rocks. She tried very hard to fit in, be one of the family, but was unsuccessful and awkward. Privately she told her husband she thought his family stuck-up and cliquy. He told her never to criticize his family or he'd belt her one. He sometimes hit her, but only when he was very drunk. He regretted it and suffered terrible remorse afterwards, but she told him that in that state his blows were inaccurate and easily dodged. So far. She lived in fear that some night he'd get lucky and hit his target and she'd fall and crack her skull. But she loved him, worshipped him even, and her starved soul put up with endless cruelties in the hope of a kindness or a need he might reveal to her. Buried in the horrors of her daily existence with him there was still that faint hope.

Ardel gave her a sherry and told her she looked the bee's knees in her frilly pink, and that made her feel much better.

Briana arrived downstairs as the birthday aunt and her family arrived. Dot and Ben Moran hugged her, and each of their eight children offered a dutiful cheek. Mary, Clare, Jamie, Roger, Angela, Tina, Dec and Maggie Moran trailed behind their mother and father like a line of ducklings. Dot and Ben were always linked. They seemed to have been born in tandem. Ben was madly in love with his wife and was not afraid to show it, much to everyone's embarrassment. Displays of amorous affection were frowned on and considered theatrical but Dot and Ben paid not a blind bit of notice to the disapproval they engendered.

'Ah, here come the love-birds,' Granny O'Shea shouted from her chair, chuckling. Dot and Ben were not put out. Dot blushed with delight and touched her husband's arm. He looked at her tenderly, and laughed. 'You can say that again,' he said, then greeted his sister. 'Oonagh, you look ravishing.'

She coloured and shook her head. 'What nonsense!'

'No, it's true,' Ben cried, and Gabriel asked what he'd like to drink.

'Ah, Dot first,' Ben said, infuriating Gabriel.

'I was going to! You're nearer,' Gabriel said somewhat sharply.

'Now, now, Gabriel, don't get irritated,' Ben said, irritating his brother-in-law even more. 'Dot is a princess and has to be treated as such,' he continued, and Gabriel realized he was clutching the whiskey bottle white-knuckled. He caught Tom's eye, relaxed and winked.

'Tell him what you did this morning,' Dot said, smiling girlishly at the company. Her long blonde hair was worn in fluffy Betty Grable curls.

'Shirley Temple, watch out,' Granny O'Shea had been heard to remark.

'Ben likes it this way,' Dot confided in Oonagh when she suggested it was time for a change, that her own hairdresser Rosie would shorten it and give it some shape and style, and perhaps a perm. Oonagh had to agree that her besotted brother still thought his wife was eighteen. She wore pink rouge and frilly little-girl frocks that Briana coveted but made Dot look like an ageing dolly.

'Tell them, Ben,' she reiterated coyly now, and Oonagh cast her eyes to heaven while Molly smiled indulgently as if Dot was one of the youngsters.

'Well,' Ben said obediently, 'I got up ...'

'Before the dew dissolved,' Dot interrupted. 'That's the nicest part.'

'And went out into the fields ...'

53

'In his dressing-gown ...' Dot was hugging herself in delight, listening, interpolating, reliving the morning.

'And picked her ...'

'A bunch of wild flowers,' Dot finished rapturously. 'Oh, he knows how I love wild flowers.'

'And I strewed them all over her bed,' Ben concluded triumphantly.

'Wasn't that romantic?' Dot asked, completely unaware of the humour she had aroused.

'Bet that jacked up the laundry bill,' Oonagh muttered to Molly.

'Don't be unkind, Oonagh. At least he loves her,' Molly whispered back. She was staring at Tom who was laughing at something with Gabriel. Peggy was hustling the young people out into the garden. Only Mourna, Banan and Emmett stayed, although uninterested in the grown-up conversation.

'What is she talkin' about?' Granny O'Shea asked.

'Ben picked wild flowers for Dot on her birthday morning, in the dew, and scattered them on her bed,' Molly said loudly.

'Oh God, damp dandelions all over the bed at six a.m.,' Granny O'Shea hooted.

'Maybe you've not had anyone love you that much!' Dot said smugly.

'I've had someone love me *this* much!' Granny O'Shea said triumphantly, pointing to a huge round pink diamond on her finger. 'That's better any day an' wild flowers.'

'Oh Gor, Ben, she's going to try to spoil my day, I know she is,' Dot wailed, and he put her in a chair while Gabriel got her another drink. 'She can't bear anyone else to be in the limelight.'

Captain O'Shea, Granny's sailor husband, had brought the diamond back to her after one of his voyages and the general consensus of opinion was that it had been stolen, or at least illegally come by. Grandfather O'Shea was a careful man who tended to frugality rather than impulsive generosity, so the family felt it must have been a bargain, and the only way such a perfect gem could have been cheap was if it had been contraband.

Granny O'Shea never questioned him. She did not care where he had got it as long as it ended up on her finger. It was a show-stopper, the kind of status symbol one couldn't argue with.

'G'wan, Granny, it was a lovely thing for Ben to do,' Molly said.

'Look, you've upset her now,' Gabriel said to Dot reproachfully. 'She's an old lady.'

Granny O'Shea's eyes were full of tears. 'No, she didn't,' she snapped. '*She* couldn't upset me. It reminds me of *him*, that's all,' she said, looking tearfully at the diamond. 'I miss him, you see. I miss the smell of him.'

'Now, Mother, don't fret,' Gabriel soothed her. Captain O'Shea was dead and gone these twenty years.

'It's the Paddy,' Oonagh said, referring to the whiskey. 'Ladies shouldn't …'

'Now, Oonagh, let Mammy have what she wants,' Gabriel said severely.

Emmett put his hand on Granny O'Shea's shoulder. Her bones were fragile and felt insubstantial as a fish's. He could not seem to get a grip on her, so he bent and kissed her dry cheek. To his vast delight she said, 'Ah, Emmett, ye have the making of a saint.'

Laughlin had reached the hall when the Bensons rang the doorbell.

'They always manage to arrive last,' Dot said to the drawing room in the silence produced by the shrill peal.

'I bet they sit in their car until they know everyone else has arrived,' Tom remarked, and Gabriel asked what it mattered if they did.

'And anyhow none of you saw them so I doubt very

much it's true,' he continued. 'Most of you 'ud kill yourselves to announce that you'd spied Colista and Eddie lurking outside in the Bentley.'

'You can't *lurk* in a Bentley ... it's impossible,' Granny O'Shea announced.

Laughlin kissed his aunt's cheek, waving to Banan and Mourna as they went down the corridor to the garden.

'Oh, Banan, don't be so boring,' he heard Mourna say to her cousin. 'Do you always have to talk politics?'

'Bypass the dining room and don't let the children in or it'll look like a plague of locusts hit it,' Oonagh instructed Peggy. 'On no account let the young ones at the food before the adults.' So Peggy was shooing the juniors down into the kitchen and out the back door into the garden.

'Aren't you looking well, Laughlin?' Aunt Colista said graciously as he kissed her cool cheek. 'Oh, such a crush!' as she looked into the drawing room. 'Your mother must be run off her feet. Everyone's here. See, Eddie?'

Laughlin looked up at his Uncle Eddie who sported a Ronald Colman moustache.

'She kept telling me we'd be late, but we're not too bad, are we, Laughlin?' Eddie appealed to him, giving him the kind of wink and nudge that made Laughlin feel very grown-up.

'Oh, no. Of course not, Uncle Eddie,' Laughlin reassured him.

He was a solid man, a manly man, with a smile that was devilish. Colista, his wife, elegant as a mannequin, was dressed with style and taste. She was wearing a wraparound dress in salmon pink crêpe, with a smart little matching hat and white gloves. Laughlin liked her perfume, the daintiness of her, her hands unspoiled by housework, and her tranquil face.

Peggy had by now moved Molly and Dot and the men into the dining room. 'Come on, help yourselves,' she called out, and noticed that Mrs O'Shea had changed the paper serviettes back in favour of the linen napkins which sat in a crisp pile on the sideboard.

'Colista, Eddie! Oh, it's grand to see you.' Oonagh kissed her sister and brother-in-law. She always felt a stab of envy when she saw those two, such a handsome couple, and they had everything that Oonagh coveted: the lovely roomy house in Killiney, the Bentley, the servants, the elegant clothes, the holidays, the circle of fashionable friends, and the easy manner of those who have no anxiety about money.

Iain Benson sauntered into the drawing room looking very much like his father, just as Oonagh, realizing that Peggy had pre-empted her and that people were eating, disturbing the elegant arrangement of food and silver and linen that she had hoped would impress the Bensons, began hustling Colista and Eddie into the next room so they could catch a glimpse of the spread before it was entirely decimated.

'Ah, Iain …' Oonagh began.

'Oonagh, how lovely! You've everything gorgeous, hasn't she, Eddie?' Colista exclaimed as she walked into the dining room. 'Mourna and Briana and the cousins are out under the trees, Iain.'

Oonagh's heart rose at her sister's words but she was careful not to show her elation. She wanted to remain casual and gracious. 'Under the trees' sounded cultivated and refined, but Gabriel spoiled it by calling out, 'Yes, they're down the back yard, Iain.' Then asking Eddie, 'Where'd you park the Bentley?'

Eddie smiled his charming smile. Molly was staring at him and Oonagh wondered if there was something the matter with her. Oonagh turned to Eddie. He was a substantial man, she thought, with wide shoulders, a strong physical presence, and a bland expression on his face.

'I parked it outside, behind Tom's car,' he said mildly.

'Why?' He had his whiskey in one hand and was eating a sandwich. His teeth were very white.

'Oh, you want to watch young Denis Cowley on his skates. He's learning and he has a habit of crashing into things. He might scrape the car. I wouldn't put it past him.'

'Oh, don't worry,' Colista said comfortably, nibbling on a salmon sandwich. 'A dab of paint'll take care of any damage, I'm sure.'

'It's a lovely gansey you're wearing, Ben,' Granny O'Shea said, and winked at Gabriel.

She's at it again, stirring, Oonagh thought, and glared at her husband.

'I made it for him,' Dot said with pride.

Everyone stared at the rust-coloured sweater that hung shapelessly on Ben. It was sprinkled with pastry flakes from the sausage rolls that he had been guzzling. He brushed at them ineffectually. They seemed to be stuck to the hairy wool.

'It's grand, Dot, grand,' Oonagh said, and wondered, Doesn't she see what Granny O'Shea is doing?

'Isn't it a bit hot wearing wool today? The weather's so good,' Granny said innocently.

'No, it's not,' Ben said firmly.

'But you're sweatin', Ben,' Maisie remarked.

'So's Joe, though not for the same reason,' he said.

'Oh, the weather's grand, thanks be to God!' Oonagh looked out of the window. She could see the girls' dresses through the trees. There were ten apple trees at the back of the garden and they were densely green, scattering the last of their blossom on the grass beneath. She couldn't see Mourna's green or Emer's blue, the foliage and the shadows were so thick. She could see their faces, moon-white, gleaming now and then through the verdant frame, and the little ones, clearly etched, tumbling on the lawn among the roses. It was a lovely view from here as long as you didn't go out and come face to face with the drains and pipes and trash cans.

She smiled at the youth out there, so careless of time, so passionate about trivialities. They were assured of bed and board and love in abundance, why should they worry so? Only Mourna didn't.

Iain was pushing Briana on the swing and little Maggie Moran was screaming because she wanted to get on and they didn't seem to pay her any heed. Peggy, standing near the door, looked tired.

'How's the factory?' Tom asked Eddie.

'Doing well, thanks be to God, Tom. Though there is always trouble with the unions. It was a sad day for Ireland when Larkin started the whole thing off and muddled the mind of the Irish working man.'

'Now, now, now, Eddie, don't talk about one of our great heroes like that.'

Banan, standing just outside the window, put his head around. 'Typical bloody British arse-licker!' he cried. 'Leeches and parasites, the lot of ye. The way you talk is sedition.'

There was a gasp of horrified astonishment in the room. Everyone paused, hands half-way to mouths, eyes wide with disgust at the violence of the language.

Molly rushed forward to her son. 'Shut up, Banan. I won't have you speak like that in your aunt's home. Keep that sort of language for the pool hall and your friends there, do you hear me? Apologise to Auntie Oonagh.'

'No, no, Molly, it's not necessary.' Oonagh didn't want to exacerbate the situation by turning it into a battle of wills between Molly and her son. 'Just let's keep off politics at this social occasion, eh?'

Molly pushed Banan further into the garden. 'Go with the others,' she said. 'Don't lurk about here. Find Mourna. She usually has a calming effect on you.'

'You don't understand,' he began. 'They don't

59

understand ...'

'Oh yes we do, Banan, but we do *not* have this kind of conversation at a party.'

'I don't see ...'

'Just go and cool off.' Molly couldn't hide her irritation.

'And if you can't keep a civil tongue in your head, then go home.'

She returned to Oonagh apologetically. 'I'm sorry, you know how he gets. He's missed a father in his life.'

'Yes.' Oonagh wondered if Molly realized how much Banan hated his step-father. However, otherwise all was going well and a little hiccup was only to be expected. She was delighted to see that Colista and Eddie were polishing off sausage rolls with relish.

'Tis well for some, having a grandfather that starts a factory,' Granny O'Shea said brightly, and Oonagh wanted suddenly to kill her mother-in-law.

'Yes, Granny. That was a great piece of luck for Eddie's father. And Eddie,' Joe said. He was steady now. He had just enough alcohol in him to keep everything together. Very soon now, Maisie knew, he'd start to fall apart.

'Oh, I don't think it was luck, Joe, so much as hard work,' Eddie said mildly, smiling his rakish smile.

'Well, my father was a labourer,' Granny O'Shea said proudly, and Oonagh sighed.

Infuriating woman! Determined to spoil my image, she thought. She keeps dragging the whole tone of the party down.

It wasn't fair. The Bensons were enjoying themselves. She looked at Colista's smiling face. She was dripping in fashion and pearls. Sometimes Oonagh forgot she was Colista's sister, so different were their lives. Oonagh felt closer to Molly. They shared the same anxieties, the same preoccupations. Colista seemed curiously alien although she was never anything but gracious. That in itself drove them apart.

60

'And the potato famine nearly carried him off,' Granny O'Shea finished, her eyes gleaming. There was a general groan.

'Oh, not that old chestnut,' Eddie muttered, and Oonagh whispered to Gabriel, 'Why does she do this to me?'

'Do what, love?' he asked innocently.

'This cake is pure gorgeous,' Colista said, sampling the sponge. 'You have the lightest touch when it comes to cakes, Oonagh. She's always been like that,' she continued to Molly. 'I was *hopeless* in the cooking department, wasn't I, Oonagh? Gabriel, you're a lucky man.'

'Sure, I know that, Colista,' he answered, smiling.

'We'll all need to have the talk about the summer holiday,' Oonagh said.

'We've left it a bit late this year, haven't we?' Tom remarked.

'Nonsense, Tom. I've got it all in hand,' Gabriel assured him.

'Emmett, why don't you go and play with your cousins in the garden?' Oonagh asked.

'No. You leave him with me. He's looking after me, so he is.' Granny O'Shea held on to the boy's hand and patted it.

'Well, let's go next door. To the drawing room,' Oonagh suggested. 'Start the meeting.'

Peggy put her head around the French windows. 'Can the children have their food now?' she asked. 'They're starving.'

'Yes, Peggy. If you and Mourna and Briana look after them I'll be grateful, while we talk about the holiday.'

'Rightio, mam.'

Oonagh clapped her hands. 'Banan! Mourna! Briana! Laughlin! Bring everyone in to eat. There's lots here. Come on, you must be hungry.'

The adults were obediently going next door. Oonagh saw Rita surreptitiously put some sausage rolls into her

61

bag. She pretended not to see. Dot and Ben were whispering. Dot seemed upset and Ben kissed her cheek and patted her hand.

She thinks I've forgotten her birthday cake, Oonagh thought, and sighed.

Chapter Eight

Molly stared at Eddie. Don't they guess? she wondered. Doesn't it ever occur to that thick husband of mine that Eddie Benson might be a temptation?

She could feel his presence from clear across the room. She knew that underneath that perfectly tailored suit and fine cotton shirt his underwear would be crisp and fresh as a Persil advertisement. Underneath that … oh, dear God, think of it! His body would be cared for, firm and tanned, the muscles taut, the skin wonderful to touch.

Money did that for you. Good soaps and toiletries made by Penhaligon of London; exposure to the sun on boats in the Mediterranean or Pacific; time and leisure to play tennis and golf, all combined to keep his body at the peak of perfection. Nature had done the rest. Yes, Eddie Benson would be beautiful, stripped.

She had been obsessed by him for so long, keeping his image in the deepest recesses of her mind, she had become used to him in her head. His place there was permanent. She day-dreamed about him, substituted his face for Tom's when her husband made love to her. She had to bite her lip in case she called out: 'Eddie, Eddie,' when she came. One day she probably would! Well, she didn't care.

Let it happen. Eddie Benson lived in her head. She had travelled a long road with him, a road he knew nothing of.

She glanced up and realized he was looking at her. What she saw in his eyes startled her. He knew! It was obvious he knew. Yet behind that look there was ... what? Contempt? Dear God, no. Not that. Then what? Certainly not a return of passion. Something chilling. He glanced away quickly, so quickly. Perhaps she had been mistaken. It had been fleeting. Perhaps she had imagined it. Perhaps she had misread his glance. Perhaps he had not looked at her at all. She was so used to his face appearing close to hers with looks so full of rapture, so full of love, that his glance, not being ardent in reality, seemed cold. She shook her head and tried to concentrate.

'Now, let's call the meeting to order,' Gabriel said. Everyone was talking together, voices lubricated by alcohol, louder than usual.

Ben and Dot sat close together, his arm around her shoulders, and Granny O'Shea had poked Tom out of the comfortable easy chair and was settling herself back in. Rita sat on an upright chair next to the china cabinet and eyed the contents.

She's wishing she could palm a trinket or two and pawn them, Oonagh thought, and felt a surge of pity. Things never went right for poor Rita.

'That was lovely, really lovely, Oonagh,' Colista was murmuring. The family had left the sofa clear for the Bensons. I wish she'd shut up about it now, Oonagh thought. She had been anxious for Colista to approve and when she did Oonagh was delighted, but she had complimented her once too often and her congratulations were beginning to irritate her sister.

'Let's call the meeting to order,' Gabriel repeated. 'Is everyone here? Then we can have the cake. It is a triumph! Wait till you see it. Oonagh has been so excited about it, haven't you, pet?'

'Stop exaggerating, Gabriel! I haven't been excited exactly, just pleased. For Dot, of course.'

Dot was squirming with delight. 'There you are, love,' Ben smiled, 'I *told* you she hadn't forgotten.' He looked at Oonagh. 'She thought you had forgotten.'

'As if I would.' Oonagh said, sounding offended.

'Oh, I didn't *really* think that,' Dot hastened to reassure her.

'Yes, you did, love. Yes, she did. I don't know why you deny it.' Ben was apologetic.

'Let's leave it, shall we?' Oonagh kept her irritation out of her voice.

'Look, let's get started, please. Can we get started?' Gabriel insisted.

'Well, Gabriel, you're the head man here, the expert. Where have you lined up for us this year?'

Every year for the first two weeks of August the families planned a group holiday together. In Ireland. No one thought of going further. In the early 1950s Europe still remained as wildly adventurous a destination as the Sahara desert. The war was still too recent.

'Well, this year I suggest Dranmore,' he said firmly. 'But I'm open to suggestions.'

'He's not really,' Oonagh whispered to Molly.

'No, no. What about Portmarnock?' Joe asked. There was an edge to his voice and the cracks were beginning to show. His eyelids seemed to have a life of their own and his hand insisted on taking his drink on a circuitous route to his mouth. 'Not that I'll be able to afford to go,' he added.

'Portmarnock is just down the road,' Ben said. 'As I live in Clontarf it's not exactly getting away from it all for me, Portmarnock isn't.'

'But it's a gorgeous place,' Joe insisted.

'I don't *want* to go somewhere that close.'

'What about the Golden Strand?' Dot suggested.

'Which Golden Strand?' Gabriel asked Dot.

'The one in Wicklow,' she replied.

'Clogher Head? Clogher Head's wonderful,' Tom said.

'Hopeless for children.'

'They're not really children any more, only Dot's last three.'

'Lahinch?'

'All right for golfers but what about the rest of us?' Molly asked.

'Kerry.'

'Clare.'

'Wicklow.'

'Dranmore,' Gabriel said firmly. 'Listen, will you? I've gone into it thoroughly. There's Mrs Flanagan's Guest-houses, four of them linked. Suit *all* our purses. She's got these houses on the head, overlooking the beach. There's her houses, a little road, a footpath and steps and the sea. Perfect for the kids. And above, on the headland itself, is the Grand. The Old Dranmore Grand. A fine hotel if anyone wants to fork out.' He was looking at Colista and Eddie. 'There's a tennis club there for them that wants it, a fair for the first week we're there, and a harbour, a yacht club and boats.'

'I love the fair,' Dot said, smiling. 'Ben and I love the dodgems.'

'Yes,' Gabriel glanced at her, then continued. 'And there's dances, and the church, and a great pub.' No one looked at Joe.

'I'd still like to go further off,' Granny O'Shea muttered.

'Well, we're going to be democratic here, and put it to the vote.' Gabriel paused.

Everyone knows we'll end up where Gabriel has suggested, Oonagh thought. No one else is going to bother organizing things. But they'll argue and if they don't like it they'll blame him.

'I suggest we have the usual arrangement for Rita and Joe. All agreed?'

Why does he always have to say that? Rita thought. Every year? In front of her and Joe. She caught his eye but he only winked at her, grinning a bit foolishly.

Everyone nodded. At least they looked embarrassed. It was the custom for the family to pay for the members who couldn't afford a holiday. Two bright spots of red had appeared on Maisie's cheeks.

'Bloody family charity,' she muttered, and Rita went back to staring at the china cabinet.

The murmurs of assent around the room died.

'You think we're a nuisance,' Maisie wailed. 'Well, let me tell you, we can …'

'Leave it, love,' Joe said wearily. 'Just leave it.'

'You're not a nuisance, Maisie dear. You mustn't think that.' Eddie was brisk. 'You're family. We look after our own. Some day when things improve for you and Joe, and Rita here, you'll be the ones asked to help.' He paused, thinking. 'Er …'

'Well, it wouldn't be you as needed help, would it?' Maisie remarked sarcastically.

'One of the children, maybe,' Eddie concluded. 'What goes around, comes around.'

I'm going to scream, Molly thought, or get up and do a strip. I wonder what they'd do if I did just that. Have me committed, probably.

'The plusses outweigh the minuses,' Gabriel affirmed. 'Dranmore will suit everyone.'

'Mam, Mam, Maggie is being sick!' Emer burst into the room.

'Oh, God,' Molly said.

'Ah, she'll be all right.' Dot, her mother, did not seem perturbed. 'She'll be overexcited, that's what it is.'

Molly looked at her curiously, and when she made no move said, 'Shouldn't you go to her? Won't she want her mother?'

'Ah, no, it's not necessary.' Dot shook her head. 'Peggy's

66

very capable.'

Oonagh nodded to Emer. 'All right, darling. Ask Peggy if she can cope.'

'Tell her! Tell her. Ye have to *tell* servants,' Dot said.

'... and has advantages for the less well-off, as well as the comfortable, *and* the children will be catered for. What more can anyone ask?' Gabriel was insisting. 'Young adults, I should say.'

'That eldest daughter of yours, Oonagh, is a dish fit for a king,' Tom said.

Oonagh smiled complacently. 'Yes,' she agreed, 'Mourna is the pick of the bunch. The diamond among zircons.' She smirked, then rearranged her face in case they thought she was smug. But no one argued with her.

'She is ... quite extraordinary,' Eddie said, almost to himself.

'Yes, well, looks aren't everything,' Molly said.

'So what do you all say?' Gabriel concluded.

'I say we better all agree because we're going to Dranmore. We always do as Gabriel says.'

'That's not fair, Tom.' Gabriel looked offended.

'We've never wanted to complain up till now,' Colista said soothingly.

'Gabriel always arranges everything so well. We're always so grateful to him.'

'And *ye* have the whole of September in Kinsale,' Joe said bitterly.

'What of it, man? It's *his* life. I'd be in Kinsale if I could afford it,' Gabriel said.

'Well, you could if your da left you a factory,' Joe insisted.

'This is getting us nowhere, Joe,' Gabriel said. 'Let's have a show of hands. Everyone in favour raise their hand.'

Most of the hands in the room shot up, and there was a cheer, and smiles and pats were exchanged.

'Against?'

67

Joe raised his hand energetically. And Granny O'Shea. And Oonagh. Maisie pulled Joe's hand down. Eddie said to Granny O'Shea, 'Well, then, maybe you'd better not come.'

And Granny O'Shea said hastily, 'No. No, I'll go. Only I wanted to sample France before I die.'

Tom looked at her open-mouthed. 'France?' he said incredulously.

Granny O'Shea nodded vigorously. 'Yes. I wanted a bit of certain sun. Now the war's over. I thought, Monte Carlo, Cannes, Nice.' She uttered the names as if they were holy. 'Captain O'Shea used to talk to me about those places and the warm dry climate and the smell of jasmine and orange blossom. I never bothered about going then, I was happy just to hear his talk. Now it's getting late and I can hear the clock ticking, so I want to go.'

'Aw, Granny, don't be daft,' Ben cried. 'How the hell d'ye think all of us 'ud be able to get to France and back? Janey, it'd be like Noah's Ark. We'd lose someone over the side or somethin'. France, d'ye hear? Think she's Lady Docker, Christ's sake!'

'Oh, hush, Ben. Don't swear.' Dot patted her husband's hand. '*And* it's selfish of you, Granny, puttin' yourself first.'

And Gabriel, who was looking at his wife's hand in the air with astonishment, cried, 'Oonagh!'

68

Chapter Nine

'Where's Joe?' Oonagh asked Molly.

'He's outside in the back garden, singing rebel songs.'
They could hear him, his voice drawing out each final note
nasally.

'Oh, the French are on the s-a-a-a-y
Said the Sean Bhean Bhocht,
Oh the Fre-e-nch are on the s-a-a-a-y
They'll be here without del-a-a-a-y …'

'He's gettin' worse,' Oonagh sighed.

'Poor man!'

'Aw, God, Molly, wouldn't you think he'd lay off it, just
for this once?'

'Maybe he did, and found he couldn't,' Molly said.
'Maybe it's in his blood, God help him.'

'I wish he'd go home,' Oonagh said.

She knocked on the bathroom door. They were
standing side by side.

'Maggie, give over throwing up. There's nothing left in
you by now,' Oonagh shouted through the closed door.

'I don't know, Mam. She ate an awful lot of rolls.' Emer's
voice floated out to them on the landing, then the sound of
the lavatory being flushed.

'Get her out of there, Emer! At once! I have to let the
guests up. I can't delay any longer.'

'They must be bursting by now,' Molly said.

'Yes, and Maggie is a little madam. Half the time she's putting it on.'

'Doesn't sound like it,' Molly remarked. Then she looked at Oonagh. 'Why did you vote against Gabriel, Oonagh?' she asked. 'It seemed so pointless, especially as the majority voted for Dranmore.'

Oonagh shrugged. 'I want him to *ask* me why I disagreed. And he will. And then I want to tell him what *I* want. You know, he never asks me. He assumes I want what he wants.' She looked at Molly doubtfully. 'And most of the time I do. But just once in a while ...' she petered out.

Oonagh resumed banging on the bathroom door. 'Come out, Maggie Moran. *At once*, you hear me? You can throw up at the bottom of the garden.' She looked at Molly. 'I'd give my right arm for another bathroom,' she said. 'And that's part of it; me disagreeing with Gabriel. We have not got the same priorities. He's not here all the time, living with the inconvenience. He says we've managed with this one bathroom so far and we'll spend the money on the roof. I tell him this is more important to *me*. It governs my life, Moll, the bathroom does. And as for Dranmore ... it's the same old thing, year after year. I'd love a change, Moll. To go away, me and Gabriel, by ourselves. Oh, the bliss of it. Be looked after. A hotel. Go to a hotel with a bathroom *en suite*, can you imagine the luxury? Janey Mac ...'

'What's that? En ... what you said?' Molly asked curiously. '*En suite*?'

'Your *own* bathroom, Molly, off your own room. Private. Can you imagine, Moll? And the sun guaranteed? Fancy that now. For once I agree wholeheartedly with Granny O'Shea.' She turned back to the door. 'Come out of there at once, Maggie Moran, I won't tell you again.' She turned back to Molly. 'In a minute she'll come out all cutesie-pie. You know, Molly, I'd worry about Maggie if I were Dot.'

'Well, you're not, so that's one problem you're spared,' Molly laughed.

At that moment Colista appeared at the top of the stairs. Molly and Oonagh stopped talking and looked a little self-conscious.

'The toilet?' she asked tentatively.

'Dot's youngest is in there throwing up … ah, here she is now,' Molly said.

Maggie, white-faced and smelling of vomit, emerged from the bathroom. She was sniffing and her face was blotched and red.

'Take her out into the fresh air,' Molly advised. Emer grimaced. 'And she's not to eat another crumb, d'you hear?'

'But I haven't had any cake,' Maggie wailed. 'I've not had me cake.'

'If you touch the cake, Maggie Moran, I'll tell your ma,' Oonagh hissed at her. The girl stared back, eyes glittering in her mottled face. 'Me mam won't care,' she said defiantly. 'She's too busy sloppin' over me da to care if I have cake.'

'Well, you can't have it and that's that,' Oonagh said feebly. 'Emer, make sure she doesn't.'

'Well, I'll try, Mam.' Emer sounded defeated.

'No, see that she doesn't,' Oonagh said.

'I bin looking after her all afternoon,' Emer cried in despair. 'An' she's hopeless! Greedy and hopeless.'

She followed Maggie downstairs, giving the girl a vicious shove when she thought her Auntie Molly was not looking.

Molly was talking to Colista who stood on one silk-stockinged leg in her salmon-pink suede shoes.

'Maggie Moran is a terror, Colista. Dot lets the children grow like weeds. She doesn't believe in discipline. Nor does Ben. The kids are wild. Except Mary, who has grown up before her time, poor lamb.'

Colista was clicking her tongue, tut-tutting in sympathy. 'Why are we waiting?' she asked Molly.

'Oonagh is just … Maggie was sick.'

71

Oonagh emerged from the bathroom where she had been feverishly tidying, wiping the toilet and sink, perfuming the air and pouring disinfectant down the loo. She had left a fresh guest towel for Colista, and ushered her into the bathroom hoping she hadn't forgotten anything.

'I was waiting too, Oonagh,' Molly whispered, and Oonagh elbowed her gently. 'Oh, you understand. You can hang on,' she said.

Colista was not long. They heard her pull the chain, then the whoosh of the water flowing into the basin. A moment later she emerged and Molly slid in.

'You want to freshen up?' Oonagh took her sister's arm and led her to the master bedroom. It was strange that she was so formal, she thought, but a distance had grown between them since Colista had married wealth. There were barriers that could not be crossed.

She had grown up with Colista. They had slept in the same room, been ill together, shared secrets, were loyal, laughed, cried and quarrelled, and yet she felt awkward with her. Molly, who was after all only her sister-in-law, was much closer. Perhaps, Oonagh mused, as she watched this slim, elegant woman, it was Colista's social position, so far above her own, that separated them, made them strangers.

Colista sat at Oonagh's dressing-table. She had taken out a swan's down powder puff in a little pink chiffon square and was dabbing it on her nose.

It was a comfortable room dominated by the bed which was large and substantial. Oonagh turned on the lights, drew the curtains, then sat on the edge of the bed and watched her sister. Colista took her lipstick out and filled in her lips, then pressed them together. Her eyes met Oonagh's in the mirror.

'You're coming down tomorrow? Brody will pick you up and drop you back afterwards. We'll be late … it'll be a late night.' She put her puff and her lipstick back into her bag.

'Oh, he doesn't need to. We can get the bus.'

'Nonsense, Oonagh. You can't, not in your evening dress.'

Oonagh didn't tell her sister that they always took the bus when they attended a 'do'.

'Besides, Brody hasn't anything better to do,' Colista said.

Brody was the handy-man/chauffeur/gardener the Bensons employed. Oonagh envied her sister his services. God, to have a bathroom on every floor, a maid and a cook, a char and an odd-job man – and to top it all, Brody! What wouldn't she give? Peggy's services seemed useless compared to that battalion.

'All right. Thanks, Colista,' she said meekly. It would be gorgeous riding in the big car with Mourna, Briana and Gabriel.

'Listen, you won't take it amiss if I offered ... for Mourna ...' Colista took a breath. 'I'd like to give you a cheque, Oonagh, for a dress for Mourna, for tomorrow. No, let me finish,' she said as Oonagh began to protest. 'You could take her out tomorrow to Switzer's or Brown Thomas's and get her something really stylish.'

Oonagh protested, 'Ooh, Colista, but ...' and her sister continued, 'You see, there's someone I 'specially want Mourna to meet. He'll be at the Club tomorrow night, and there's no one to touch Mourna in the length and breadth of Ireland so ...'

'Oh, who is it?' Oonagh was breathless. Her heart jumped in excitement and she hung on what her sister said, repeating salient words.

'He is, my dear, marvellously eligible.'

'Eligible ...'

'Yes. And he's rich.'

'Rich ...'

'Yes. He has a house in Tullamore, and an apartment in Fitzwilliam Square.'

'Fitzwilliam Square ...'

'Yes. And he's German.'

'German!'

'With a charming accent.'

'German?'

'He's extremely attractive.'

'Yes, but … German?'

'Oh, he got out during the war. His parents escaped with him.'

'Yes, but German. Not Irish?'

'It's a remarkable story. They took all their art treasures out, bit by bit, then got trapped.'

'Still, Colista, I don't know. I was hoping for a nice Irish boy. Or an English gentleman wouldn't have been too bad for Mourna. I'm not crazy about the idea of a German.'

Colista raised an eyebrow and looked at her sister quizzically. 'A fabulously rich German, although he is older than …'

'How old?'

'Oh, thirty odd.'

'Oh, well, that's not too bad. He'd be sensible by now.'

'Yes. And Oonagh –' Colista clasped her hands and looked at her sister with shining eyes '– he's a Count!'

Oonagh had been dithering. A German, however rich, was a foreigner, a stranger to their ways, but the title clinched it. Mourna would be a Countess! It was grander than any vision Oonagh had dreamed. A Countess!

'I thought that might interest you, Oonagh. He's bought Ardmar House and has moved in, set it all up very luxuriously, very grandly. It's like a palace. He has only the best. Mourna could queen it there.'

She had turned to her sister and now she leaned forward. 'She'll never have to wet her fingers. She'll live in the lap, as they say. So *please* let me buy her a dress. Call it an early Christmas present. I want her to be a knock-out. Trust me, Oonagh, I have a reason. First impressions are everything, don't you think?

74

'Of course,' she continued, 'they may not like each other. Then there's no harm done.' She sighed. 'Then Eddie'll have his way and she'll marry Iain. But let's keep him in reserve.'

'There's nothing I'd like better,' Oonagh said, 'Iain and Mourna.'

Colista winked at her. 'Better the German, though.'

'Eddie said it could be arranged; the problem of the first cousin element. Consanguinity, you know. A little money, he said, a greased palm will get you anything in this country, in spite of John Charles McQuaid.'

'But the German first, Oonagh. Let me tell you, he's handsome and sophisticated. Mourna's bound to like him at the least. And she's a treat, Oonagh. You can be proud as Punch there.'

Her handbag slid to the floor from her lap and she bent to retrieve it. She took out her chequebook as she spoke, and a gold fountain pen, and scribbled on the cheque, tore it off and handed it to Oonagh.

'Get something lovely, she deserves it. There. Take it and no nonsense! I'm not giving it to *you*, I'm giving it to Mourna.' She rose briskly, smoothed her skirt. 'I think we'll be on our way, Oonagh.' She pressed a cool cheek to her sister's. 'Eddie has a game of golf at the crack of dawn and I'm playing tennis at ten.'

'Oh, but wait for the cake. Dot'd be mortified if you didn't.'

'Yes, well, after the cake.'

'Peggy'll be bringing it in any moment. I think she's just waiting for us to go down.'

Oonagh held the door open for her and she exited, leaving a waft of Coty's L'Aimant on the air behind her. Oonagh followed, murmuring, 'Countess. Countess ...'

'So we'll send the car about seven-thirty, no rush, and see you when you arrive,' Colista rambled on. She was putting on her gloves. She doesn't care about the cake,

Oonagh reflected.

'Oh, Colista, thank you, you're so kind,' Oonagh murmured.

'Not another word! It's been a lovely evening. Lovely food. Gabriel is great at making all the arrangements for the holiday. We'll book into the Grand. If things go well tomorrow night, Count Kurt Von Mensil (she pronounced it 'Koort' in an exaggerated, foreign-sounding voice that Oonagh found irritating) will be joining us there.'

They went down the stairs together. Peggy saw them coming and hurried into the kitchen. The cry went out: 'The cake! The cake!'

The young people came in from the garden, into the dining room, in a crush. The lights were turned off. The adults stood in the double-doors between the drawing and dining rooms. Dot and Bob stood in isolation beside the table.

'Why on earth did you do that, Oonagh? Put your hand up and make a show of me?' Gabriel asked, joining Colista and his wife.

'Oh, you wouldn't understand,' she said.

'Hoist me up, Emmett darlin', I can't see a thing,' Granny O'Shea called.

At that moment Peggy came in with the pink-iced cake, the top covered by a myriad tiny candles all aflame.

'Happy birthday to you,
Happy birthday to you,
Happy birthday, dear Dot ...'

Dot was sobbing happily, holding tightly on to Ben's hand, looking around at the circle of faces. Her blonde curls trembled and she smiled tremulously, the make-up running on her old/young face. 'Oh, thank you, Oonagh – Gabriel, thank you.'

Some of the children clustered at the door oohed and ahed, chanting excitedly, 'Mam, Mam, can I have some?'

Maggie sidled up to her mother's knee and whispered in the most alluring way, 'Oh, Mam, can I?' Molly drew in her breath sharply. Dot laid a hand tenderly on her daughter's head. 'Of course you may, love,' she said. 'Of course.'

'Make a wish, Dot,' Tom shouted, face becoming redder as the whiskey hit him.

'Sure, I have everything I want.' Dot smiled at Ben.

'Well, make one for me then,' Joe shouted. The whiskey had already slaughtered him and he'd passed the bonnets-over-the-windmill time, Maisie noted with a sinking heart.

'He's past the point of no return,' she muttered to herself in despair, and Emmett looked at him in horror.

Dot blew out the candles. The children let out a collective breath and the adults clapped. Ben put his hand over Dot's and they cut the first slice.

'Just like a wedding,' Emer breathed.

Maggie, quick as a flash, grabbed the slice of cake and ran into the garden with it.

'Little brat,' Oonagh said.

'I'm *not* goin' after her,' Emer announced firmly, 'I'm *not*. Someone else can hold her head this time.'

Chapter Ten

Granny O'Shea held Emmett's hand in her claw-like grasp. She had managed to beat Tom to the chair after the cake and was ensconced snugly in it in the drawing room. She had had three large Paddys and her false teeth had come loose in her relaxation. She had a habit of easing them out a little when she got to a certain stage.

'Don't let them stop you, Emmett,' she said, peering at him, her sharp little eyes raking his pale face. 'Don't let anyone stop you doin' what you want. You've only one life to live. No one told me that. All my life I kept thinking, tomorrow I'll … or, one day I'll … and now it's too late. Don't you come to the end of your life, Emmett, never having been to France, wonderin' what it would have been like if you'd tried to make your dreams come true. If you fail, you fail. You can do what they want then; at least you've tried.'

He nodded. He understood what she meant. The others didn't but he did. Emer said Granny O'Shea was a silly old cow, and Briana and Laughlin and Mourna listened with one ear while they thought of other things, so they missed the essence of her. They didn't know her at all. And Ardel flirted with her and made her laugh so much that she never told him anything, never got the chance. However, as he thought about it, Emmett realized it didn't seem likely that anyone could prevent Ardel doing what he wanted.

Emmett said now, 'I want to go to Africa, Granny.'

'God bless us, that's the end of the world.' Granny looked at him with new admiration. 'Isn't that a grand ambition, Emmett?'

There were full ashtrays on the floor beside the chairs and dirty, empty glasses. The standard lamp was on, but no one had switched the overhead light back on. It was dim in the room and easy to talk of dreams.

'Yes, Granny, Africa.' He breathed the word with reverence. 'Africa. Hot and dusty and dry. There are wild animals there, and huge insects, and little black babies. There's the tundra and the bush and villages like beehives where they've never heard of Jesus. It's a golden country and there's gold in it for greedy men. Can you imagine, Granny? Can you?'

'Yes, I can, Emmett. Janey Mac, it must be wonderful.

78

Hot and dry. No more of this pissy rain. That's why I want to go to France. It's hot there too, in the South. See hibiscus, see bougainvillaea before I die. I've never seen those for real. Only pictures. They sound lovely Emmett, don't they? Bougainvillaea and hibiscus. Gorgeous! The colours brighter than anything here. Bright and clear. God'n it must be wonderful.' She looked at him. 'But I left it too late, Emmett.' The old woman's eyes were sad. 'I couldn't make it there now. I cod myself that I could, but I couldn't. It's too late. Don't you make that mistake, y'hear me?'

'No, Granny, I won't.'

'Tell me about Africa, Emmett.'

'Well, it's hot and dry and the sun looks like an orange. It sits on the horizon, then drops. I saw a film about it once. I never forgot. People have strange customs and wear hardly any clothes because it's so hot. There's lions and zebra and …'

She nodded, listening, drowsing. She sat up with a start when Tom burst into the room, turning on the overhead light. Emmett jumped too.

'Home time,' Tom sang out. 'Home. Colista is leaving.'

'She's not the bloody Queen,' Granny shouted.

'She's talking to Mourna, but she's saying her goodbyes, so we better start moving you, eh, Granny?'

'I don't see why we have to go just because she is,' Granny said.

Tom paid no attention to her. He never listened to Granny O'Shea.

'By the time we have you sorted out they'll all have gone, so we better start moving.'

Granny O'Shea said, 'Don't forget, Emmett. Don't let them stop you. Don't listen to sense.'

'Do you hear her?' Tom boomed. His voice hurt Emmett's ears, atuned to the quiet of the room. 'Preaching sedition. Of all the cheek, Granny.' He pulled her up a

79

little more roughly than he should which hurt her and she knew he had done it deliberately. She looked at him and let him know she knew.

Oonagh came into the room and began tidying up, gathering the glasses and full ashtrays.

'Open the window awhile, Emmett,' she said. 'Let the smoke out. Tom, you looking after Granny? How kind.'

Granny O'Shea harrumped and Oonagh noted that one of her Dresden figurines had gone from the china cabinet. She'd have to take the key out when Rita came to visit. She wondered if she would succumb to temptation if she was in Rita's position and decided she would not, she'd beg first. She tried to quash her anger at the loss of a precious piece of china, and sighed watching Tom propel Granny O'Shea out of the room, not registering his careless handling of the old lady.

'Colista is looking for Eddie,' she said. 'Tom, have you seen him?'

'Mister High-and-Mighty! Yerra, sure he's just gone out in the garden to have a smoke. Colista won't let him smoke in the house, God help him.'

'Well, he could've here,' Oonagh said, but Tom shook his head.

'No. He has to behave the same everywhere, she says.'

Eddie Benson was just outside the French windows in the garden, smoking his cigar peacefully. The tip glowed in the dark.

He was ruminating on the unsatisfactory food situation. After he had had a picky snack with his in-laws, Colista never allowed dinner. Sausage rolls and sandwiches were no substitute for a sirloin and onions. It was too late, she always said, and it would be greed to eat steak after all that starch. She looked after his health. She wanted to keep him fit, she said, but Eddie hated it at times like these when his stomach, although full, felt empty.

'Like a bloody Chinese meal,' he muttered.

Dusk had thrown a blanket over the garden and the first stars pricked out the midnight blue sky like candle flames. The garden was full of shadows and he could hear what sounded like giggles from behind the apple trees. Whispers and sighs and a little laugh. Then he noticed, near him, another shadow.

'Who's there?' he called softly. He knew who it was.

'It's me, Mourna.' The girl made no move.

'Come over here, Mourna, where I can see you.'

The girl moved closer. He could see her now, beautiful face, floating hair, like a girl in a dream.

'You're very lovely, Mourna,' he whispered. People always said that to her. She did not react, just stood there, her face bathed in moonlight.

'I'm your uncle, Mourna. I'll always take care of you.'

'My da can do that.' Her tone was sharp, bringing him up shortly.

'I'd like you to marry Iain,' he said.

'Yes, I know. You've told me before. Da says I can marry who I like.'

'But I know you, Mourna. You'll never be satisfied with some struggling young student. You need security. Iain is an only child. My heir.'

She said nothing. They both heard the giggles from behind the apple trees.

'I'm going in now,' she said, suddenly moving past him. But he caught her arm and held it. Then he kissed her cheek lightly, and released her. 'Remember what I said,' he called after her as she fled into the house.

He thought about food again. He hated meals at odd times. He liked routine. Weddings, funerals, all these affairs where snacks were served, disrupted the pattern and caused him a dislocated feeling of dissatisfaction.

Ah, well, he would have to accept the fact that there would be no more food that night. He wished he had eaten another sausage roll. He turned and looked back into the

81

dining room but there didn't appear to be much left.

Oonagh and Gabriel always made him feel that he had missed something. Something essential. He hated the feeling. He, Eddie Benson, had everything.

Being in this house made him feel uncomfortable. There was, to him, something small and mean and stultifying about such accommodation; such a large family living on top of each other. There could be no privacy, no space.

A memory shivered in the corner of his mind. He tried to shove it away but it obtruded insistently and made him quail.

He saw the face of his father, darkly angry. Why was his father always angry? He was ordering Eddie out of the dining room, a large room, an echoing room, vast in the eyes of a child. All the rooms of his childhood had been enormous and he had been very small, very alone. There had been no other children and he had no friends. They did not ask other boys to the house because of his mother. His father was shouting at him, 'You are stupid, boy, you know that? Stupid! How did I manage it? But it is your mother's fault. You are *her* child, gormless bloody eejit!' And the blow on the side of his head that made his brains rattle. But it was not the pain that made him cry, it was the humiliation he felt at his father's scorn.

'Bloody stupid boy!' His rich and powerful father's voice, full of contempt.

His mother said nothing. She never uttered a word. Too scared, Mary McC., his nurse said. She was terrified of his da, Mary McC. said, that's why she raided the sherry bottle. 'Sometimes she's out to lunch, your mammy, clean not there in her head.'

He remembered her face, not dear, not fondly recalled. It was an empty face, devoid of emotion, devoid of love. His father, red-faced, was calling him. 'Stupid boy! Come here or I'll tan your hide.' And where was he? Somewhere hiding. But the voice always found him. 'Stupid boy!'

82

At that moment a hand on his shoulder made him jump. He turned around violently, arm raised, fist clenched, ready to ward off a blow, ready to deliver one, but the hand turned out to belong to his brother-in-law, Joe Moran.

'Hey! Hold on, Joe,' Eddie yelled. 'Whoah!'

Joe was unsteady and fell backwards in the force of Eddie's violent reaction.

Recovering, he looked at Eddie with hostility alternating with servility, his eyes glazed.

'Caught ye on the hop, din' I?' he slurred, and winked. 'Made ye jump.'

'Take it easy, Joe,' Eddie said equably. Joe stood before him, swaying, peering blurrily at him.

'Y'wan' make an issue?' he asked belligerently, then in a lightning change of mood he leaned against the back wall beside Eddie and said, 'I'm all fucked up, Eddie. Need your help.' Eddie's eyes probed the darkness. 'Hush, Joe. The kids are about. Watch your language.'

"S all very well for you. Father left you a factory. Nice house. Servants. Boat. Oh, 's all very well for some.'

Eddie turned towards his brother-in-law. 'Look, Joe,' he said, an edge to his voice, 'I'm tired of you saying that, I really am. I work damn' hard for my money and …' He looked at Joe's slack face, his unfocused eyes. 'Oh, what's the use?' he finished, shrugging.

Joe pulled himself together and for a moment seemed sober. 'Listen, Eddie, lend me some money, please? I need it bad. I'm askin' you. I'm up the creek, Eddie, an' I need your help.'

'Don't ask me, Joe. Don't do that.'

'Why not? You can afford it. I don' like askin' – think it costs me nuthin'? Stand here and grovel? Jesus' sake, Eddie, a little something, tide me over?'

'No, Joe! The answer is no. Everyone in this family has given you money and where has it gone? Eh? Down your gullet, that's where. No money, so you can quit asking.'

'Please, Eddie, I'm beggin'.'

'No, Joe. I'm sorry. Pull yourself together, man. We pay for your holiday, you and Maisie, but enough is enough. There is no way I'm going to give you even a bob.'

'You'd give it to a cripple, wouldn't you? Not ask questions. Jesus, must there always be a price to pay? Can't anyone just open their hands, no conditions?'

'You've heard what I had to say. That's all, Joe.'

Joe gathered himself together, raised a fist to hit his brother-in-law, but Eddie grabbed him by the shirt collar and slammed him violently against the wall.

'Don't you ever try that again,' he said through his teeth. 'Not ever, do you hear?'

He slammed Joe's back viciously against the wall again, his fine teeth biting through the cigar he had clamped in his mouth, then he let the drunk slide, moaning and sobbing, down the wall until he sat, slumped against the drain-pipe. Eddie spat out the cigar, shot his cuffs and smoothed back his hair.

'Eddie? Eddie? Where are you? We're leaving, darling.'

It was Colista's voice and she popped her head around the French windows. 'There you are!' she exclaimed. 'At last. I was looking for you everywhere. I wondered where you'd got to.' She scanned the garden, looking into the middle distance with narrowed eyes. 'Come along, dear. We're going. I just have to round up Iain.'

She did not notice Joe half-lying, half-sitting, crumpled up on the concrete at her husband's feet.

'Okay, dear. I'm coming,' Eddie said, stepping over Joe and leaving him there in the dark without a backward glance.

'I can't find Iain,' Colista rambled on over her shoulder. 'Have you seen him?'

Eddie shook his head. 'No, my dear, I haven't.'

'Where on earth can he have got to?' she asked abstractedly. She pushed her husband aside and leaned out into the garden, calling, 'Iain? Iain? Come along. We're going home.'

'Shush,' Iain whispered under the apple trees. He held Briana by her elbows. She was trying not to laugh out loud. 'Shush. It's Mother. Don't laugh, Bri. Don't. You'll spoil everything.'

He touched her cheek with his finger and looked at her, his love and lust and tenderness clear in his eyes. 'You're beautiful, y'know.'

'Not as beautiful as Mourna.'

'Oh, she's *perfect*. Who wants that? No, you're gas Bri. You're fun. You are the nicest, sweetest person to be with. Oooh, yes!' he said, sighing contentedly.

'Really?'

'Really. You make me go hot and cold. I feel like a movie star when I'm with you. I feel important. When I'm with Mourna I keep apologising, as if I'm not good enough.'

'Your mother wants you to marry her,' Briana said. He shrugged. She could not see him clearly in the dense shadow beneath the trees. All she saw was his outline and the white curve of his jaw, the blur of his hand clutching the branch. They could hear Emer and Brigid giggling somewhere near, and there was the feel of others about.

'I think it's Father wants us married. Keep the business in the family. Mother has other fish to fry now. Like this German ...'

'German?'

'Shush. Yes, German. He's a bastard in my opinion, but what would I know?'

'Oh, go on!'

'Yes. Mother hopes Mourna will like Kurt.' He imitated his mother's exaggerated German pronunciation of the name. Then he grinned. 'So do I.'

'Mourna'll never marry a *German*.' Briana stared at the

85

white cheek above her. She wanted to touch it, so she leaned forward and trailed her fingers across his skin. He gave a little shiver, then smiled at her and took her hand.

'Oh, don't let's bother about them.' He took a step towards her, caught his breath at the nearness of her face, leaned over and kissed her clumsily. The kiss landed at the side of her mouth. Instinctively she turned, and tenderly, lips acutely sensitive, they kissed briefly, parted and stared at each other.

'Iain! Iain!' Colista's voice floated through the garden in a dying fall.

'You better go,' Briana whispered, her knees shaking. He nodded, squeezed her hand, and they came out from the pitchy darkness of the trees, walking to the French windows, hand in hand.

'Oh, look, someone's there on the ground,' Iain said.

'It's Uncle Joe. He's drunk.'

They too stepped over him and went into the house.

Chapter Eleven

When had it started? When had it gotten out of hand? When had he lost control? When had it all become too much?

Joe remembered a young convivial man, life and soul as they used to say, girls mad about him, always a jar in his hand. Could take it or leave it, he always said. Then, with a laugh, 'Only I prefer to take it. Har, har, har.'

There was nothing convivial about him now, lying on the ground, on the cold concrete, and not for the first time. He was unable to move for the moment. So he lay there. That was usual too. Being there, on the floors of the world, a shell, unfeeling, inanimate. Oh, Jesus H. Christ, when had it started?

He could not remember. It had crept up on him slowly, imperceptibly. The celebration days into the desperation days; the change from a great night's drinking into the acute *need* for booze, when body and nerves screamed out for the stuff, would not be stilled without it.

He yearned for something. What, he did not know. Deep in that darkness that engulfed him there must be a tiny light, there must be hope.

The shame of it! The terrible humiliation. The loss of his pride, his dignity. Eddie despised him, they all did. Lying there, in the gutter in the O'Sheas' back yard, he disgusted himself. He was revolted by his behaviour, wished he was someone else, not this sick, pathetic man. If he could be Eddie, maybe, with a house and a car.

When he came to, each morning, stumbled to the basin (there was no bathroom in the caravan) and threw up, hands shaking, stomach heaving, he faced two alternatives: to cut his throat or to fix himself with a Paddy, down a whiskey and follow it with a Smithwick's – in fact, anything strong, fierce or lethal. Shake himself like a dog, then face the day. Unsteadily, true, but face it all the same. Otherwise cut his throat.

Maisie, God love her, nagged him, but he didn't blame her for that, except when he was drunk and then he threatened or even hit the poor cow. The shame of the aftermath of that, the guilt! Who else would put up with him? No one, he knew. Who else would put up with the lies, the broken promises, the spoilt dreams?

If only life had given him some advantages he would not be like this. But even as he told himself this he knew it would have made no difference.

How to escape his predicament? He couldn't get a job.

No one would employ him. Eddie had given him work in the dim and distant past. A job as a messenger boy was what he was asked to do by his brother-in-law, Eddie bloody Benson. A messenger boy! Him! Brother-in-law of the boss. For a while he'd stuck it but then the inevitable happened. He'd blown it. Got in a fight one day when he'd had one too many at lunch. Heck, one? More like three. Or six. Or ten. This geezer says, as he's leaving the office where he'd just delivered a message, 'Hey, you,' he goes, 'you've brought the wrong instructions to the wrong place. Eejit! God-damned jumped-up piss-artist.' Everyone looked around at him. Girls stopped typing. Joe had stuck his fingers in the air. 'Fucking twerp!' he went. Nothing too clever. Nothing too inventive. He was sorry at once because the girls were very distressed. They weren't used to foul language. Then he'd said it again, even though he was ashamed, 'Fucking twerp!' The guy reported him. Reported him to his brother-in-law.

Eddie'd sent for him. Eddie sitting in his huge leather chair in his huge office, looked like a Goddamned hotel lobby, and said, 'Joe, old man, this won't do!' Sat there reeking of money, sleek and healthy, his golf clubs near the door of the Goddamned hotel lobby-cum-office, his yellow cashmere cardigan folded neatly on the chair beside the golf clubs.

Those things – the cashmere cardi, the golf clubs – spelled out to Joe the difference in their positions. They conjured up pictures of Eddie walking with prosperous men over green velvet courses, taking deep breaths of sea air and exchanging titbits of stock-market advice for the knowledgeable. They silently spoke of invigorating showers after healthy exercise, of Eddie draping the yellow cashmere carelessly over shoulders; shoulders held back in pride and well-being and lack of worry, of Eddie eating lunch with silver utensils, attentive waiters hovering, or drinking wine from sparkling glass, the menu bountiful: steak, salad, smoked salmon and trout. Whiskey and wine.

Ah! That was the rub. There lay the trip-wire. Alcohol. Joe knew, even then, looking at the golf clubs and the yellow cashmere, that *he* would never have left the club house, never have played the game, never have picked up on the deal-talk.

He would have been hooked into the booze at the bar in his favourite stance, elbows on the counter, holding a drink in one hand, a cigarette in the other, an ocean of booze in the offing. Nothing would prise him away; not healthy showers, nor games across green swards, nor brilliant opportunities.

Eddie had eventually sacked him. Another grievance to fuel his resentment. Another valid reason to find it impossible to escape from the vicious circle he found himself in.

Maisie worked, God love her, sustained them, or God knows where he'd be. She was loyal, faithful to him, no matter how tough things became. She bore him like a warrior, battle-weary, pushed to limits yet game to go on till the end. Bloody but unbowed. Without Maisie ... He could not think, would not contemplate it. He would be lost.

Yet, again, the drink made him treat her like an animal. No, worse. No, then again, the drink didn't *make* him. He drank the drink himself. No one forced him. It was the craving. Jasus, if he could only stop! He'd tried often enough. Once he'd given up for a whole week, Friday to Friday. Then Saturday he'd felt good. Vigorous. Full of get-up-and-go. He'd dappered himself up and gone to the pub. Talk to the boys, his friends. Show Maisie he could have one, maybe two, and leave it. Stop. Two days later he swam home, pressed suit covered in stale vomit and blood, vigour all gone. No get-up-and-go left at all.

Still Maisie stuck and the family despised her, looked down their noses at her pink nylon blouse and awful colour sense. He hated her clothes, her manners irritated him. But who was he to talk? Beggars can't choose and he reckoned he was lucky.

He moved carefully, first one leg, then the other. Maisie had pressed his suit to come to Oonagh's today. It was in a mess now. He moved his other leg again, put the soles of his feet flat on the ground, knees in the air, and pushed. The feet slid over the concrete and his legs were stretched before him on the ground again. His body hadn't risen an inch. So much for that. Trouble about being drunk was that your movements escaped you, like an infant.

'Ah, love, look at yiz. Here, let me get ye up an' out an' we'll go home now, *alanna*.'

Maisie's hands were under his armpits and she was hauling him to his feet. Maisie was a nurse. It helped in this situation.

'Now, let me brush ye down.'

'Jasus, I'm not a fuckin' baby.'

'Come on then, Joe. We'll go out the side. I said to Gabriel we'd be on our way.'

'Fuckin' bastard.'

'Ah, he's a nice man, Joe, and we can't afford to offend him. Now one last push ...'

'I'm not some fuckin' mother in labour, Maisie, leave me be,' he yelled, and nearly toppled them both on to the ground.

'If I lave ye, ye'll be down on yer backside in a flash. Come on now. We'll slip out the side.'

Out the side again. Hurrying away or being hurried away in shame and embarrassment. Maisie near to tears, trying to hide them, putting on a brave face. Jeez, it broke your heart.

Hang your head, Joe, hang your head! Shame! Shame! Shame!

Chapter Twelve

Ardel had heard Briana and Iain. Further down the garden, near the ivy-clad back wall where the oak tree grew in the next garden, spreading its heavy shadow on to the small path in the O'Sheas', he had listened and laughed silently to himself. In and out of the apple trees, Briana and Iain were not the only ones! Emer and Brigid had giggled together and Laughlin had stood alone, staring at the clear and lovely stars above him. Ardel had seen Joe and heard him mumble obscenities. He had heard Maisie's soothing. He had listened to the family singing 'Happy Birthday to You' to Dot, and he felt himself no part of it.

They were fools, living in a fools' paradise, happy with so little, the cracks in their lives covered with hopes that would never be realized, dreams that would never come true. He saw himself as a realist and decided that the only member of the family he understood and respected was his Uncle Eddie. There was a man who knew power lay in position and wealth, not hymns and breast-beating, tender consciences, rectitude and honour. What did all that matter when it gave so little? Ardel wondered. He wanted success and he was determined to get it.

'Hello, Ardel. How're you?' It was Mena, Molly's girl. A lurky girl, a girl who slipped through life without being noticed, yet wearing the kind of clothes that drew the eye. How she managed it Ardel did not know, but it was a talent.

He said nothing. Her remarks did not seem to need a reply. Her arms hung by her side, bare, the skin soft as silk, and she moved closer and closer to him, slowly, until she was pushing him with her breasts, but he did not budge.

There was no sound now in the garden. Only a buzz from the house could be distantly heard, and Mena kissed him.

It was a melting, deliberate kiss. A professional kiss he would say. He wanted to be in charge so he slipped out and around her until he could push her gently against the back wall, holding her helpless there, and this time *he* kissed *her*.

Angrily he realized she was playing a game with him, a power game. She kept her mouth open and allowed his tongue to wander about over her teeth, but there was no response this time. He pressed himself against her, feeling himself growing hard, feeling her pressing against him, moving her body against his. Ardel pulled up her skirt,

'No, Ardel. No,' she whispered, suddenly returning his kiss, glueing her mouth to his, making him moan softly.

'I won't hurt you. Just let me put the tip in, just the tip.'

He was feverishly trying to get her skirt right up and his trousers open when she pulled away, laughing.

'No, Ardel. Not that way. Not tonight.'

She looked at him and he knew he was helpless before her, knees trembling, trousers in disarray.

'Bitch,' he said.

'But you want me, Ardel. Look at you.' And she ran away from him, up the path towards the house.

He had not succeeded in dipping his wick with anyone except Dodie Donnelly in the grass in Phoenix Park. She was obsessed with sex was Dodie. She got all the boys to sit in a circle and show her their equipment, teasing them unmercifully, then choosing one and doing it with him while the others sat around and watched, bug-eyed, and often involuntarily came. It was great gas, that. She rolled her buttocks around underneath him and he had to get Brendan Riley to stuff his cap in his mouth in case someone might hear him yelling. Dodie loved it but she was the only girl he knew that did. All the others were freaky about sex, said their mams would kill them, said it was against their religion. What had it got to do with their mams anyhow? Only if he got them pregnant, and he had no intention of doing that, not if he didn't come inside them. It was impossible, he'd been told on good authority. It was a pity you couldn't get condoms in Ireland except on the black market at exorbitant prices. Dodie didn't seem to worry and he saw no reason to take precautions if the girl felt okay about it. And Dodie had done it with all of the guys, the six in his bunch and who knew how many more, so he was off the hook there. No one could pin the blame on him, for sure.

He thought of Mena, of her hard little elfin face and crop of black curls. Her eyes were hot when he looked at her. Well, he'd teach her a lesson, that was for sure. He thought of her last words to him, called up the garden path,

'Ye want everything at once, Ardel O'Shea, can't wait. Well, this time ye'll have to.'

Bitch, he thought.

He always got what he wanted. By fair means or foul. He smiled suddenly, took out his packet of Craven A and lit one, smoked it until his nerves had quietened down.

He'd go to the city tonight, down to Molly's pool hall. Auntie Molly wouldn't be there, she rarely was, and he didn't go when she was. He didn't want his mother finding out how much time he spent there. What she didn't know wouldn't hurt her. He liked to avoid trouble whenever possible.

Uncle Tom would be there but he wouldn't tell Oonagh about him. Ardel had seen him in the pool hall kissing a waitress from The Hot Chicken next door. The waitresses wore cute little red rah-rah skirts and frilly pants, low-cut peasant blouses and elasticized belts that clinched in their waists. Ardel loved to put his finger down the belts and pull and snap, see the angry girl turn, jumping. He'd seen Uncle Tom kiss this girl, Tina or Gina or something was her name, in the back passage of the pool hall, and he had let his uncle know that he'd seen them. He'd cleared his throat, standing there, lighting his fag, and Uncle Tom looked up from the girl's face in mid-kiss, startled, and saw his nephew standing there.

Afterwards Ardel had said, polite-like, 'I'd rather you didn't tell Mother I come here,' and all subdued his Uncle Tom said, 'Of course, Ardel. An' why would I?'

Ardel speculated on his plans contentedly, out in the dark, smoking. He'd go down the pool hall, have a beer, a bet, a game. He always won. Never lost. They called him Lucky Lad.

He dropped his fag, ground it underfoot, making the decision. He'd slip out the side after Aunt Maisie hauled Uncle Joe to his feet and got him sorted. He'd cadge a lift from somone. Eddie and Colista might not have gone yet. He could ride with them in the great big car. He hadn't heard it leave. Well, maybe if he vaulted into Deeny's next door and hurried around the front, he might still catch them.

He heard Colista's voice. "Bye, Oonagh, 'bye, Gabriel.' And the car engine started. Yeah, he could make it, tell them he was going to the Pro Cathedral. Would they fall for that? Yeah, of course they would. From him. He'd smile at them, turn it on. He could get away with murder. Yeah.

Chapter Thirteen

Everyone had gone or was going.

Oonagh said, 'All you children, help Peggy. She's inundated. Laughlin, where's Laughlin? Mourna, Briana, quit mooning and help Peggy. Emer, gather up the plates.'

'Oh, Mam, I'm exhausted from Maggie,' Emer cried, whingeing a little, telling the truth. Her greedy little cousin had worn her out.

Oonagh went out to wave to Ben and Dot and their brood. They walked down the street hand in hand, Dot's blonde curls bouncing youthfully, the crocodile of kids following, two by two. The other Morans were piling into their battered old Ford, Tom telling them to squeeze up together, Mena complaining, Banan remote and louring as usual, Roac, nervous and irritable, wanting to stay.

'Well, you can't,' Molly snapped and smacked his knee.

Denis Cowley was still practising on his skates. He waved to Oonagh as he whizzed by, and lost his direction and hit a lamp-post quite hard. Oonagh saw that the Bensons had backed the Bentley, turned it, and now it rolled past sedately, Colista waving, Eddie serious over the wheel — and surely that was Ardel in the back? She looked again as the car glided smoothly down the Avenue. No, she decided she must have been mistaken. She shook her head as she caught sight of Maisie, Joe hanging out of her, staggering down the street after Ben and Dot and the crocodile. Shame on him, she thought, a grown man, God help us, a disgrace. As she watched, Maggie Moran, at the rear end of the crocodile, turned around and looked at Joe and stuck out her tongue at him.

Everyone had gone. Gabriel said he'd sit out of the way in the drawing room.

'Tom says Molly's going to cause trouble on the Quays tomorrow,' he said to Oonagh who had begun to get out the hoover from under the stairs.

'Ah, well, you know Molly.'

'He says she's doing it so's Eddie will spring her. That's what *he* says.'

'Oh, Gabriel, that's nonsense. He's probably jealous, casting mud, because … well, you know.' Then suddenly, firmly, 'I don't want to talk about it, Gabriel. Now out of my way.'

He went into the drawing room. It had been cleared of ashtrays, empty plates, dirty glasses, and a cool breeze blew in through the open window from the street. He could hear Denis Cowley whizz past on his skates every ten minutes or so.

He could have a crack at the newspaper at last. The *Evening Herald* lay folded neatly on the top of the china cabinet where he had carefully put it at the beginning of the evening. He loved a quiet read of the paper. He loved to hear the women busy around the house, to smoke a pipe in peace.

Just as he had shaken the folds out, Mourna came into the room. She entered surreptitiously and carefully, noiselessly closing the door behind her, and he realized she had something to say to him. He smiled at her fondly.

'They'll never miss me, Pa,' she said.

'You'll be lucky!'

He could hear the noises from the dining room and kitchen, the high octane activity, duties squabbled over, orders flying about, his family contradicting each other as cutlery, glass and china were cleared, washed and dried, the hyperactive buzz of female diligence that warmed his heart and gave him a feeling of security and reassurance.

Gabriel loved women. He loved their soft shapes, their hectoring ways, their nagging and concern. He loved their smell, the feeling of being looked after, his needs being taken care of, he loved their unselfishness. Most of all he loved his wife Oonagh, whose body he had watched change a little more after the birth of each child and the passing of the years. He loved her with absolute acceptance of the woman she was, the woman she had become, the woman he had helped to shape. He loved the signs he saw of the girl she once was, the girl he had courted and married, and the occasional glimpses of the old woman she would become. She was his wife, his other half, his dearly beloved partner for life, and life encompassed all these things; time represented in her.

He loved his children too, but often felt remote from them. Their experiences were strange to him, he did not intuitively understand them. But he was scrupulously fair with them, strict but kind. Tom said he was too lenient.

'They're not afraid of you, Gabriel, and they should be,' he said.

Gabriel did not agree but he did not argue. It was his way. He disliked arguments but, as with the decision about Dranmore for the holiday, he had an uncanny knack of getting his own way without fuss. So his children both obeyed and trusted him.

He looked at his daughter now. She put her finger to her lips and sat opposite him.

'I've got to talk to you, Pa,' she said softly.

'Shouldn't you be helping your mother first?' he asked mildly.

'It's too important. It's about Laughlin.'

'What's the matter?'

Mourna looked at her father, her cornflower eyes wide and clear. 'It's difficult, Pa. I don't know how to begin, or even if I can tell you. I don't know if I understand.' Her brow was creased, her beautiful face troubled, but he gave her time and waited, silently. 'See, Pa, there's this Brother, this Christian Brother …'

He knew immediately what she was going to say. He had wondered how he would react if anyone tried to interfere sexually or harass one of his children. He knew now. The rage in him was barely containable. It boiled within him, threatening to erupt.

'This Brother is, er, touching Laughlin in, well, funny places …'

Gabriel couldn't remain sitting. He rose abruptly, jack-knifed out of his chair, fists clenched.

'I understand what you're trying to say, Mourna. You need go no further,' he said gruffly. He went and poured himself a whiskey to give himself a little time, to calm himself.

He noticed his hand was trembling. He took a gulp, steadied himself, and turned his face to his daughter.

'What is this Brother's name?' he asked, his voice sounding harsh.

Mourna gave him a swift inquiring look but the glance he gave her in return was reassuring.

'Nathan. Brother Nathan. Laughlin wanted to come and tell you, Pa, himself, but he was a bit shy.'

'I'm very proud of you, Mourna, that you told me. Very grateful he came to you, that he trusted you. Tell him, will you, that the matter will be taken care of? That he needn't worry any more.'

'Okay, Pa.'

'And Mourna …'

'Yes, Pa.'

'Tell him before he goes to bed. It'll ease his mind.'

'Okay.'

She went to the door.

He said again, 'And Mourna …'

She turned. 'Yes, Pa?'

'I'm that proud of you. Thanks.'

'Thanks, Pa.'

Impelled by a rush of love she ran over to him and hugged him. Then awkwardly she turned to leave the room.

'Thanks, Pa,' she said again over her shoulder, and left.

Chapter Fourteen

That night he told Oonagh that he had decided to take Laughlin away from the Christian Brothers and send him back to Belvedere. She was stunned.

'But why, Gabriel? What has happened?'

'He's not like the others, love,' he said. 'Ardel is a real tough guy and Emmett loves the Brothers. Laughlin is not happy there at all, and if we're careful we can just about afford it.'

'But it means such sacrifice, Gabriel. There will be no extra bathroom, will there?'

'I'm afraid not, my love. But Laughlin's happiness comes first.'

He carefully put his waistcoat on the hanger, put his jacket over that, shook them, smoothing them and putting them in the wardrobe. He unbuttoned his trousers and took them off, arranging the legs carefully in the trouser-press. Now came the difficult part. He wondered how she'd take it. He snapped the press shut and looked at her.

She sat on the side of the bed, pulling off her lisle stockings. No Colista she. No silk, no nylon stockings, no

L'Aimant, no manicured hands. He remembered her sitting just like that on their honeymoon in the hotel in Kerry. Her legs were slim then, her waist eighteen inches around. He looked at her with compassion and love. She had sacrificed her waist, her breasts, her legs, willingly, and she had borne her children with joy. Now his heart flooded with love for her.

Oonagh had been about to tell him she was pregnant. She had been steeling herself when he had made this announcement about Laughlin. She put her hand to her heart. She waited for what he was going to say. Something terrible had happened to make Gabriel do this, something awful. She knew her husband, she was not a fool. He did not do things suddenly like that without powerful reasons.

She shivered. 'What is it, love? What's wrong?' she asked.

Gabriel knelt at her feet. 'Why do I always underestimate you?'

She smiled. 'Why do we underestimate each other?' she replied.

'I wasn't going to tell you, thinking you would not understand. Oh, darling.' He held her arms and she looked at him intently.

'It's serious, isn't it? Don't be afraid to tell me.'

'One of the Christian Brothers … Laughlin was …'

As usual she surprised him. 'Oh, no! Not that!' she cried and he realized that she, like he, had guessed instantly.

'Nothing too bad, my dear. Let's leave it at that. Laughlin asked Mourna to tell me. Poor lad was nervous. Understandable, really. I couldn't have told my da. But, love, it's holidays in three weeks. Let's keep him home and send him to Belvedere and the Jesuits in September. We can just manage it if we're careful.'

'How bad was it? Did he …?'

'Rest easy, my dear. Mourna said "touched him where he shouldn't". She's pretty accurate and I got the impression that she was quoting Laughlin. In any event we mustn't dwell on it. It's over and we must put the whole unpleasant incident behind us. I'll see the Head and give him my reasons for taking Laughlin out of school.'

Her lip trembled. She wanted so badly to tell him about the baby, return trust for trust, but she could not. Not now, not with this new expense. Suppose, when he heard her news, he decided that Laughlin had to stay with the Christian Brothers? (That filthy man, that dirty beast, interfering with her angel!) She knew he wouldn't. Gabriel wouldn't leave Laughlin in that situation. But suppose? Suppose her news meant he had no choice? She said nothing. She drew in a deep breath and smiled back at him. 'Whatever you decide, my love, will be right.'

He hugged her, then asked, 'Why'd you vote against the plan for Dranmore, pet?'

She blushed. 'I suppose I wanted to … oh, it sounds silly now, Gabriel, in the light of these, more important matters, but I wanted to assert myself, I suppose. Sometimes I long for us both to go away, just ourselves, like it was that time in Kerry.' So fleeting, their time alone, a short, precious memory. 'And if we couldn't have that, then just *our* family alone, not the whole tribe.'

He shook his head. 'You know, pet, that that's not possible. There's my mother.' No, they couldn't just forget about Granny O'Shea.

'Then Rita and Joe, what would they do?'

He was so very Christian, she thought, like Christians ought to be, concerned about others, responsible. Duty came first. Deep in her heart she wished that just once he'd throw it all to the winds and sweep her away on a dream.

'You're good, Gabriel. You're a very good man,' she said, ashamed of her thoughts.

He put his arms around her, kissed her lips and asked, 'Can I, tonight?'

She nodded, smiling. What irony.

'Oh, yes,' she said, thinking of the warm coupling, familiar and loving, that brought them close as two people could get.

'Is it safe?' he asked, meaning could he come inside her? It had been a careless yes to that question that had got her into the predicament she was in now.

'Oh, yes, darling, it's safe,' she said. 'It's very safe.'

Chapter Fifteen

Ardel stood in the dim smoky pool hall, leaning against the wall, casing the place for a likely mark. He wanted someone who would be fooled by his youthful appearance into thinking him an easy victim. Although only eighteen, Ardel, sharp as a razor, had taken many a forty-year-old cocksure expert to the cleaners both at the pool tables and also the card games that sprouted illegally around the hall and its environs. They thought him young and inexperienced, and, determined to teach the young whippersnapper a lesson, show him how cards or pool should *really* be played, ended up sadder, wiser and poorer. They learned painfully not automatically to associate youth with ignorance.

The pool hall was an enormous dark basement room in Abbey Street. There was a semi-circular bar, oak-topped, scored and stained by a million glasses of Smithwick or Guinness. There was a mirror behind. It was so dimly lit it was difficult to see what you were drinking. Below was the windowless hanger-hall filled with green baize tables, the 'pock-pock' sound of cues on balls a constant background noise.

Ardel shot a game with a bleary-eyed punter and won two pounds. The punter was asthmatic and coughed just before he shot the ball which meant a lot of his shots went wild. He was an old-timer and played not to win or lose but simply for the joy of playing. It was the only time he was really alive, forgot his aches and pains, enjoyed himself and savoured life. He didn't mind losing at all.

Tom Moran had seen his nephew come into the pool hall and had given him a wide berth. He hated Ardel O'Shea with a passion only exceeded by his loathing of his step-son Banan. Ardel had something on him, something lethal, and it made Tom acutely uneasy that the boy had that power.

He'd use it too, Tom had no doubt. He was quite ruthless, was Ardel O'Shea.

Tom didn't like to contemplate what would happen if Molly found out. He was quite sure she didn't know of his little strayings from the marriage bed, his Tom-cat couplings with plump little girls in uniforms. The Hot Chicken waitresses from next door were tasty as the sauce with which they smothered the food they served. He could no more resist them than a gourmet could pork crackling.

But Molly was a fierce and fiery woman, quite unlike Oonagh or Colista, manageable females in his opinion. She'd massacre him, destroy him, if she found out. She'd turf him out; he'd lose his job, managing the place, for the pool hall was hers. He'd be for the high-jump and out the door quick as a flash; he doubted she'd even let him pack. The thought made his blood run cold, and he shivered. She'd have no qualms, he thought. Like Joe he'd have to live in a caravan or, worse, roam the streets of Dublin homeless. Jasus, it made him sweat to think of it.

Yet he couldn't stop the philandering. God knows he'd tried. He knew it was dangerous, he knew the score, yet he couldn't stop any more than Joe could stop drinking. It was like a disease. Like a drug-addict, he had to have his fix.

There was a concealed window in the office where the

staff could observe the pool hall, and if there was trouble, phone the police. It was the policy of the place that the staff did not intervene. It would be a fool-hardy thing to do, so any problems were sorted by the Garda Shiochanna.

He peered out now, saw Ardel pocketing the quids, shaking hands with the old-timer, nodding to him and returning to his favourite position; leaning nonchalantly against the wall. The boy's long lanky frame was as relaxed and ready to spring as a leopard dozing in the shade, and just as lethal. Tom shivered again.

As he watched he saw Banan arrive, look around, see Ardel and go over to him. Tom's heart sank. He wondered did they talk? Did they gossip? Exchange notes about the family? Ugh! Jasus, he'd be destroyed. Ardel was shit-mean but Banan was meaner.

Banan hated his step-father and if he found out about the floozies Tom knew he was a lost man. Banan'd make a meal of him. But there he had a little power, he thought smugly. Tom Moran knew of his step-son's association with an I.R.A. group and Banan dared not allow the animosity he felt for his step-father to show too much or Tom might just shop him to the authorities. They were very anxious, since Ireland became a Republic, to stamp out any trouble of that sort, and there were rewards.

Actually, the only reason Tom didn't inform on his step-son was the fear of reprisal. That organization, or the fanatics who were left in it, not accepting the peace, determined to continue the war, was lethal, and tenaciously pursued anyone who betrayed one of its own. Tom did not want to be looking over his shoulder for the rest of his life.

The old Irish Republican Army had been disbanded when Ireland was given self-determination and attained independence. Yet there were some who would not let the fighting die, were not content with half (or, to be precise, three-quarter) measures. England still held the North, with her golden-guinea shipyards and cotton mills, and there were those who wanted a United Ireland, an island whole under the blue flag with the golden harp, not the make-shift green (Erin), white (peace) between, and orange (for the North, the land of William of Orange, King Billy). Green, white and orange, not the blue and gold it should be. So these people, some set in the ways of violence, some genuine patriots and idealists who could not settle with the division, some used to the life, the excitement it engendered, incapable of adapting to peace, formed groups and battled on, while the vast majority of Irish men and women settled down to freedom, to making their own government work, to forming their own Army, Navy and Police Force, to stimulating their country's productivity, making it economically viable if not wealthy.

Banan O'Rourke had only this legacy from his father, Sean O'Rourke, an Irish hero in the struggle, a martyr, a hard and angry man who said with his dying words that he couldn't rest until Ireland was united. Banan had inherited his father's nature, his resentment, his incli- nation to blame his bad luck and wasted life on politics rather than his own disposition. Banan had seized on the ideal of a united country and held to it tenaciously, closing his mind, neither bending nor bowing to the changing climate of the times, blaming his own belligerence on the policies of the Irish Government, and fighting for the I.R.A.

Banan hated Tom Moran as vehemently as his step-father hated him. He resented his presence in his mother's bed, resented his management of the pool hall which, he felt, was his domain. It was a perfect cover for the meetings and a place that should be dubbed a 'safe house', guaranteed. But bloody Tom Moran made that chancey.

Tom watched his step-son with distaste. He was jealous of the boy's youth, his looks, so like his mother's – wild black hair and fierce blue eyes – jealous of his relationship

105

with Molly. He feared Banan, and anyone Tom feared, he hated.

What were they talking about? He wished they were right under the concealed window so he could hear, but Banan knew of the peep-hole and would be certain not to risk saying anything near it. Tom watched with narrowed eyes and felt sure that something was brewing. He determined to find out what it was.

~~~~~~~

Banan said, 'A courier, Ardel. That's all. The pay is brilliant.'

'Much?' Ardel took a drag on the Craven A and looked into the hard blue eyes level with his own.

'Tenner a go. Sometimes twenty. Sometimes, if you're lucky, more. You'll take in more'n your da, promise.'

'Hey, what about danger? It's illegal, isn't it?'

Banan shrugged. 'Oh, Ardel, nuthin's for nuthin'. It's illegal all right. What isn't? Anyhow, you don't earn that class of money over the table, Ardel, c'm'on!'

'What'll I carry?'

'Parcels. No questions, no prying.'

Now it was Ardel's turn to shrug. He took another pull on his fag. 'Where?'

'Here and there. Not far. If it's any distance you get paid extra expenses. We're not mean.'

'Okay. What do I care? It's money.'

'Jesus, Ardel, you got no patriotism? You do this for money? What kind of a man are you? This your country after all.'

'Keep calm, Banan. We're not all heroes.' Ardel smiled. 'What you care anyhow 's'long as I do the job?'

'Okay. But don't get any ideas, y'hear? It'd be more'n your life is worth. Understand? You'd have to drop off the edge of the world.'

106

'As if I would. What kind of an eejit you take me for?'

It was precisely what Ardel had been thinking and he was not frightened by Banan's warning. Get their trust, he thought, make the dough, then when he had enough, disappear. Carry a consignment (what would it be? guns? money? drugs? something saleable) right out of Dublin, on to a boat and off to where they couldn't find him. Easy.

'You'll do it then?'

'Sure. No worry.'

As if he read Ardel's thoughts, Banan said, 'Our arms are long. They stretch to England and further. And we're patient. We get there in the end. Informers, traitors, Judases, smart alecs rarely live to tell the tale. Remember that.' He stared at Ardel a long moment, then said, 'I'll be in touch.'

He gripped Ardel's hand, shook it once, and turning on his heel left the hall. But before he reached the exit he deliberately looked up to the spy-hole and made an up-yours sign to Tom, grinning mirthlessly.

Ardel stared after him. The cigarette smoke was thick now and it seemed to reflect the green of the tables so that Banan appeared to move in a verdant haze, blurry and somehow menacing. Ardel shivered, then his natural buoyancy returned and he stubbed out the cigarette on the linoleum, ground it beneath his heel and looked around for another gormless eejit to take.

He made a fiver that night, the hard way, he thought, and remembered Banan's promise.

He left by the back entrance, a lane off Abbey Street. As he emerged into the night air he heard someone softly calling his name.

'Ardel, Ardel, here.'

The voice came from above. He looked up to see Mena leaning from her window. Mena with the wicked eyes.

'Hello. You been conning the old pros?' She sounded mocking.

'I did all right,' he said, and laughed. 'Got no complaints. What you doin' up, kid like you?'

'I'm eighteen,' she said.

'Never!' he teased. 'I thought you were twelve!'

She giggled. 'That'd make what I did to you in your back garden illegal.'

There was a street-lamp under the window. He could see her face clearly, the hot eyes, the cigarette she was holding.

'You got no conscience, Mena?'

She tossed her cute black curls.

'No,' she said. 'None.'

'How come?' he asked.

'Me da has it off with the chicks next door, or anything that moves and is young. Me mam is deeply in love with someone else. Banan is a murderer, and poor Roac really believes none of this is happening. So what use are morals?'

He was taken aback by what she said. Then he thought, Typically female, exaggerate everything.

'Da is a bundle of guilt,' she continued. 'Mam can't sleep, she hasn't the courage to *do* something, and Banan spends his life making excuses for himself, saying he's killing people in a good cause. You ever hear anything so silly? So daft? Horse shit! That's morals for you. Uncle Eddie and Colista, they got no morals. They're top of the heap. That's where no morals gets you. See what I mean?'

He shook his head. 'You talk just like a woman.'

'That's another thing,' she said, eyes fierce. 'No one – repeat *no one* – will ever pull that male stuff on me! No man is ever going to boss me, bully me, force me to do anything I don't want.'

'Whee! Like to see you stop a great big hunk,' he said derisively. He was out of his depth. He didn't understand her at all.

'Like to see him try,' she said quietly. 'Like to see him try.

108

Well, night, Ardel. Nice talkin' to you. Remember what I said.'

He looked up and she was gone. The street was dark and deserted. He turned up his jacket collar and headed home, his footsteps echoing on the cobblestones.

Chapter Sixteen

The next morning Oonagh took Mourna shopping. Gabriel was hurt that they didn't go to Barnet's but his wife said firmly, 'No, dear, this requires the most stylish dress available and so we'll go to Grafton Street.'

'But I could have got you a discount,' Gabriel said.

'Well, with Colista paying that's not necessary,' Oonagh replied in a voice that brooked no argument.

Peggy was putting the house back in order. Emmett had gone to early Mass and communion and the others were sleeping.

When Mourna left Briana was still in bed. Soundlessly, Mourna took out her evening dress, the sea-green taffeta Briana loved, and hung it in her sister's part of the wardrobe. Bri would understand and it would make up for the fact that she was not included in Colista's generosity.

They took the bus into town. They saw a lot of people they knew on the journey and Oonagh said the same thing to them all: 'We're going into Brown Thomas to buy Mourna a special frock. We're going to Kilcrony Country Club tonight, y'know, for the dress dance.' Oonagh's face wore an excited flush and she bustled about with an air of importance. 'That'll give them something to think about,' she whispered to Mourna.

They had a pleasurably anxious time selecting from a gorgeous collection in Brown Thomas. They chose a black lace sheath that was strapless and hugged Mourna's figure perfectly.

'It's dead plain, Mummy,' she said happily.

'Classy,' Oonagh said, nodding, satisfied. Mourna's shoulders rose from the soft material like columns of marble, and the dress outlined the curve of her breasts. The *décolletage* was perfect, Oonagh thought, discreetly revealing the blue-veined slopes.

'None of yer Restoration wench, modom,' the saleswoman said in a ripe phoney accent. 'More Carole Lombard, eff you know what I mean. Ladylike.'

They bought shoes to match and Oonagh said, 'You can have my black *diamanté* evening bag if you can manage to squeeze in my lipstick and powder. We'll share it, love.'

'Oh, Mam, that'd be great!'

'Mummy, darling.'

They had coffee in Mitchell's, sitting in the window, watching the fashionable parade pass up and down Grafton Street. Pretty women from Stillorgan, Dalkey and Killiney, looking to see what was new in the windows of Switzer's, or sitting all around them in couples and groups, chatting over coffee and cream cakes. Lawyers hurried past holding sheaves of papers clutched in their arms, intent on reaching Molesworth Street and the Four Courts. Actors, perfectly groomed, dapper or glamorous, strolled up to the Gaiety to rehearse.

'Oh, Mummy, look!' Mourna pointed, directing her mother's gaze to where Diarmuid McDiarmuid was emerging from Weirs & West. Actor, poet, wit, he flashed his famous smile haphazardly about and the crowds parted respectfully to let him through.

'They must be playing in the Gaiety,' Mourna said, and

110

continued to sip her coffee.

Her mother nodded. 'Yes. *Midsummer Night's Dream.* Diarmuid McDiarmuid is playing Oberon. And then they go on tour. I read it in the papers.'

'Oh, Mummy, look! Isn't that the handsomest boy you've ever seen?' she asked, and Oonagh didn't have to enquire who she was talking about. Beside the great actor was a young man, tanned, with a swashbuckling charm. He was laughing. Everything about him was captivating.

'Yes, well, actors, you know.' Oonagh's mouth narrowed. 'That's Hector Breen. Now come along, Mourna.'

Oonagh's one fear was that Mourna would, as she put it, throw herself away on a pretty face. Someone like Hector Breen. So she hurried her daughter out of the coffee shop and they were home in time for lunch.

The afternoon was a hectic swirl of activity as Mourna, Briana and Oonagh prepared for the evening. There were dresses to be tucked and ironed. (Not the new black lace, of course.) There were shoes to be refurbished and polished, bags that needed attention, a sequin sewn on here, a *diamanté* stud there. There was hair to be washed and curled and set, and they all had to share the bathroom.

Emer sat on the stairs in the curve of the flight, waiting for her period to come. She sat alone, close against the wall, and the family ignored her as they passed. She was quite content now that she was wearing a sanitary towel. She sat there and read *Jane Eyre* and dreamed of Mr Rochester and becoming a star.

Ardel was nowhere to be seen but there was so much going on that no one missed him. He had been asked to join the party but had refused on the grounds that he had no evening dress. He simply didn't want to go.

Laughlin was in great form, he had taken his togs and a towel and bicycled off to Dollymount Strand with Denis Cowley for a dip. Emmett, who had returned from Mass in

111

St Agnes', ate an absentminded lunch then went to the bottom of the garden to swing.

Gabriel kept out of the way in the drawing room and looked at the *Herald*, which he had been prevented from reading last night, as well as this morning's *Independent* and *Irish Times*. He asked Mourna to bring him a coffee and send Laughlin to him. The interview was brief.

'Sit, son,' he said when the boy entered, looking acutely uncomfortable. 'Your sister talked to me last evening.'

'Yes, Da.' Laughlin blushed, looked flustered, and shifted from foot to foot.

'Sit down, boy. There, that's better. I'm keeping you home these next weeks.'

'But, Da ...' Laughlin wasn't sure he wanted that. To be out of it all, away from the school altogether, the routine, the rough-and-tumble, the cameraderie. To be at home alone, but for Ma and Peggy busy about the house, getting in their way, under their feet, would be a pain.

'Listen, Laughlin, I'm sending you back to Belvedere.'

His heart rose.

'What I want you to do – promise me faithfully, it's like a trust – is to spend the day here, in the drawing room. No one comes in here of a morning or afternoon. Study here, like you were in school. You can come out for lunch, but back after. We'll make a timetable from the one you have. You got the picture?'

'Oh, yes, Da.'

'Promise? Otherwise, no deal.'

'Promise, Da.'

'It's only for three weeks, two really. I remember the last week at school before the long vacation, no work was ever done. I don't expect things have changed that much?'

'No, Da, they haven't.'

'Then in September you'll go back to the Jesuits.'

'Oh, yes, Da.'

'All right, Laughlin. That's all.'

'Thank you, Da.'

Laughlin turned and went to the door.

'And, Laughlin?' his father said.

'Yes, Da?'

'You did the right thing … going to Mourna. Good lad. Never keep things to yourself. They fester.'

'No, Da.'

'Well, well, off you go. Tell Mourna to bring me in the coffee. It's a mad house out there and I've no intention of joining it.'

'Okay, Da.'

~~~~~~

Tansy sat on the end of Briana's bed while Mourna got ready in the master bedroom.

'God'n you're lucky, going to Kilcrony.' She gazed admiringly at Briana in Mourna's sea-green taffeta. Briana had strict instructions from Oonagh not to sit down and get it creased.

'But it'll get all scrunched up in the car,' Briana said, and Tansy fingered the shimmering material enviously and said, 'No, but Briana, I know what she means. The *less* you sit, the *less* creased it'll get.'

'So I haveta stand. I feel like an eejit.' She stood at the window watching for the car.

'Isn't Ardel going?' Tansy asked.

'He *says* it's because he has no evening clothes but I don't believe that. Da said he'd rent some from Bourke's but Ardel refused.'

'Why?' Tansy tried to appear casual. She was mad about Ardel though he never appeared to notice her. Briana shrugged.

'Oh, it's hard to tell with Ardel. He's got other fish to fry.'

'Like, maybe, a girl?' Tansy kept her voice light.

'Oh, no! Ardel's not that interested in girls. He likes

them but they're not important to him. No, he's ambitious.' Briana looked vague. 'I dunno, Tansy. I don't understand Ardel. Never did.' She leaned closer to the window. 'Will you look at that?' Her voice sounded incredulous. 'It's Denis Cowley out there in the dark, practising! Can you believe it?'

Tansy was silent, realizing that the vein had run dry, that Briana had nothing more to say about Ardel, and at that moment her friend shrieked, 'The car's here! The car's here! Mam! Oh, Mam!'

The car, driven by Brody, had arrived sedately at the door. It was exactly seven o'clock.

'Don't keep him waiting.' Oonagh, who had been ready since six o'clock, fussed over last minute touches to Mourna's coiffure.

'Isn't that what he's paid to do?' Gabriel asked mildly, deftly arranging his bow tie. He'd left it a bit late to get dressed and now Oonagh chivvied him to hurry up.

He looked very attractive in his evening clothes, she thought, even as she hectored and drove him on. His dinner jacket was of a slightly old-fashioned cut. Nevertheless, she was proud and happy that she was married to this man.

Oonagh sat beside him in the car, on the soft well-sprung leather seats, Briana and Mourna opposite them. She thought, I could live like this, this is the life. This is the way to travel. She lapped it up: the smoothly rolling automobile, the driver, smartly uniformed, her best dress on her, her husband, band-box fresh beside her, and her two daughters, lovely as flowers, opposite. Briana, in Mourna's sea-green, looked fresh and pretty. She had a becoming flush to her cheeks and Oonagh was glad she had not succumbed to her daughter's pleas to wear make-up. In the frame of her dark hair, the soft curves of youth, the sparkle of excitement in her eyes, were enough.

And Mourna looked, as usual, breathtaking in the black

114

lace which made her skin seem whiter, her hair seem darker, and her eyes more like violets than ever.

'It's us she chose,' Oonagh crowed to Gabriel, thinking of Colista. 'Us. Not the others. She's cultivating us, Gabriel. Because of Mourna, I suppose. And because I know how to behave and what's done and not done. They have powerful connections, pet, and they could be a great help in placing the boys and finding suitable matches for the girls. Introduce them to the right class of boy. Oh, we're on our way!'

'Don't get over-excited, dear.' Gabriel patted her hand but Oonagh would not hear him. She had a vision of endless parties, of tennis in the summer and riding in the winter, of boating and sailing, of swimming and young people drinking champagne – and her girls there, participating, part of the privileged group. After tonight anything was possible. A Countess! Mourna could be a titled lady!

She gave herself over to the enjoyment of the drive, queening it in the back of the car, looking graciously out on the populace. She hoped a few of the neighbours had seen her.

They crossed the city in style. Past the Gresham, Nelson's Pillar, the Metropole, the Liffey. Over the bridge and out to the south side. The houses here were bigger, detached. Cars parked in driveways beside manicured lawns, groomed homes; all the signs of affluence.

When they arrived in Dalkey, when the car swept up the drive, when Brody jumped out and opened the car door for them, handed her out, then Mourna and Briana after her, and they mounted the steps to the open door of the square Georgian mansion, Oonagh felt positively regal. She savoured the grandeur of the moment, the servants taking her tippet, the fox cape Molly had lent Mourna, and Briana's taffeta stole. Standing in the spacious hall, being received, knowing she was welcome, knowing she belonged, was family, she had a moment of pure ecstasy.

Then she saw Ben and Dot and her bubble burst. If

Colista had asked *them*, and she obviously had, then there was no real advantage, this was no honour, and there was nothing to crow about. Tonight was a poor relations night, a night geared down to them rather than a party to elevate the O'Sheas into the higher strata as she had at first supposed. Janey Mac, Dot and Ben!

Colista was greeting them, presenting a cool cheek to be kissed. She wore beige chiffon and looked extremely elegant as usual, willow wand-slim. How did she do it? Oonagh wondered, then knew: one child, and money.

'Oonagh, how smart you are as usual,' Colista said graciously. 'Mourna, Briana, you're both heavenly. When I see you I'm quite cast down that I never had a daughter.' She sighed and smiled at her sister. 'Well done, Oonagh.' Then to Mourna, 'Perfect choice, perfect. Gabriel, the men seem to be gravitating towards the smoking room – to the right, as you probably remember.'

She looked at her sister, sensed her agitation, followed her gaze. 'Yes, Oonagh, it's Dot and Ben.' She leaned forward until her face was close and Oonagh could see a fine film of moisture on her upper lip. 'I couldn't get out of inviting them. They practically asked themselves yesterday. They heard me talking to you, Dot did, I think, and she thrust herself at me, saying in her little-girl way ... so phoney, don't you think? ... "You must ask birthday girl, Colista." So I *had* to. Anyhow, come along with me, into the drawing room. Follow us, Briana, Mourna. She goes – Dot, that is – "Ben and I would love you to ask us." So what could I do?'

Colista paused at the door, hand on knob, still talking to Oonagh. 'You know what she's like. I tend to give in to her so that she has no complaint, then I don't have to see her for, well, as long as I can possibly make it. I don't want to cause a rift though, do I?'

She took Mourna's arm, leaving a distinctly relieved Oonagh to follow with Briana. People turned as they

116

entered. Iain rose from the settee he was sitting on with a bunch of young people and hurried over, his face turned to Briana, but his mother intercepted him and paired him with Mourna.

'Take your cousin and get her a drink, Iain,' she instructed. Then, to Oonagh, 'Come and meet everyone. The Count is not here. He said he'd meet us in the Club. Now let me see … Mrs O'Brien, Mrs O'Shea. Lord Davenport, Mrs O'Shea. Lady Davenport, Mr O'Sullivan-Moore, Mrs O'Shea.'

Drinks were served. All the ladies seemed to be having gin and it, confirming Oonagh's conviction that it was the fashion in high society. She floated on a cloud of social success, chatting with the rich and famous as if, she said afterwards to Gabriel, she'd been born to it.

The men who had been in the smoking room joined them and Oonagh was able to hang on Gabriel's arm, proud of him, more confident with him. He was much better looking than a lot of the men in the room, and even if his jacket was a wee bit ill-fitting he was holding his own with a Lord and a solicitor!

'You know, Lady Davenport, I had exactly the same problem with my Emmett. Sucked his thumb until he was eleven. Still does it now and then, when he's tired and worried, and, I assure you, it never spoiled his mouth. So you needn't worry about it.'

'That makes me feel much better, Mrs O'Shea. Is that your daughter over there? I heard Colista say … she's beautiful. You must be very proud.'

Oonagh's smile was gracious. She was pleased with the way Lady Davenport leaned towards her as if they were old friends, and received her advice so eagerly. She accepted the compliments on Mourna with a dignified nod of acceptance.

After about an hour of chit-chat some of the people there began to take their leave, talking of dinner. Dot,

117

looking more incongruous than usual, a riot of curls and frills and rouge, topped by a huge artificial flower that defied classification, at her bosom, came over to Oonagh.

'You're going to the Club?' she inquired fiercely.

'Yes, Colista insisted.' Oonagh had not realized her sister-in-law had only been invited to the Bensons' house, not the party afterwards. She felt a mean glow of triumph envelop her and she was ashamed. All she wanted was for Dot to disappear and not embarrass her in front of these people.

'It's because of Mourna,' she whispered to Dot, pouring balm on her hurt. 'She wants to introduce Mourna to someone special.'

'My Mary'll never look like Mourna,' Dot said emotionally.

'Well, she'll be herself, Dot. She'll be pretty when she's a little older, you'll see.'

'Oh, it's not fair!' Dot said, and people began to turn their heads to see what was happening. Colista whisked Dot and Ben outside, put them in a car, and they were away before Dot could do any damage.

The favoured ones were scooped up, Oonagh amongst them, moved out into the balmy night, slipped into cars, made comfortable, and feeling relaxed and genial were borne smoothly along the coast road, where a necklace of lights shimmered in the dark, until they reached the Club.

Once again doors were opened for them, this time by uniformed doormen, and the sound of music, romantic and lush, started faintly and grew louder and louder as they checked their wraps, put the little tags in their purses and entered the dinner-dance.

The room was large, a chandelier and candles in delicate little storm-globes lighting it softly so that the women acquired a sheen that made their skin luminous. Around the dance floor people sat at tables laid for dinner with white linen, cut-glass, silver cutlery. The band wore white jackets and changed now from playing 'La Vie En Rose' to 'Abba-Dabba-Dabba-Dabba-Dabba-Dabba-Dabba Said the Monkey to the Chimp'. Their leader turned every now and then to show his teeth in a wide smile to the members and their guests at the tables. The couples on the dance floor didn't look at him.

The Bensons' table was the best in the room. They took their seats, one chair remaining tantalisingly empty. Drinks were ordered, and they sat and smoked and ate and drank and then danced, and the chair was never filled. Oonagh didn't care whether the Count ever came or not, she was having too good a time, but Colista seemed restless and kept looking around the room, searching.

Eddie pressed his napkin to his mouth and bowed to Mourna. 'Will you dance with me, Princess?' he inquired, and she laughed and put out a hand to accept.

At that moment Colista called, 'Oh Kurt, Kurt, you naughty boy, where have you been?' to a man crossing the floor, a tall blond man with a military-straight back and a handsome if severe face.

'I'm so sorry. I was delayed,' he said, bowing over her.

'You're atrociously late.' Colista lightly slapped his hand, and pulled Eddie towards her. 'Now, my husband you know. Who have you not met?'

'Where did you buy your daughter's frock?' Lady Davenport asked Oonagh.

'Brown Thomas,' she replied, looking at the newcomer with appraising eyes.

'It's lovely,' Lady Davenport said.

His accent was slight and his eyes very light blue. They searched the table, then relaxed and smiled. Oonagh, following his gaze, saw he was looking at Mourna.

'Ah, there she is,' he breathed, and Oonagh felt a sudden surge of resentment. Mourna was not a prize.

Oonagh waited to be introduced. She glanced at Eddie and saw that he was staring, eyes narrowed, at Iain and

Briana on the dance floor. Oonagh stared too for her daughter's head rested comfortably on Iain's shoulder with a familiarity that was surprising and touching at the same time. Eddie looked angry, but there was nothing he could do. As they watched, the music swelled and 'Who's Sorry Now?' saturated the eardrums with a surge of romantic violins, and Briana lifted her face from Iain's shoulder and looked at him – a private, loving, sweet exchange that astonished Oonagh and made her gasp,

'Briana!'

'Well, Colista, well?' Kurt looked at his hostess and she smiled and drew Mourna to her.

'Kurt, this is Mourna. Mourna O'Shea. Oonagh, Kurt.'

He fixed his light blue eyes on Oonagh and smiled. She smiled back. She decided he was charming but, as yet, an unknown quantity. Gabriel, she noted, was very wary. Everyone else seemed to know Kurt.

Oonagh watched her daughter closely as she met the man her aunt and mother hoped she'd marry. She smiled at him shyly, modestly, nothing effusive about her yet obviously not disliking him. Who could tell? It was too soon yet. The German was admiring and at once asked her to dance. Mourna inclined her head and he led her on to the floor.

They made an attractive couple, moving to the music, graceful together, well-matched, the right height. The band played, 'I've Got You Under My Skin'. Would they remember, Oonagh wondered, in after years? Say to each other, 'When we first met they played "I've Got You Under My Skin" in that club in Wicklow, in Ireland.' Where would they be then? Perhaps standing on the steps of a castle in Germany? Looking at a sunset in France? Count and Countess.

She felt suddenly emotional and overcome with nostalgia; for her own youth and the romance she had known, for Kerry and her so short time alone with Gabriel, and the knowledge within her that things always change.

120

She had said to Gabriel the other day, 'Remember Kerry? That summer? When you stopped the trap and plucked a branch of blossom from the hawthorn tree and put it in my hair?'

And Gabriel, to her delight, said, 'Yes, indeed I do.' Then spoiled it, adding, 'God, you were a mess that day! We'd come in from haymaking and your hair was full of straw. I leaned over to take some out. It stuck every which way.'

'Not to put the blossom in?'

'No. Not at first,' he said casually. Then asked, 'When's dinner?'

She had been shattered. All those years she had seen that moment as the encapsulation of their romance, the moment they knew they loved each other. The memory shone, a picture in a golden summery haze as if shot through gauze. And now Gabriel had torn the gauze away and revealed the reality underneath. For him there had been no romantic scene. Two memories of the same incident, so different.

She caught Gabriel's glance and smiled at him. He nodded but she could not tell what he was thinking and that irritated her. She looked back at Mourna, moving confidently in the arms of the stranger, and wondered what they were saying.

'I hope Mourna is not seduced by this silly idea of Colista's?'

Oonagh looked at Eddie in surprise. His tone was unusually sharp, lacking its even tenor. He stood just behind her chair and was staring at the couple on the dance floor.

'Why, Eddie? Don't you like the Count?'

'He's German,' Eddie said coolly. 'What do we really know about him?'

Oonagh blinked. She didn't want to think about anything taxing this evening.

121

'Oh, Colista is beguiled by his money and his title,' Eddie continued. 'It would be advantageous for him to be related. She would love to have him in the family. But, Oonagh, I've wanted Mourna for my daughter-in-law, to marry Iain, for a long, long time now, you know that.'

'Yes, Eddie.' Oonagh felt trapped, unsure how to react and unwilling to pursue the argument further. She said nothing, then he turned and asked Lady Davenport to dance. Colista moved up a chair to the one beside her sister.

'Why does Eddie want Mourna to marry Iain?' Oonagh asked Colista when she had settled. Colista looked agitated, flustered, and for her that was very strange.

'I would have thought that obvious,' she said, and shrugged. 'Iain is our son and heir, our only child. Eddie would like to keep the business within the family. Iain is charming but needs, er, guidance.' She narrowed her eyes. 'He's ... weak. He can be manipulated. Eddie is afraid another girl, an outsider, and her family could influence Iain. Could make things, well, difficult.'

'Don't you think that's a bit premature? A bit far-fetched?'

'Far-fetched or not, it's what Eddie believes. He's paranoid about Benson's. I think it's because of the way my family – oh, not you, Oonagh, or Gabriel for that matter – will chide and chivvy him about business. And he had all that trouble with Norman.'

Norman was Eddie's young brother. A wastrel and ne'er-do-well, he had nearly destroyed the whole company during the short time he had spent within the factory walls and Eddie had had to sack him.

Both women looked out into the ballroom at Eddie.

'He always gets what he wants,' Colista said, and stubbed out her cigarette.

Chapter Seventeen

'Father's seen us. He's clicked,' Iain said in Briana's ear.

'Oh, Iain, what'll we do?'

'Nothing, my darling. It's just as well anyhow. Better for them to know.'

'Will he try to stop us?'

'I can't work it out, Bri. Why is it okay for me to marry Mourna and not you? It seems silly, doesn't it? The only impediment is consanguinity and that applies to Mourna as well as you. I don't know why he's so set on it, I really don't.'

'I do, Iain. Mourna is so beautiful, you see. She's like first prize. She would be an ornament in the Benson crown. You have to admit your father is very proud. He likes to possess the best.'

'You're the best,' he whispered. 'You're worth ten of Mourna.'

He gave her a twirl and for a moment she left the secure circle of his arms, did a dizzy little pirouette, then returned to his embrace.

'Do you know how good it makes me feel to hold you like this?' he asked her, putting his cheek against hers.

'I know. I feel the same.'

'You're so lovely, Bri.'

'Mam's watching,' she said.

'Let's get out from under their eyes.'

He guided her across the floor away from the table. She

123

loved the feel of his hands taking charge of her, and smiled at him tremulously.

'Oh, I hope they'll leave us alone,' she said.

He shook his head. 'They won't. But we mustn't let it matter. I have a plan of campaign. What we do is, we wear them down. I'll do everything they ask of me. I'll be tractable and biddable – oh, Briana, just wait and see me! But I'll marry you. You've got to be strong, Bri.'

'I don't know if I can.'

'You can. It will be all right, I promise.'

'But …'

He put his finger on her lips to silence her. 'Hush. I promise. Let's go in here,' he said. 'It's quiet.'

The bar was more or less deserted. A lush in evening clothes leaned drunkenly on the white leatherette banquette, eyes half-closed, mouth slack, immobile, a drink half-way to his lips. A peroxide blonde in a tight gold dress leaned on the glass-topped bar and held the bartender in conversation, laughing, a little shrilly, topping up on the drinks available in the ballroom. The place was dimly-lit, cosy, conducive to a romantic *tête-à-tête*.

There were booths opposite the bar and Iain slid into the one farthest from the door and pulled Briana in after him. He looked at the bartender to order something to put in front of them but the man was occupied with the blonde and didn't notice them.

'What'll we do?' Briana asked. 'What do you mean, saying you'll wear them out? If your da and my mam know …'

'We'll take it little by little,' he said, touching her hair. 'People get used to things. Habit is wonderful. If I'm always near you, always with you, people will start thinking of us as a couple. I won't *argue* about not taking Mourna out. I'll tell Mother I'll ask her, then not bother. Mourna doesn't want me anyhow. They'll get tired.'

Briana smiled into his eyes.

124

'We don't have to turn it into a battle, Briana,' he said. 'It's like passive resistance. Gandhi, in a minor way.'

'Oh, Iain, I love you,' she said.

'And if they get really stroppy, well, we'll run away and get married.'

'Oh no, Iain, you can't. It'd kill Auntie Colista. You're all she's got.'

'Well, it's my life. *Our* life, Briana. But we don't have to think about that yet.' He frowned. 'What we have to do is let them get used to the idea of us this summer in Dranmore. They can't stop us from seeing each other with all the family there, now can they? It'd be most peculiar.'

'No.' Briana sounded doubtful.

'We'll be going to Dranmore in a few weeks. It'll be all right.' He was so certain, expecting her to trust him as a matter of course. 'I love you, Bri. Never forget that. I always have. I always will.'

His eyes were wide and he looked at her achingly. He looked vulnerable, emotionally exposed. It took courage, she thought, to open yourself like that. Her heart went out to him and she wanted to kiss him so badly.

'Do you think anyone else ever felt as strongly as we do?' she asked him.

He nodded and cleared his throat. He found it difficult to speak. 'Yes,' he whispered, 'Romeo and Juliet, people like that.'

He was sensible, she thought. He would do nothing wild or abandoned. He would always act with her best interests a priority. He would take care of her. She shivered with pleasure, with a feeling of completeness, being here in the cosy bar, in the booth, with him looking at her that way, his love in his eyes.

All he could see was her mouth. He stared at the petal-soft lips, half-open, and he leaned over and kissed her. It was so soft, so tender, a touch so gentle yet so passionate, it seemed to deprive them of their senses, making them both light-headed.

The blonde snorted, jerking her head towards them. 'Young love,' she chortled, and the barman laughed, a knowing lewd laugh.

'Long may it last!' he said. 'They'll learn soon enough!'

They heard a cough near them and looked up. Eddie Benson stood over them, looking at them quizzically, his crooked smile on his face. Iain pulled away from Briana.

'Don't let your mother see you kissing Briana, Iain. Or anyone else for that matter,' he said gently.

'Father, it's none of your business who I kiss,' Iain said.

'Now, now, Iain, calm down.'

'Well, Father, it's no use. Match-making went out in the dark ages and Mother can't just foist me off on whoever she choses. It's not on. And even then, it's only if Mourna turns down the German.'

'Don't be silly, m'boy. Your mother won't foist you on anyone. You know that. You've got plenty of time. Briana dear, could you excuse us, please? This is a matter between me and my son.'

'If you'll excuse me, I'll go to the ladies,' she said with some dignity. She was embarrassed and disliked intensely the way Iain and his father talked about something she felt was so private.

'Now, Iain,' Eddie smiled charmingly at his son, 'I'm well aware of your childhood interest in Briana ...'

'Not childhood, Father, we ...'

'No, Iain, I'm not prepared to discuss it with you. Let's not quarrel about this. It's a dance — romantic lights, music, and a lovely girl. Briana *is* a lovely girl. She's a little sturdy for true beauty. She hasn't got Mourna's delicacy ...'

'Father, don't! I can't have you ...'

'Iain, let me finish. I want you to think about something. I'm a very rich man. My wealth provides you with cars, comfort, an enviable way of life. You'll have it all when I retire. But only if you do as your mother and I feel is best for you. And, Iain, it's a very cold place out there without the cushion of my money, and you're not used to it.

His son was staring at him. 'Are you threatening me, Father?'

Eddie smiled again. 'Yes, son, I am.' He clipped a cigar and clamped it between his teeth. 'We've made arrangements to send you to Edinburgh tomorrow. You are to stay there with Auntie Ag until we go to Dranmore. Understand?'

'Yes, Father.'

'Good. Then that's settled then.'

'Yes, Father. Whatever you say.'

'And, Iain, think about Mourna, please. She's the perfect wife for you. Oh, you're young now, but you'll mature. Your tastes will change. Don't do anything foolish, all right?'

'Yes, Father. I promise I won't do anything *foolish*.'

'You don't want to upset your mother, do you?'

'No, Father.'

Briana went to what was labelled the Powder Room. It was like a padded boudoir, plushly carpeted, with neat little stools with pink brocade seats in front of oval, gilt-edged mirrors. The loos were white marble with polished wooden seats. The toilet paper was pink and there was a bowl of face-powder with a swan's-down puff on the vanity table. Briana had never seen such grandeur.

'Isn't this the height of it?' Oonagh was sitting in front of the glass making liberal use of the face-powder. She twinkled at her daughter and Briana couldn't help but smile at her mother's enthusiasm and wonder. 'Isn't it though, Bri?'

'Yes, Mam. It's fabulous.'

'Mummy, Bri. How many times … Aren't we the lucky ones though?' She looked shrewdly at her daughter's hectic colour, at the dazed glitter in her eyes. She knew

127

what it meant. She remembered looking into the mirror in the hall at Granny O'Shea's, and the old lady (not so old then) coming upon her, saying, 'Yer in love wi' my Gabriel. No, don't deny it. It's written all over ye.' It was written all over Briana now. That glow, that suspension of any other interest or feeling, everything concentrated on the loved one.

'Briana, sit here beside me.'

'Yes, Mam.'

'It's Iain, isn't it?'

Briana looked at her mother sharply, brought back to earth by her words.

'Don't go sharp on me, Briana. Don't get spikey. Just take my advice, play it calmly for a while. You'll wear them down,' she said. Briana was surprised. Iain had advised the same thing.

'But Uncle Eddie wants Iain to marry Mourna. I can't think why he minds me so much. I …'

Oonagh frowned. 'Neither do I,' she said.

'Oh, I know she's much more beuatiful than I am. But what's that to him?'

'Yes, Briana. What *is* that to him?' Then shaking her head to evict an unpleasant thought, she said, 'Well, you see, your Uncle Eddie is used to getting his own way and he tends to think he's God.'

'Oh, Mam … Mummy, will Iain have the courage to stand up to his da?'

'Well, it hasn't come to that yet, Briana,' her mother said sharply. 'And I hope there'll be no trouble. Uncle Eddie has been so good to us. There's such a lot he can do to help us, all of us. He has such influence. I'd *hate* there to be a conflict. It would really be a tragedy.'

'But, Mummy, I love Iain.'

'I know you do, Briana, but you have to remember your father, your brothers and sisters. All of them need your Uncle Eddie's help. And I know how you feel. So keep everything quiet for a while.'

'That'll be easy. Iain wants it that way.'

'Sensible boy,' Oonagh said, relieved. 'Things at your age are so desperate, I remember. But they work out. They usually work out for the best.'

With that Briana had to be content. She returned to the dance with her mother. The band was playing a samba and Uncle Eddie asked her to partner him. She felt like a will-o'-the-wisp in his arms. He was a very good dancer and she laughed with the sheer joy of movement to the Latin beat and being alive. Mourna flashed past, dancing efficiently and smoothly, without frills or exuberance.

'I enjoyed that, Briana,' Uncle Eddie said to her when it was over, bringing her back to the table, taking out a large handkerchief and dabbing his brow. 'I've told Iain he's going to Edinburgh, tomorrow. Until we go to Dranmore. In case you were making plans.' He patted her cheek. 'I'm so fond of you, Briana. I only want what's best for you.'

She smiled at him dutifully. 'I know that, Uncle Eddie,' she said meekly. He looked at her, a little confused by her reaction, then turned to Oonagh. 'She dances well, Oonagh,' he said.

'Well, well, well, look who's here.' He was waving a small dapper man over to the table, as everyone seated themselves and sipped their drinks.

'It's Mr Wilmot,' Colista said, looking slyly at Gabriel.

'Dave, Dave, how nice to see you. Do have a drink with us.'

Mr Wilmot flushed with pleasure. 'Oh, how kind, Mr Benson.'

'You know my brother-in-law, I believe? Eh?' Eddie waved the waiter over and the man came scuttling. Mr Benson was a good tipper, the best.

'Now what are we all having?' Eddie asked, and Mr Wilmot sat down beside Gabriel.

Oonagh was ecstatic.

'Look at Daddy,' she said to Briana. 'Hob-nobbing with his boss in this company. It'll do him the world of good in Barnet's. Oh, Briana, we mustn't do anything to rock the boat.'

It was almost a plea and tears came to Briana's eyes. Why did the grown-ups make it all so difficult?

Mourna and Kurt had not left the floor.

'You are a remarkable woman, Mourna,' he said. She thought it strange, the word 'remarkable'. She put it down to his translating from German. She smiled at him. His skin was fine and he had a blonde moustache. She liked the feel of his strong grip. She liked him.

She knew what was expected of her and she looked at him to like him. It was not difficult. He was a handsome man. But she felt him alien. He did not smell or speak or think like her kind. Uncle Eddie and Uncle Ben and Da, Ardel and Iain and Tom, smelt of tweed and tobacco and had that salty, heathery smell that was for her the essence of the masculine, and that Kurt had not. She did not yet know how he smelled or thought. She was intuitive about the men she knew. She could anticipate their reactions and act accordingly. She could deflect criticism or anger or hurt or impatience, steer clear of challenging avenues of debate and lead the conversation into safe channels. She knew too the cadence of their speech, the underlying moods, meanings, temperature.

Kurt was speaking in a tongue foreign to him. His speech was stilted and flat like recordings she had heard of Edward VIII. She could not begin to guess what lay beneath the spoken word, she was in uncharted seas. Yet the very strangeness had an attraction that was in itself potent. The German voice was seductive, the foreignness appealing.

She would wait and see. Meanwhile she smiled at him and they turned and turned to the music, assessing each other, weighing up, deciding it was not going to be too difficult.

'The next dance is "Goodnight, Sweeheart",' Eddie said.

130

'Goodnight, Sweetheart' was always the last dance. 'Iain, why don't you dance with Briana? I want to dance with your mother, and I'm sure Gabriel wants to dance with Oonagh. Mourna and Kurt are lost out there on the floor.'

Colista glanced at her husband and Iain and Briana looked confused. Mr Wilmot took his leave and everyone obediently paired off as Eddie suggested for the last dance. The lights were dimmed. The violins swelled. The women rested their heads on their male companions' shoulders. The evening was over. Oonagh sighed. It had been wonderful, but it was over. She kissed Gabriel's cheek.

'It's been lovely,' she said.

'Yes, my dear. And so are you.'

I could tell him about the baby now, she thought. But the feeling was sweet and warm. They were close and harmonious with each other, it would be a pity to spoil it. She decided to wait until tomorrow.

Chapter Eighteen

Briana laid her head on her mother's shoulder on the way home in the big car.

'I had a lovely time Ma ... Mummy,' she sighed, and nodded off to sleep.

Mourna rested her head against the cool leather of the seat. 'Yes, Mummy, lovely.'

'You like the Count?' Oonagh asked hopefully.

'Oh, yes. He's very nice,' Mourna said.

Nice! It wasn't wild enthusiasm but it was better than nothing.

Oonagh looked out of the car window at the lights in the dark. She could smell the sea. She felt very warm and protected in the leather womb of the Bentley, as if nothing could touch her, nothing could harm her. She looked at her girls and her heart swelled with pride. They were a credit. A credit. She looked at her husband. He smiled back at her readily and she thought, nothing can hurt us when we love each other so. I'll tell him tonight about the baby.

But she didn't tell him. She was too upset and worried by the fact that when they got in at three-thirty a.m., Ardel was not in his bed.

'Where could he be, Gabriel?' she whispered to her husband on the landing.

She had looked into all the rooms as she always did when they were out late, kissing the occupants, appreciating for a moment their special place in her heart.

Emer caught her arm and stared at her, large-eyed, drenched in sleep. 'I got it Ma – tonight! My period. I really got it.'

'Isn't that great, lamb? Now all your worries are over,' she said.

Poor Emer. Her worries were just beginning, Oonagh thought, but why distress her about that now?

'I kept awake to tell you. It's very late, isn't it?' Emer held on to her mother. 'I heard Margaret Price, Ma, tonight. When you were out.'

Margaret Price lived opposite them. She had 'turns' which the O'Sheas had got used to but which frightened Emer. Margaret Price would lean up against the barred window and scream into the street.

The story was that she had got pregnant and the man responsible had run off and deserted her. She had gone to England and got rid of the baby. Went to some back-street abortionist. She'd never been the same since. She came back to her parents in Griffith Avenue and every so often she would run into the street in her nightie, wringing her hands. 'Like Lady Macbeth,' Briana had said.

She lived with her parents who took to locking her in, and then the bars appeared on her window upstairs.

'What else can I do?' Mrs Price asked Oonagh, and she shook her head and clicked her tongue against her teeth in sympathy.

' 'Tisn't right,' Mr Quin, Tansy's father, said. 'She should have professional help.'

But Mrs Price wouldn't send her only child away to one of those institutions. She lived in the community, and they could hear her every so often, screaming. Briana sometimes talked to her over the gate. She sat in the porch on sunny days when she was having a good spell. No one except Briana stopped to talk to her. Briana told her mother that she was just like anybody else at those times, yet at others all the street could hear her shriek and shake her barred windows, and people could see her tearing her hair.

'My mother doesn't want me to go the lunatic asylum,' she told Briana, 'but I don't think I'd mind. I've been in St Pat's and the nuns are kind and you're not ostracized there like I am here, on Griffith Avenue.' She sighed. She had yellowish skin and her teeth were bad, but her eyes were innocent as a spring morning in spite of what she'd done. Like a baby's, they were.

'People are not nice, Briana,' she confided. 'They do such terrible things to each other.'

Briana thought of the war, of the newsreels she'd seen of those poor Jews staggering out of concentration camps, skeletons covered in yellow tissue-paper that was their skin, and she pressed Margaret's hand and said nothing.

'Don't be afraid of her, Emer,' Oonagh whispered now. 'She's a poor, sad, harmless girl, so she is, an' we should thank God every day our family is safe and sound and well.' Emer's eyes were drooping in sleep. 'Now you've got your period, Emer, you're too grown up to be afraid. Pray for that poor troubled soul. All right?'

Emer nodded. 'Now, Emer, say after me, "God bless Margaret Price".'

Emer murmured, ' "God bless Margaret Price." '

Oonagh continued, ' "And soothe her troubled mind".'

Emer repeated it. ' "And Lord, preserve me from crime, tragedy and accident and keep me safe in your arms O Lord. Amen." '

Emer gave a little contented grunt and slipped deep into sleep.

'Now you can rest,' Oonagh said, and tucked the girl in and left her, curled up under the eiderdown, sound asleep.

Emmett had his thumb in his mouth and Oonagh smiled and thought of Lady Davenport. He was clutching a rosary, and, not for the first time, Oonagh wondered what would become of him. He was too good, too hopeful, too trusting to get far in the world, or even in the priesthood – perhaps especially in the priesthood. She kissed his forehead, then glanced in on the girls who were getting undressed in weary silence.

'Keep the sound down, girls, everyone is fast asleep,' she said, rather unnecessarily. Then she looked in on Laughlin and Ardel. Laughlin lay in total abandon on his back, arms and legs sprawled. He's happy now, she thought, he's at peace. And she felt a fierce stab of anger against that Christian Brother, whoever he was, who had interfered with her son's innocent trust. Damn him, she thought. Damn him.

Then she turned to Ardel's bed and saw it was empty. She wouldn't have worried if it had been midnight, twelve-thirty or even one o'clock. But three-thirty! Gabriel would kill him. Fear entered her in a rush, a thousand 'supposings' and 'what ifs' running around in her brain. If he'd had an accident? Suppose he'd been kidnapped?

Suppose he'd been killed, was lying in a ditch somewhere, suffering? Where could he be? Her heart jumped in anxiety at every sound, and bizarre thoughts and suppositions found foothold in her mind.

Dear God, let him be safe. It's all I ask. Let him be safe.

Gabriel was furious. He was feeling mellow and content. The evening had been lovely, he had been delighted for Oonagh that his daughters had been a success, and his talk with Mr Wilmot had been very promising. He had looked forward to the comfort of his bed, his wife's arms and the sweet oblivion of sleep. And now this! How dare Ardel!

'I'll murder him when he gets in,' he said. 'I'll bloody kill him.'

'Oh, don't say that, Gabriel. There's no need for bad language, and God might take you up wrong. Let's just pray and watch.'

They sat in their bedroom on the window-seat and Oonagh said a Hail Mary every now and then and promised God anything and everything if only He'd send her son home safely to her.

Chapter Nineteen

Ardel had gone to the pool hall as soon as the girls and his mother and father had left in the car for the Bensons'. He wondered why he had not gone with them. He might have met powerful people, influential men. Opportunities might have presented themselves. Who knew what might happen? Yet he had refused the invitation.

In his heart he knew why. If he was honest he knew all

135

right, but he did not articulate it to himself.

The reason he did not accept Eddie and Colista's invitation was that he did not trust himself to play a fair game with friends of theirs he might meet, and he did not want to spoil things for Mourna and Briana. His talents were not geared to honesty and straight dealing, and although his instincts told him that Eddie was a kindred spirit, he knew too that his uncle would never be found out. He would cover his tracks too well. Ardel had not perfected his double-dealing yet. He was still an amateur. He might be found out and that would never do. His father would be lethal. He'd break his mother's heart. Not yet, he told himself, not just yet.

His Jesuit master in Belvedere said he was as crooked as a coast road and he should succeed in anything he did provided it needed guile. 'You'd be at home, Ardel O'Shea, in the court of the Medici,' Father Ambrose said. If an opportunity presented itself later, when he felt ready, he'd avail himself of it. So he went to the pool hall.

He was always on the look-out for a scam. The people there were more likely to be dazzled by his baby-blue eyes than the nobby crowd at Kilcrony.

He sauntered in, mooched over to the side and propped up the wall, waiting.

It was quiet for a Saturday night. Old Blackie White, lips stained brown from tobacco, eyes scrunched up against the permanent curl of grey smoke from his cigarette, was aimlessly poling at the table, not looking for company, not giving Ardel the time of day. Ardel knew Blackie meant, 'Leave me be,' so he did.

He wondered was there a match on in Croke Park? After the hurling or the football everyone was in the pubs. But, no, it was the wrong time of year.

At first he didn't see Banan. All he saw was a hand beckoning him out of the darkness. The brightness in the hall spilled directly on to the green tables from the overhead lights. The rest of the room was shrouded in shadow.

There was only one light on tonight: at the table Blackie White was using. The rest were dark.

Ardel saw the hand. He wondered if Uncle Tom was looking through the peephole. He glanced at where, last night, Banan had made his rude gesture, but of course could see nothing. He didn't think Banan would drop him in it so he crossed the room to where the hand waved him on in ghostly detachment.

He knew as he neared it that it was Banan's hand because of the gold Claddagh ring. Banan wore the Celtic ring and a Faine in his lapel that meant he spoke Gaelic. He was very patriotic, Banan was. Ardel thought patriotism a waste of time. He believed more in the every man for himself doctrine, like the Americans, and had often thought that if all the boundaries in the world came down it would even everyone's chances.

'Then we could all have a go. Like a race,' he said.

But his father had replied. 'That's typical of you, Ardel. You want to win the race without running it! Sure, it's not very stimulating to come in first if you've put no effort in. 'Specially if you cheat.'

Ardel didn't understand why. He thought it just dandy to win without effort. He never understood why cheating was frowned on. It took brains and nerve to cheat.

Banan didn't understand Ardel. 'You a communist or something?' he asked, completely misunderstanding Ardel's theories. Banan always managed to irritate Ardel. There was an unbridgeable gulf between them.

Banan grabbed Ardel now and pulled him into the passage where Ardel had seen his uncle kissing the Hot Chicken girl. 'Can ye do a job tonight?' he asked in an urgent whisper.

'That was quick!' Ardel had not been expecting a commission just yet.

'Can ye?' Banan's voice tightened.

'Yeah, I guess. Mam and Da are at …'

'I don't give a fuck where your ma and da are!' Banan interrupted. 'We've got a van has to be driven to Dun Laoghaire.'

Ardel didn't tell Banan he couldn't drive and whether he chanced his arm or not depended on how much he was offered. He leaned against the wall, his eyes half-closed. Banan stood opposite smoking, dragging the smoke into his lungs greedily, very little filtering out afterwards. Ardel could see his eyes glittering in the dark.

'How much?' he asked.

'Jesus, you're mercenary! Ye haven't a patriotic bone in your body.' Banan sounded disgusted.

'Sure, it's all *over*, Banan,' Ardel sighed. 'The war's over. We've won. Nobody told you? We got our independence.'

'It'll never be over until we are a united Ireland. Never, you hear?'

'Your problem, Banan, is that father of yours. Bloody Irish hero! You don't know when to stop, do ye? We've got to get on now wi' it, but ye can't leave it be, can ye? The North doesn't *want* us, Banan, don't ye see? Just some fanatics like yourself.'

Banan grabbed Ardel's jacket and slammed him against the wall. 'Don't call me a fanatic, Ardel, you value your life, you hear?'

He put his arms up in a gesture of surrender and smiled, shaking his head which ached from the bang.

'Okay. Okay. How much?' he asked mildly, and Banan let him go in disgust.

'Four twenties,' he said.

Ardel whistled. 'When? Where?' He'd get the hang of driving on the way. That was wealth!

'Ye have te go *now*. To Drimnagh. A garage there. I'll give ye a note. Pick up the van. It's not too big. Drive it to Dun Laoghaire to just the other side, past the pier, a

138

building site – I've drawn a map for you. Leave it there with a guy called Sean Duffy. Got that?'

'Yeah. That all seems simple. What's in the van?'

'None of your business.'

That murderous gleam shone again in Banan's eyes so Ardel backed off. Banan looked at him contemptuously.

'I'll give you two twenties now, then Sean'll hand over the other two an' you deliver the van, okay?'

'Okay.' Ardel thought, He's got no sense of humour at all. And Banan gave him the note with the Drimnagh address on it.

'This is a serious business, Ardel. No slip-ups, okay? Or your skin's on the line.'

'Jeez, you're scarin' me to death,' Ardel said sarcastically, then stopped, for something in Banan's face made him shiver.

'I mean it, Ardel. And I meant what I said last night. We've long arms. We've long memories.'

'Okay. Okay. Keep your shirt on.'

'Here, then.' He handed over two crisp twenties, more money than Ardel had ever seen.

'Off you go. Good luck.' Banan gave his version of a smile, tight lips stretched, teeth bared.

Ardel slipped out the back way into the alley. He looked over his shoulder before he closed the door behind him. Banan waved the Claddagh-ringed hand in salute. The rest of him melted into the shadows.

Chapter Twenty

They watched in disbelief outside the garage in Drimnagh as the van scuttered drunkenly along the road, ploughing up the grassy verge, tyres screeching over the sidewalk curb and zig-zagging down the street bordered by little council houses. Ardel uprooted a sapling, a bed of roses, took the paint off a fence and turned the corner, leaving the man who had handed over the van and two twenties, his two friends and a few faces at lighted windows, staring after him, crossing themselves.

He laughed to himself as he got the hang of it. 'Twas easy. Dead easy. He wasn't too happy twisting and turning in the city but once he left it, got outside, it was easy as falling off a log. And the man had given him the twenties. He had not expected them till later, at Dun Laoghaire. And now they were snugly tucked into his wallet in his back pocket. Eighty fuckin' quid. And he was zooming along in the high seat, his hands on the wheel.

He found the sensation exhilarating. Up there, looking down on the populace going about their pleasure of a Saturday night. Girls and fellas courtin' in the darkness of shop doorways 'cause they'd no place else to go, drunks throwing up against the outside walls of pubs, revellers leaving for a party somewhere, shouting happily to each other. Posh couples going to dress-dances in the big hotels, all tarted up, girls holding their long skirts with one hand and their partner's arm with the other, crowds queuing for the last show at the cinema, larking about, gurriers selling papers and officiously directing traffic, a grubby palm never far away, open for small change.

It was a starry night, and warm, tempered by the cold sea-breeze that always whipped Dublin.

He did not know how to stop the van, so when the traffic got light on the Blackrock Road he practised. Stopping, having a fag, starting again. Stopping again, another fag, and off once more. He was enjoying himself hugely. Sitting in his small cabin on a comfortable seat, wheel under his hand, cigarette in the other, breeze through the open window, the money in his back pocket. Great! The world was his. He threw back his head and laughed.

The hand on his shoulder gave him the fright of his life. His stomach nearly left his body and he dropped his cigarette and nearly crashed the van into a chemist shop.

'Holy Mother of Jesus!' he screamed, battling with the wheel to keep control. The car did its contrary piece, refusing to obey him, and he reeled the steering back and forth in demented fury and fear.

'Who the fuck …?'

'Quiet, man, God's sake!' a voice from the back hissed.

It had not occurred to Ardel that he could be carrying human cargo. He had figured on guns, money or dope. Something not somebody.

'Give us a fag, will you?' the voice asked harshly. 'I'm gaspin'.'

'Shit! Who the hell are …?'

'Never mind that now, y'hear? Just light us a fag.'

The man had a Northern accent. Ardel, recovering from his shock, breathed deeply, trying to work out what this startling change in his assumptions meant. One thing he knew: a bloody human being was unpredictable, therefore dangerous. If he'd known he'd have asked for more money. No wonder they paid eighty smackers. But without telling him? Jesus H. Christ.

141

He lit a cigarette from his own with trembling fingers, then held it over his shoulder. He felt a hand fumble with his and take the cigarette. The rough material of the curtains that separated the driver's cabin from the rest of the van scratched his arm.

'Who're you?' he asked.

'Naver ye mind.' The voice was hard as concrete. 'I just had te have a fag. Ye lightin' them up, me smellin' the smoke. More than a mon could bear.'

'Well, shut up now an' let me drive.' Ardel felt irritated and disconcerted.

'That's another thing that's drivin' me crazy. Ye're a terrible driver.'

'Shut up,' Ardel ordered.

He needed time to think. All his good humour had evaporated. Transporting inanimate freight was one thing, he could rely on his nerve, his gift of the gab, his own wits, but another human being was a quite different responsibility. You never knew what someone else was going to do in a crisis, how they would behave. The more he thought about it, the madder he got.

Still, there was nothing he could do now. He'd have to make the best of the situation and have a talk with Banan when he saw him again. Explain that wasn't the deal he'd agreed and if he wanted this type of transaction again he'd have to pay more. Banan was a humourless bastard but he didn't scare Ardel. Banan was inflexible and Ardel knew that you had to be flexible to survive.

They had reached Blackrock when the man surfaced again. 'Another fag,' he said, whispering through the curtains in Ardel's ear.

'Jasus, don't *do* that,' Ardel said, nearly jumping out of his skin, 'I'll go into something.'

He lit the cigarette, wondered why the man was hiding, what he'd done. Then he said, 'Here's the fag,' and held the cigarette over his shoulder as a car came up behind him. He shifted his eyes to the rear-view mirror to see the car and instead saw the man's face.

It was a well-known face, its familiarity shocking to Ardel. He'd seen it so many places. In papers, magazines, in books. Janey, he had a famous wanted man in the back of the van and now the man knew he'd seen him, recognized him.

What was he wanted for? Ardel couldn't remember. Only that he was a Northern Ireland leader of a banned group. Ulster. Bloody Ulster. But there was more than that. He had done something terrible. Ardel wished he could remember what it was.

The man had a neat beard and cold eyes. Mean eyes. 'Keep calm, boy,' he said, and disappeared.

Ardel was shaking now. His throat felt tight and he didn't like the feeling in his stomach. He put his foot on the pedal and urged the van forward.

'Take it asy. Do ye want tay kill us both?'

The voice was in his ear again and he clenched his hands on the wheel, white-knuckled.

He looked in the mirrors, the one overhead and the one at the side. Was anyone following? Jasus, he'd *kill* Banan when he saw him. He must think me an eejit, Ardel thought bitterly. Eejit, eejit, eejit, he told himself, over and over. Banan'd probably think it an honour! Think he was doing Ardel a favour. Shit, he would too. For the unification of Ireland! Sure, who the hell cared? Not Ardel.

He was nearing Dun Laoghaire now. He'd have to cross through the town, get to the other side, to the building site.

He suddenly remembered what the man had done. This guy had killed a policeman. Killed a fucking policeman! An Irish policeman. One of his own. Ardel couldn't remember the details. He was mulling over the facts he did remember about his passenger when he felt himself grabbed again.

'The polis is follyin' us,' the man whispered. 'Go asy now.'

Ardel hadn't heard the siren. He'd been too preoccupied with his thoughts.

'What the fuck'll I do?' he hissed.

'Talk it through. Delay. Think of somethin'. You better or there's a death penalty on you! I'll get outa the back of the van soon's you stop, soon's it's safe. Make my way to Sean Duffy. We're nearly there.'

'What about me?' Ardel asked.

'Fuck you!' the man snarled.

Billy Macken. That was his name. Billy Macken.

The Gardai were waving him down. He was petrified for the first time in his life. Thoughts ran around his head like squirrels. If he was implicated in any way in Billy Macken's attempts to get out of the country, they'd put him away for ever. And why else would he be going to Dun Laoghaire and the ships and the B & I, the Irish Mail bound for England? Billy Macken, Garda killer. Mountjoy Jail forever. Ardel's blood ran cold as death.

A possible solution came to him. He relied on his wits and they did not desert him now. He rearranged his face. It was not difficult to look as terrified as he felt.

The police hailed the van to a halt. Ardel drew up very inexpertly. He shook and shivered and pointed behind him frantically. The policeman looked confused.

'Out, lad. Out.' The Dublin officer motioned with his head. 'Sure, you're drivin' like a lunatic, all over the place, a danger to the countryside, never mind yerself. Why, what's the matter, lad?'

He had registered Ardel's not completely assumed mask of terror, Ardel just wished he'd keep his voice down. Still he felt confident the man in the back couldn't hear.

He felt his knees buckle beneath him as he got out of the van. It was not difficult, he felt paralyzed with fear.

The second policeman came around the van. 'Got his driving licence?' he asked, twinkling. 'Joy riding, were ye, boy? Got a girl wi' ye? Showing off? In the back? Well, we won't be spoilsports ... why, what's the matter, lad? Hey-up, tell us. Don't be afraid.'

144

'Billy Macken,' he said softly.

'What? Speak up, lad. What?'

'Billy Macken,' he whispered, careful to keep his voice down. At this moment his own skin was more important than anything else. He hoped Billy Macken had run off. It would help if he didn't get caught, but informing seemed the only way out. Ardel couldn't lie to the police. He knew that. He'd be found out sooner or later. They'd remember him and his bad driving. Only thing to do was to be honest. Well, bend the truth a little …

'What's he on about?' The older cop, the big one with the twinkle in his eyes, caught his shoulder. 'Billy Macken? What about Billy Macken?'

'He forced me! Thank God you came. He's gotta gun.' It seemed likely.

'Where is he?' The police were galvanized into action.

'Was in the back. Hey, look, there he is, in the field.'

The younger Garda ran off into the field. Ardel and the older man moved around the bonnet of the van to see. In the distance the bobbing head of Billy Macken rose and fell amid the wheat, a swaying silver sea under the moon.

'He'll get away,' the older cop shouted. 'Don't loose him, Liam. To your right, man. To your right.'

The policeman's helmet bobbed behind Billy Macken and he seemed to get closer and closer. Then they both disappeared.

'He's got him,' the older man said beside Ardel, punching his fist jubilantly into the palm of his hand. 'Liam bloody Gleeson! One-miler, best in Ireland. Holds a record second only to Ronnie Delaney. Good on yerself, man.' He looked at Ardel. 'Now, lad, don't be frightened. Tell me what happened.'

'Was jumped,' Ardel stammered. 'Forced me, he did, at gunpoint to drive him to Dun Laoghaire.'

Billy Macken appeared out of the field as he said this, handcuffs on. He would never forget the look Macken gave him as he passed by. The cold, lethal eyes, promising, promising. As he was pushed past Ardel, he spat at him, hitting him full in the face.

'Informer,' he snarled. 'We'll get you for this, I promise yew. We'll get yew.'

'Shut up, Billy,' the older man said calmly. 'This boy didn't tell us a thing. That's not nice. That's not nice at all. Anyhow, you'll not be in a position to get anyone for a long, long time.' He handed a large handkerchief to Ardel. 'Mop yer face wi' that. Good on ye, boy. Well done, Liam. That was some sprint. Janey, wait'll the chief hears!

'Now, Billy, in ye go. I don't think I can promise ye a good time from now on. Twas a Garda from our own barracks ye iced. 'Twas a well-liked boyo he was too. Now get in there an' shut yer gob, y'hear me? Contemplate the pleasures in store for ye when my lads get their hands on ye.'

~~~~~~

They treated Ardel very well, made a fuss of him, gave him tea and sent out for fish and chips for him. He said he'd been in Drimnagh, visiting a girl-friend. On his way to see her he had passed a van, stationary on the road. Billy Macken had put a gun in his back, forced him into the van, forced him to drive … an' he'd never driven in his life, didn't know how.

'I'll swear to that', Liam Gleeson was heard to remark. 'You shoulda seen him. All over the road he was.'

Billy Macken had ordered him to take him to Dun Laoghaire at gun-point. 'He din' have no gun,' the older Constable O'Brien said, 'or he'd 'a used it. He must have thrown it away.' The best moment of his life, Ardel told them, was when he saw the police wave him down.

'We'll make sure he believes you said nothin' to us,' the Constable assured him.

146

They never doubted him for a minute. It reinforced his belief in his ability to extricate himself from most unpleasant situations. He thought about Billy going to jail for a long, long time and his confidence returned. He began to enjoy himself getting all the praise. Everything had turned out for the best and he had eighty quid in his pocket. Life suddenly seemed very rosy.

Oonagh and Gabriel were overwhelmed to see him, relieved to have him home. They were watching for him when he arrived with the police. Far from them being in charge of him, as Gabriel first thought, they were an escort, praising him, complimenting them on their brave son.

'He's a grand lad, Mrs O'Shea. Did a very courageous thing tonight. There is probably a reward in it for him. You've every reason to be proud of him.'

Gabriel gave him a narrow look, but he was so relieved that Ardel was safe and sound that he quashed sceptical thoughts and simply hugged his son, something he rarely did. All in all, Ardel felt he had come out of the whole escapade better than could reasonably be expected.

His mother gave him a nasty turn by asking as they mounted the stairs to bed, 'What girl-friend in Drimnagh? I didn't know you had a girl-friend in Drimnagh.'

He didn't reply, making non-committal sounds in his throat, saying he was worn out.

If only he could forget those eyes, that promise: 'We'll get you for this.'

And if only Banan wasn't family.

Chapter Twenty-One

Rita sat on the side of her single bed and stared at the piece of paper in her hand. If she did not pay the interest on her loan by Monday they would crucify her, and she had nothing left to hock/pawn/sell. Only Oonagh's Dresden figurine, and that would merely buy her a little time.

In her hand to mouth existence Rita couldn't afford scruples. The children needed food and clothes. Oonagh didn't understand how terrible it felt to have to send them to National schools. Oonagh wouldn't even miss the Dresden figurine. She had so much that was extra, over and above what was necessary. As for the Bensons, they were opulent in their life-style and if she ever got invited across *that* threshold she'd have no compunction over taking as much from her sister as her handbag and coat pockets would hold.

Neither Colista nor Oonagh had any idea what life was like for her. Never enough money, never getting ahead of herself, always behind, begging time, begging credit, begging bargains. No, Oonagh and Colista hadn't a clue.

It was no use asking them for help. They thought they had fulfilled their duty, been wonderfully generous, paying for Rita and the children to have a holiday. But it wasn't enough. Rita would have preferred the money. A holiday was luxury. Extra. She could have paid rent in advance, got some new shoes for the children, given something to the wretched loan company.

It was the loan company that frightened her most. They were sharks. They had no pity. And they had bully-boys who carved up your face and broke your bones, no questions asked.

She shivered. When Steve had died he had left nothing. He'd been a good man, a kind man, but he'd never expected to be taken off in his thirties and had made no provision. Rita's first mistake was to let the house go. She should have made a deal with Eddie Benson to continue mortgage payments, at least she'd have had a home. But she needed the money for the funeral and what she got on her husband's share of the house seemed a lot, enough to last forever. Rented accommodation didn't seem too bad, and the children were younger then. It was only supposed to be *pro tem*. She would get a well-paid job. They would be all right.

But the children needed her, the money dwindled, her qualifications were rusty and minimal, she looked anxious, seemed tense, and the quality of her clothes deteriorated as time passed, and so people did not employ her. Hope dwindled. Then the borrowing began.

She had never had to work, never expected to have to. Steve had a good job in the Post Office. Offig an Phoist paid well and looked after its employees. It was safe and secure, a Government job, and Steve would have been promoted. She would have stayed at home and looked after the children. She might, eventually, have taken a part-time job to supplement their income, but it had never dawned on her that she'd have to support the family on her own.

At first she got a job as a receptionist in Jury's Hotel in College Green, opposite the Bank of Ireland. It was well-paid and there were tips involved, though in her time there she had never received any. Perhaps this should have warned her. She was not there very long when the manager told her he was sorry but he could not keep her on. He explained that there had been complaints about her manner.

'You look worried all the time,' he said. 'Anxious. We need someone happy to welcome visitors.'

'I *have* been worried, sir,' she told him. 'I have to arrange for someone to pick up my children after school and look after them till I get home.'

'I'm afraid that's not my concern, Mrs Maguire. My concern is this hotel and a bright and helpful receptionist to welcome our guests. *Caid Mile Failte*, and all that. A worried mother is no use to me at all.'

Eddie got her another receptionist's post in a solicitor's office, but they too sacked her. They also found her manner off-putting and said she lacked charm and got flustered too easily.

Then she got a job on Gabriel's recommendation in an underwear shop in O'Connell Street, Madam Nora. Uplift bras, 3/II. Padded 4/II. The staff there found her stuck-up and said she spoke with a grand accent and they didn't get on with her, she just didn't fit in. So she lost that job too.

Finally she got the position she had now: receptionist in the Mater Hospital. It didn't seem to matter there if your manner was anxious and you lacked charm, but she received a small salary and there were no rosy prospects.

Expenses became higher than her salary as the children grew. In desperation she hocked what she had of value, not much, and gradually she was sucked into the game of borrowing to pay a debt, then borrowing to pay the borrowed-from. It was a vicious circle, a no-win situation, a merry-go-round that she couldn't get off and was bound to lead to disaster.

She sat on the bed looking at the figurine, a great and overwhelming ache inside her. She felt tired unto death and her teeth hurt. Tears spilled on to the china shepherdess and washed it clean of dust. She smoothed

150

the delicate face with her thumb. How terrible life was, she thought, how terrible and frightening unless you had someone to protect you.

She leaned down and picked up a newspaper from the floor. She had ringed an announcement in black ink. She read it again. LISDOONVARNA FESTIVAL.

It was an old festival, it had been going on for hundreds of years. Bachelors went there to look for wives. Out of the wilds of Mayo and Sligo they came, ripe and ready to go, frustrated and feisty, looking for a woman. Obviously not the most attractive of the young (or indeed older) male species, or they would hardly have had to go there to find mates. It had been started originally for farmers who lived in isolated places and needed a woman, a wife. It was the same as looking for a servant.

Rita looked at herself in the mirror balanced on the chest of drawers in the mean little room. She looked jaded, depressed, not even remotely tasty. Well, she thought, some of those fellas might not see the anxiety, the despair: some of those guys were pretty desperate. And well-to-do. Most of them had money stashed away. They had little to spend it on in those remote places.

Would she have the nerve? Would she be able to do it with someone she did not love? She did not know but she'd sure as hell try. She wondered if Lisdoonvarna was far from Dranmore.

Chapter Twenty-Two

'What's the matter with my Dotty?' Ben asked, looking at his spouse.

She sat brushing her blonde curls in front of the dressing-table mirror in their bedroom. The dressing-table had a pink frill around it and there were dolls scattered about the room, lined up along the window seat, on a little vanity chair and on the bed. They had to be taken off the pink satin embossed spread every night. Dot collected dolls.

Ben did not see the lines on her face, the bags, the crêpe texture of her cheeks. She was still his sweet girl, pretty as Doris Day, sexy as sin. He'd never known any other woman except his mother, never loved anyone but his Dotty.

Tonight he knew there was something upsetting his petal. 'What is it, Dotty?' he asked.

She tossed her curls in a fashion he found unbearably provocative. She wore a pink satin frilled negligee.

His lips were dry. He licked them and she rose and went to the bed and began putting the dolls on the chest at the foot of the bed.

'It's just ... it's just ... Benny baby, we weren't asked to *stay*!'

She slammed down the last doll, pulled back the sheets and slid into the bed, still frowning. Hastily he got in beside her, reading her face.

'Don't let that bother you, Dotty,' he said. 'You know the Bensons.'

'No, I don't! That's just it. Oonagh and Colista are like that.' She crossed her fingers. 'An' I don't get a look in. What about Mary? What about Clare? Much chance they have up against Mourna or Briana, I ask you!'

He put a hand on a satin-clad thigh. 'That'll be over soon. They want Mourna to marry a German. Then she'll be off the market. And a good thing too, no one stands a chance up against her.' He rubbed the satin up and down. Dot clasped her hands behind her head.

'Really? Oh, Benny, you always console me. You always make me feel better.'

He carefully began to push up her nightdress.

'They didn't ask us to go to Kilcrony though,' she moaned. 'I was so disappointed. I was sure that at the last moment they would relent. I thought they'd never let us actually leave. But Colista is a cold cow. She's like a rock when it comes to getting her own way.'

'Then it's likely Mourna'll marry the German. Eddie wants her to marry Iain.'

'That's consanguinity.'

'But it's not too difficult to get a dispensation.'

His hand had travelled right up to her private little place, the place he thought of as his own. He felt himself grow hard, excitement mounting. This was his dearest Dotty in pink satin. He began pushing down his pyjama bottoms with his other hand.

'I'd like once, just once, to go there, Benny,' she said, sweetly reasonable. 'That's not much to ask.'

'I'll work on Eddie, dear,' he said, a trifle breathlessly. 'Eddie is easier than Colista.'

'Oh, would you? Yes, I must say I agree. The women in our family are awful. Except Oonagh. But then, she's a snob.'

'Um.' He prised open his little place.

'Rita is a disaster. I wish she'd keep her troubles to herself, where they belong.'

153

Over and in. He was in. 'Ah … ah … ah …' Pump, pump, pump. Up and down. Up and down. Good. Oh, good!

'And as for Maisie! She's a disgrace to the human race.'

'Ah … ah … AH … AH … umm … umm … AH.'

'I know what I'll do, Benny love. I'll work on the Bensons in Dranmore. We'll both work on them. We'll go up to the Grand …'

'AH … um … um … AH …'

'… and have tea with them. If I say it outright they can't refuse …'

'Oh … OH … OH …'

'Colista liked the sweater I knitted for you, Benny …'

'OH … OH … AH …'

'I might even knit one for Eddie. Yes, that's a good idea.'

'Ah … ah … AH … OH …'

'A very good idea.'

'AHHHH … ACHNG … Ng … ng … ng.'

'Was that nice, Benny? Was that good for you, my lovely boy? Yes, that's what I'll do. I knit one for Eddie. Night, night, dear old Benny. Sleepy tighty.'

'Um. Thank you, Dotty. Thank you.'

'What for, Benny love? That's what wives are *for*. Thank *you* for this morning. Nighty night.'

'Nighty.'

She clicked the side-light off and settled down to peaceful sleep.

PART II

Chapter Twenty-Three

They came to Dranmore in every form of transport; bus, train, car, pony-and-trap.

The Bensons came by car with a huge picnic hamper which they raided beside a lake in Wicklow. Brody drove them, served them and looked after them. He laid out the rug beside the purple water, the soft lapping sounds mingling with bird-song. He arranged their silver on a damask cloth, served champagne in crystal. The quails' eggs were excellent, the caviar golden, the crisp rolls fresh, the salmon and salad perfect, the strawberries dewy-moist and juicy. Colista insisted they travel with their own cutlery, glassware and linen and expected hotels to accommodate her by using them.

Iain was not with them. Colista had written to friends in Edinburgh, Irish friends who sent their son to Blackrock College and had been with Iain there, friends who owed her a favour. She had looked after them while in Dublin, so now she despatched her son to their care. Mrs Ag Prudy, called Auntie Ag, was delighted to return the favour and have Iain come to stay with her in Scotland until it was time to go to Dranmore.

'You know, Eddie, I must have been wrong about Iain's interest in Briana O'Shea,' Colista said, dabbing her mouth with her linen napkin, then re-applying her lipstick, peeping in the mirror of her gold compact.

Eddie brushed down his grey flannels. 'Maybe,' he said non-committally.

'He made no fuss about going to Mr and Mrs Prudy and he hasn't asked how Briana is in any of his letters.'

Eddie said nothing, contenting himself with a nod. Colista was naïve. It did not occur to her that the 'children', as she called them, could write to each other quite independently of her. In fact, even though it infuriated him, he had to admire his son's and Briana's patience. He thought their behaviour sensible and alarming. Its very maturity gave him pause for thought.

'Let's get along now, Eddie.' Colista held out her hand to be helped up. The sunlight played on the water, turning it into a sheet of dancing golden light. Eddie doubted she noticed the beauty. Her sensibilities were finely attuned to the sheen of silks and satins, not sunlight.

He raised her up and she smiled at him, coaxing him, flirting with him, reminding him of their linked past experiences. And underlying this expression of her love for him there was a plea. He understood it and his consciousness flinched away from that unasked request.

'I suppose it won't be too awful, darling?' she said lightly, looking away, having received no reply, no reassurance.

'What, dear?' Brody was packing the hamper, folding up the rug.

'The Grand. Dranmore.' She sighed. 'With all the relations. I don't know why I let myself in for it, year after year.'

'Well, at least we have Kinsale to look forward to next month,' he said, and then in silence led her back to the car.

~~~~~~

The O'Sheas took the train from Amiens Street. Only Mourna was missing. Kurt Von Mensil had called for her that morning in his Riley. He had brought a beautiful bouquet of pink roses for her. He always arrived bearing gifts of flowers and chocolates.

158

For a moment, Oonagh was confused. 'Why did you bring them when we're going away?' she asked, looking at the flowers, thinking of the waste. The beautiful plump pink buds smelled so exquisite. 'What'll we do with them?' she asked Kurt, but he was not looking at her. He stood in their little hall looking at Mourna, filling it with his largeness and his strangeness.

Oonagh never called him by name. She felt that 'Kurt' was too intimate for someone she did not know well, and she couldn't seem to bring herself to call him 'Count'. It sounded silly, as if she was in a movie. So she spoke to him without using a name at all, which was awkward.

'Never mind, Mother, I'll take them to Dranmore with me,' Mourna said tranquilly. 'They'll brighten up my room there.'

Oonagh hadn't thought of that. She was amazed at how swiftly Mourna adapted to what must have been a strange and taxing existence. Kurt had drawn her into an unfamiliar society and she had adjusted with an ease that surprised her mother. She was proud of her daughter, the relaxed poise with which she acclimatized herself to Kurt's socially demanding life, as if she had never known another, as if she was used to batteries of cutlery, knew instinctively how to address titled people, what to wear to cocktail parties or musical evenings or boat-races or soirées – all of which would baffle Oonagh.

But she didn't know what Mourna was thinking. She was remote as a film star, familiar, admired, but unattainable. At least she obviously enjoyed the new life-style.

Oonagh had always found her daughter enigmatic. She had a reserve that revealed little of how she felt, and now Oonagh wished she was closer to Mourna. She showed a contentment, a satisfaction, she had not revealed before. All Oonagh prayed for was her happiness.

Mourna had seen a lot of Kurt Von Mensil since that night in Kilcrony. Since then he had taken her out three or

159

four times a week and for whole weekends to his country house – chaperoned, Oonagh was assured, by either Colista or someone known to her. They had gone dancing and dining in all the best places, with all the best people. He had taken her on picnics, to the races and the theatre, and everyone waited, expectant, and Mourna revealed nothing. When Oonagh asked her she said, 'I like him very much, Mummy. We'll see.'

Colista asked Oonagh again and again what Mourna revealed about the relationship, and Oonagh could tell her little. Colista took to inviting her sister for afternoon tea in the fashionable places she frequented, and Oonagh was only too delighted to accept.

'But she must have given you some indication,' Colista insisted over tea in Mitchell's, but Oonagh shook her head.

'No, she has not.'

Colista rolled up the veil on her little pill-box hat to light a cigarette while Oonagh tackled an éclair.

'It's impossible to tell what she's thinking, what the situation is,' Oonagh continued. 'I'm sure she likes him but that's as far as I can truthfully go.'

'We'll have to be patient,' Colista sighed.

Oonagh was quite happy that the Kurt and Mourna affair had brought them together. She was much less in awe of her sister since Kurt Von Mensil had come into their lives. These little *tête-à-têtes* in the Shelbourne or Mitchell's, gossiping and exchanging views and ideas, progress or the lack of it, delighted Oonagh who welcomed the break in the monotony of her housewifely curriculum.

'In a way, Colista, I'd rather she didn't marry Kurt Von Mensil,' Oonagh confided. 'I'd really prefer her to marry a nice Irish boy. I wouldn't lose her so completely then. This way she goes to a stranger who'll take her away from us.'

To her surprise her sister paled. Her face took on a sick look and she clutched Oonagh's hand, eyes wide and scared.

'Oh God, Oonagh, don't say that.'

For a moment she didn't know what to say or do. Colista's reaction was so sudden and surprising as thoroughly to confuse her and she stared in astonishment.

'Why, what's wrong?' she asked eventually.

But Colista had recovered, quite quickly, and for a moment Oonagh thought she had imagined the whole thing.

'Oh, Oonagh, no matter who she marries, you'll have lost her,' Colista said in a light brittle voice.

Oonagh didn't agree. There was no necessity for that, she thought. She'd hoped to welcome the children's spouses into the family. She wanted to be a generous and loving mother-in-law but she couldn't see herself being like that with Kurt. She would not know how to begin.

The Sunday morning they left for Dranmore they missed Mass. Emmett was upset.

'It's not right, Mam,' he said.

'Don't be daft, Emmett,' Oonagh cried, shoving a hot-water bottle into her case. 'Travelling, you're exempt. Ask Father Maloney. Ask anyone. There's only one train to Dranmore and we're on it.'

Emmett looked at her, his big eyes blank. She knew he was thinking of something else. He's thinking of the black babies, she thought. She knew she should be grateful that he was so ... well ... religious. But sometimes he irritated her. She looked at the hot-water bottle then out at the daffodil yellow day. Birds sang and bees hummed. She'd hardly need it. Then she remembered other holidays and the weather turning cold suddenly, and rainy, and her shivering in a strange bed and wishing for a hot-water bottle, so she put it in and closed the case.

She was wrong about Emmett. He was not thinking about the black babies. He was thinking about Laughlin. He had been confused by his brother staying at home to work, so he asked Laughlin about it.

'Why you staying at home from school?'

'Never you mind.'

'Don't be so touchy, I only asked.'

'Well, it's none of your business.'

It was Denis Cowley who told Emmett a few days later why Laughlin had been taken away from the Christian Brothers. Unfortunately the story was exaggerated.

'One of the Brothers did things with his willy to Laughlin. Can you imagine?' Denis said, relishing every word and Emmett's horrified reaction.

'I don't believe you!' Emmett screamed.

'Well, it's true. Ass Laughlin yourself. The Brother is sent away to an island. Gerard Mahally says the Brothers willy was cut off an' he did such bad things wi' it, an' now he's sorry he ever touched Laughlin.'

'Shut up! Shut up! You're filthy, Denis Cowley. You're a pig. A pig!'

Emmett was stunned. That such a thing could happen to anyone, let alone Laughlin, was a terrible shock to him. He had not known it was possible. He knew the facts about mating, something dreadfully unpleasant that a man had to do to his wife if he wanted children. It caused him to shut his eyes and shudder just to think about it. His own da must have done it, gosh, eight times at least, probably twelve times in all, to his ma. It made him want to throw up. Thank God Catholic priests didn't have children!

He had found this out a few weeks ago and now, every so often, he slipped into a perplexed trance, thinking about Laughlin, worrying about it all.

'Who else is coming on the train, Mam?' Briana asked.

'Ben and Dot, probably Joe and Maisie. Tom'll drive the Ford and the family down.'

'I suppose the Bensons ...' Briana paused.

'They'll drive down too. Brody will take them. Now, children, don't forget to take your coats.'

'But, Mama, it's *hot*. It's so *hot*.'

162

'You can't depend on the weather, Emer. Not in Ireland. Better to be sure than sorry.' Oonagh looked at her husband. 'Gabriel, have you ordered the taxi? Remember, we have to pick up your mother.'

They reached the station in plenty of time. It was full of holiday-makers on their way to the sea. Children screamed, husbands carried suitcases, buckets and spades; mothers carried babies.

They were travelling first class, a luxury Gabriel insisted on, saying that second and third were more suited to cattle.

'There's Auntie Dot and Uncle Ben,' Briana called, waving madly. Dot and Ben and their offspring were boarding a second-class carriage and Oonagh felt embarrassed in case they thought the O'Sheas were showing off.

'She'll think we're coming the heavy,' Oonagh whispered to Gabriel, who shrugged and said, 'So what?'

Dot wore a nylon dress covered in a cabbage-rose print. She teetered along on high-heeled white shoes, wore her white gloves and had a little plastic envelope bag.

'We'll never all fit in one carriage,' Dot cried, tap-tapping up the platform to the O'Sheas, the high heels clicking merrily, kissing Oonagh when she drew opposite her, Oonagh saying, 'We're in this one, Dot,' Dot not listening, too busy explaining her point of view. 'Ben got ever such a nice one for us. We'll see you at the station the other end.' And she hurried back to Ben who was herding the crocodile on to the train.

'Let's follow her example and get on,' Gabriel said.

One carriage was hardly big enough for the O'Sheas. It was lovely, though, with plush seats and head-rests and little linen antimacassars, and above that there was a panel of wood, a mirror and two prints, on one side of the Wicklow mountains, and the other of the Gap of Dunloe. Above the prints there were string-mesh luggage racks.

Oonagh said, 'Isn't it gorgeous!' She felt a glow of content spread through her, a keen feeling of physical well-being. This was the life!

'It's great to feel affluent, Gabriel,' she whispered to him as they settled themselves. 'To feel top of the heap. I know it's snobby but I don't care.'

She had not told him yet about the baby. Somehow it never seemed the right time.

Gabriel felt exactly as he thought a husband ought to feel. He was proud to be seen with his family, proud of their good looks, proud of their neat, well-groomed appearance. Barnet's and the family discount was responsible for that and he thought himself lucky. He was going on holiday and they were travelling first class. Oonagh could indulge in a feeling of luxury, and it was all thanks to him. What more could any man want?

Chapter Twenty-Four

Granny O'Shea sat in the corner, her back to engine, with Emmett in attendance. 'I hope this train doesn't crash!' she kept agonizing, and Emmett replied, 'Ah, sure, if it does we'll be with God, won't we, Granny?' And she said, 'Not *yet* Emmett. I'm not quite ready just yet!'

Laughlin sat beside his father. He had worked hard and obediently on his schedule, but Oonagh worried about him for he seemed unusually malleable and obedient. Too much so, and she didn't trust that.

She worried too about Ardel who had also changed. He had clung to his home ever since that terrible night the terrorist had kidnapped him. He hardly went out at all. Oonagh could understand the change in both boys. Poor Laughlin was, she felt sure, suffering from the shock of that awful Christian Brother's despicable actions and Ardel, who had thought he was a tough guy, was trying to adjust to finding out he could be terrified.

Actually Ardel had clung close to home because he did not want to meet Banan. He wanted to vanish from his cousin's orbit. He had avoided it so far by keeping away from all his usual haunts, particularly the pool hall. He didn't reckon his chances much longer. Banan would sure as hell pitch up in Dranmore and the music would have to be faced.

Ardel had spent the eighty quid and the fifty pound reward the Gardai had sent for his part in the capture of Billy Macken. He had bought everyone in the family a present. He had given Laughlin a new pencil-case, Emmett a brown rosary with wooden beads, Emer a bottle of Midnight Magic, a strong-smelling perfume that she had once said she liked and that she received ecstatically. Oonagh had not the heart to forbid her wearing it although it reeked of the cheap ingredients it was comprised of, manufactured as it was in a factory in Finglas.

'Smells like fly-killer,' Laughlin said.

'Well, they make that there too,' Oonagh remarked. 'Still, it was lovely of Ardel, spending his money on us. Don't spend it all now, will you? Put some into the Post Office.'

He had given his mother a rope of pearls he had bought in Woolworth's and his da a book-mark purchased ditto. To Mourna and Briana he had given lace-edged handkerchiefs.

'Save some of it, Ardel,' his mother admonished, but he could not. It was as if he had a compulsion to get rid of it all as quickly as he could. He bought himself a new outfit

165

and had himself a glorious evening in the Red Bank and Davy Byrne's, drinking, living it up, trying to forget Billy Macken's words. He had made a lot of new friends in the convivial atmosphere of the pubs, friends whose names he never discovered and whom he never saw again.

Now, money all spent, he shivered in the corner near the corridor and wondered what would happen to him when Banan caught up with him. Billy Macken's face haunted Ardel's dreams and Laughlin often shouted at him in the night to shut up, he was having another nightmare.

Laughlin was subdued because he felt he was on the edge of something terrible and did not want to travel too near. He did not know what it was, this edge, he just knew it was lurking in his mind somewhere and when he tried to catch hold of the reality of it, it slid away. He did not try too hard to pin it down because he knew it would be a frightening revelation. Sometimes he even thought he knew what it was, but he drew back, not wanting the knowledge, rejecting it subconsciously. Bemused, he had drifted through the strange days of studying in the drawing room at home, which was very odd. Being by himself was even odder. Life felt peculiar, as if time was out of joint. There was no one to test himself against and this curious lack of competition left him relaxed and reflective. He could pursue avenues he had neither the time nor the opportunity to in school. He also could not help wondering about what had happened to him.

There were so many assumptions that had proved false. He had always been told that priests and Brothers were holy men, goodness personified, and therefore to be trusted. Yet he had found out that the reverse was true. The holy man, the very person he should have been able to bank on, had let him down, led him into evil ways. Emmett, in his boring self-righteous way, talked about 'God's pattern'. What was that? Laughlin wondered. Did

God move us around like chess pieces? Emmett said that Father Maloney had told him that nothing happened by accident, and that there was good to be found in every situation. Well, what good could come from Brother Nathan fumbling him? He'd like to know that.

The other thing, completely unexpected, that he had learned was that his father was his friend, not someone to be frightened of or ashamed before. Oh, his da hadn't said a word, made no comment, and Laughlin wouldn't have wanted him to, but he was *there*, supporting not condemning.

'You all right?' Briana asked him now. His eyes slewed away from her. Why did he feel guilty?

'Course,' he said. 'Course. Why wouldn't I be?'

His father glanced at Laughlin. He smiled at him and laid a hand on his shoulder, squeezed it, then patted his back. Laughlin felt a wave of relief sweep over him and smiled back.

Briana went to the window and hung out. Oonagh watched her and wondered who she was looking for.

'Bri, sit down, darling,' she said, and saw Briana's face suddenly light up, like a torch being switched on. She leaned further out of the window so that her mother, alarmed, caught the hem of her skirt and held on.

'We're here. Here, Iain. Over here,' she yelled, waving.

Emer, who had up to then been lost in a dream, made a face and the next moment the door was yanked open and Iain Benson bounced into the carriage, bringing with him an air of energy and excitement.

'Well, well, well, what a surprise,' Emer murmured sarcastically.

Gabriel could see Iain wanted to embrace Briana, but he held back with amazing self-control.

'Hello, Uncle Gabriel, Auntie Oonagh. Just made it. I'm right off the train from Dun Laoghaire,' he said breathlessly.

167

'He's just got back from Edinburgh,' Briana said, hardly able to contain herself, looking at him with shining eyes.

Their bodies were like magnets, Oonagh thought, and shivered. They are drawn involuntarily and unerringly towards each other.

'Where's your luggage?' she asked.

'I left it in Dun Laoghaire in the left luggage,' Iain said. 'It was delaying me something shocking.' His hands reached for Briana's, touched, then parted.

'Ah, sure, what's your hurry?' Gabriel asked, a twinkle in his eye.

'I'll get it sent on,' Iain looked at Gabriel anxiously. 'I can do that, can't I?'

Gabriel nodded. 'Yes, of course.'

'Oh, Briana, it's so good to see you,' Iain said, hugged her suddenly then let her go, quickly, as if she had burned him.

'There's nowhere for you to sit,' Emer said, staring at them with avid interest combined with pity.

'Ardel, get up and let Iain sit. Ardel!'

He didn't seem to hear. He was staring absently into space.

'Mam, can I ask Auntie Dot for a loan of her white stilettos?' Emer asked out of the blue.

Oonagh looked at her in astonishment. 'What on earth for?'

Emer blushed and hesitated. 'A ... project,' she said defiantly.

'Well,' Oonagh was doubtful, 'I don't know, Emer. Wait and see.'

'That's all I ever get, "wait and see".'

'Emer, don't be rude.'

'Well, it's true. I never ask for anything, ever, and when I do I always get "wait and see".'

'Yes, but, darling ... Auntie Dot's shoes!'

'That's weird, Emer.' Briana looked at her sister. 'Wouldn't my sandals do?'

Emer shook her head. 'No. They have to be Auntie Dot's. For the project.'

'Weird!' Briana repeated, and turned to Iain. 'Let's go and get a drink. I'm thirsty. I'd like some tea or orange or something.' He nodded in urgent agreement, a private look passing between them making Emer grimace. They left the carriage, taking with them the excitement that Iain had brought.

'They've gone to find an empty carriage,' Emer remarked. 'And then they'll snog.'

Laughlin blushed.

'Don't be rude, Emer. How many times must I tell you?'

'Well, they won't find one, the train's packed,' Ardel said, coming out of his trance.

'Isn't Molly coming?' Gabriel asked after a while.

'Tom is driving the family down,' Oonagh said, not looking up from her magazine. 'They'll be there before us.'

'So they'll take all the best rooms,' Emer said, swinging her legs, banging her heels on the bottom of the seat.

'Emer, you're appalling,' Oonagh complained. 'Even to think such a thing! And stop kicking.'

'We're in four houses anyhow,' Gabriel said, 'so it's not going to make any difference. We have one, Molly's family have one, Dot and Ben have one ...'

'And poor Auntie Rita is landed with Uncle Joe and Auntie Maisie,' Emer crowed, giving the seat one last wallop.

That was true. Oonagh shrank away from the hypocrisy that underlay the general consensus that Rita would be more comfortable with Joe and Maisie. As if anyone would!

'It's her punishment for being poor,' Emmett said, and Granny O'Shea, who had been reassured by him that the train wouldn't crash, said, 'What? What? I don't know if I'm goin' to be able to sleep in a strange bed. I like my own bed!'

'She says that every year,' Oonagh said to Gabriel.

'What's the matter with Ardel?' Granny O'Shea asked.

169

'I don't know.' Oonagh glanced at her eldest son. 'Is anything the matter, Ardel?'

'No, Mam. I'm fine.' Ardel didn't look at her. He seemed subdued, so unlike his usual self.

'He's very quiet,' Granny O'Shea remarked loudly.

'I'm fine, Granny,' Ardel said, wishing it were true.

Doors slammed, whistles blew again, and the train shuddered into action. It gathered speed, and Oonagh settled back contentedly with *Woman's Home Journal* which was her favourite magazine. It was an American publication and had glossy pictures of unheard-of luxuries like pantyhose, blouses that fastened under the crotch and would never ride up, showers in bathrooms, and recipes for Aunt Sarah's sour-dough bread and chocolate-chip cookies and blueberry flapjacks, all with prices beside them in dollars. It was riveting stuff.

'I'll stretch my legs,' Gabriel nodded to his wife and stood up.

'You're not stretching your legs, Da, you're going to check on Bri and Iain,' Emer said, and Gabriel tweaked her hair.

'You're much too clever for your own good, Emer,' he laughed, and went out into the corridor.

He walked down the now speeding train to the restaurant. He could see from outside the door his daughter and Iain, elbows on the table, fingers folded into each other's hands, talking earnestly. They were oblivious of all else in that impenetrable circle lovers draw around themselves. They did not see him, they did not see anybody, and he moved back up the corridor, lit his pipe and pushed down the window.

He watched the fields race by, green as emeralds, moist under the eternal dew from the lakes and streams and rivers. This was his land and he loved it. It nourished him. He drew in great draughts of the damp air, smelled the grass and earth and the trees.

He felt Briana's touch before he saw her. She linked her arm in his and pressed her face against his sleeve.

'It's lovely, Da, isn't it?' she sighed, looking out over the spreading countryside. 'You can't hear the birds though.'

'No,' he said. 'You can't. The train goes "to-po-cco, to-po-cco" all the time.'

'I'm so happy, Da,' she whispered, looking up radiantly at him, and for some reason he felt a great sadness come over him. Happiness is such a serious business, he thought.

'I'm glad, Bri. Hold on to it, love. It's all too soon over.'

But she could not visualize that.

'I'm off to the lavvy,' she said, gave his arm a squeeze and left.

He watched her slim figure in her flowered print dress, Barnet's best, move away from him down the train.

Temper her emotions, Lord, he prayed silently. Help her not to feel too intensely.

Briana's intensity sometimes frightened him. She immersed herself in her feelings, not holding back. There was no reserve. Tears flooded, laughter bubbled, exuberance threatened sometimes to overwhelm her. He worried about her being hurt and knew he could do nothing to save her. She might drown in her pain. On the other hand she had her mother's common sense. She had dealt with Miss Marshall, her Maths teacher, who neither understood nor liked her, with admirable philosophical acceptance. However, he could smell trouble ahead.

Eddie, to put it mildly, liked his own way. He wanted Mourna to marry Iain, unless Colista had her way and she married the German. If she did, then the Bensons both wanted their son to marry one of the Fitzwilliam twins, high society debutantes, rich and fashionable. Eddie said that not only was Colista dead set against Briana O'Shea, she would be incensed beyond enduring if Iain took the law into his own hands. Gabriel knew she would fight tooth and nail for her son and Colista Benson had never lost a fight yet. Ah, well! They'd have to wait and see.

He smoked, peacefully puffing his pipe out of the window, and Briana returned, her arms out, hands touching the sides of the swaying corridor, balancing herself as she made her way towards him.

'Iain's buying lunch,' she said, winking at him. 'It's just an excuse.'

'Ah, yes. We'll have the packed sandwiches Peggy made.' Gabriel smiled.

'Poor Peggy spends her life making sandwiches,' Briana retorted, laughing, and passed by him back into the dining car. The attendant was to be heard in the distance shouting something about 'Faaast Lunch ina Dining Caaaar'.

When Gabriel eventually returned to the carriage he found poor Rita had arrived. He always thought of her as 'poor Rita'. There was something so defeated about her, so hopeless. Brigid, her daughter, was with her and was engaging Emer in animated conversation.

'I feel sometimes, Oonagh, like I'm holding on by my finger-nails,' Rita was saying to Oonagh, who gave Gabriel a pregnant glance as much as to say, get me out of this. 'I feel I'm going to drop off the world.'

'Now, now, Rita, that's a silly thing to say. How could you?'

'Don't you even understand that?' Rita cried.

There was no place for Gabriel to sit. Rita was in his seat and Brigid had squashed up beside Emer.

'She's talking nonsense, Gabriel,' Oonagh said briskly. 'She's letting her nerves get the better of her.'

'No. I mean it, Oonagh. You just don't understand, do you?'

'I know you've had a hard time, Rita,' Oonagh said patiently. She wished Rita'd go away. She was spoiling the lovely opulent mood that travelling in a first-class carriage had induced. She was making Oonagh feel guilty.

172

'If you put sixpence between yer thighs, an' another sixpence between yer knees, an' another where yer calves touch,' Emer was saying to Brigid, 'it says here,' she pointed to the *Woman's Home Journal* that had slipped from her mother's knee while she was speaking to Auntie Rita, 'if you can hold sixpences like that, you have perfect legs!'

'Who has three sixpences? Gawney! Wealth!' Brigid cried.

'I have.' Emer looked meaningfully at her cousin and they both jumped up.

'Got to go to the lavvy, Mam.'

Oonagh hardly noticed them.

'All right,' she said automatically. 'Remember, don't sit on the seat.'

'All right, Ma.' Giggling, they both left, and with a sigh of relief Gabriel sat down.

'Ah, the war was a great time, Emmett.' Granny O'Shea sounded regretful. 'A great time. It was all black-and-white though until the Yanks came, and then everything went technicolour.'

'Well, what I wanted to say,' Rita told Oonagh tensely and glanced at Gabriel, then looked away as if she was ashamed, 'what I wanted to tell you was … that …' She took a deep breath. 'Well …'

'Spit it out, Rita,' Gabriel said impatiently.

'Well, I'm off to Lisdoonvarna for a … a … while, once we get there. Get to Dranmore, I mean. I'll leave the children with Maisie. She's a nurse so they'll come to no harm.'

'What?' Oonagh looked dumbfounded. 'What are you talking about?'

'What on earth are you on about, Rita?' Gabriel looked perplexed. 'Have I missed something? You're not making any sense.'

'I'm off to Lisdoonvarna,' Rita said in a tremulous voice.

'But we're going to *Dranmore*,' Oonagh said. 'How can you be going to Lisdoonvarna, Rita? How?'

'When we get there I'll settle the children and then I'll go.' Rita said, looking out of the window and fidgeting in her seat.

'But you can't do that,' Gabriel said. 'You can't afford …' He stammered to a halt. 'After all, we …' he petered out as he realized what he was saying.

'You mean, how can I afford to go to Lisdoonvarna when I can't afford to pay for my holiday in Dranmore?' Rita turned on him, furious. 'Well, let me tell you, I can't afford *either*. Only no one ever asks me if I want this holiday. My wishes are never consulted. I suppose because I'm charity.' This irritated Oonagh for it was exactly how she felt herself. Not the charity part, but the being asked.

'But it's a treat for you, Rita.' Oonagh was, Gabriel saw, confused by what she saw as Rita's ingratitude.

'Rita, why Lisdoonvarna?' he asked curiously.

'Don't you know?' Rita said harshly, looking at him with cold eyes. 'Can't you guess?'

Light dawned on Oonagh. 'Holy Mother of God! Yer not going to the marriage market? Rita, ye wouldn't.'

'Oh yes I would, so there!' Rita said defiantly. Gabriel looked from one to the other, mystified.

'She's going to find a husband!' Oonagh said. 'Aren't you a bit old, Rita?'

Rita's pale face flushed angry red. 'Are you suggesting I'm over the hill?' she bristled.

'A husband … Oh, I see.'

'Well, Gabriel, now that the penny's dropped I suppose you're going to start in on me?' Rita enquired sarcastically.

Gabriel shook his head. 'No, Rita, I'm not. What you do with your life is your affair.'

This made her feel very lonely. It was worse than Oonagh's outraged disapproval. He was telling her obliquely that on her own head be the consequences of her actions. It cut her off and frightened her. She wondered briefly if she'd told the O'Sheas in order to be persuaded not to go.

174

'Well, I think you're mad, Rita. Who'll you meet there but randy old men looking for some young chickabiddies to warm their beds?'

'I've thought of that, Oonagh, and I think that warming a farmer's bed in Kerry or Galway or Mayo, an' he'd look after me and pay my debts and for the last of the children's education, would be far better than the spot I'm in now. One room in Gardiner Street and not a penny to my name.' And she burst into a torrent of tears.

'Good God, what's the matter with Rita?' Granny O'Shea broke off her conversation with Emmett. 'Are they putting on the grand act with you, Rita, eh? Well, don't let them. We should look after our own.' She winked at Rita. 'I'll have a word with Eddie and Colista, never fear.'

Rita stood up, horrified. 'Oh no, Granny, don't do that. For God's sake, no!'

'Why not? They can afford it.'

Rita despaired of anyone ever understanding. How could she tell them that if Granny O'Shea spoke to the Bensons, Eddie, only too delighted to help, would lecture her, then take out a tenner or two from his pig-skin wallet, give them to her and say, 'That'll keep you going for a while, Rita,' and everyone would think him grand, and she would have to be terribly grateful.

And it *would* keep her going. For a while. Make a small dent in her loan and buy her time from the sharks. But only a little time. Then it would all begin again, all over again, and she couldn't keep asking.

She wanted security. She wanted not to have to worry about loans and debts ever again. The anxiety was killing her.

'Well, I think it's disgraceful ...' Oonagh began, but just then Dot burst into the carriage carrying a Switzer's bag and followed by two of the crocodile, little Dec and Maggie.

Maggie stood in the centre of the compartment, sturdily steady on her two fat legs, stoically swaying with the motion

175

of the train on the tracks. She fixed large eyes on Granny O'Shea who stared back at her. Little Dec burrowed into his mother's skirts, sometimes chewing the indestructible nylon fabric, sometimes making faces at his sister.

'Ooooh! First class, I see, Oonagh,' Dot remarked on entering. 'How grand! It's well for some! How are you all?' Then, not waiting for a reply, anxious to get her news over, bursting with excitement, 'We're having tea with the Bensons at the Grand tomorrow. Alone. Think of that. Private, Colista said. A little chat about the children and Ben's position in the Post Office.'

She was bristling with self-importance and having delivered her news, with pride and triumph, she opened the bag to reveal what it contained. She shook out an extraordinary mohair pullover in green, white and yellow wool.

'The colours of patriotism, Oonagh,' she cried, shaking out the garment. 'The Irish flag!'

'Well, isn't that gorgeous?' Oonagh said in a small strangled voice.

'Yes, *I* think so.' Dot smoothed it on her lap, and when little Dec began to finger it she removed his hand gently. Dot didn't believe in corporal punishment.

Gabriel cleared his throat. 'I don't think Ben'll get much wear out of it in this weather, Dot,' he said. 'It's beautiful quality, beautiful, but not for summer.'

'It's not *for* Ben,' Dot said. 'It's for Eddie! I made it myself.'

'Yes, we can see that,' Oonagh put in hastily. 'It bears your stamp, Dot.'

Gabriel was at a loss to know what to say. The picture of Eddie Benson in the green, white and yellow gansey was a thought not to be dwelt on in case of hysteria.

'Excuse me, will you?' Rita got up.

'Don't do anything hasty, Rita, not until we talk,' Gabriel said.

Dot's head swivelled around, suddenly aware that there was something going on, instantly alert.

'Oh, shut up and leave me alone,' Rita said bad-temperedly, and left.

As the carriage door closed behind her, Dot asked, 'What's up with that wan?'

'You've got green stuff on your teeth, Granny O'Shea,' Maggie piped up, swaying gently with the carriage.

'Don't say things like that, Maggie,' Dot admonished her youngest mildly.

'Why not? It's true,' Maggie loudly insisted.

'One doesn't make personal remarks about others,' Oonagh said waspishly, giving Maggie Moran a hard stare, which was returned with interest until Oonagh withdrew her gaze under the unnerving insolence of the child's scrutiny.

'What's Rita on about?' Dot persisted.

'She's going to Lisdoonvarna to find a man.'

Dot screamed. 'What? What? I don't believe you.'

'Well, it's true. She's going to find a man with money.'

'I think she meant a husband,' Gabriel interpolated, and his wife glanced at him with withering scorn.

'Well, I should hope so.'

'You having me on?' Dot asked incredulously. 'You're having me on!' she said.

The carriage door slid open.

'We've got perfect legs, me an' Emer,' Brigid announced. 'Me an' Emer did the test in the lavvy an' we've got perfect legs!' She bounced on the seat beside Ardel.

'Isn't that grand news, Brigid?' Gabriel said absently.

Emer saw Maggie and cried, 'Oh, no!' and Maggie smiled at her evilly.

'Can Emer take me to the lavvy, Mammy?' she shrilled.

'Why don't you just go away?' Emer hissed.

'She can, can't you, Emer? There's a dear. Oonagh, that's all right, isn't it? She loves Emer, don't you, pet?'

177

Maggie nodded violently and Emer looked pleadingly at her mother who was staring in disbelief at the sweater as it disappeared into the Switzer's bag. Then she looked at her father, but he was settling Granny O'Shea. She sighed.

'C'm'on then,' she said resignedly to Maggie, and took her hand. 'But you'd better behave, I'm warning you! C'm'on, Brigid, help me with the little gurrier.'

Gabriel took his pipe out of his top pocket, but Oonagh glanced at him and shook her head, 'Not here, Gabriel,' she said, and he quickly replaced it.

Dot said, 'What's all this about Rita? What does she think she's doing? Is she off her rocker or what?'

'It's just that she wants some security, I think,' Gabriel said, then decided he didn't want to hear another apalled conversation about Rita, with Dot and his wife shaking their heads in disapproving condemnation. He wanted a few puffs on his pipe so he left the carriage again.

No one had paid any attention to Ardel in the corner next to the corridor and so no one noticed when he too left the carriage. He had not listened to what either Dot or Rita had talked about so lost was he in his thoughts. Somehow all other concerns seemed trivial when compared to his problems.

He mooched down to the restaurant car, saw Briana and Iain enthralled with each other. He turned around quickly and retreated the other way. He passed his father leaning out of the open window, hardly noticed him and did not return his greeting.

He got to the toilet, saw the red engaged sign, moved towards the last first-class compartment and leaned against the door, waiting for the lavatory to be free. He could hear Emer and Maggie in there. Maggie was shouting, 'Hold me over the lavvy, Emer, don't let me fall in. Me mam says not to sit on it or I'll be sick.'

He noticed that the blinds were drawn in the compartment. That was odd in the middle of the day. A

178

honeymoon couple, he thought, couldn't wait! The blind twitched. Ardel shrugged and lit a fag.

What happened next was so swift he had no time to think or prepare. The compartment door opened. He stumbled as hands grabbed him and he was yanked into the carriage, the door slammed behind him and a huge fist connected with his jaw, another with his solar plexus. Involuntarily he sat down on the seat, clutching his stomach, fighting for breath against the overwhelming agony that threatened to engulf him. The pain felt as if it was splitting his face in half. He looked up to see two men towering over him. He had never seen either of them before.

'Who're you?' he gasped stupidly, rising unsteadily. 'What do you think you're doin'?' He knew. Of course he knew. He sounded feeble, and scared as well.

'We're friends of Billy Macken,' one of the men said, and Ardel felt his stomach sink in terror. These were the hard men, the ones Banan had threatened him with. These men never let go. Were they going to kill him? Dear Jesus, no! He looked at the men, fear in his eyes.

One of them had thick caterpillar eyebrows and a thatch of black hair growing low, bull-like, down on his forehead. The other was thin and tall, like a string-bean, with a flat lizard head and small icy eyes.

'Yeah,' he said, 'we're friends of Macken's.'

'We've come to warn ye.'

'Yeah.'

They were a double act but Ardel didn't feel like laughing.

'He wants his money back. The money he gave to Banan an' Banan gave to you.'

'Strictly speakin',' the other said, 'it's not *his* money, y'see. It's *ours*. It belongs to the organization.'

They both had sharp Northern Ireland accents that scraped Ardel's nerves.

'He wants it soon.'

179

'Yeah!'

'We're messengers, see?'

'Listen, fellas, you gotta understand,' Ardel pleaded, searching for a way out. 'It wasn't my fault. The polis came up behind the van an' I had to stop ...'

The bull-like one shook his head and whispered, 'We don' care! See, we know nuthin' about that. We don' even know why we're doin' this. We bin' told you bin naughty, takin' money, not doin' the job. Your mam not tell you it's bad to steal? It's a matter of honour. An' *we* obey orders. You should too. It's good advice.'

He punctuated each sentence with a blow, hitting Ardel again and again. 'It's just the money. No hard feelin's.'

Ardel's muscles bunched in protest when he saw the blows coming. Bull-head didn't seem angry, he just hit efficiently and effectively as if he were practising on a punch-bag until Ardel felt as if he was wrapped in barbed wire.

Lizard-head hit him in the stomach, kneed him in the balls, nearly broke his nose, smashed his face and slapped him around the head, saying rhythmically, 'We want the money, understand?' in a sing-song voice as if he were at choir practice.

Then suddenly they were gone.

He lay on the floor of the empty carriage, spitting blood, holding himself together, arms around himself, moaning, rocking with the train. The pain sloughed over him in waves of nausea and agony, and ploughed through his body. Nerves jangled like broken glass, jumping, screaming, throbbing in his head. His face felt scalded and raw and he had wet his pants. He didn't feel like a man now, he felt like a little boy. His teeth were chattering and his tongue found one of them loose. His mouth was full of blood.

Painfully he drew one arm from around his body and felt his jaw. He yelled out. Was his jaw broken? Every bone in his body ached. His stomach felt bruised and hollow, like

180

gravel had been rubbed in an open wound.

He heard Maggie Moran outside, taunting Emer. 'Neh-neh-ne-neh-neh! If ye follow yer nose ye'll go straight to heaven, Emer O'Shea.'

'Oh, shut up, you little termite. If your mammy only knew what you were really like.'

'Well, she doesn't, an' so there!'

He pushed himself up on one elbow. It took all his courage and determination.

'Ugeeeerrr ... Emer!' It came out in a screaming cry that exploded from him uncontrollably.

'Janey Mac, what's that?' Maggie's voice was scared. 'Emer, what's that?'

'It's the bogey man come to *get* you,' Emer replied with relish.

'Ah ... h ... h ... h ...h!' a frightened yell diminished as Maggie fled down the corridor, her fat little legs flying, and after a moment the carriage door opened cautiously and Emer's head appeared around it. 'God, Ardel, yer pulp! What happened?'

He was glad it was Emer. She was stalwart. You couldn't shake her.

She pulled out her handkerchief. 'Here, let me help you up, then I'll go and wet the hankie an' we'll try and mop you up a bit before Da sees you. Now don't try to say nuthin', Ardel. You know Da'll have to see you an' it'll be okay but we don't want to give Ma a heart attack, you lookin' like that, now do we?'

All the while she talked to try to keep his mind off his agony. He kept seeing her face fade away in black shadows and return, and fade and return, as pain washed over him like a tide.

It was a slow process getting him up, sitting him on the seat. 'Now don't you move till I get back with the wet hankie,' she told him, and left the carriage. As if he could have moved when all movement was agony.

Outside she leaned against the door and took deep breaths to try to calm herself. Her heart was racing and she suppressed a desire to throw up. She didn't want to admit it but Ardel's appearance had shocked her. He looked like nothing she had ever seen. When Jimmy Cagney punched people they vanished off the screen and you didn't see them again and anyhow it was all in black and white. She had never seen a victim of violence before and Ardel's blood was very dark red, almost purple, and he was covered in it. He looked very messy and quite frightening.

She wet the handkerchief under a trickle of water from the tap in the toilet and hurried back to the compartment. The blinds were still down.

'Did you see anyone?' Ardel asked through stiff swollen lips.

She shook her head. 'No, I didn't. I think you should have a couple of aspirin. It would help the pain. As soon as I've cleaned you up a bit. Sorry, sorry!' He was wincing and moaning and she tried to be careful. 'I'm going to get Da. He's in the corridor further along the train.'

Ardel was too defeated to protest. His brain had shut down while he coped with his injuries and his pain. Emer left him propped up against the seat and went to find her father.

He was still at the open window in the corridor, puffing his pipe. He turned when she pulled his sleeve.

'Why, Emer, what's the matter? You look as if you've had a fright.'

It was a relief to unburden to him. 'It's Ardel, Da. He's hurt. Come with me.'

'Oh God, what's happened?' Gabriel's face lost its colour.

'No, Da, he's all right. Just bruised and …'

'Bruised? Bruised … how?'

'Come, Da. Come with me. He's in the last compartment down here. I don't want Mam to …'

'Oh no, no, of course not,' he said, following Emer's train

182

of thought. 'Well done, Emer.'

He went with her down the corridor to the carriage and entered after her.

Chapter Twenty-Five

The sight of his son shocked him. Ardel sat, face swelling, one eye closing and turning an ugly purple, clothes torn and in disarray, nose bleeding – a mess.

'Ardel, son, what in God's name happened to you?'

'It was nothing, Da. Nothing. Two men ... er ... attacked me. It's okay. I'm okay.'

'No, you are not. I never heard such appalling ... I'm going to stop the train. This is insufferable. These men are dangerous. It was not a little scuffle, I can see that. How dare they! If they're still on the train, we'll catch them.'

He had been sitting beside his son and stood up as if to pull the communication cord, but Ardel grasped his arm, wincing at the effort.

'No, Da, don't!' He tried to think, to gather what remnants of reason he could together, to use the wits which seemed sadly scattered. 'Look, Da, it's better not.'

'Why not, son? What really happened?'

'They were ...' Ardel hesitated. 'They were friends of Billy Macken.'

'Oh God! This is preposterous. This is the Irish Free State after all. Who do they think they are?'

'But it's better to let it lie, don't you see?'

'Yes, well, those guys!'

'It's better, Da.'

'But why? Why did they beat you up? What do they want?' Gabriel looked narrowly at his son. There was an evasiveness about Ardel that worried him.

'Are you telling me the whole truth?' he asked.

'Of course, Da. All they wanted was to teach me a lesson. That's what they said. You know what they're like.'

'It seems odd to me. We'll have to report it, though. I suppose there's no need to pull the cord, but we must report it.'

'I don't see why, Da. I don't think it's a good idea to cross those guys. I think the best thing would be to forget all about it.'

'No, Ardel.' Gabriel sounded implacable. 'No. We are law abiding citizens. We have done nothing wrong.' He looked keenly at Ardel. 'That I know of. And as we have not, we must do as the law advises. These people must not be allowed to get away with violence.'

Ardel could not prevent his father from reporting the incident. He had not the stamina to argue further.

'There's the ticket collector, Da,' Emer said.

'Call him, pet.'

The ticket collector, a weasel of a man with darting eyes, turned pale when he saw Ardel and promptly did a Pontius Pilate.

'Beaten up, sur? Yis, I can see dat, sur. Yis, I can indeed. But what do ye expect me to do, sur? Dere's nuthin' in de rules about dis.'

He was less than useless. He stood in front of Gabriel, blinking rapidly, shifting from one foot to the other, dying to escape.

Gabriel gave up. 'I'll want it reported,' he said, 'I insist on that.'

Emer had gone back to their compartment and Oonagh immediately demanded to know what was wrong. When Emer told her she fled to her husband and Ardel, burst into the carriage, clasped her son in her arms, cradling him to her bosom and demanding something be done at once.

The ticket collector stared at the ceiling, pursed his lips stubbornly and reiterated, 'Nuttin' I can do. Nuttin'. It's not my business, sur. Nuttin' to do wi' me. I'm only paid to collect the tickets, sur.'

'All right. All right. We can report it in Dranmore,' Oonagh cried. 'Oh, pet, are you all right? Let me get you something to drink and some aspirin. Come back to the compartment ...'

'Do you think that's wise, love? Granny and Emmett are there. They might be upset.'

'They'll have to see him sooner or later.'

'Well, I'd rather it was later,' Gabriel insisted. 'At the station in Dranmore there'll be such bustle and fuss it won't be so remarkable. People will be preoccupied with their luggage, you know what it's like. Then we can get Ardel to the house as quietly as possible.'

He was quite correct. When they reached the station at Dranmore there was a huge commotion. Dot and Ben, the O'Sheas, their respective families, Rita and her children, and last but not least Joe and Maisie, all emerging from the train, made it easy for Gabriel and Oonagh, supporting Ardel, to whisk him without much fuss into one of the pony-and-traps that Mrs Flanagan had sent to pick them up. One by one the mothers and fathers, aunts and uncles, sisters and brothers, sorted themselves out and into the waiting vehicles provided. They were much too busy collecting their luggage and bits and pieces to notice Ardel O'Shea's pathetic condition.

The sun had come out and Mrs Flanagan, who had come to supervise said, 'There now, ye see? The sun got up for ye.'

She was a warmly stout woman with a brisk manner, a florid, faintly mauve face and shrewd eyes.

'Ah, now, I haveta get yiz right ... Mr and Mrs ...

O'Shea? Ah, yes. Mrs Molly and Mr Tom Moran arrived earlier, by motor vehicle. You are? Ah, Mrs Maguire. Ah, yes. And Brigid … Mary … Maggie … Well, let's see, I'll get used to ye all, so I will, never fear.'

She spied Ardel, her face fell and she hurried over to the O'Sheas who had grouped around him, as if, Emer whispered to Brigid, they were ashamed of him. 'In the name of God and his Holy Mother, how'd he get himself into that state?'

'My son's been hurt. We need to get back to the house as soon as possible,' Oonagh said.

'But he's a mess! I never seen the like …'

Joe, who had spent the whole journey in the bar, created the desired diversion, staggering up, dazed by the sunlight, Maisie trying to help him, and bumping into Granny O'Shea.

'Sorry, Gran. I'm that clumsy,' he said.

'You're that drunk!' she replied tartly.

'Your lipstick is all over your face,' Emer whispered to Briana, who didn't seem to care, and the tense moment was over.

'Can't we go *on*! I bin standing here ten minutes!' Granny O'Shea said loudly. 'An' Molly an' Tom have already hoofed it to the best rooms.'

'She's got no patience,' Joe said. 'She can't wait for anything.'

'Uncle Joe, you keep your gob shut about Granny,' Emmett hissed at the sottish, swaying man. The contempt in his voice made Joe blink and look at his shoes, and Maisie, trying hard not to cry or show her irritation, pulled his arm.

'Where's the houses?' she asked. 'Just let me get to the house we're in.'

'Ye each occupy a house and they're identical, so there's no advantage in arriving early,' Mrs Flanagan said firmly to Granny O'Shea.

Dot looked at Ben. 'Joe's in no condition to look after their luggage,' she whispered. 'Benny lamb, do you think you could …?'

'Oh, sweetness, of course. Of course. Though it would serve him right if …'

'Now, Ben!' Dot gave him a reproving glance and then a loving smile.

At last they were all transported to the four houses. Their anxiety and irritation calmed when they found themselves in four identical buildings snuggled down in the shade of two huge Monterey pines and set in surroundings of such beauty that it drove all petty argument from their minds. It was a breathtaking scene. Green of earth, blue of sea, gold of strands and sunlight on water, the bays lay before them, circling the headland, red cliffs dropping sheer, the harbour full of dancing boats and fishermen's nets. The shoreline, dented by bays, some sandy, some pebbly, stretched around below them, shimmering in the sun.

Molly was there to greet them and seemed perplexed when Oonagh avoided her and hurried Ardel inside. She could not see the boy for the dazzle of the sun in her eyes. Gabriel steered her away towards the trees, looking out over the magical horizon.

'It's gorgeous, Moll, isn't it?'

The houses, linked by connecting doors and passageways, sat close together on the rise above the bay called Golden Strand. Collectively they were called Kincora, Mrs Flanagan informed them. 'Not that ye'll need to know it!' she laughed. 'But just in case ye get lost.

'Yiz have a common dining room in the centre building,' Mrs Flanagan informed them. 'Breakfast is at nine o'clock. All together, I'm afraid. We tackle the lot of yiz in one go. Otherwise,' she shook her grey curls, 'it's murder!'

There was a general laugh. People stood around, grimacing as they held the heavy luggage en route to their

187

rooms. They were half in and half out of the houses. Mrs Flanagan continued, 'There's a timesheet on the door of the dining room if ye forget. Dinner is at one o'clock, on the dot, and tea is at six, an' then the kitchen closes – an' no raidin'.' She fixed the youngsters with a beady eye. 'Anyone late misses the lot,' she said. 'I'll not have the guests puttin' me in the hospital above.'

Oonagh was pleased, if not enchanted, with Kincora. It was not top-drawer after all. It was not the Grand. The euphoria of the first-class carriage had evaporated and she was suffering from delusions of grandeur and disappointment at the decor. The bedrooms were certainly not the Grand, or what Oonagh imagined the Grand to be like. The mass-produced furniture, the inferior linen, the nylon bed-spreads and gaudy orange Tintawn that covered the floor, were not to her taste. However, it was comfortable, and when she realized that Gabriel, watching her, had read her feelings in her face, she was ashamed and set about reassuring him.

'It's lovely, Gabriel, lovely.' And she looked at him and smiled. 'At first it's always a shock because other people never furnish a place like you would yourself.' That satisfied her husband and she set about adapting herself to her new surroundings and making the most of them.

Dot was much more impressed. Her own home in Dublin was in a constant state of turmoil and untidiness because of the children. Kincora seemed to her total luxury.

Molly was indifferent. As long as the mattress was comfortable she was content. The room she occupied hardly impinged on her. All she saw was the view from the window. The perpetual motion of the sea, the red cliffs and the dark green mass of the pines. She felt she could gaze forever at what lay before her and be content.

Maisie was too worried to register the view or the decor. She was frayed by the fact that Joe was already drunk and that Rita seemed to be leaving Brigid and Des in her care. Maisie didn't like children, had no desire to associate with the offspring of her unfortunate sister-in-law, and thought Rita's assumption that she would not mind looking after them high-handed to say the least. After all, this was her annual two-week summer vacation. But she couldn't think of how to refuse without sounding churlish. That was the problem with being a recipient of charity.

'They'll be no trouble, Maisie,' Rita assured her. 'They're very good youngsters. All you have to do is see they don't get in late and are on time for meals. That Mrs Flanagan is obviously a stickler for punctuality.' She smiled nervously. 'Oh, an' see they don't drown.'

As if I hadn't enough to do looking after Joe, Maisie thought to herself wearily, but she hadn't the nerve to refuse Rita. It was a holiday for the others, not for her. She had to see Joe didn't disgrace himself – as if that was possible. The anxiety and fear that his behaviour engendered in her were the same here as in the caravan, only here she had the added strain of the family's presence, the shame she felt under their contempt.

He can't help himself, she thought. Don't they know how he tries?

It was all ahead of her; his too-loud singing, his tasteless jokes, the gaffes and the embarrassing remarks he made, the bumps and falls he was prone to that stopped her heart and made the others giggle, the children snigger into their hands, Colista, Oonagh and Eddie look at him with disdain and Emmett O'Shea with fear and loathing.

Only she knew his pain. Only she knew his remorse, the effort he put into trying to stay sober. Only she knew his gaiety of spirit when he managed to, his loving, yearning soul. Only she wiped his tears when in despair he told her he wanted to die.

Rita had returned to the station, going back in one of the traps with a small grip and a vanity case, its handle

189

bound together with elastic bands. She's going to need that, Maisie thought, and then reflected that as usual she was left with the inconvenience.

She looked out through the window, but unlike Molly she saw nothing, her mind picking over and over her problem. Emer was walking past, looking right and left as if she sought someone.

'Where's your mam?' Maisie asked her through the window. The girl turned, the sea breeze whipping her flaming red hair.

'She's lying down,' she said. 'I've never seen her do that before, Auntie Maisie. She said she deserves it. She doesn't look right though.' Emer wrinkled her forehead. 'But she had a shock.' Unable to keep it to herself any longer: 'Ardel was beaten up on the train.'

'No!' Maisie leaned out the window, her curiosity aroused.

'Yeah.' Emer nodded importantly. 'Some thugs, friends of Billy Macken. You know, the guy with the gun who stuck up Ardel.'

'Yes, I heard. But he's in jail.'

'Yeah, well, these are friends of his. And my da's gone to the Garda Shiochana to report it.' Emer had by now lost interest in the whole subject. She squinted up in the sun. 'Auntie Maisie, are Brigid and Des there?' Maisie nodded. 'They are indeed, an' I don't know how it happened but I seem to be looking after them. Your Auntie Rita has taken herself off an' left me in charge. Of all the cheek!'

'Don't worry, Auntie Maisie. Brigid and Des are able to look after themselves. They are really. Will you tell them, after tea we're going to the fair? There's a fair down the road. Great gas! Tell them we'll call for them tonight. Okay? Tell them bring their pocket money.'

Maisie looked down on Emer. 'Why don't you tell them yourself? At tea? You'll see them then.'

'Ah, sure, ye never know. They might ask me to look after

190

Ardel. Just tell them, will you?'

'Yes, I will.'

'An' tell them to bring some money.' Emer's voice floated away.

'Sure, we don't have any,' Brigid whispered to her brother who leaned out of the window of the room next to Maisie's and yelled after Emer.

'We'll see ya at tea, Emer. We'll be after you to the fair.'

'We got no money,' Brigid wailed, turning into the room as Emer waved and vanished out of sight.

'Aw, shut up,' Des said as he turned towards his sister. 'They'll help us out, the O'Sheas.'

'But I *hate* it that they have to. It's so humiliating!' Brigid moaned.

'Still, Ma's gone, an' this is better than the little room behind we were going to be in.'

The room designated for them, and all the younger ones in the four houses, was small and poky, while the front rooms were large and bright and had a view of the ocean and the purple headland, the rocky islands set in the jewel-bright sea.

'Oh, the room! Who cares about the room? I want to be able to pay my way, Des. Like Emer, Laughlin and Emmett.'

'We'll manage somehow, Brigid.' He scratched his head. He suffered from dandruff and eczema and was often itchy. 'Do you think Mam means to find a husband?' he asked after a pause.

Brigid nodded. 'Yeah. Gawney Mac, Des, what'll we do? We'll have to live in bloody Mayo or Kerry or somewhere out in the wilds.'

Des scratched again. 'Well, it might be better.'

'Better?' Brigid screamed.

'Shush. Yes, better. I *hate* that little room in Gardiner Street. I *hate* us all sharing it. I *hate* Mam sleeping in the same room as us. I'd do anything to have my own, an' if she was married I'd have to, wouldn't I? I *hate that National school Mam'll have to send us to in September*. I *hate* our lives. I *hate* it all, do you hear me? I *hate* it.'

'Hey, hang on, Des.' Brigid had never heard her usually quiet brother talk like that before. 'I didn't know you felt like that. You never said.'

'Oh, what's the use? No one could *do* anything. At least now Mam is trying to get us out of it.' He looked at Brigid. 'How can you bear listening to her crying every night?'

Brigid hung her head because she never heard her mam crying. She always fell asleep as soon as her head hit the pillow.

'Poor Mam. I wish I could help her, Brigid. She's so brave. She hangs on in there, surviving. She deserves better and I hope she finds it.'

He looked out of the window. Evening was coming on. Clouds chased across the Madonna blue sky and the sun sent shafts of golden light over the red stone of the cliff, turning it bronze. The sea shifted and heaved its pale grey mass, and frills of white foam decorated its surface in abstract design.

'I didn't know she cried,' Brigid whispered, ashamed.

'I know. You're always asleep.'

'That's not my fault! I can't help getting tired.'

'I know it isn't, Brigid. I never blamed you. I wish I was asleep too. But I can't help thinking, *anything* is better than that room and sharing the bathroom and the lavvy.'

'But we don't know what he'd be like – he might be awful.'

There was a crash from the next room. A loud drunken voice uttering profanities was raised and Maisie's voice saying, 'Hush, Joe, hush. You'll frighten the children.' Another crash, then utter quiet.

'Joe's arrived,' Brigid said, and lapsed into silence. In the distance a bell rang.

'Tea, children,' Maisie called, rapping on the wall. 'It's tea time.'

'Ma might be getting someone like *him*.' Brigid nodded to the wall behind which Joe now snored. Her eyes were wide with fear.

Des shook his head. 'No, she won't,' he said firmly.

'How'd you know?'

'She's not falling in love,' he replied. 'She's picking someone out. That's the difference. She'll chose carefully.'

Brigid sighed. 'Come on,' she said, and left the room.

'You go on,' he cried after her, 'I'll catch up with you.'

He heard her run down the corridor, heard Auntie Maisie call out something and Brigid answer.

He looked at his bag on the bed. It was a torn grey grip, worn thin and patched in places with tape. It contained all he owned. He thought of his mother's tired face. It was permanently exhausted and hopeless. He sighed and shook his head angrily. She tried so hard, so very hard, and it broke his heart. Doing well in school, getting a good job … it would be too late. With certain knowledge he was sure that she had not much more to give; to lose. She was empty. He prayed silently that she'd find someone, anyone, to help her in Lisdoonvarna. He stood scratching his arm absently, then heard a loud snore from the next door.

He'd had an idea.

He went into the hall. There was no one about. He turned the handle of the next-door room, very gently, very cautiously. He paused on the threshold, his eyes adjusting to the gloom. Maisie had drawn the curtains against the glorious view and Joe lay on his back on the double bed, snoring. His mouth was open, dried saliva and alcohol caked in the corners.

Des's eyes raked the room. Ah, there it was – Joe's jacket on the back of a chair. He tiptoed over, glanced at the bed, and nearly died to find an eye open, a bloodshot, glaucous, viscid eye, staring at him fishily. For a moment he stood frozen, paralyzed with fear, then he realized that his Uncle

Joe slept that way and did not see him. The eye was asleep but not closed. Des moved. The eye followed. There was no recognition there, no awareness. It gave him the shivers.

He searched the jacket, the eye staring at him all the time, giving him the creeps. He found some loose change, the twisted stubbs of the train tickets, Eddie Benson's signature on a note enclosing them with wishes for a good journey, and a bottle opener. He put his hand in the inside breast pocket. A crumpled ten-shilling note was lodged under a dirty handkerchief. Des removed it, stuffed it in his trousers pocket just in time as he heard his sister calling him.

'Where are you, Des? You coming?'

'Yes, Brigid. Yes,' he shouted when he had closed the door behind him. 'I'm on my way.' He looked over his shoulder, picturing his sleeping uncle. 'It won't go through me like a dose of salts,' he said, and followed his sister into the dining room, a spring in his step.

Chapter Twenty-Six

They were all seated, family by family, around four huge mahogany tables. In the centre lay plates of sliced ham, chicken and cold beef. There was lettuce in a bowl, and scallions, dishes of tomatoes red as pomegranates, sliced white pan and doorsteps of nutty homemade brown bread. There were artistically made pats of butter in glass containers and brown eggs in chaffing dishes, jars of home-made jam and pickles, fat and green. It looked very

194

appetizing and the buzz of chatter rose in anticipation as Gabriel and Tom and Ben, at their separate tables, rubbed their hands together and watched their wives pour out the strong black tea from institutional teapots. Maisie presided over a sadly depleted table as Rita and Joe were missing.

Mrs Flanagan, followed by two maids, marched in with hot scones and boiling water to top up the teapots.

'Everyone settled in?' she enquired, and without waiting for a reply, 'This is Dymphna and Aggie. They'll look after you.' She gave the girls a severe look. 'Now behave and help serve the tea. Help yerselves, ladies and gentlemen. Don't stand on ceremony or ye'll go hungry. As you see it's cold food of an evening, hot at dinner at one. I can't help it if you don't like it, it's our way. Fish on Friday. Hope everything's to your satisfaction,' she said and left.

She had discovered years ago that questioning the guests was a mistake. If you worked things out to your own satisfaction and told them what to expect it saved an awful lot of trouble. If you asked them their opinion they'd find a million things they'd like changed and you wasted a lot of valuable time because the next person would have another idea altogether and you'd spend your life trying to please all the people all the time which, as everyone knew, was impossible.

'Where's Joe?' Tom called over to Maisie.

'Resting,' she replied, and Tom snorted. To change the drift Maisie said, 'Rita's gone.'

Molly looked over in astonishment. 'But I saw her arrive,' she said.

'Well, she's gone.'

'Where?'

'To Lisdoonvarna,' Ben informed her, nodding his head meaningfully.

'Lisdoonvarna?' Molly looked puzzled.

'Tell you after,' Gabriel remarked, winking at her and jerking his thumb towards the children.

195

'Come to that, where's Ardel?' Molly asked.

'He got beaten up by two thugs on the train,' Oonagh replied. 'I've never been more shocked in my life, Molly. He says they were friends of Billy Macken.'

Molly turned very pale and for a moment she looked frightened. Oonagh was surprised at her reaction but shrugged it off.

'I got no satisfaction from the Gardai,' Gabriel said. 'Waste of time when I could have helped Oonagh with the unpacking.'

'What'd they say?' Ben inquired.

'Nothing. Took the facts – boy beaten up by friends of Billy Macken who is in Mountjoy Jail – then asked what did I want them to do? Said they were delighted that he'd been caught and anything they could do to help, but they thought the perpetrators would be long gone now and as it had happened on the train it really wasn't their jurisdiction. Even asked me where we were at the time, the train moving and that. Like what county.'

'Janey Mac, did you ever hear the like?' Dot asked. 'I expect they wanted to shunt the responsibility on to the polis of whatever county the train was going through at the time. Janey Mac!'

'Mam, can we go to the fair?' Emer asked in the high piercing voice she kept for requests. 'There's a fair up above. A carnival. It's got hobby-horses, a ferris wheel, dodgems, a ghost-train – oh, all sorts. Oh, do say we can go, Mummy? Daddy?'

Oonagh thought, she always remembers to call me Mummy when she wants something.

'Is he all right now?' Molly asked, looking anxiously at Oonagh.

'Who? Oh, Ardel? Yes. He's resting. I'm taking him in some food when we're finished,' Oonagh told her.

'There'll be enough,' Tom laughed. 'Mrs Flanagan has a lavish hand, no doubt about it: sure, there's enough here to

196

feed an army.'

They tucked into their meal, conversation flagging while they ate. Mustard was spread on ham, pats of butter smoothed on crunchy brown bread, pickles forked with cold meats; it was a feast for the travellers with only sandwiches all day to keep their hunger at bay.

'If you're going to the fair, let's see, who'll be in charge?'

Oonagh wrinkled her forehead in thought, and then laughed at the whoop of delight that echoed around the room when the children realized that she had given her permission. 'I'm not letting you lot out in the night without supervision.'

'Briana,' Gabriel said.

'What?'

'Briana can supervise.' She cast her eyes up to heaven and Emer muttered, 'Bang goes the plans. What'll Iain do?'

'Why does it always have to be me?' Briana asked. 'Why isn't Mourna here?'

'And Roac.' Molly looked at her second son. 'Roac, will you watch the youngsters?'

'All right, Ma. But I'd like to know where Mourna is too.'

'Where's Banan, Moll?' Gabriel asked.

'Questions! Questions!' Molly laughed. 'Banan is at home looking after the pool hall. He'll be here later in the week. Maybe not until next week.'

Oonagh noticed her distress and wondered what was wrong with her and decided it was Tom shamelessly ogling Dymphna whose nubile shape in her maid's uniform was exactly to his taste. The girl's uplift bra hoisted her breasts unnaturally high and Tom peered down her cleavage whenever she came near him. Oonagh shuddered and looked over where Maisie, in her frilly pink blouse, was sitting silently between the equally silent Des and Brigid. They were lonely for their mother, Oonagh decided, and thought she would see that Emer and Laughlin kept a

197

friendly eye on them. Emer and Brigid were very thick, she knew, and got on well, but Des and Laughlin were oil and water, although they should be friends, she thought, both being nervy types. But they weren't at ease in each other's company.

Granny O'Shea had gone to bed. Exhausted, she said, after her long journey. And although she hated to miss any meal, especially tea, her appetite had got very small over the years and it was as well, she said, to sleep off the excitement and have a bumper breakfast in the morning.

'If I can! If I can! I can't usually get off unless I'm in me own bed,' she said pessimistically.

Nevertheless, when Oonagh looked in on her on her way to the dining room for tea, she was out for the count, relieved of her false teeth which reposed in a tumblerful of water beside her bed. Oonagh decided to move it in case the old lady woke in the night and drank from the glass.

At Dot and Ben's table pandemonium reigned. The children were behaving outrageously as usual, ignored by their mother and father. Oonagh was horrified to see bread being thrown and tea spilled on the immaculate tablecloth. Totally absorbed in each other, Dot and Ben seemed oblivious of their children's appalling manners. Maggie had tomato everywhere; on her dress, in her hair, on her face, and, as Oonagh watched the child grabbed another out of the bowl and squeezed it between her fingers, screeching with over-excited laughter as the juice of the squashed tomato squirted everywhere. Oonagh couldn't bear it any more.

'Dot, Maggie is making a bit of a mess,' she called across the room. A sudden silence descended. Everyone looked at Maggie who started to wail theatrically. Dot looked up vaguely.

'Oh, the maids will clear it all off,' she said. 'Don't worry, love,' she added fondly to her youngest, who immediately stopped in mid-cry.

'I think Oonagh means the maids shouldn't *have* to,' Molly said mildly.

At that moment Mrs Flanagan entered the room. 'I just want to make sure everything's all right.'

'Oh, it's grand, Mrs Flanagan, grand,' Tom assured her.

'Absolutely first-rate,' Gabriel said to a chorus of agreement and wifely nods.

'Holy Mother of God, what's this?' she exclaimed, sighting the Moran children's havoc-ridden table. 'Oh, this won't do at all, not at all.' To everyone's astonishment, most of all Maggie's, she went around the table smartly smacking the children's hands, saying, 'Naughty! Naughty!' at each firm blow, and not one whit discomfited by Dot and Ben's horrified faces.

'We don't … we don't …' Dot stammered.

'We do *not* hit them,' Ben said loudly.

'Well, you *should*,' Mrs Flanagan said with determination.

She faced the children, arms crossed.

'Now ye listen to me. This is *my* house an' you'll behave like civilized human beings while you are under my roof. Not like animals, understand? Although that's an insult to Tatty, our cat. A tidier creature would be hard to find. Any more throwing about of food an' the culprit will be whisked into my kitchen an' can finish their meal in there with my cook. Shamus!' she called out.

The cross-door opened and a huge fat oriental-looking man emerged. He wore a white overall, a chef's hat, and carried a large kitchen-knife. He looked exactly like the illustration of the genie in 'Aladdin and his Wonderful Lamp' in their book of *One Thousand And One Nights*.

The Moran children gulped and shrank back in their chairs, staring at him round-eyed. Mrs Flanagan nodded to him and he returned from whence he came.

'Do you understand?' she asked, her voice crisp as lettuce. The children nodded. No one had ever spoken to

199

them like that before and they gazed at this dragon-lady warily and with interest.

Dot and Ben didn't know what to do. They could hardly object to her laying down the ground-rules in her own house, yet, at the same time, she had crossed the boundary of what was permissible with other people's children and what was not. They looked at each other and at her open-mouthed.

A flurry of conversation and tea-pouring broke out in the room, bridging the embarrassing pause Mrs Flanagan's behaviour had precipitated.

'Is it *quite* understood?' Mrs Flanagan repeated, bending down, her face close to the children who stared back at her wide-eyed. They nodded.

'Right,' she said, straightening. She smoothed her apron. 'I'm glad that's settled.' She looked around at the others. 'There's a wonderful production of *Midsummer Night's Dream* outdoors, in Sneadhach, about a mile away along the coast. They tell me it's not to be missed. It's Diarmuid McDiarmuid an' his company from Dublin, professional actors all. An experience, I'm told, ye'll never forget. Thought I'd mention it. An' the children know about the carnival. The older ones, I mean. Well, I'll leave ye an' love ye. G'night all. I hope ye sleep well. Breakfast nine o'clock.' She turned to the cross-door, looked over her shoulder. 'An' no noisy return's late at night. Me an' my staff deserve our rest, y'hear?'

There was a chorus of, 'Yes, Mrs Flanagan,' a chorus that included parental voices, sounding very subdued and obedient. She departed, leaving behind the feeling that the Reverend Mother had just exited. Gabriel burst out laughing. 'I feel like a school kid.'

'Like the bloody Pope, she is,' Ben ventured.

'She's got no right to smack the kids,' Dot said firmly, with an assurance she had lacked when Mrs Flanagan had been in the room.

'Ah, now, she's got a point,' Molly said reasonably. 'It's better to know the done thing than maybe upset people.'

'I suppose you're right, Moll.' Gabriel rose, dabbing his mouth with his serviette. 'Anyhow, I'll guarantee you I'll not be making any noise tonight, that's for sure. I'm knackered.'

'There's little to do here of an evening, I suppose,' Tom sighed.

Oonagh wondered why Gabriel's speech always deteriorated in the company of other men. 'Aren't you going down the road for a drink?' she asked them. She knew that's what they wanted to do and she would be glad of the privacy.

She liked to be alone, relax and unwind as she took off her make-up with Pond's Cold Cream – 'Light as a Feather on Your Skin'. She only wore powder, Coty Peach, a touch of Bourjois Rosette on her cheeks, and a dab of lipstick on her mouth. She enjoyed the ritual and it was not possible when Gabriel was there. If they talked, her concentration was on what he was saying, not on the Pond's Cold Cream.

Tom was looking optimistic and Gabriel said, 'Yes, love. There's a pub along the boreen. We can have a jar there.'

'There's Mass,' Emmett piped up defiantly and everyone looked at him, their glances ranging from cold to incredulous. 'If you want it,' he added nervously.

'That boy's not normal,' Tom muttered.

'We must see about the tickets for the Shakespeare,' Oonagh said. 'We *saw* Diarmuid McDiarmuid in the flesh, Mourna and me, in Grafton Street.'

'We're off to the carnival, so we are,' Emer cried, and nodded to Brigid who whispered to Des, 'We don't even have the entrance money.'

Her brother winked at her. 'I do,' he said.

'How?' she asked, open-mouthed.

'In the Name of the Father, the Son and the Holy Ghost. For what we have received may the Lord make us truly thankful,' Gabriel said, and they all chorused 'Amen', Dot and Ben bemused, Oonagh and Gabriel replete and content, Molly worried, Tom lusting after Dymphna, the children and young adults excited about the fair, and Briana thinking about her date with Iain and wondering how she was going to be able to keep it.

Before they left the room Mrs Flanagan put her head around the door.

'Mrs O'Shea, yer daughter Mourna telephoned, says she won't be down till after dinner. She's eating at the Grand.' She managed to make this sound an upstart sort of thing to do and snorted as she said it. 'An' I hope that's the last of it for tonight,' she added crisply, and left.

Chapter Twenty-Seven

'Would you like to come for a jar, love?' Gabriel asked Oonagh. His wife looked up at him and did not reply. Nor did he pressure her. It was a formality, his way of announcing his intention of joining the other men in the local without offending her or allowing her to feel neglected. But he knew she wouldn't come with him. She loathed the atmosphere that he and Tom and even Ben found so convivial. She loathed the smell of beer, the pall of smoke that hung over the deep gloom of pubs the length and breadth of Ireland. She hated the careless eroding of the niceties that overcame even the most gentlemanly of men in that atmosphere. Their language slipped, their manners coarsened, their intelligence became fuddled. 'Unlaced,' she said, 'they become unlaced.' But she would never try to stop her husband. It would not occur to her to do so. She was his wife and he was the master. If he wanted to go to the pub he must go, but she would rather he went without her.

She looked pale tonight, he thought. The long journey probably accounted for her pallor, and Ardel's beating-up had probably shocked her more than she cared to admit.

She sat at the little balsa-wood dressing-table applying her cream. He touched her shoulder affectionately. A feeling of perfect tenderness overcame him.

'I love you,' he said. She smiled at him through the blotched mirror.

'Gabriel, I …'

'I'll take you to dinner or lunch at the Grand,' he announced, wanting to give her something special, make some gesture. 'How about that?'

She gulped. 'Would you? Oh, Gabriel!'

She had been on the verge of telling him about the baby but his announcement stopped her. He might not want to splurge on an expensive meal out in a grand hotel if he knew there was another mouth to feed on the way. And the idea of eating in the Grand was heaven. It would be a memory to cherish, something to treasure. 'Oh, Gabriel, I'd love that,' she said, eyes shining.

He felt suddenly sad. He wished he could always make her eyes sparkle like this. She didn't ask that much. It must be wonderful for Eddie, able to bestow gifts, fulfil desires, indulge generous impulses. He sighed, kissed the top of her head.

'Don't wait up for me, Oonagh,' he said. 'Rest, love.'

'Be quiet when you come in. You don't want to waken the dragon,' she giggled.

'I'll be as quiet as a mouse.'

He would only have a couple, she knew, and felt grateful she was not poor Maisie. But how was she ever going to tell him about the baby?

203

She watched the door close behind him. She gathered the hair from her brush into her palm, rolled it together to form a little ball, then went to the window and released the tangle for the birds. They would use it in the making of their nests. She looked up at the bright silver moon. The baby had no reality for her. All her other children had been real from the moment of conception. This little embryo had no place in her heart and she did not know why. She felt as if it would never really live for her.

Maybe I'm too tired, she thought. Then, I'm going to lose it. This is God's way of preparing me.

Still, if she was honest she knew that she did not really want the baby. The miscarriages she had had since Emmett's birth had been painful experiences. Her sense of loss had been extreme, her grief overwhelming. She had wanted those children. *They* had lived for her.

This time it was different. Whoever it was within her felt alien. There seemed to be no ties, no bonding.

I'm tired, she thought again. I'm being fanciful. She closed the curtains, sighing. I'll see Ardel's all right, then I'll sleep. And after the meal in the Grand I'll tell Gabriel about the baby and maybe then it'll become real to me.

She wished she was English and could have that wonderful barrier between Gabriel's potency and her womb, but John Charles McQuaid, Archbishop of Dublin, had put paid to any such convenience. She knew the arguments and did not agree with any of them. She could see nothing wrong with limiting a family. She felt she had done her duty as regards having children and could not believe it would be a good thing to refuse Gabriel her body on the grounds that love-making was for the creation of children and nothing more. Never! Never! Never! And to say that saving the baby was more important than saving the mother seemed crass stupidity to her. She couldn't understand the reasoning behind it. Only a fool of a bachelor would suggest such a course of action. But weren't they all bachelors in the priesthood? And looked after well at that. By women.

She thought of the vast army of willing females, usually ugly to avoid gossip, washing, ironing, cooking, house-keeping, fiercely protecting the clergy from Dublin to Boston, Rome to Rio de Janeiro. What did that crowd of over-protected men know about the marriage bed that they felt they could issue edicts that killed women, broke their husbands, and allowed unwanted children to come into an already hostile world?

If she died in childbirth what would happen to her family? Would they remain staunch members of the Holy Roman Catholic Church? Without her guidance she doubted that Ardel, Laughlin, Mourna or Emer would bother with the observation of their faith. Briana would go because she was dutiful and she had been told she should attend church each Sunday, and Emmett would go until he found out that God expects you to love his people, then he would become an agnostic. As for Gabriel, so bereft would he feel, so angry at her unnecessary death, that his fury and loss would likely drive him to hate the Church whatever his feelings for God might be.

She sighed, fixed the last slide into the last curl at the nape of her neck, and rose and went to the back room Ardel occupied.

He was sitting up in bed, puffing a cigarette and reading a comic. He had been patched up by the local doctor, his ribs strapped, his eye stitched. Bruises distorted his face horribly and he smoked gingerly, barely putting the cigarette to his lips, inhaling, then blowing out a grey stream.

'Ardel, I wish you wouldn't smoke.' She regretted it as soon as she said it.

'Aw, Mam! It's my only pleasure. Sure, what can I do here? I'm stuck in bed an' everyone else out enjoyin' themselves.'

205

She nodded and touched his hand, then realized she had hurt him. She touched his hair and he winced again, so she folded her hands in her lap and wondered what he was thinking.

He would have loved to have gone to the carnival. He liked the atmosphere. He felt at home in the tawdry world of tipsters and barkers, gamblers and card-sharpers, illusionists and shady chancers, who were here today and gone tomorrow. They attracted him and he was seduced by their slightly dodgy moral code and the places the fair was pitched; piers and sea-sides, village greens and the back of pubs. He liked the honky-tonk music and the nocturnal lifestyle they lived. Everything about the life of a fairground worker was alluring to him and he made up his mind that if things got worse for him he'd slip away into that world and disappear with them to wherever they were going. When they pulled up sticks and left Dranmore, he'd go with them. It seemed an obvious thing to do. Depending on what happened.

His mother was watching him, her kindly face creased with concern. He wished she wouldn't make him feel guilty. He didn't like anyone worrying about him. Hated it. Wished they'd leave him alone.

'Was there more to this, Ardel, than you're telling us?' she asked now, sitting on the bed, hurting his leg where the mattress dipped under her weight, forcing his bruised thigh sideways, putting pressure on it.

'No, Mam. Why'd you think that?'

She was shrewd, his mother. It would be silly to underestimate her. He laughed. It came out all wrong and hurt him, but that didn't matter because his eyes mirrored unconcern. He hoped.

'Good heavens, Mam, what are you imagining?' he asked lightly, 'Don't you think what happened was bad enough? What else could there be?'

She smiled back at him and seemed relieved. 'I don't

206

know. I thought you would tell me.'

'Well, there isn't anything else.'

'All right, son. I suppose I'm being silly. But if there was something …' She hesitated. 'Anything, I hope you'd trust me and your father to help. We'd do anything for you, Ardel, you know that, don't you?' He nodded. 'You've eaten nothing.' She glanced at the plate of cold meats and salad on the bedside table.

'No, Mam. It was too difficult,' he said, ruefully touching his mouth.

'But you can smoke?' she couldn't resist remarking. This was when he liked her least. He cast his eyes up to heaven.

'Yes, Mam,' he replied patiently. 'That's puffing and blowing. Eating's chewing. It's more difficult.'

She nodded, slightly mollified. 'The doctor says you must stay in bed at least a week.'

'Yeah, Mam.' He thought it a good idea in any event. Keep a low profile. 'Mam?' he said hesitantly.

'Yes, Ardel?'

'Can you mention to the others not to talk to strangers about me? Not to anyone who might ask if I'm here.'

'Why?'

'In case those guys try again.'

'Why would they?'

'I don't know, Mam.' He tried not to sound impatient. 'But they might. If no one says I'm here, then they'd go away.'

'Well, Ardel, I'm not sure …'

His face lit up as another thought struck him. 'Better yet, Mam, if you and the family put it out that I am in hospital then they'd leave me alone. Can you tell them, if anyone asks them, to say I'm in hospital?'

'But that would be lying, Ardel.'

Jesus Christ! He asks her to help and she talks about lies! They want to murder him, turn him into mince-meat, and she balks at lies! Jesus H. Christ. Women!

'Listen, Mam, Billy Macken is a hero to these guys. They want my guts for garters.'

He looked at the honest dismay on her face. She was so innocent. She'd never known any violence in her life. His beating was the first time anything unsavoury had even brushed close to her. Auntie Molly would be far more use to him in this predicament. She understood violence, his mother did not.

'Oh, read your Irish history, Mam. It's awash with the spilled blood of informers.'

She cried out in pain. He saw her face and was immediately flooded with guilt and resentment.

'But the Garda distinctly said you *didn't* inform,' she protested.

'Oh, Mam, quit worrying. Just ask everyone to say I'm in the hospital. No.' The rabbit-warren of his convoluted thoughts took another direction. 'Tell them I really am! Yes, that's it. Tell them, the family, I really am in hospital.' He waxed enthusiastic at this new idea which suited even better. 'Tell them I was taken in tonight. By ambulance. They'll believe you. No one except you and Da need know I'm here.'

'Don't be silly, Ardel.' His mother briskly nipped his hope in the bud. 'They'd smell a rat. They're not fools, you know. Anywhow, they'd want to visit whatever hospital I said you were in. Molly'd set off tomorrow, you know that.'

He had to admit she was right. It was all this family-love shit he could do without.

'And there's Mrs Flanagan. She has a nose like a hound. She'd suss you out, never fear. And the maids ...'

'All right, Mam. All right. You win. It was an idea.'

A wonderful idea if only it would work. He wanted to disappear. He wanted not to be. Simply not to exist. Vanish. But with this lot around that was impossible.

'I think you're being paranoid, Ardel. After all, if they'd wanted to kill you, God forbid, they had ample opportunity on the train. I think they put scare into you so that you wouldn't talk to the police again, though why you should is beyond me.'

She could not understand why they should bother her son again unless he had not told her the full story. She looked into his eyes. They were clear and guileless as a child's. She sighed and rose. 'I'll ask your father, Ardel, see what he says.'

And with that he had to be satisfied.

Chapter Twenty-Eight

The men walked down the road in companionable silence. The moon was up and Gabriel was humming, 'She Moves Through the Fair', the slow mournful notes of the song hanging on the still air. The boreen was bordered by curling green ferns, waist-high, and they could hear the crash of the sea beating on the shore. The road led them inexorably to the local shebeen. A crooked sign outside read: 'Drat Regan's. Bona Fide. Travellers Welcome'.

They ducked their heads as they crossed the threshold, feeling a warm wave of conviviality wash over them as they entered. The ceiling was low and they walked stooping to the bar and ordered the best porter. Tom had whiskey.

The place was full of smoke and the ripe smell of the land-folk. 'This is the life,' Tom said, smacking his lips.

'You'd soon tire of it if it was permanent,' Gabriel remarked.

'Ah, it's all right for a while,' Ben said, 'but I'd be happier though an' Dot were here.' The other two looked at him pityingly. They amused themselves separating the visitors from the locals. It was easy. The locals were ruddy-complexioned and the clothes they wore were heavy; tweed jackets and caps even in the heat of summer. The visitors wore flannels and pullovers and were bare-headed. But in the crowd two unidentifiable strangers stood out, two men difficult to categorise. One was tall and thin with a lizard face and a flat back to his head. He wore a shiny suit and crocodile shoes. The other, thick-set, hirsute, wore a white jacket and black trousers.

'What on earth class of fellows are those?' Gabriel speculated.

'They look like some of the oddballs, think their God's gift, come into the pool hall,' Tom remarked.

'Well, I'll tell you one thing – they're up to no good.'

'An' are you stayin' below in Mrs Flanagan's?'

It was a large jovial man, substantial of frame, with abundant grey hair and hands like hams. 'You're visitors, I can see that.'

'Sure we are,' Tom said, sensing a kindred spirit.

'Will ye join me in a jar?' the stranger asked.

'That'd be grand.'

'Ah, Mrs Flanagan's a fine woman,' the man said and squeezed his way over to the bar, ducking the cross-beams above him automatically.

Gabriel and Tom sat on upturned wine casks that served as seats and Ben stood nervously behind them. He was never too comfortable in pubs, he felt threatened in all-male company, uneasy without Dot beside him.

'There isn't a woman in the place,' he remarked.

' 'Tisn't a place for talent,' Tom said.

'I'm Barney Boland, by the way,' the stranger said, plonking down a couple of pints on the round wooden table and returning to the bar for the rest. There were Guinness signs over the bar and an advertisement for Gordon's Gin.

'I have the newsagent's and sweetshop down below at the harbour,' Barney said when he rejoined them. 'Now, are we all okey dokey? Good!'

They introduced themselves to the newsagent and then gave themselves up to the enjoyment of the black porter. They didn't talk much at first, concentrating on downing the pints, content to sup the stout and take in their surroundings.

'It's a nice place to live,' Gabriel said as their companion rubbed his hands together then lifted his glass to his lips. He took a great draught, half emptying the glass, wiping his mouth with the back of his hand and letting out a long contented sigh.

'Ahaaa! Sure, it's grand. 'Tis a gorgeous place. Do enough business in the summer, well,' he amended, 'end of May to middle of October, to make the few bob, then I migrate for the cold months. Man, it's cold here in the winter, facing the ocean. The wind is a slicer. Shocking!'

'Where do ye go in the winter?' Ben inquired timidly.

'Oh, I go off to Florida or the Canary Islands. Or the South Seas. Somewhere nice and warm.'

They looked at him amazed, mouths open, porter held half-way between the table and their chins.

'Go on!' Tom murmured in disbelief.

'Ah, yes.' Barney Boland talked about it as if going to Florida in the United States of America were the most everyday thing in the world.

'Well I never!' Gabriel shook his head in astonishment.

''Tis grand,' Barney Boland said in the most matter-of-fact way. 'There's only myself, y'see.'

'Ah!' Ben said, as if that explained everything. 'Yer a bachelor then?' He shook his head in sympathy.

'Aye. So I'm me own master.'

Tom looked at the sweetshop owner in envy. 'Yer own master?' he muttered.

'Aye. It's a nice little business I've got. Can't help but be.

211

I'm the only shop sellin' papers an' magazines an' sweets in the whole of Dranmore. There's nowhere between here an' Waterford 'cept myself. Sure, how could I fail? Ah, tis a grand life, grand.'

For a moment Tom and Gabriel let their minds dwell on the thought of tropical beaches, hot sun, boats bobbing on turquoise seas, exotic flowers – and, for Tom, exotic maidens. And the man did it for months! Not for a couple of weeks snatched from dark and cheerless days in ill-lit offices, but from October to May. He never *saw* winter.

'*All* winter? Yer away the whole time?' Tom asked incredulously.

'Aye. I leave end of October. Sit in the sun. Charter a boat. Do a little fishing. A little sailing. A little exploring. Come back April, thereabouts.'

'It's well for some!' Tom said reverently.

'Aye, I have it arranged to suit myself,' Barney said.

'Ye have that,' Gabriel agreed.

'Those two fellows over there?' Barney asked, shrewd eyes narrowed. 'You know 'em?'

Gabriel shook his head. 'Never saw them before.'

'Thought they might be relations.' Barney glanced at them. 'Though on second thoughts, maybe not,' he said, and winked. 'Not really your sort, eh? Mrs Flanagan told me there were four families commin' to Kincora.'

'Five.'

'Isn't that grand? And these are none of your lot? That's odd. Wonder who they are?' He scratched his thick hair, then rose, 'Sure, what does it matter? It'll be all the same in a hundred years. Let me get another. Same again?'

Tom pushed him down. 'No, it's my turn,' he said, and furridged off to the bar.

Ben had relaxed after a second drink. He sat down and sipped his pint with the others. Sometimes there was a burst of laughter in one or other corner of the little pub. The drone of conversation mingled with the hacking coughs of smokers and the shouts of orders given in an undecipherable code. Someone had begun to sing 'The Mountains of Mourne' when Joe burst into the bar. He stood swaying at the door, peering into the smoky gloom, trying to focus his eyes, searching for then finding Ben and Gabriel and Tom.

'Oh, bloody hell! This one *is* one of us!' Gabriel watched as Joe weaved his way over to their table.

'Yerra, so he's had a few, so what? It could happen to a saint,' Barney Boland said, standing. 'One for the road, boys?'

'Jasus, he's like this twenty-four hours a day, fifty-two weeks a year,' Tom grumbled.

'Oh, it's like that, is it?' Barney murmured as he went to the bar.

'I think I'll vanish now,' Ben said, nervous at Joe's arrival.

'No, you will not. We'll be with you, Ben.'

'How're you buggers?' Joe stood grinning at them through slitted eyes. Then he sat down abruptly. 'Gave other half the slip,' he slurred.

'Hey, it's my shout,' Gabriel called to Barney.

' 'S done now. Ye'll have chance enough to stand your whack unless you're plannin' to leave tomorrow.'

'Ah, there's such a yearnin' in my soul, boys,' Joe said, smiling at them foolishly.

'What'll you have? I'm Barney Boland, by the way.'

'An' I'm Joe Moran. The original Wild Colonial Boy, though I've never strayed over the water away from this beautiful country in my entire life.'

'Then how could ye be Colonial?' Ben ventured.

'Ah, pay no attention to him, Ben. He's three sheets in the wind.'

'None of yiz know the half of it,' Joe mouthed, and took a gulp of the pint Barney set before him.

'Well, I think that's fine coming from you,' Ben said indignantly. 'All the cheek … '

'I'm not sure it's a good idea to give him drinks,' Tom whispered to Barney.

Joe grimaced up at them. 'Heard that, so I did,' he said quite distinctly. 'Heard that. Think I'm a half-wit or something?'

'Leave him be. Leave him be.' Barney pulled over another stool because Joe had occupied his wine-cask.

'I've had my ten shillings stolen,' Joe said, peeking at them.

'But he talks rubbish,' Ben said. Barney turned to him.

'Can't you see the man's in pain?' he asked, thoroughly confusing Ben who moved away from Joe and looked around the bar.

'That pair've gone,' he said. They all knew who he meant. Barney and Gabriel, who sat with their backs to the bar, looked around.

'They have that,' Gabriel said.

'Who? Where?' Joe peered around.

'Wonder who they were,' Barney mused.

'They'll belong to the fair, shouldn't wonder,' Tom said. 'Didn't like the look of them. Hope the kids are safe.'

'Oh, Roac is with them,' Tom said.

'And Briana will stick close,' Gabriel remarked, taking a good gulp of his porter. 'She's very conscientious is Bri.'

Chapter Twenty-Nine

Briana sat on the beach listening to the carnival music. It came from the hobby-horse carousel, she decided, churning out 'Over The Waves', round and around. She could see the lights above her on the hill spotting the water with discs of blue and yellow and red. Dancing lights. There was a buzz of concentrated noise from the fair that echoed around the cliff-face. The dark sea pounded against the foot of the headland that marked the coves: Badgers Cove, Pebble Beach, Gentleman's Cove, Golden Strand, Ladies Cove. They curved around, one after another circling the bay.

She sat now on the Golden Strand, directly below the carnival. In the shimmering shadows she could see the lights on the boats bobbing just inside the harbour and stared at them, hugging herself. The sea shush-shushed against the ribbed strand. She had taken off her shoes and her legs were bare. The sand felt lovely between her toes. She felt warm in the Aran sweater she had pulled over her dress.

She had been happy all day. 'It's a beautiful day, Lord, never let it end,' she prayed.

Seeing Iain after all these barren weeks was like a blossoming of everything, an opening out, an embrace. She felt as if waiting, holding on to herself in anticipation, she had been guarding herself fiercely, her emotions, her love, even the movements of her body. Now her hands unclenched and spread themselves wide, each vertebra softened, her knees grew weak and the tension in her face disappeared. She wanted to shout 'Hooray!' to release the triumph inside her.

She dug her toes in the sand, feeling it cold and hard under the soft top layer.

Roac would look after the younger ones. She'd asked him, told him she had to see Iain. He'd made no comment. He was a serious boy. With Banan around he'd learned early to keep his mouth shut. Banan, angry at the world, had turned his half-brother into a cautious responsible adult before his time.

She felt Iain arrive before she saw him. Her heart lurched, the pulse in her throat pounded, and she turned to see him running down the narrow steps cut out of the cliff that led to the cove. She waved and he returned her salute, then paused to roll up his grey flannel trousers.

She sat waiting, trying to still her heart, listening to the far-off pounding of the music from the fair 'Put Another Nickle in, in the Nickleodeon, All I want is Lovin' You and Music, music, music.' And the waves sighing softly on the sand.

He put his arm around her, pulled her in towards him and laid his cheek on hers. They both stared out to sea.

'Oh, I love you,' he said. 'It's like coming home. You're in my heart's core, Briana. You belong there. You fit.'

'I know, Iain, I know. I feel the same.'

She was calm now, at one with everything. Deep within her she felt a stillness so immense, so serene, that it was like the quiet depths of the ocean. She knew this feeling was happiness. It was love. Not how the books described it at all. Just calm and certainty and a brimming over of life.

'You haunted my dreams, Briana. All those weeks I was in Edinburgh I couldn't sleep.'

'I don't want to be in your dreams, Iain,' she said. 'I want to be here in your arms.'

216

They sat there quietly listening to the carnival noises, the waves, the sound of the sea-breeze stirring the trees, and the beating of their hearts.

'I want to marry you, Bri.'

'Yes.'

'And keep you beside me always.'

'Yes.'

Someone screamed very loudly and they looked back to where the ferris-wheel had started to pick up speed.

'They'll make it difficult.'

'You mean your mother'll make it difficult.'

'No. It's Father. But we'll persist. We won't give up.'

'No, we won't give up.'

His lips trembled when he kissed her and his hands cupped her breasts. She could feel him become excited and she turned to him, her body drawn, magnet-like to his, her flesh cleaving to his, wanting to become part of him. But he gently held her away from him.

'Oh God! Oh God, Briana, I want you so much. But I want it to be right. I don't want to do anything, anything at all, to hurt you. I don't want them to have a thing to reproach us with. I want to be able to look them in the eye knowing I behaved honourably.'

She was glad about his attitude to her but her body protested. She ached to be one with him, yet knew she was not ready for that in these circumstances. She wanted, like him, to be clear-eyed before her parents and his. She did not want the burden of guilt. She took his hand and rose from the sand.

'Come on,' she said. 'Let's go find the children.'

Chapter Thirty

Mena Moran had searched for Ardel but when she found
him in his room he told her to piss off and even she could
see he was in no condition for a bit of fun. Disconsolate she
wandered around, catching up with Emer and Brigid on
their way to the carnival. They froze her out quite firmly
so she sat down in the boreen, plucked some honeysuckle,
crushing it between her fingers, and moped. She could
hear the sea crashing below on the cliff-face and the
setting sun, a disc of burnished gold, touched the
headland, spreading a shimmering mantle over the black
velvet water.

She hated the sea. She didn't like the discomfort of sand
in everything and getting wet and the curl going out of her
hair. The seaside bored her. She liked the local hop where
she knew all the boys, and they knew her, and she could
exchange smart remarks, and they understood the crack,
and the vernacular was familiar. She liked Dublin and the
dangerous atmosphere behind the pool hall. She liked
hanging out there and letting the good-looking guys have
a feel, but only if she felt like it. She liked night-time, and
the city, and familiar people and places, and being in
charge.

Laughlin came down the road. She stood up as he
approached. 'Who's that?' he asked, a little nervously.

'Scared? 'Sme, Mena,' she said. 'Here, sit with me for a
minute, will ye, Laughlin?'

'Why?' God, she thought, stupid eejit! 'I'm off to the fair.' She could kill him. Wouldn't you think he'd know? Play the game with her. But no! Ardel O'Shea would have been ahead of her.

'I'm bored, Laughlin,' she said, and thought, but didn't add, and Ardel isn't available and I want a bit of excitement.

'Aw, sit down a minute, then I'll walk wi' ye to the carnival.'

Laughlin wasn't sure he wanted that. He really wanted to be alone. However, he sat down beside her obediently.

'Hope I don't dirty my trousers,' he said. Janey Mac!

'Aw, Laughlin, don't waste time worrying about things like that. Here, sit near me. It's warm here.'

'It's warm everywhere,' he said, but sat. She snuggled up near him, making him nervous and uncomfortable.

'Here, smell this, Laughlin. It's honeysuckle. Isn't it lovely?'

He sniffed, then nodded. He could feel her breath on his cheek and tried to move away but found he couldn't.

'I'll let you do something … something very exciting, if you like.' He was going to say no, he wanted to leave, when she caught his hand and put it under her blouse on to her breast. He was touching the soft naked mound, the hard little nipple which she rubbed against his fingers. She gave a little grunt of satisfaction but he let out a yell that ricocheted around the cliffs and pulled his hand away as if she'd scalded him.

'Janey Mac, what'd you think you're doin'?' he screamed. 'Have ye no shame?'

Angrily she rose to her feet. 'Don't you talk to me like that, you … you freak! Yer an eejit, Laughlin O'Shea. Haven't ye ever been with a girl or what? Ye never gone in fer pettin' with the Christian Brothers? Ignorant, that's what ye are, pig ignorant.'

She was shouting after him as he ran down the road

219

away from her, running as if the devil were at his heels. 'Laughlin O'Shea's pig ignorant. Laughlin O'Shea's pig ignorant,' she chanted after him, buttoning her blouse.

She felt near to tears. No one had ever rejected her before. It was all she was good at, all she could offer. She was not pretty like her mother or the O'Shea girls. She wasn't clever like Roac or smart like Banan. All she had was a good body that pleased men. She enjoyed pleasing them. She liked them gasping under her hands, eyes squeezed closed. She liked to see them cry for more, liked it when their heads drooped on her breast and their bodies went slack. It made her feel powerful.

And she was still a virgin. No one could slag her off on that count. Oh, there were ways and ways without going the whole hog, as the priests put it, and she had no intention of getting pregnant. It was a terrible threat, pregnancy.

Bloody Laughlin O'Shea. She'd get her own back on him for what he'd done, see if she wouldn't.

The others were coming down the boreen now. Dot and Ben's children in their crocodile, Des Maguire on his own. He scratched a lot did Des, and his skin was lousy and she was finicky about skin. But he was tall, he had nice teeth, a nice smile.

She stuffed her blouse into her skirt and called out, 'Des! Des! C'mere. I've a splinter in me finger. Can you help?'

Chapter Thirty-One

The music was so loud in the fairground they couldn't hear each other speak so they shouted and laughed and their voices were soon hoarse. Roac bought them candy-floss with money his mother had given him. In the darkness, the fairy lights and arc lamps, red and green and blue, faded the moon to a pale backdrop.

'Don't get lost,' Roac called, 'If anyone gets separated let's meet at the coconut shy.'

The coconut booth was under a chestnut tree and it was very easy to see.

Roac wasn't worried about the kids. As long as Maggie Moran wasn't there. At seven she was too young to stay up, and despite making an outrageous fuss, this time she had failed to get her own way. The others would stick close and not try any stunts. Roac watched Briana slope off and leave him to it. He didn't care. He just wondered when Mourna would show. Where was she? He didn't want to ask again, draw attention to himself. She hadn't travelled with the O'Sheas and there had been no sign of her all day. He had not heard Mrs Flanagan relay her message to Oonagh, so for all he knew she was not coming to Dranmore at all. Maybe she was going to someplace else where he wouldn't see her all summer. All he wanted was for her to be there, where he could see her, where he could feast his eyes on her beauty. That was all.

Brigid and Emer were waving at him from the

ferris-wheel. Both of them had mouths open, screaming. When the turn was over and the ferris-wheel came to a stop they tumbled off it, still screaming, and could not stand up.

'You're reeling around like two drunken ould wans,' Roac yelled bad-temperedly at them over the jingly music, now at ear-splitting level. They fell over each other, speechless with laughter, tears pouring down their faces. Roac was fed up with them both. Not feeling in the least like laughing himself, their hilarity irritated him.

'Janey Mac, it was great.' Brigid sank on to the ground beneath the wheel, panting.

'God, you girls are *boring*!' Roac shouted and wandered off chewing the inside of his cheek.

'What's the matter wi' him?' Emer asked, then added, 'Jasus, it was grand.' They were breathless and sat back to back on the sandy grass.

'Tell you somethin', Brigid, if you promise not to say a word,' Emer yelled, cupping her hand so that her voice was aimed directly into her cousin's ear.

'What? Tell me what? What?' Brigid shrilled.

'Ah, hold yer horses. Listen.' Her lips were touching Brigid's cheek. 'Can't you hear?'

Brigid frowned and stood up, pulling Emer with her. She jerked her head sideways and Emer followed her as she led them past the hobby-horses endlessly circling, churning out the hurdy-gurdy music, past the dodgems and the screams and shrieks as people crashed into each other, until they came to the fortune-teller's tent where relative quiet reigned.

'I've entered the Beauty Contest, so I have,' Emer said to Brigid.

'You did what?'

'I entered the Beauty Contest. The Miss Dranmore.'

'When? You didn't have time.'

'Ages ago. From Dublin. I did it from Dublin. I saw it in the paper. They have one every year.'

'Gawney Mac, Emer! Wow! Your mam will be *mad*.'

'I don't care about Mam. She mightn't find out.'

'She'll find out if you win,' Brigid said, making Emer's heart jump. She had thought Brigid might laugh at her, ridicule her. Brigid was not noted for her tact. Instead she actually entertained the thought that Emer might, could just possibly, win! She hugged Brigid.

'Hey! Hey!' Brigid cried. 'I think you're great, Emer, doin' something like that.'

'Will you help me?' she asked.

'Sure. 'Course I will.'

'I'm worried there isn't enough of me to fill a thirty-six bra. I want to look like Janet Leigh.'

'You can stuff some cotton-wool in,' Brigid said placidly.

'The coins between my legs worked so they must be all right.'

'Your legs are gorgeous, Emer O'Shea. Only no one ever notices because of Mourna.'

Emer nodded. 'You're right, Brigid. No one even *sees* anyone beside my sister.' She wrinkled her forehead. 'But she is useful. I can borrow her make-up. Or Briana's. That'll be a breeze. But most of all I *have* to get Auntie Dot's white stilettos.'

'Oh, Auntie Dot'll give them to you. She's ever so sweet and generous like that,' Brigid said, her face excited. 'What'll you wear?'

'I have a yellow one-piece Mam let me choose in Barnets. She didn't notice how sexy it is. She was too busy concentrating on Mourna and Bri.' Emer stuck her chin out. 'Those two! They get all the notice. How'd you like to have sisters like that? I have to do *something* to get myself noticed.'

'Yeah, I can see it'd be difficult.'

'You will help me, won't you?' Emer asked, and Brigid squealed.

'Emer, I can't wait. Gosh, it's so exciting.'

'But you won't breathe a word, will you? Promise.'

Brigid shook her head solemnly.

'You little ladies alone?'

The man with the lizard head tried to smile but his face split in a weird grimace.

'You dirty ould man, talkin' to little kids!' Brigid yelled at the top of her voice, and several people hurried over as she shrilled, 'I'll tell my mammy on you, so I will.'

Lizard-head moved rapidly away. Brigid took Emer's hand and ran in the opposite direction. A woman stopped them. She had an officious manner and seemed to be spoiling for a fight.

'Did that man say something to you? What did that man say, little girl?'

Brigid stared at her. 'He said he wanted to put his hand up my knickers,' she shouted. The woman blanched and turned.

'Mister, you stick to your own age-group. Pervert! That's what you are. Pervert!' Lizard-head quickened his pace as the woman ran after him.

Brigid dragged Emer away. They mingled with the crowd.

'Let's go into the ghost-train. I want to get *really* scared.'

'Janey, you're a glutton for punishment,' Emer laughed, but was more than willing to join her friend.

The thick man with the beetle brows was licking an ice-cream. Roac wandered over. He was looking around him, searching for the girls.

'You lookin' for someone?' the man asked the boy, licking his lips.

'No. It's okay. Well, yes. Two girls. My cousins. Want to keep my eye on them.'

'One got red hair, bobbed? One wearing a check cardigan?'

'Yeah, that's them.'

'They went in the ghost-train.'

'Well, thanks.'

'You visitors?' the man asked casually.

'Yeah.'

It was proving difficult, talking to kids.

'Wise to keep your eyes on them. Lota violence these days.'

'Sure.'

'Someone told me a boy'd been beaten up on the train.'

'Yeah.'

'You hear that?'

'Oh, yeah.'

Jesus, where was the kid's *mind*? He wasn't paying any attention and Beetle-brows wanted to shake him, beat it out of him. But that was against the rules. He wasn't allowed to do that. Well, they'd just have to wait for Banan to arrive, see where the kid was staying. Find him. Get the money. Then they could all go home, out of this tiny God-forsaken hole.

Roac had moved off into the dusky evening light. The man popped the cone into his mouth and sucked the last dregs of ice-cream swiftly down the back of his throat, then crunched the cone between his teeth until it was gone.

Chapter Thirty-Two

Laughlin mooched around the fairground, keeping out of the others' way. He didn't want to think about what had happened in the ditch, didn't want to remember his embarrassing behaviour or Mena's. They'd said she was a nymphomaniac, whatever that was; something to do with sex, and he didn't want to know. If it was a sickness that entailed the sort of encounter he had endured, he had no desire to be enlightened. The less he knew about anything that had to do with Mena and girls who put your hand up their shirts, the better he'd like it. It was obscene, that's what it was. It made him feel sick. It had spoiled his whole evening.

He saw Roac talking to a strange-looking giant of a man. Doesn't he see he's a hooligan? he wondered, but had no intention of getting involved. Let him find out for himself. Bloody Roac. He wondered why he felt such hostility. Maybe because he was Mena's brother.

Laughlin felt ill at ease with the rest of humanity, out of humour, out of tune. Alone, he took a shy at a coconut and missed, took a shot at a moving target and missed, had a go at an Aunt Sally and missed. Thoroughly browned off with life he left the fairground, moving away from the garish lights and raucous music, moving over to a parapet that overlooked a sickeningly sheer drop to the cove below. He stood there, staring out unseeing.

'It's Gentleman's Cove,' a voice said, and he turned, startled, slipping against the parapet.

'Steady on. You could kill yourself.'

The man was about twenty-five, terribly handsome, like a film star. He held Laughlin at arm's length, hands gripping his elbows to steady him, and Laughlin felt suddenly safe as if he'd been rescued from some terrible fate, as if he'd been made very secure. He righted himself with the stranger's help, staring at him in the moonlight. The wind lifted his blond hair from his forehead. His eyes were dark in this light and Laughlin guessed them to be blue. His face was classically featured, narrow and tanned. He looked American but had not sounded so.

'You okay now?' The stranger let him go and Laughlin came to himself.

226

'What? Oh, yes. Yes. I'm sorry.'

'What for? *I* startled you. *I'm* sorry. I'm Hector Breen, by the way.'

The stranger put out his hand and Laughlin grasped and shook it. 'My name is Laughlin O'Shea,' he said.

Hector Breen leaned on the parapet. He wore a pale blue cashmere sweater over his checked shirt.

'The sunset is mighty,' he said, looking out over the sea at the huge orange disc in the sky. 'Sun and moon out together. So very beautiful.'

His voice was marvellous, Laughlin thought, like an organ, a musical instrument. He said nothing in reply. There was no need. The stranger gave him a comfortable feeling of serenity. He leaned on the parapet beside Hector. They stood together like that for a long while without speaking. Then Laughlin said, 'I love the smell.'

'Um, it's like salt and iodine and grass and heather and sand. The world!' Hector laughed. 'Maybe that's what God smells when he looks down.'

Laughlin had never heard anyone talk like that and the sound was like singing, like poetry. He liked the idea of God leaning down smelling his world.

'You live here?' Laughlin asked. It seemed unlikely. Hector was too glamorous to belong to this unsophisticated Irish sea-side hamlet. He seemed to come from some exotic place only seen in American movies. But he said, 'No. I'm from Dublin.'

'So'm I. I live on Griffith Avenue.'

'Know it well. I'm from Donnybrook myself.' He smiled at Laughlin, a wide warm smile.

'We're on holiday down here, me and my family.'

'Brothers and sisters?'

'And cousins, aunts and uncles, old Uncle Tom Cobley and all.' Laughlin laughed, too, feeling very at ease.

'No!' Hector looked amused. 'When you say family, you really mean family.'

227

'Oh, yes.' Laughlin nodded. 'There's, let's see, Mam and Da, my two brothers and three sisters, my Auntie Molly and Uncle Tom and their kids, Roac and … '

'Hey, hey!' Hector exclaimed in comic disbelief and Laughlin continued, practically boasting, as if such a large family was remarkable, 'Auntie Maisie and Uncle Joe, no kids, and Auntie Rita and two, Brigid and Des, and Auntie Dot and Uncle Ben … '

'Hold it, hold it.' Hector was laughing with Laughlin now, sharing the joke of the large family.

'Yeah. Down in Kincora. Four houses of us. And more in the Grand.' He indicated the large building behind them on the cliff. 'Auntie Colista and Uncle Eddie and my cousin Iain. That's all.'

'All?' Hector hooted, incredulous. 'All?'

'All!' Laughing again.

He had never felt so easy in himself, so relaxed. He felt he could say anything he liked to this guy, share anything. It was the sort of friendship you read about in books; the sort of companionship he had longed for but, which so far had eluded him.

He didn't want to move, didn't want to break the spell.

'You on holiday too?' he asked Hector.

'No. I'm working.'

Laughlin didn't understand. 'You mean, you work at the carnival?' he enquired. Hector didn't seem the type. He was anything but spiv-like and Gabriel said carnival workers were mainly spivs.

Hector laughed, showing fine white teeth. 'Oh no, I'm an actor. I'm playing Lysander in *Midsummer Night's Dream* over in Sneadhact.'

'Oh!' Laughlin was thrilled. An actor was a glamorous thing to be. It meant he was right in his assessment of his new friend. You had to be sensitive and talented to be an actor. You had to be intelligent. And he was a member of Diarmuid McDiarmuid's Company, the best in Ireland.

228

'You'll come and see the play?' Hector asked, turning his face to look at Laughlin.

'Oh, yes! My mam's getting tickets.'

'Well, if you have trouble, let me know. Though they'll only let me have a couple of comps.'

'What?'

'Complimentary tickets. I couldn't manage for your whole family. That'd be asking a bit much.' He laughed infectiously and Laughlin joined him.

He was going to go. He had made no move but Laughlin knew. He was tightening up, his attention gathering itself, leaving Laughlin, his focus until now. He was going to leave. Laughlin didn't want him to go just yet.

'You not on tonight?' he asked.

'No. It's Sunday. We don't play Sunday,' Hector said. He had put his hands in his pockets. The moon hung sharp-edged in the sky, silvering everything over. The sun had long since disappeared. Hector had moved a few paces away. Laughlin watched him, helpless to stop him. But Hector turned.

'Maybe ... if you get bored ... we could have tea in the Grand? I'm staying there. Or, if you'd prefer, drive some-where? I know a few places along the coast road.'

'I'd love that.' Laughlin was breathless with excitement but he tried to keep cool. 'Might have to talk to Uncle Eddie at the Grand ... ' He stopped, realizing what he was saying, the implication that he wanted to be alone with Hector, which he did. 'I mean, I ... '

'That's okay. We'll drive along the coast then. Keep in touch. Ta-ra.'

And he was gone, taking the brightness with him, like a lamp going out. He left Laughlin feeling more alone than he had ever felt before. He hunched his shoulders and looked at the bright carnival lights, then up towards the Grand, hearing the faint sound of an orchestra begin, some moon in June melody. He decided he would go home to bed. The evening for him was over.

Chapter Thirty-Three

With a flourish the quartet brought to a finish a selection of Gilbert and Sullivan with which they had been entertaining the guests in the lounge of the Grand Hotel, Dranmore. Groups of fashionably dressed people sat around and sipped their after dinner coffee at the small tables, their conversation muted, half-listening to the music.

The seats were curved, padded and covered in wine brocade to match the wine carpet on the vast expanse of floor. A huge Waterford cut-glass chandelier hung from the ceiling, dazzling lights sparkling from its myriad diamond drops and balls, loops and necklaces. Uniformed waiters moved about the discreetly lit room, replenishing cups and glasses, serving liqueurs, coffee and brandy. Couples in evening dress moved in from the dining room. The women laughed softly, long skirts rustling, and the men lit cigars.

'She'll stay here. I insist,' Eddie Benson said, looking at Mourna.

'Of course she should,' Kurt Von Mensil agreed, looking worried, 'but *I* cannot suggest it, it would be improper.'

'Of course not, Kurt. Leave it to us.' There was a proprietary note in Eddie Benson's voice.

Colista protested, 'Oonagh'll miss her. We must *ask* her first, not *tell* her, Eddie.'

Her husband replied, 'Nonsense!'

230

'Where's Iain got to?' Colista asked, glancing around the crowded room. 'He disappeared directly we left the dining-room.'

She looked about the room, nodding here and there to acquaintances, and sighing. A waiter swiftly materialized at her side and refilled her *demi-tasse* with coffee. Later there would be dancing in the ballroom just beyond. Phil Grady and his swing orchestra would strike up any moment and at midnight a Latin American combo would take over, playing tangoes, rhumbas and sambas.

Mourna was wearing her blue taffeta. She wished it was chiffon. Taffeta was becoming *passé*. The Fitzwilliam twins, acknowledged leaders of fashion, were wearing chiffon; Amanda white, Dodo black. They looked ultra-chic and Mourna was glad she had her black lace in reserve.

She had been surprised to find the Fitzwilliam twins staying at the Grand. The gossip was they had followed Iain here. Wherever he went the Fitzwilliam twins were bound to pitch up, and people speculated which one would catch him. They were persistent females. 'Perhaps he'll marry both,' the jokers said.

The Count sat near Mourna. He was very proper. He smelled of cologne.

Amanda Fitzwilliam had asked Mourna in the powder room what he was like, the Count. Misunderstanding, Mourna had replied, 'Very nice. He's a gentleman,' and the twins had sniggered into their handkerchiefs and what they really meant suddenly became clear. They also had a repu-tation for being fast. It was said they had got themselves 'fitted out' in London, not only in Harrods but Harley Street as well.

'Their mother is taking no chances,' Auntie Colista had said. 'And it gives them an unfair advantage over the other eligible girls.'

'He's a nice man,' Mourna had repeated to the grinning Amanda.

231

'I heard he was a Nazi,' Dodo said. 'You know, tortured Jews and things like that.'

Mourna was shocked. 'Oh, I don't believe that,' she protested. 'He's so kind.'

'You mean he buys you flowers,' Amanda said, and nodded. 'I must admit he's good in that department. When he took me out he always arrived with roses and chocolates.' Her bright malicious gaze was fixed on Mourna. She could see she had shocked the O'Shea girl.

It was news to Mourna. It had not occurred to her that Kurt had taken out other Irish girls, yet when she thought about it, it seemed logical. But she was not at all sure she liked the idea.

'*All* well-brought up boys bring you flowers and chocs,' Dodo said.

'Yes, but it's usually a ghastly orchid that clashes with *everything* and you *have* to wear it,' Amanda said. 'You know, the beastly flower is purple and you are wearing shell-pink.' She screwed her eyes up and added, 'And a grim box of chocolates, squashed Cadbury's.' Mourna liked Cadbury's. She didn't like Amanda Fitzwilliam.

'Anyhow, he's a great petter,' Amanda said. Mourna said nothing. She left the powder room lost in her own thoughts, leaving the twins frustrated.

Mourna wished Amanda had kept her mouth shut. She had succeeded in disturbing the untroubled relationship she had with Kurt, putting thoughts into her head that she'd have liked to keep out. Now she'd always know he'd kissed Amanda and, well, done things with her. Mourna was angry at being enlightened. She'd much rather have remained in ignorance.

Kurt turned to her now. 'Are you all right, Mourna? You look pale.'

She shook her head, picturing him with Amanda, imagining his lips on hers.

'I'm all right, Kurt.'

'We'll dance later,' he said.

He was a good dancer and she liked being partnered by him. Other boys jerked her around, pulling her into their rhythm, or were awkward and tentative. Kurt was firm and sure and in command, yet respectful, and she imagined that the way they danced would be a blue-print of their lives together. If it lacked a certain excitement, the thrill of discovery, then they were emotions she could do without. Modest and shy for all her beauty, Mourna was beginning to believe that Kurt would be the perfect husband for her. He was calm and mature and in charge. If only Amanda Fitzwilliam had kept her mouth shut.

The orchestra next door was playing 'You Are My Lucky Star', and Uncle Eddie bent down, asking her to dance. Auntie Colista glanced at him sharply and said, 'I'll telephone Mrs Flanagan and arrange about Mourna. You have your bags here, don't you, Mourna? We don't have to have anything brought up?'

'No, Auntie Colista. They're with the hall porter. But I'll be okay with Mummy and Daddy. I can easily go down after the dance.'

'Nonsense, dear. It's all settled. We'll all be together here. It's more convenient.'

For what? Mourna wondered. For whom? For Kurt and herself certainly, but what would Uncle Eddie get out of it? Uncle Eddie, Mourna knew, always got something out of his generosity, he always had ulterior motives. She thought she was the only one who knew that. The others didn't seem to understand.

'We've got Dot and Ben coming up for morning coffee tomorrow, remember?' Colista said, frowning. Eddie grinned at his wife, who cast her eyes up to the chandelier.

'Couldn't you cancel?' he asked. Colista shook her head.

'Better to pretend we forgot,' she said.

'Oh, you can't do that,' Mourna cried. 'Auntie Dot and Uncle Ben would be so humiliated.' She knew the store

233

Dot would put on a visit to the Grand. She would never come here without an invitation, she simply hadn't the nerve.

'Whatever you decide, dear.' Eddie laughed and turned to Mourna. 'How lovely you look tonight,' he said, grinning at her. She fought down her dislike of him, feeling like a traitor.

They had been so good to her, yet they repelled her. It worried her that she should react so negatively to two such popular relations. 'Dance with me, my dear?' Eddie smiled his rakish smile.

He always held her too close. She could feel him against her and the sensation unnerved her. It was too urgent, too raw. She was not prepared and she felt insulted. The Fitzwilliam twins would not feel like that and she wondered if there was something wrong with her attitude.

She was not crazy about Colista either. She was watching them now like a cat, lazily alert. She arranged events, manipulated people. Did anyone really know what she was thinking? Eddie was so good to everyone. He had helped Tom over a rough patch with the pool hall, Mourna had heard Molly tell her mother. And he had been very good to Molly herself over some trouble that nearly sent Banan to jail. Eddie had had a word with the Chief of Police and the whole thing was smoothed over. He'd helped Ben, securing him a post a notch higher up in the Post Office, because Eddie Benson was a friend of the Minister of Posts and Telegraphs and that Minister owed him a favour and was only too glad to assist in Ben's advancement.

Then there was her father. Eddie had been at pains to show his brother-in-law how chummy he was with the Managing Director of Barnet's. Mourna felt her heart flutter at the thought of the father she adored at the mercy of a word from Eddie Benson.

Yes, Eddie was good to all and sundry. True, he expected loyalty and gratitude in return, but that was normal enough. Why then did he make her uneasy? What was it about him that caused her to back away?

'You're so good, Mourna, aren't you?' he whispered. 'So very good.'

'Oh, no, Uncle Eddie, I'd not say that,' she replied, blushing. He made her self-conscious when no one else did.

'Such goodness is always corrupted,' he said. 'Sadly so.'

'Is it?' she asked. 'We were brought up to be good.' It sounded prissy but she didn't care.

'Ah, well, it doesn't last,' he replied cryptically. 'It is something you just have to get over.'

Mourna thought about that word 'good'. He used it with reference to herself and she had thought it of his actions, the help he gave her aunts and uncles, her mother and father. She thought of Emmett and his pious quotation about what you give you receive back, and felt muddled. No one she knew had any ambition to be good. Except Emmett and he didn't count. He was only a child. It was all very difficult trying to read between the lines, trying to decipher what people *really* meant.

These were the facts of life, she thought as he held her in his arms, this tall handsome uncle, guiding her around the floor to the music of Phil Grady playing 'You Were Never Lovelier'. She kept her face averted from him and supposed she was ungrateful.

There was a multi-coloured globe overhead that sent slivers of coloured light carouselling around the ballroom. Her uncle loosened his hand from hers and tilted her face towards him, smiling, showing his even white teeth. 'You're very lovely, Mourna,' he said softly. 'Like the song says. You have grown into a beautiful woman.'

She wondered why he took so much trouble with her, what he wanted. She came to the conclusion that it must be something to do with Kurt. Perhaps his position, his title, irked Eddie Benson who was not happy in the company of his social superiors.

His body was hard against hers as if he was trying to tell her something. She turned her face away again, looking over his shoulder. Kurt was dancing with Colista who was watching them. When Mourna's eyes met her aunt's, Colista glanced hastily away.

'I've arranged a dinner-dance here, did I tell you?' Eddie said, so normally that she decided she was being fanciful and unfair. He guided her back to the table, sitting her down on the padded seat. 'I've asked Mr and Mrs Wilmot. They'll drive down for the week-end, stay overnight. Dave Wilmot loves his game of golf. I want your father here, Mourna. It will be good for him. The job of second-in-command in Barnet's is coming vacant, Maurice McLaglan is retiring. Tell your father, Mourna.' He raised his brandy glass and took a gulp. 'And, Mourna?'

'Yes, Uncle?'

'You'd do well to think of Iain, get this German out of your hair. He's Colista's friend, as you know, and my wife's taste can be ... well ... faulty.'

'Yes, Uncle Eddie.'

'I have this dream, Mourna. I see you marrying my son, becoming the daughter I never had.' He glanced at his wife as he said this. She was walking back to their table, Kurt holding her elbow. They reached the table and sat down.

'Yes, Uncle Eddie,' Mourna said.

'And enough of that Uncle Eddie stuff. Call us Eddie and Colista, eh?'

Colista nodded, her eyes scanning the room. 'Yes, Mourna. Auntie makes me feel so old. I wonder where Iain can have disappeared to? He really is a naughty boy.'

'Will you dance with me?' Kurt asked her, and looking at him, into his clear blue eyes, she felt suddenly safe and secure. She smiled at him and nodded.

Chapter Thirty-Four

It was past ten o'clock and the men not returned when Mrs Flanagan drew Oonagh back from the edges of a nightmare in which two huge thugs were beating her son to a pulp. Mrs Flanagan was knocking at their door with an impatient rat-a-tat-tat.

'In the name of God, have you forgotten your key, Gabriel?' Oonagh cried, leaning out of bed to turn on the bedside lamp. She groped for her dressing-gown as she heard Mrs Flanagan shrill, 'It's me, Mrs O'Shea,' for all the world to hear. Oonagh sighed. 'Yes, Mrs Flanagan?' she called out. 'What is it?' wondering why she felt guilty. She had done nothing.

'I've had *another* phone call from the Grand! The Bensons said to tell you Mourna is staying up there, they hope you don't mind,' she chanted. Her voice dripped ice. 'It's more *suitable*, they said!'

'All right, Mrs Flanagan. I'm sorry they disturbed you.'

'So well you might be!' came the acid retort. 'They asked will you and Mr O'Shea have lunch (they mean dinner, I expect) there tomorrow? And, Mrs O'Shea, I hope in future you'll see to it that your friends and relatives realize I am *not* a messenger-boy!'

And with that Mrs Flanagan flounced back to her room muttering, 'The cheek of some!'

~~~~~~

237

The men came quietly down the road from the pub. It had been a pleasant evening, except for Joe passing out in the gents.

'I hope to God he's not going to keep it up,' Tom remarked. Tom had taken him home earlier, walked him up the boreen and silently delivered the helpless man to Maisie who was waiting in the window, a dark silhouette. She had made no comment, just bowed her head in acceptance and guided Tom who supported the limp drunk into their bedroom. Tom lowered him on to the bed where he lay inert.

'Sorry, Maisie,' Tom said apologetically.

'It's not your fault,' she sighed wearily. 'He'll have the shakes in the morning.'

Tom had left him there and returned to the pub for the last half-hour. The crack was great, and they'd made new friends, and when they got home their wives were asleep which was just as well for they were far too limp from the jars to have accomplished much more that night.

'Just right. It's been perfect,' Gabriel muttered to his pillow.

The young people drifted in and were asleep before they had finished undressing, their faces stained with candy-floss and ice-cream. Last to arrive home, Briana was last to bed and sleep. She leaned out of her window staring at the moon as a thousand lovers had done before her. The pale silver globe hung like a lantern in the sky and seemed to her more beautiful than anything in the world. The Monterey pines were dark masses against the midnight blue velvet sky, pricked with shimmering stars. She wrapped her arms around her own body and smiled into the night at the wonder of it all. She felt at one with the world, everything seemed right, perfectly in tune. When, much later, she slid between the sheets and laid her head on the pillow, it was to dream of her love, a smile on her lips.

Chapter Thirty-Five

Dawn broke over Dranmore. The countryside was drenched in dew and a pale sun, hardly a relative of last night's fiery ball, peeped up over the green land behind the Grand, flooding the sky with primrose light. The sea sang its gentle lullaby and tiptoed on to the strand and over the rocks where yesterday evening it had thundered. It crept up over the cold hard sand and shuddered back as if afraid, leaving a border of white foam.

The children awakened first, rising early in excitement, pushing and shoving each other, horsing around, throwing pillows. The older ones groaned, turned over and tried to hold on to the last remnants of their sleep, but soon joined the little ones: fighting for the bathroom, retrieving socks and sandals, wiping their faces in careless excitement, preparing to enjoy their first day in Dranmore.

Maggie Moran had been up and about and very busy. She excelled herself that morning by pinching Mrs Flanagan's apples, taking bites out of half a dozen and leaving the remainder to go brown on the grass beneath the trees. She raided the bushes and consumed huge quantities of blackberries, both ripe and unripe, and so at breakfast it was not surprising that she looked faintly ill.

The food at breakfast proved that last night's feast had not been a fluke. They had grapefruit segments and orange juice, porridge and cereal, bacon, eggs, sausage, black and white pudding, tomatoes and mushrooms, tea, toast, brown and white breads, marmalade of the thick and thin varieties, and jams. Even Granny O'Shea stopped complaining about the bed and how she hadn't slept a wink, being out of her own, tucked in and managed to put away cereal, fruit, a sausage, an egg and some toast.

'I checked her a couple of times last night,' Oonagh mouthed to Molly, 'and she was out for the count.' Then, loudly, 'This is first-class fare, Mrs Flanagan.'

'Ah, sure, you can't go wrong with a fry,' Mrs Flanagan replied, and whisked some dirty dishes into the kitchen, shooing the maids before her and returning with plates piled high with fresh baked buttermilk scones.

'It's a smashing spread, Mrs Flanagan,' Molly echoed Oonagh and added, 'Tell the cook for us, will you?'

'An' give him a swelled head?' Mrs Flanagan hooted. 'Yerra, not on your life. Ye can show yer appreciation at the end of the holiday.'

'Is there a Mr Flanagan, may one ask?' Ben enquired. 'If so he's a lucky man!'

'Been in his grave these ten years so I don't suppose he'd be considered lucky,' she laughed. 'D'ye think I'd be doin' all this work if he was alive?'

They sat for a while after the meal, chatting, a lovely feeling of indolence overwhelming them. No need to hurry, they had all day. Dot was bragging about her impending visit to the Grand and her date with Eddie and Colista, and Oonagh forebore to mention the fact that she and Gabriel had been asked for lunch.

Outraged yells brought the peaceful mood abruptly to a halt and they hurried outside to see what was wrong.

'It's got to be Maggie,' Molly whispered to Oonagh as they emerged into the sun.

She was right. Maggie Moran had topped twelve of Mrs Flanagan's red geraniums. They grew in halved wine-casks outside Kincora. Cerise and crimson, white and pink, packed in with white alyssum and purple aubretia, they made a brilliant splash of colour against the walls and Mrs Flanagan was justifiably proud of them. She had gone out to empty the tea-leaves into the casks for fertilizer and had been appalled at the sight that met her eyes: Maggie Moran, caught in the act of beheading the lush blooms, surrounded by decimated crimson blossoms. She smirked up at the infuriated landlady who picked her up, put her across her knee, pulled up her skirt, her frilly panties revealed for all the world to see, and in front of her brothers, sisters and cousins was spanking her firmly and thoroughly on her bum.

'How *dare* you!' Dot squealed. 'How *dare* you touch my child?'

'She asked for it, missus.' Mrs Flanagan was breathless and unapologetic. 'Never saw such a termagant in my whole life. Nearly as wicked as I was when I was her age. Try anything. Needs a firm hand.'

'You *dare* touch her again and we'll leave,' Ben echoed his wife.

'Well, go then,' Mrs Flanagan said tranquilly, taking the wind out of their sails. 'But ye'll still have to pay the whole whack!'

'Oh, come now, don't talk of leaving,' Molly said. 'Mrs Flanagan is right. She did ask for it, Dot. Look at the devastation.' She pointed to the beheaded flowers.

'I don't care,' Dot protested, 'they're only flowers. Maggie's a baby. You're right, Ben. We'll have to leave.' He looked a bit taken aback at these words and Dot pulled a surprisingly silent Maggie to her. To everyone's surprise she firmly detached herself from her mother and ran to Mrs Flanagan.

'Don't *want* to leave,' she pouted. 'Want to stay here. With her.' She pointed to the red-faced landlady.

Dot was dreadfully put out. She stared at the six-year-old who looked defiantly back at her as if she was a stranger.

241

'Maybe she wanted to be told to behave,' Oonagh said mildly. 'Come on, let's go down to the beach. It's a gorgeous day.'

They all vanished to their rooms to change into their swimming costumes and collect towels and lotions and books to read.

Oonagh and Gabriel discussed the Bensons' invitation and decided on prudence.

'We'll have to limit our visits up there, Oonagh,' Gabriel said. 'I'll have to offer to pay at least once, pet, and you know how these things go. Sometimes you get stuck with the bill by accident.'

He was putting on his swimming trunks, bending over, steadying himself on the bedpost. 'And the prices at the Grand are exorbitant. It would really set us back, cramp me for the holiday.'

She held his arm, helping him to keep his balance, and to his surprise agreed. She usually ached to frequent places like the Grand but now she said, 'You're right, Gabriel. We should refuse today.'

The reason was simple. She had three outfits suitable for the smart hotel, so she would limit her visits to the number of outfits. She did not want anyone there to think she was a poor relation.

'We'll accept the invitation to the dinner-dance, and we'll go up one more time, perhaps if Mourna gets engaged ... '

'Oonagh!'

'Well, she might. At least after this holiday we'll know what she feels about Count ... Count ... '

'Count Von Mensil. Kurt.'

'And you haven't forgotten your invitation, Gabriel?' she asked him shyly.

'My darling, no. Of course I haven't.'

'It's not really fair, Gabriel, asking you to be on duty, as it were, with Mr Wilmot. When you're on holiday, I mean.'

Mourna had phoned at breakfast and told them.

'Well, I don't mind. It will be a great opportunity. I must say, Eddie has been very kind.'

'Yes, and they'll appreciate us more if we're not there all the time,' Oonagh said.

'Would you prefer lunch or dinner, pet? At the Grand, I mean?'

'Lunch,' Oonagh said firmly. 'Lunch, please, Gabriel.'

'If that's what you want, pet.'

'It is,' she said firmly. 'It's what I want.'

So Gabriel went to the telephone in the hall in his swimming trunks and booked a table for two on Thursday for lunch, and asked them to give Mr and Mrs Benson a message to say that the O'Sheas would not be lunching with them today. And while he was doing that Oonagh steeled herself to trot along to Dot's house and ask her if she by any chance possessed a pair of pink shoes. She didn't like asking for favours but she had no choice and Dot was famous for her collection of shoes.

Dot was trying to tie the strings at the back of Maggie's elasticized swim suit. The child was squirming in her grasp, slippery as a new-caught trout.

'I don' wanna wear *anything*,' Maggie yelled at her mother.

'That wouldn't be modest, pet,' Dot cried. 'Come in, come in, Oonagh. What can I do for you? This child has become impossible since we came to Dranmore.'

Become? Oonagh thought, and said, 'I wondered if you had a pair of pink shoes I could squeeze into, Dot?' Oonagh knew she was gushing but couldn't stop herself. 'I left mine behind and I thought, you being famous for your shoes, you might help me out. Gabriel and I are going up to the Grand on Thursday, and, as I say, I've left the very shoes I need for my rose dress in Dublin.'

'The Grand? Oh?'

'We are not going at Eddie's invitation, Dot. Gabriel is

taking me.'

'Oho! Aren't we toffs? Janey Mac, Oonagh, there's no stoppin' you, is there? Well, as you know, we're going up there this morning.' Then she added, '*All* the O'Sheas musta left their shoes at home.' She was watching Oonagh closely, glad to catch her surprise.

'Which O'Shea are you talking about?'

'Wasn't Emer in earlier askin' for a loan of my white stilettos? I told her what I'll tell you – yer welcome to anything I have, with a heart and a half.'

Oonagh wondered briefly about Emer's request but was too grateful to give it the thought it would otherwise deserve. You had to admit one thing about Dot: she was generous to a fault. She thinks she's got everything, Oonagh thought. She has no axe to grind.

Oonagh despised her for this, deploring her lack of ambition, but just at this moment, looking at the confident badly made-up face and the crown of blonde ringlets, the kindness writ large, she felt that perhaps her contempt was misplaced and Dot was, in fact, the lucky one.

'I'll need these ones today,' Dot said, pointing to a pair of emerald green strapped high-heeled sandals. 'For the morning coffee with Eddie and Colista. I've got the gansey to deliver.'

'Ah, yes.'

'Any others you're welcome to.'

'You're very kind, Dot,' Oonagh said, feeling an unfamiliar rush of affection for her sister-in-law. 'Very kind indeed.'

'It's a pleasure,' Dot said, pink-cheeked.

Oonagh took the shoes back to her room. They matched her outfit in the shade of the room but Oonagh doubted the colour would be exact in the sunlight. However, there was nothing she could do about that.

They spent the morning on the beach. The sun shone in cloudless skies. The sea sparkled. Rocks covered in slippery green fern were watered over by lapping waves and black seaweed swayed in the pools on the shore encrusted with cockles and mussels alive, alive-oh. Boats bobbed, children screamed in delight and excitement, the sandy beaches were covered with the brightly coloured paraphernalia of the young: gaudy tin buckets, spades, beach-balls and other leisure toys. Adults turned nicely pink and fell asleep under the sun.

Oonagh led the families down a little path past Gentleman's Cove to the sandy beach which she had purloined for the family. 'We'll keep away from the riff-raff here,' Oonagh said, staking her claim on the cove beneath Kincora. What she really meant was that *she'd* keep the riff-raff away from them. It would be a brave body indeed who would dare to breach the phalanx of O'Sheas, Morans and Maguires.

They encamped there, spread themselves widely the length and breadth of the cove. Any stranger with enough temerity to venture actually on to the beach soon fled, defeated by the wall of disapproval and cold hostility that greeted their arrival. And of course the presence of Maggie Moran.

This was where the *enfant terrible* came into her own. Sand-kicker and pebble-pitcher *par excellence*, she would put a saint off, so the families' claim on the beach was more or less absolute. Lunch, which Mrs Flanagan called dinner and was served hot, comprised of a substantial Irish stew, and a rhubarb tart and custard. During the meal Dot seemed very subdued. In fact, there were distinct signs that she had been crying.

'How'd you enjoy your morning coffee at the Grand?' Oonagh asked, thinking to cheer her up by giving her a chance to brag. To everyone's consternation, Dot burst into tears. She jumped up from the table and dashed out the door.

'What is it, Ben?' Gabriel asked, perplexed. Ben stood up.

He too seemed near to tears.

'Bloody Eddie and Colista!' he cried, his voice shrill. He pulled his serviette from under his chin. 'They've upset my precious.' He glanced around at everyone. 'They didn't turn up,' he said defiantly, then sat down again. 'Forgot,' he whispered.

'Oh Ben, no! How awful.' Gabriel glanced at Oonagh who went and put her arm around him.

'We walked up there, in this heat,' his lip trembled, 'Dot carrying the bag with the sweater. She worked so hard on that sweater. A labour of love it was, only you knew.' He wiped his arm across his eyes. 'We asked for them at the desk, sat in the lounge, waited. Like eejits! All morning. Dot was like a statue, frozen. Sitting there with her Switzer's bag clutched in her hands. My poor love. Never forgive it. Never!' he shouted and banged the table with his fist. 'Then we get up to come back here and as we leave Eddie breezes in. Sees us. Looks amazed. Says, cool as a cucumber, they forgot! They forgot!'

'What'd you do?' Tom asked, 'I hope you gave him a piece of your mind?'

Ben lowered his eyes, staring at his plate. 'We left. We just left.'

'Ye didn't say anything at all? Tell him off?'

Ben looked at his brother. 'How could I, an' he a friend of the Minister? How the hell could I? Don't you think I wanted to? But the family is dependent on my job an' Eddie Benson is a friend of the Minister, so I kept my mouth shut. But I'll never forgive him. Never!'

He stood, knocking his chair over backwards, and hurried out of the room.

Maggie began to bawl. 'Mary's got a bigger helping an' me. 'S not fair. 'S not fair.'

At that moment Mrs Flanagan appeared at the cross-door to inquire if everything was all right and Maggie, on sight of her, stopped in mid-yell.

Oonagh went to see Dot after the meal but Ben met her at the door saying they were all right and Dot was resting. Oonagh thought of her sister-in-law's kindness to her earlier in the day. 'If there's anything I can do, Ben, please let me know,' she said. He nodded and went back into the room.

Oonagh went down to the cove. A young couple had arrived while they were at lunch and had spread themselves out on the strand. Tom and Molly quickly followed Oonagh down and Gabriel came soon after. Within minutes the young couple left, deciding it must be a private beach.

'It's just as well we refused the lunch invitation if they're in such an absent-minded mood,' Gabriel said to Oonagh who nodded in agreement.

'I didn't know they'd asked you up to lunch,' Molly said.

'Yes, well, we didn't want to steal Dot's thunder,' Oonagh replied. 'But now it seems … '

'Nice of you though.'

'Well, Gabriel decided it might be a bit steep.'

'Oh, Eddie would have forked out,' Tom reassured him.

'Yes. I'll give him that. He does. But sometimes, only sometimes, one gets stuck with a round, a very large round, and I'm just not up to it, Tom, the way things are.'

'Quite agree with you, me boyo. Know just what you mean.' Tom smiled.

'Still, I don't think he'd forget Mourna's da.' He grinned at Gabriel who was puzzled by the implication and did not understand it. One of the problems of family holidays was having constantly to avoid taking sides. It was a major rule Gabriel had made, the only way to keep the peace. So often he did not pursue a topic if he felt it might contain innuendo best left unexplored.

They swam and the sea was perfect, warm, with a chill as you struck out. It restored their tranquillity and they stopped thinking about Dot and Ben and feeling sorry for them.

'Work up a sweat, then dive in,' Tom shouted.

Emer kept out of the sun in a huddle with Brigid, and once Oonagh asked her why she borrowed Dot's shoes but Emer pretended not to hear her.

Roac read a book in the shade. Des, nervous as a kitten, jumping at the slightest remark, blushing for no reason, dodged everyone, thwarting kindly attempts to incorporate him in beach activities. His eczema had flared up overnight and Oonagh was quite worried about him.

'Leave him be,' Gabriel advised her. 'He doesn't seem keen at all to join in and he's entitled not to.'

'He's missing his mam,' Oonagh said.

They went to bed early that night, all of them too tired to go anywhere after tea at six o'clock. Faces felt hot, skin was burned, camomile applied, and they fell into bed, exhausted and blissful.

Chapter Thirty-Six

The next morning, routine established, they breakfasted in the now familiar room, got into their togs and took their towels down to the beach. Oonagh picked Des up, determined to look after him.

'Where are Tom and Molly?' Gabriel asked Roac who shrugged.

'Where's Mourna?' he inquired.

'She's staying at the Grand,' Oonagh said, squinting up, and Roac ran away from them across the beach.

'He's got a terrible crush on Mourna,' Emer said to Brigid.

'He'll have to join a queue!' was Brigid's tart reply.

'Where's Molly, dear?' Gabriel persisted.

'I don't know, Gabriel,' Oonagh said. 'I saw her get in her car. I called out to her but she didn't seem to hear me.'

'How odd,' Gabriel mused. 'How very odd.'

'That's what I thought,' Oonagh said. 'She seemed upset about something and she was all right at breakfast. Anyhow she drove off. Where, I don't know.'

She put on her sunglasses, settled down on her towel and gave a contented sigh. Gabriel decided to follow her example. It was fruitless worrying about other people and it solved nothing.

Molly had taken the Ford and just gone. She had no idea where she was headed, she simply had to leave the vicinity of Kincora. She knew she couldn't go down to the beach with the others the state she was in. She drove the car, shaking, trying to get a grip on herself, not seeing Oonagh waving to her.

How could he? she agonized. How could he here, where the children, the family, anyone could see? Anyone could have walked in. Shaming her like that.

She had left the house key behind her in the dining room after breakfast. Going back to get it she had stumbled on a scene she had always dreaded: her husband in action. She had known about his exploits but she had never actually caught him and the sight of him pawing the struggling maid sickened and shocked her. Knowing about something like that was one thing, seeing it was quite another.

He was pressing Dymphna against the wall, his hands all over her, his knees bent, looking like a dog in heat.

Dymphna was pushing him away. In his feverish state he was at a disadvantage. Young and strong, she did not have much trouble with him. She brought her knee up and shoved him against the table with her two hands, shouting at him, 'Get off me, get off! Old fart like you should have a

249

knot put in it, by law!' And she flounced out the cross-door as Molly closed the other gently and glided away. She fled out to where the cars were parked, away from the pathetic and disgusting little scene.

~~~~~~

In the bright sunny day the local boys sat on the sea-wall like a row of birds; preening, alert, ready to hustle and move at the first indication of adventure, eyes cocked for the main chance.

Mena walked past them slowly, taking her time. She had left the top button of her blouse undone and now, as always, she managed to give the impression that her clothes were on the point of falling off, or at least coming adrift. The boys watched, at first swaggering then puzzled as they realized that she was pointing at them and counting. One, two, three, four.

It dawned on them that she was counting them off. Was *she* going to choose? Six, seven … They were annoyed. She was breaking the rules. *They* were the sex that chose. Yet there she was: countdown! There was something exciting about it all the same. She was some hot chick. But she should have left it up to them.

'What are you doing, Mena?'

A woman had driven up in a Ford. 'Mena, come here at once!'

The girl shrugged and turned her back on the boys.

'I will return,' she called, and opened the door on the passenger side and jumped into the car.

'Gee, Ma, did you *have* to?'

'Mena … what I saw … what were you up to?'

'What you saw, Ma?' Mena said coldly. 'I was up to boy-stalking. That's what I was *up* to.'

Molly stared at her daughter. 'Sometimes I don't know you, Mena. You're a stranger to me. Why can't you be more like Briana or Mourna or Emer?'

'Because Auntie Oonagh and Uncle Gabriel are a real family who love each other and talk to each other and … '

'Oh, Mena, Da and I love each other and … ' Molly thought of the little scene she had just witnessed and shivered.

'Ma! Who do you think you're kidding? You and Da *hate* each other. You can't bear to touch him … '

'Shut up, Mena, do you hear me? Shut up.'

There was denial on Molly's lips but reluctantly she bit denial back. She drove for a while in silence, not sure where she was going.

The trouble was that she had not got this far herself. She had not reached the point where she could admit to herself that she hated Tom. She was achingly aware that he hurt her, that she despised him, but she had not chosen to look too closely at the death of her love for her husband.

When had it happened? When had she started lying to herself about him? When had the light gone out and the darkness fallen? Not this morning, that was certain. This morning had been the final curtain, the play over by then, well and truly over.

'Listen, Mena,' her knuckles were white on the wheel, 'I'm not going to tell you this again – no daughter of mine will behave like a slut. You go on like this and I'll send you back to Dublin.'

'That suits me just fine,' her daughter said triumphantly, 'I'd much rather be there than here.'

Molly glanced at her in surprise. She was telling the truth. Mena would prefer to be at home, which meant, Molly realized, that she didn't know her own daughter at all.

The sun was hot and Molly wiped her face with her handkerchief. She didn't know what to do, didn't know what to say. She drove along the coastline, the wheel clutched between slippery fingers.

'Where we going, Ma?' Mena asked.

'I don't know.' Molly hadn't the strength to lie. She hadn't the ability to keep up a pretence.

'Look, Ma, why don't you throw him out?'

'Mena, you're speaking about your father!'

'I know, I know, but I despise him. Think I don't know about him? Think we're all blind? Can't you see what you're doing? Banan's like a raging bull and Roac gets deeper and deeper inside himself every day. I'm hardened, but Da and his floozies … '

Molly lifted her hands off the wheel and the car skidded sideways. 'Don't, Mena! Don't, do you hear?' she screamed.

Mena gripped the wheel and her mother took it. 'Be careful, Ma. I don't want to die just yet. Things are bad, but not *that* bad.'

Molly got the car under control. Her head was throbbing and she felt as if someone was driving a corkscrew into her temple and out the other side.

'You haven't faced up to it, have you, Ma?' Mena looked at her mother pityingly. 'Look, stop the damned car a sec, or you'll kill us both.'

Molly drew to a halt. The car stopped on the headland looking out over a mild blue sea, the waves crashing at the feet of the purple rock, the stony islands, like a string of crouch-backed turtles straying out into the blue-grey ocean. Crows skeetered and dipped and journeyed to and from the trees, and seagulls stood on spindle-legs at the water's edge raising their heads to the wind.

We are like a couple of sightseers, Molly thought. Her daughter touched her arm but she couldn't bear even that and gently pulled away. She was contained in her own misery. She could feel Mena's hurt but there seemed nothing she could do about it. She clutched the wheel, sitting beside a slumped Mena, staring out at the wonderful panorama, not taking it in.

252

Mena was frightened at this show of weakness from her mother. 'Look, Mam, there's Iain and Briana.'

They could see the tiny but unmistakable figures on the pebbly beach, sitting close together. Mena was instantly sorry she'd said anything. Iain was sitting against a rock, his arms around Briana. They looked so accustomed to each other, their bodies familiar, content and at peace, there was a oneness there that made Mena remark, 'They must be doin' a line.'

Molly thought, That'll drive Eddie mad, but she didn't say anything.

From where they had parked above the bay and below the Grand, she could see several of the coves. Briana and Iain were alone on their pebble beach, isolated, encircled by the aura of contentment that emanated from them. Around the corner in the next cove that lay beneath the cliff, Molly could see all the children jumping at the water's edge. Roac, in his anxiety, was watching them. Maggie was splashing him. A couple of smacks from Mrs Flanagan had subdued but not squashed her.

We get what we produce, Molly thought, and remembered all the days she'd started on a promise to forge a friendship with Roac and Mena and how evening had fallen without her having made a move. Why? She had not been overly busy. Oonagh with double, no, treble her work load had achieved an enviable closeness to her offspring. You could see it in Briana's trust and peace with Iain and in Mena's derisive temptation of the boys at the sea-wall.

Molly had to admit, reluctantly, that her negligence had been born of lazy procrastination. Was tiredness an illness? she wondered. Exhausted beyond belief she rested her head on her hands and heard Mena's soft, 'Mam?', felt her timid touch on her shoulder, and Molly suddenly cracked. She burst into a flood of tears that, released like a broken dam, gushed from her unrestrained.

253

'That's it, Mam. Let it all out. That's it.'

Mena put her arms around her mother and held her close until the storm had passed. Their roles were, for the moment, reversed. When it was over Molly raised her head, kissed her daughter and started the car. They drove back to Kincora in silence, not looking at each other, but every so often Molly laid her hand on her daughter's and gently squeezed it.

Chapter Thirty-Seven

The long summer days slid past, sand-between-the-toes, red backs and noses dabbed with camomile, the sea-salt scalding peeling skin and making soft hair sticky.

Granny O'Shea had to be transported down the steep incline to the beach each day, a danger to life and limb.

'We should have thought of that contingency before,' Ben said, 'If they fall it'll be up with them all, never mind her.'

Roac and Mena, or Laughlin and Emer, made a seat with fists clenched on wrists, and Granny sat on the seat with her arms around their shoulders and issued instructions and warnings. 'Look out – the branch'll hit me. Down, Laughlin, *down*, or I'll fall. Begob, where are yer brains at all? In yer bums be the look of it.'

'Ah, Granny, say a prayer. Our Lady of Lourdes will see ye right,' Dot called out as the old lady made her way down.

Strong young legs did a lot of running up and down on messages; forgotten necessities.

'The sun's gone in. Get your mammy's sweater, Mary.'

'I forgot the camomile, Emmett, can you get it for me?'

'Maggie is thirsty, Emer, take her up and get her a drink.'

Maggie buried little Dec in sand which nearly proved fatal. The sea sucked the caverns in the rock-face and the young folk were warned not to go in there.

'There's a dragon in there, Dec, wi' yellow teeth like Granny O'Shea, an' he'll eat you effen you go in,' Maggie informed her brother.

'Maggie says the dragon in the rocks'll eat us,' little Dec told his mother as she wrapped his shivering body in a towel to dry it off after he'd spent too long in the sea and turned a funny mauve colour. Dot loved the feel of his chunky little body under the towel and said, 'Nonsense, Dec. Nonsense,' as his teeth chattered and she rubbed a little warmth back into him.

Above the beach the boys with bikes gathered, keeping an eye open for talent and making remarks whenever anyone passed by. Far out at sea they could see the porpoises, sleek grey backs sliding gracefully over and under the waves, and at the shoreline the gulls cried out as if in pain and great swatches of seaweed wrapped itself around the driftwood.

Back at the house Ardel got restless. The memory of the beating, although his injuries still pained him, was fading from his mind and he hated being shut up all the time.

Maggie Moran piped up one morning at breakfast, 'Two men're lookin' fer Ardel.'

'Where? Where'd you see them?' Oonagh asked, fear clutching her heart.

'Outside the poob.'

'The pub?'

'Yes. Thas' what I said. The poob.'

'What were you doing there?' Dot asked.

'Doesn't she drink then?' Tom asked sarcastically, and

255

Molly gave him a glance of withering contempt. He had been in a foul mood since Dymphna had spurned him. His nose was out of joint because, worse, she had been flirting with the battered and bruised Ardel, driving Tom crazy with frustrated lust.

Dot hadn't heard his remark, or if she did hadn't thought it worth comment. It was irritating, Tom thought, how difficult it was to get a rise out of Dot. It seemed impossible to annoy her. Yet she got right under his skin with her innocent goo-goo eyes at Ben and her total lack of discipline for the children. She was far too treacly for him and he had not been able to prevent himself feeling a certain satisfaction that Eddie Benson had let them down and not turned up for the morning date. However, she seemed to have made a quick recovery from the incident even though he, Tom, had not been able to resist making several snide remarks about the slight.

'What did they say?' Oonagh persisted. She looked upset as well she might, Tom reflected, for if 'that lot' were after Ardel there was no hope at all for him. He wondered did any of them know of the connection with Banan, and glanced at his wife. He met a look of such vitriolic contempt that he suddenly felt very afraid, almost as if those guys were after him.

'They said, "Sixpence for anyone knows where to find Ardel O'Shea",' Maggie chanted, delighted to be the centre of attention.

'Did you tell him?' Oonagh asked. Maggie rolled her eyes.

'Course not! What you take me for? 'Sides, sixpence!' she said with withering contempt. 'If it had been five bob now ... '

'They been askin' fer *days*,' little Dec piped up, drumming his heels on the dado behind him. He always did that when he spoke, from nerves. He beat a tattoo loudly with his heels.

'Who's been asking?' Gabriel inquired.

'Two men. One is stringy, thin like a pole,' Maggie said.

' 'N the other's like a gorilla!' Dec yelled, knocked over his milk and started to cry.

'I'll mop it up for you,' Mary Moran said. She mothered all that family while Dot concentrated on Ben.

'The pair we saw in the pub. We couldn't place them, remember?' Tom said to Gabriel who nodded.

'Sure I remember. What did you mean when you said they'd been asking for days?' Gabriel asked little Dec, but the boy was still choking on his food and was not listening.

'Maggie, do you know?'

She, happy to oblige, feeling important, said, 'Oh, *yes*. They assed us at the carnival, they assed us in the boreen, they assed us outside the poob, and they assed us *in* the poob … '

'You were *in* the pub?' Ben sounded mildly surprised and the children around that table looked suddenly very innocent. Little Dec stopped crying and choking.

'Yes, well, we went in the snug an' collected coasters. Wi' designs on,' Maggie said, and chancing her arm added, 'It's for a school project, Mam.'

'Oh, then that's all right,' Ben said, looking relieved.

'I don't believe it!' Tom marvelled.

'You saying she's lying?' Ben asked Tom, a coldness in his voice that surprised his brother.

'No, no, no. I meant … '

'He was surprised you'd let her go in the pub at all,' Oonagh remarked mildly. 'That's all, Ben.'

'*An*' beside the ice-cream shop near the harbour,' Maggie added loudly.

'We'll have to sort this,' Tom said, and Gabriel nodded.

'No,' Oonagh said loudly, 'I don't want you ending up like Ardel. No, Gabriel, I forbid it.'

'No, Da. It's my problem,' Ardel said. 'I don't want you mixed up in it.'

'Well, lie low, son, for the time being.'

'Janey Mac, I'm bored senseless in that room, Da. I'll go crazy if I'm shut up in there much longer.'

Nevertheless he would do what they told him.

He could hear their voices as he lay in bed while the sun blazed down outside and the sea shushed against the shore. Why did people always shout on the beach? he wondered. Why did they always sound so excited? And they laughed a lot, immoderately, like at a party. He could hear them in his cramped little room on his hot little camp-bed. He wished like Mena he was back in Dublin. He could get lost in the city, stay with cousins in Clontarf or Whitehall. But here! If he went out here, stuck his nose out an inch, they'd know. He'd be as obvious as the bloody lighthouse.

'Well, did anyone tell where Ardel was? That's what I want to know? Better say now if you did.'

Little Dec was trying to slide under the table as all the others said no in firm chorus.

'You did, din' ye? Fer what? Fer sixpence?' Mary Moran screamed at him, pulling him up by the back of his gansey.

'No! No!' Little Dec began to cry again and Dot said, 'Leave him alone, Mary. Sure, he meant no harm.'

'Jasus!' Tom ejaculated.

'What did you take from him, that man?' Mary asked.

'An ice-cream cone. A strawberry ice-cream,' little Dec wailed.

'Have'n I tole you an' tole you not to take things from strangers?' Mary asked.

'But it was'en poisoned. I saw him get it from the ice-cream man,' little Dec protested, and Mary picked him up and shook him like a rat, paying no attention to their mother.

Dec's teeth chattered. 'Put me d-d-d-down.'

'Put him down, Mary,' Ben said. 'You'll achieve nothing like that. I'm sorry, Gabriel. I'm sorry, Ardel. You know

258

we'd never harm you. He's only eight!' he added as if in mitigation.

'He wouldn't live to be nine if he were mine,' Tom said.

'Where'd you say I was?' Ardel asked through clenched teeth. He was glad he was not near little Dec Moran or he'd have bloody strangled him.

'Where you are!' little Dec said, his eyes sliding nervously away from his cousin. 'In Kincora, first house on the right.'

'Then they'll go there. They mustn't find anyone. It must be empty.'

'You tell them the exact room?' Little Dec nodded, petrified by the enormity of what he had done.

'They'll get me,' Ardel said. 'They'll come after me. I'll get you for this, you little informer,' he added, staring at little Dec.

'It's not *him* you should call informer,' Tom said. 'If there's an informer, isn't that yourself, Ardel O'Shea?'

Everyone looked at him. 'Shut your mouth, Tom.' Molly's voice was cold.

'But that's why he's in trouble with these men. He informed, didn't he?'

Ardel bit his lip and wished he could tell them about the money. But that would be a much worse sin in his parents' book.

'Where'll we put him?' Oonagh asked.

'I know. Let him have Rita's until she comes back. If she ever does.'

'You heard from your mam yet?' Tom asked Des and Brigid.

'No, we haven't, Uncle Tom,' they answered in unison.

They hadn't thought about her much, in their unaccustomed luxury, not going into the room they should have been in, leaving it small, cold, uninhabited. They didn't want Ardel O'Shea to put them into it as he surely would. They didn't want him there at all but they couldn't think of a way out of it, a way around Oonagh's determination.

'Then that's that,' Gabriel said to Oonagh. 'Shift him in there after breakfast, Mother, and make sure he goes down the corridors and through the cross-doors and doesn't put his nose outside.'

'And you kids,' Tom added, 'if those men ask you again, say Ardel O'Shea has gone back to Dublin. Hear me? Gone back to Dublin.'

They all nodded solemnly, thrilled at the seriousness of the affair. It made them feel grown-up and responsible.

'We've been sleeping in the big front room,' Des said to Oonagh.

'Well, I'm afraid you'll have to go to the rooms you were meant to be in. It's safer.'

'I don't see why, Auntie Oonagh,' Brigid said stubbornly.

'It's safer because those men will not be expecting him to be in an adult's room, that's why. By now, thanks to little Dec – ' little Dec shrank into his skin – 'they'll have an idea of the geography of the place. I'm sure they've asked others. So the last place they'll look is in a room supposed to be occupied by an adult.'

'Then it's decided?' They all agreed, and Des and Brigid sighed for lost comfort, shrugged, and decided to go out into the sun.

Chapter Thirty-Eight

Briana was not at breakfast. She told her mother she was not hungry of a morning and preferred to wait for lunch. She would pick an apple from the tree and that would do her.

Each morning she pulled on her shorts over her swimsuit and ran barefoot over the grass under the pines springy as a race-course, the needles softened by the dew and smelling fiercely sweet. She ran down the steps to the Pebble Beach, wet-footed from the moist grass, and there Iain would be waiting for her, to hold her, hug her to him, kiss her cheeks and her lips. Then, unable to bear their ripe promise, he would race her to the sea. Stones hurt their feet. They yelped and yelled at the hardness of them under their insteps.

Engulfed by the waves, the breath knocked from their bodies, but both strong swimmers, they would strike out from the shore to a rock that rose like a seal's back, smooth and round, with one ledge cut by the tide that gave them just enough room to stretch out, damp and sleek as the porpoises further out to sea, and just as playful. They were too young to worry, too much in love to think of much else than how they felt about each other, and too inexperienced to realize their helplessness. Life for them was simple. Their happiness depended on only one thing, their proximity to each other.

Time was their friend. They were not in any hurry.

Unlike their parents they had no ambitions except to be together.

That Thursday Oonagh and Gabriel walked up to the Grand, hand in hand. Her tea-rose dress and matching jacket gave Oonagh a look of Queen Elizabeth at her most feminine and she felt stylish and elegant. Gabriel looked smart too in his linen jacket and light flannel trousers. The effect was somewhat spoiled by the fact that he wore sandals, and her feet were squashed into Dot's pink satin stilettos which were pinching her mercilessly and had actually drawn blood under her ankle. But Oonagh was not going to let something so trivial spoil lunch at the Grand. She didn't think people would notice her feet. They would be tucked under the table once they sat down.

The building had a pillared porch entwined with wistaria that earlier in the year had hung heavily in misty azure bunches. Young people in tennis whites with cardigans over their shoulders wandered to and from the tennis courts, swinging their raquets.

Oonagh and Gabriel entered the cool foyer. It was carpeted in moss green and there were green brocade seats on the chairs scattered about. Elegant ladies sat there, sipping coffee and aperitifs and flicking through magazines.

Gabriel went to the desk clerk. 'I've booked a table for two for lunch.'

'Yes, sir. Name?'

'O'Shea.'

'Yes, sir. We've been expecting you.'

He flicked his fingers and a waiter in white jacket and black tie materialized beside Gabriel, saying, 'This way, sir,' and guided them towards a large sun-filled room with a huge chandelier and a fountain splashing in the centre.

'It's fabulous!' Oonagh breathed, holding Gabriel's arm tightly.

'I've put you near the window but in the shade,' the waiter informed them, and Gabriel basked in the man's consideration. He knew it was the policy, he knew the waiter would expect to be handsomely tipped for his courtesy and would have forgotten them the next day, but he didn't care, it made him feel grand.

They were handed two huge menus and Gabriel was given a wine list. Oonagh drew in a contented breath. It was exactly how she had imagined it. The view from the window showed the huge headland promontory cut clear against the pale blue sky, dipping into the glittering sea which crashed at its base in a spraying cascade of foam. They could see the dark olive of the Monterey pines, and the red of the rocks, and the white sails of the boats bobbing out on the ocean's heaving bosom. The sun turned the sea gold and the light would have blinded them, only the waiter had placed them at a table where the window frame cut off the sun.

She loved the good glass, the silver with 'Grand Hotel, Dranmore' engraved in curling script on the handles. She loved the single pink rose in the crystal vase in the middle of the table, and she loved the elegance and quiet voices of the other people around them. She loved the long mirrors and the vision of herself in them looking right and suitable in her surroundings. She loved the gilt and the light airiness of the room.

'It's perfect, Gabriel. Perfect,' she whispered, and he smiled at her.

'What will you order, love?' he asked.

'I know just what I want,' she said.

'You can have anything you want, dear,' he said, and groped for her hand across the table. 'You are lovely, Oonagh O'Shea, you know that? There's not a woman smarter than you here today.'

It was not true, she knew, but she loved him saying it, believing it about her. She looked good and right but there were women here, her quick eye told her, who were wearing Christian Dior and Molyneux and Cardin. But she did not envy them. Sitting here with Gabriel in her smart tea-rose frock, seeing the admiration in his eyes, she was perfectly content.

'I want,' she said, without looking at the menu, 'smoked salmon to start, then duck, if they have it, if not black sole on the bone. Then I'm going to have Strawberry Galantine.'

He laughed at her. 'You knew what you wanted. You planned it before you came.'

She nodded. 'Oh, yes.' Then she cocked her head, cheeks flushed with excitement. 'Listen, do you hear?'

The quartet had filed in and taken their places on the small raised dais at the end of the room. They had begun to play 'I'll be your Sweetheart'. Gabriel held her hand tighter. 'Ah, Oonagh, that brings back memories.' A long time ago, a ballroom, pink ribbons in her hair, his Adam's apple wobbling above his black tie, both so very young.

She nodded and whispered:

> ' "I'll be your Sweetheart,
>   If you will be mine,
> All my life I'll be your Valentine … " '

The waiter returned and took their orders. 'And to drink, sir?' he asked.

'Champagne.'

'Oh, my dear, dear Gabriel.'

'Certainly, sir.'

They sat allowing the gently reassuring atmosphere to wash over them, happy and at peace in each other's company. Then the bubble of content was abruptly burst as they heard their names being called out.

'Gabriel! Oonagh! Why on earth didn't you let us know you were lunching here?'

Eddie's presence filled the room, shattering the peace.

He crossed swiftly towards them, waiters parting before him, following him in droves. Oonagh watched his approach with sinking heart. It was over. Their little *tête-à-tête* interrupted. Why couldn't he greet them, then leave them in peace? But that was not Eddie's way.

Oonagh saw Mourna, Colista and Iain, and behind them the tall German in the doorway. Her daughter, she thought, looked very lovely, ethereal in her summer dress of airy voile, her black hair a cloud.

Her feelings deadened. She knew the occasion was spoiled, she knew what was going to happen, and of course it did.

'You *must* join us, I insist. Seamus, cancel that order. Add another two places at our table. Come along, Oonagh, Gabriel.'

They were given no choice. It never dawned on Eddie that they might not want to join his party. As usual he was managing the event and no one ever gainsaid him.

The Bensons' table was situated between open French windows in the centre of the room. The fountain played directly behind them and a cool breeze blew gently from the sea. It was by far the best table.

'Oh, yes. This is *much* better.'

He says it as if he brought us in from Outer Mongolia, Oonagh thought resentfully, and was angry with herself for being angry with him. It was silly to resent someone else's kindness. Eddie couldn't help the way he took over. It was his nature.

'Oh, Mummy, Daddy, it's lovely to see you,' Mourna was saying, hugging them.

How gracious she is, so grown up, my little girl, so sophisticated. Oonagh smiled at her daughter and thought suddenly that it was not Eddie's fault, it was her own. How ungracious to mind being whisked over to this table with her daughter and relations who were eager to see her.

'I hope you didn't mind my staying up here with Auntie

265

Colista and Uncle Eddie?' Mourna was looking at her with sparkling eyes.

'Of course not, pet. Daddy and I were, are, most grateful.'

The waiters had set extra places, one at the head of the table and one at the foot. Eddie put Oonagh at the bottom and Gabriel at the top. So far from each other. Oonagh felt a pain at the smashing of their lovely mood together and tried to quash her sense of grievance. After all, Eddie was just being a good host, and, using common sense, with Mourna here it might have looked funny if they had eaten separately in the same room. I'm a selfish old woman, she thought, and determined to enjoy the meal.

'It's been lovely having Mourna,' Eddie said to Oonagh. 'What a triumph she is. A thing of grace and beauty.'

'Oh, Eddie, she's not a "thing".'

'Er, that was a quotation.'

'She's a person.'

'Yes, of course. Everyone settled? What shall we start with?'

Oonagh beside him said, 'I thought a little smoked salmon … ' She loved the woody fish-taste, the smooth satiny texture, the bite of the lemon juice and the sharpness of the pepper. She had been looking forward to it.

'Oh no, Oonagh, that's pub food. No, let's have *foie gras*. Yes, the *foie gras*, and bring plenty of toast, waiter, please. And to follow, perhaps the poached sea-bass. Yes, bring the whole fish. I'm sure between us we'll manage to polish it off. Fine. Now, wine. Let me see the list.'

Oonagh caught Gabriel's eye. She had a large lump in her throat no matter how hard she tried to control her emotions. Gabriel raised a shoulder imperceptibly and spread his hands in a helpless little gesture. They both hated *foie gras*.

'Now, everyone, I want to hear how the rest of the

family are doing down in Kincora,' Colista pressed, and the conversation moved on. Gabriel gave them the news, omitting the trouble with Ardel. Gabriel and Oonagh were aware that it was not only the fact that beatings up and threatening pursuers were not suitable lunch-table topics that prevented them from disclosing the brutal facts, but a feeling of shame about the situation, a feeling that it somehow reflected badly on them.

'You haven't mentioned Rita? Poor old Rita. How is she?' Colista was asking.

'Oh, Rita is not there,' Oonagh said.

Eddie seemed astounded. 'Not there! Not there? Well, where in God's name is she?'

'Lisdoonvarna.'

'Lisdoonvarna? How did she …? Why?'

'She is going to find a husband. At least, she hopes to.'

Eddie's usual calm deserted him. 'What the hell does she think she's *playing* at?' he said, teeth clenched.

'I don't think she's *playing* at anything. I think she means what she says and has decided to find herself a farmer who has a few bob and marry him.' Oonagh was pleased that Eddie seemed put out by Rita's odd behaviour, and she wished she wasn't. She wanted to be calm again, at peace with Gabriel, not have all these emotions churning up inside her.

'Well, we'll have to get her back before she makes a complete fool of herself,' Eddie said firmly.

'How will you do that, darling?' Colista asked sweetly.

Eddie glanced at her but said nothing. Oonagh turned to her daughter beside her and Mourna smiled at her mother.

'You've got a tan, Mummy. You look lovely.'

'How are you getting along up here, darling? I haven't asked you.'

'Oh, very well. I'm happy. It's lovely here.'

'Yes, it is.'

'I think I want to marry him, Mummy.'

Oonagh had hardly given the Count a thought or a glance. Now she looked at his handsome profile, head bent, listening to Colista.

'Do you love him, darling?' she asked.

'Oh, yes. Not passionately like you read about, but I care for him deeply and I'd be happy to spend the rest of my life with him. He teaches me so much. He knows such a lot. All about music and painting.' She frowned, glancing at her mother from under long lashes. 'Funny though, I get the feeling Uncle Eddie is against the idea. I don't know why, Mummy.'

Oonagh sat, nodding and smiling, trying to be social, knowing only that she wanted to sit with her husband, feel his presence near, and talk to her daughter privately, not here in a crowd. She supposed that meant she was provincial, unsophisticated, a bumpkin not suited to society, ill equipped to belong to the glittering scene, hopelessly middle-class. She didn't taste what she ate. The *foie gras* was heavy, too luscious, and the sea-bass seemed tasteless, and anyhow she only got a tiny bit with a lot of bone. They had sorbet for dessert and the iced sweet hurt Oonagh's teeth as she knew it would. The Strawberry Galantine would have melted in her mouth.

She was relieved when it came to an end and the waiter brought them coffee in the lounge.

'I think you must be wrong about Uncle Eddie, darling,' Oonagh said to Mourna. Then thought. No, it was Colista who had been pushing all the time for the match between Mourna and the Count.

When she had finished her coffee she suddenly felt queasy and, excusing herself, went to the ladies. The powder room was empty and she sat on a vanity stool and dabbed her face with her handkerchief. Mourna, who had followed her mother, came and sat beside her.

'Are you all right, Mummy?' she asked.

268

How can I tell her I feel sick and I'm pregnant? Oonagh thought. Oh Lord, what am I going to do? I'm not myself today.

'Yes, dear,' she said firmly. No need to alarm Mourna, who was so kind and considerate. 'It's nice to see you here. See you happy.'

'What is it, Mummy? There's something wrong, I always know.'

To her horror Oonagh felt tears prick her eyes. 'Oh, darling, I feel so stupid.'

'Come on, Mummy, tell me. You must or I'll worry. What's wrong?'

'I'm pregnant, darling.'

'Is that all?' Mourna laughed. 'Oh, Mam. I thought something *awful* had happened. You had me worried.'

Oonagh instantly felt better. 'Your father doesn't know. I've told no one. Only I don't know how we're going to manage with another mouth to feed. Things are stretched at the moment as it is.'

Mourna put her arm protectively around her mother's shoulders.

'Don't worry, pet,' she said soothingly. 'You'll be all right. Kurt and I will help. You'll see.'

'Oh no, darling, I wouldn't expect that.'

'It's not a matter of expect, Mummy, it's a matter of what I want.'

'Anyhow, your father is bound to get Mr McLaglan's job. With Uncle Eddie behind him, he can't fail. And it can't be long now before he retires, poor Mr McLaglan. He tilts over around four o'clock every evening, Gabriel says, and begins to doze off at a sort of Pisa angle. He really can't last much longer.' Oonagh giggled and Mourna laughed.

'Oh, darling, don't worry. Everything will come out right, you'll see.'

'Don't let on to your father about me. I'd like to tell him myself.'

269

'Course not, Mummy.' Mourna leaned over and kissed her. When they emerged moments later, Colista beckoned from the lounge where Kurt waited with her.

' 'Bye, darling.' Oonagh kissed her daughter. 'And, thanks.'

' 'Bye, Mummy.'

They took their leave, thanking Eddie for lunch and departing the hotel with relief not regret.

Gabriel held Oonagh's hand as they walked away from the Grand. 'I saw the bill, Oonagh,' he said in awe-struck tones, 'Eddie turned it over and signed it. It came to more'n a week's wages and he was tipping here, there and everywhere. Janey Mac, I wonder what it must be like to be able to do that.'

'Well, I'd rather be us,' Oonagh said a little tremulously.

A heat-haze cloaked the sea and shimmered over the land. Annoyed with himself for not having somehow stood his ground and remained at their little table for two, Gabriel did not at first notice that she was crying. Then to his horror he felt the trembling in her hand and arm, and looking at her saw huge tears pour down her face.

'Darlin', don't!' he pleaded, totally unmanned. It destroyed him when she cried, and she never broke down in this way, not in public. 'Darling, don't, please.'

'I know now how Dot and Ben felt,' she whispered. 'There's something there makes me feel awful.'

'Well,' he tried to comfort her, 'aren't you better off down in Kincora without someone hoverin' at your elbow when you take a forkful or blow your nose?'

They walked along the headland, the sun blinding them. Oonagh pressed his hand. After a while she said softly, so he could hardly hear, 'It's all right. It's just that I … I'd hoped … '

'I know,' he replied. 'But you've got to think, Oonagh, how trivial it is compared to what we've got. It's not important really.'

'I feel I've behaved like a baby, like Maggie, not getting her own way.'

'Tell you what, when we get back to Dublin we'll have a grand lunch or dinner in the Gresham.'

'It wouldn't be the same,' she said. How to explain? How to explain to him, or anyone, her feelings? How to describe the satisfaction of leaving their guesthouse where they were staying on holiday, where she did not work, had no responsibilities, and dressed in her best, after taking as long as she liked to prepare, sauntering up the hill to the opulence of the Grand, to eat with her husband *tête-à-tête*, relaxed, away from it all, in the euphoric world of holiday? It would not be the same thing at all at home, dressing up in Griffith Avenue, beset on all sides with the evidence of pending chores, with demands for fresh shirts, ironed blouses; then getting a bus to the Gresham, still worrying about the family – their wants, their needs – preoccupied with the routine and discipline of home, in a hurry to get back. Not the same at all. Still, she reflected, it was not fair to make poor Gabriel pay for Eddie's high-handed lack of sensitivity.

Was it only lack of sensitivity? she wondered. His desire to make others bend to his will? She looked at her husband, saw the concern on his face.

'You are right, Gabriel,' she whispered. 'We *are* lucky. And it is not important.' Wanting now more than anything to alleviate his distress at her disappointment. 'We have so much more than they do. We have our children. Each other. We are lucky, Gabriel.' Smiling at her own words, knowing them to be true.

'Yes,' he said, 'but it's more than that. There's something – not quite right about that crowd up there.' He turned to her, 'I'm not very good at explaining.'

'I know what you mean, love.' She visualized Eddie's feverish excitement, his will to dominate everyone, even the waiters. Her sister's watchful eyes following him everywhere.

271

'If I had my way,' Gabriel said, 'I'd bring Mourna down from there now. Take her to Kincora and her own room there at once. Into the real world, the world where she belongs.'

Oonagh thought of Mourna's face, sweet and young and hopeful. 'She said she loves him, Gabriel.'

'She can love him from Kincora as easily as from the Grand.'

'Yes, but ... ' There was a brief struggle in Oonagh's breast. Ambition won. 'I'm sure she's all right. She's a sensible girl.'

Gabriel nodded. 'Yes, in spite of her beauty, she's got a sensible head on her shoulders. She'll be all right, love. I think we're both being over-sensitive today. Let's go home now. Back to Kincora.' And they walked, hand in hand, down the hill.

Chapter Thirty-Nine

Later that afternoon Rita returned looking woebegone. For one moment Oonagh thought that Eddie had somehow kidnapped her from Lisdoonvarna and whisked her back to Dranmore, but she realized this was not so.

Rita had walked from the station and her ankles were swollen, her face wet with perspiration. She leaned over the parapet and yelled down to the families on the beach. 'I'm back!'

Dot and Ben waved. They had forgotten she had gone and why. The children went on playing. Only Oonagh got up, albeit reluctantly, and pulling on her skirt over her

272

rucked bathing suit, said to Gabriel as she picked up her towel, 'I'd better pop up, see how she is. Although I think I've had about as much as I can handle for one day.'

'Would you like me to go?' Gabriel asked from under the straw hat he had over his face.

'No, love, what would you say to her? No, she'll want to tell a woman whatever her news is, though it's not good by the look of her.'

Gabriel took the hat off. 'She looks terrible,' he said, waving up at Rita.

'Your chest's getting red. Turn over, love. And can you keep your eye on Dot's children?'

'But she's here,' he replied, squinting, the sun in his eyes.

'Well, but *she* doesn't. I always feel we should.'

'All right, but I don't see why.'

'It'd make *me* feel easier,' Oonagh said firmly. 'Wish me luck!' she said, and prepared to climb back up to the house.

Rita had bumped straight into Ardel in her room.

'I need privacy, Ardel,' she was saying when Oonagh came in. Her mouth was tight, her voice edgy. 'I want you out *now*, repeat *now*. Jasus, my bed's a mess.' She saw Oonagh. 'Can you get your son outa here pronto? All I want, Oonagh, is to have a rest in my fresh bed. Is that too much to ask? I've been looking forward to it all the way on that terrible train journey. And walking from the station here, all the way, I've been saying to myself, as soon as I reach Kincora I'll collapse into the fresh sheets and loose consciousness. And what do I find? Him! In my bed which is messed-up, cigarette ash everywhere. A pig-sty.'

'Ardel, get up and go to our room, Daddy's and mine. You can stay there for the present till we discuss it. Rita, I'll have this fixed up in no time. Have a bath, love. Use my Coty salts. They're L'Aimant. I can't afford the perfume but I can afford the salts. Indulge yourself. Go on. And when you come back it will all be ready for you.'

'Oh, all right. Where are the children?'

'They're out on the boat with Laughlin, Emer and Roac. They're fine.'

'Thank you, Oonagh. I'm sorry, I'm … '

'Off you go now.'

Oonagh was quite happy in her task. She would worry about Gabriel and herself and where they'd sleep later on. After all, it was their problem. Ardel was their son.

She aired the room, trying to rid it of the heavy smell of tobacco. As she worked, the window open wide, listening to the raucous calls of the seagulls and the shouts of the children below, she thought she saw someone moving in the undergrowth where the tall ferns waved and the blackberries grew.

She walked to the window, shaking out a sheet, crisp and fresh from the laundry, looked out and decided she'd imagined it. She'd tell Gabriel though. Just in case. Get the men to beat the bushes tonight before they went to the pub and perhaps afterwards as well.

When, half an hour later, Rita returned, she found her room spotless and sweet-smelling. With a huge sigh of relief she took off her dressing-gown and crawled between the sheets, laying her head against the plumped up pillows.

'Well,' Oonagh said, sitting on the edge of the bed, 'tell me about it or I'll burst.'

'Thank you, Oonagh. This is bliss.'

'Well, an' what happened?' Oonagh couldn't conceal her curiosity.

'It was terrible, Oonagh. Worse than anything you could imagine. Nothing you said could have prepared me for it. And, I may say, you and Gabriel were right.'

'Tell me about it,' Oonagh repeated.

Rita's face looked curiously young without make-up, but she looked very weary. She turned and propped herself up on her elbow, looking levelly at her sister.

'First, Oonagh, I've got something to tell you. Something to confess.'

'Sure, I know, Rita. I know.' It was about the china Rita had stolen. Oonagh knew that was what her sister was referring to.

'No. Listen, Oonagh, I've got to say it or I'll do it again, telling myself you won't notice.' She sucked in her breath and closed her eyes. 'I took your Dresden figurine.' She said it bluntly, then opened her eyes and Oonagh saw they were full of tears.

'Sure, I knew you wouldn't do it, Rita, unless you had to,' Oonagh said. She had tied a scarf around her hair to keep it tidy while she cleaned the room. She pulled it off now.

'Oh, I'm so sorry, Oonagh. I'm so sorry. I even persuaded myself that you wouldn't notice.'

'Yerra, don't fret yourself,' Oonagh said gruffly. 'It's all forgotten.'

'I'm such a failure, Oonagh.'

' 'Twasn't your fault! How can you blame yourself, pet? You did your best.' Then, looking at her sister, she asked, 'What was it like, Lisdoonvarna?'

'Gross! It was gross, Oonagh. I don't know what possessed me. They came out of the hills these ... these Neanderthal men, smelling of stale sweat and onions, dirty socks and bad teeth. There wasn't one of them had a full set! Of teeth, I mean. God, Oonagh, an' you saw them, you wouldn't believe! And the worst part, they were choosy! Thought they were God's gift! Thought they were Errol Flynn and Cary Grant combined. Janey, Oonagh, most of them had beer bellies on them make the Michelin Man jealous.'

Oonagh had begun to laugh. 'What'd you do?'

'Mingled, Oonagh, mingled. On parade. On show. Up for auction. And guess what? I got rejected! They were looking for young meat.' Rita began to laugh too, joining her sister's giggles, 'This guy, fat as Falstaff and ripe as rotten fruit, smelling to high heaven, well, he sidles up to me in the bar and says, whispers in my ear ... ' She could hardly speak for laughter now, Oonagh guffawing and wiping her eyes. 'Whispers, "Let's give it a try, gorgeous, see if we suit?" Can you believe it? He meant to go to bed together. When I looked at him he rolled his eyes up to indicate the bedrooms, and all I could see were the whites! I ran. I got out of there fast as I could.' They laughed some more and then their laughter died naturally and they sat in silence awhile.

'I wanted to lay down a burden, Oonagh. I didn't realize that to do that is to die.' Rita sighed. 'Somehow we'll all survive. I'll pay my debts. I'm not sure how, but I will. Now, let me sleep. I feel as if I've been trounced and I'm knackered. I need rest.'

She slid down into the bed, sighing contentedly, and was asleep almost instantly. Oonagh tiptoed out, leaving her alone.

Chapter Forty

Emer had borrowed the shoes from Dot. They fitted her perfectly. Dot had small feet, an attribute she was proud of, and whilst Oonagh had had to squash size fives into four-and-a-half, they were just right on Emer.

Having padded one of Mourna's bras (stolen when packing: 'I can say it got into my case by accident,' she told Brigid) and wearing a dress Briana had said was too sexy for her ('Mrs Taylor has cut it too *low*, Mam, I don't want to look like a tart!'), Emer slipped out the back way and tiptoed past her parents' bedroom. She saw Ardel staring out. He gave her a fright. Still, she thought, he has a view of the sea now. It was only fair in Emer's estimation as he had to sit in the room all day looking out, whilst Mam and Da were only there in the dark.

She left the house and made her way towards the tennis club that overlooked the club house, over the courts and out around the harbour. Brigid was sitting in the hedgerow waiting for her. She had been pulling at the cow parsley which grew there thickly. Emer put out her hand and pulled her up.

'I've snagged my dress on the blackberry bushes,' Brigid complained. 'Mam'll *kill* me. It's my only good one.'

Emer had noticed her cousin's lack of wardrobe and pitied poor Brigid who didn't seem to mind too much. All she cared about was what her mam thought.

'She's back without a man anyhow,' Brigid said. 'Me mam.'

Emer said nothing. There was nothing suitable to say. The sea was very still today, a calm bright blue satin stretch with ships in the distance, motionless, like a picture.

Emer felt sorry for Brigid. She couldn't imagine what it would be like if Da wasn't there; if he was dead, a cold headstone visited once a year. She couldn't imagine how it would be if Mam went off to Lisdoonvarna to get a man, and couldn't imagine what it would be like if she came back without one. No one knew how to behave around Auntie Rita. Being poor was very embarrassing.

'Des is mortified,' Brigid said, brushing down her skirt. 'He's scratching all the time. Seems to be consumed by itch. Means he's worried. But we'll survive,' she said, echoing her mother.

'Now, listen,' Emer said briskly to her cousin, 'I'm eighteen, okay? I look it in this make-up. And you're my little sister.'

Brigid nodded, glancing sideways at Emer. She had been too busy thinking about her mother's return really to

277

look at her cousin. 'You'd never know,' she breathed now. 'You'd never think you was only fifteen.'

Emer's short red hair gleamed in the sun and the padding had pushed out her dress in a very Lana Turner way that was sexy. The dress itself, bright red cotton with white wavy braid trim, hugged her waist and revealed her long legs and slim ankles in the stiletto heels. She had left her pale gold skin free of foundation and slashed on loads of Pillarbox Red lipstick on her wide and generous mouth and glued up her eyelashes with four coats of black mascara. The result was, in Brigid's estimation, spectacular, and Emer had rounded the whole effect off with a Margaret Lockwood mole (a dot with a black pencil) high up on her cheek-bone. She looked fabulous, just like Rita Hayworth, and Brigid had every confidence that no one would query her cousin's age.

Entering the competition from Dublin, sending in her form, Emer lied about her age. She had received a note in return asking her to register in person in Dranmore by the ninth of August at the Dranmore Tennis Club and that was what she was doing now.

Dranmore Tennis Club consisted of six hard tennis courts, two lawn courts and a Nissen building, one-storey, with a wooden floor and a long chrome bar. The room was meant for the dances that were held nightly during the summer. The music was loud, and the chairs and tables looked as if they'd been borrowed from the local school (which indeed they had, it being closed for the summer vacation), and the place was always packed. No one knew, exactly, why it was so popular but people crowded in in droves, mainly visitors to Dranmore.

There was a knees-up night when they also had a community sing-along, a firm favourite with the over-fifties. The band played, 'A Long Way to Tipperary', 'Danny Boy' and 'The Mountains of Mourne'. There was a Latin American night when everyone ended up doing the

Conga in a long snaking line around the harbour, up and down the pier on to the Dranmore Road, and around and back to the club. There was a teenage evening, 'Youngsters Wednesday' it was called, when the roof was raised with bee-bop and jive and the older folk shook their heads and said youngsters were going to the dogs. There was a 'Romantic Night' when they played Strauss Waltzes and music from light Viennese Operettas. They had raffles and competitions, one of which was the Miss Dranmore Beauty Queen, the most beautiful bathing belle for that year. Emer wanted the title so badly that she could hardly sleep nights thinking about it. It was to be the first step on her carefully planned road to stardom.

They came in out of the dazzling sunlight to the dark and shadowy interior of the club. Emer blinked and tried to adjust her vision but she couldn't see anyone.

'Can I help you, little ladies?' a male voice inquired, and someone emerged out of the gloom.

The man was large and jovial. He wore glasses that were almost opaque and he kept cracking the most terrible jokes. 'Naw then! Naw then! I can see yer here, as the actress said to the Bishop. No doubt about it, but yer a gorgeous piece. So don't tell me, let me guess, yer here for the Beauty Contest?'

Emer had felt sick with apprehension and it took her a moment to absorb the fact that the jolly man had immediately twigged her purpose and saw nothing odd about her entering the contest. The fact astounded her. She had been prepared to wheedle and beg, to plead if necessary. But it had not been necessary and she could not believe her luck.

'Yes,' she replied, confidence growing, 'I registered last month from Dublin. You'll have my name there. Emer O'Shea. Over eighteen.'

The man nodded appreciatively. 'Yeah, I can see that. I got eyes, haven't I?'

He looked down the list, then gave it a triumphant bang with his finger. 'Yeah, it's here, Emer O'Shea. Got it in one, as the actress said to the Bishop.'

'What do I do next?' she asked.

'Let me see, tick you off my list, as the … '

'Actress said to the Bishop,' Brigid finished.

'Yeah, let's see. Just show up here Saturday, bring your bathing suit, which you'll be wearing. The changing facilities are not very good, I warn ye. The ladies loo is a nightmare so I'd wear the swimsuit under a coat. Be on the safe side. If in doubt ask for me. Bob O'Brien's the appendage, if yer interested.'

'No, Mr O'Brien, but thank you. What time Saturday?'

'Oh, we start the ball rolling at nine p.m. so if yer here at eight – give you loads of time.'

'Thank you, Mr O'Brien.'

'Bob. Fancy a beer?'

'Only if I win Saturday.'

'Well now, I've no influence there unfortunately. My role is hosting the show. If I had any pull you'd be my choice.' He winked at her. 'Then again, yer first to register.'

He put his hand under his floral shirt and scratched his belly. 'Is there a lot of competition, Mr O'Brien?' Emer asked.

'Well now, there is an' there isn't, if you see what I mean.'

Emer shook her head. 'No, I don't.'

'Well, we'll have a full complement. Twenty girls, no more, no less. Sometimes the talent is cream of the milk, others it's a farce, so it is. Depends.'

'Well, thank you, Mr O'Brien.'

'I told ye – Bob. See ye later, alligator.'

'In a while, crocodile,' Brigid quipped back.

'Come back soon, as the actress said to the Bishop,' he called after them.

They fell out into the sunlight stupefied, collapsing in helpless mirth at the side of the road.

Chapter Forty-One

Emmett had struck up a friendship with the old parish priest in St Brendan's on the hill. The old man was white-haired with a face coloured by the winds above Dranmore and days spent in his little boat – 'Catching the sweet fish the Lord provided for the Presbytery table', in his words.

The bell tolled twice a day. At seven-thirty a.m. when the sky was pearl grey and the dew still fresh on the grass and the sun still slowly rising, a golden streak splashed across the water. It tolled then for eight o'clock Mass.

Then it tolled once more at five-thirty p.m. for the six o'clock service when the children, hot and cranky after a long day on the beach, were coming up for tea and the boats were beginning to return to the harbour, and the sun, still high, shimmered on the sea, turning it into a shining sheet of bronze silk.

Emmett went to both services. The old priest talked to the boy, for such behaviour was unusual to say the least. He listened to Emmett, who opened up under his silence, confiding his plans and hopes and dreams.

'I want to be a missionary, Father. Go to Africa. Convert little black babies. The others laugh at me, Father, when I tell them. They make fun of me. Not me mam or Mourna or Granny O'Shea, but the rest of them do.'

'Ye have a large family?'

'Very large. Me Uncle Tom is always smirking at me when I tell him my ambition is to be a priest. They think I'm a goodie-goodie.'

'And are you?'

The boy blinked nervously and shook his head.

'I don't think so. I try to be good, of course. I try very hard so's I can be a priest.'

'How do you try to be good?'

'Keeping the Commandments. Doing what God told me to do.'

'And do you succeed?'

Emmett nodded, 'Oh, yés, I do. I almost never have much to tell in confession.'

'I see.'

'Not like Uncle Joe.'

'Who is Uncle Joe?'

'He's a drunk. Commits the sin of drunkenness all the time. Never stops. He's disgusting.'

'I see.' The priest cleared his throat and sighed. 'Ye don't *like* people, do ye?' the old man asked, his voice scratchy from the foul pipe he sucked. 'Ye better give up the idea of priesthood with these thoughts in yer head, boy. Ye can't be judgemental. Ye have to love them as they are. Sure, they're shit, but the Lord himself on earth chose the dregs rather than the rich and beautiful, didn't He? If He was here now, 'tisn't at the Grand He'd be, but down with the crowd on the lower beach.' He peered out from under his thick white eyebrows at Emmett. 'Not where yer mammy is, I bet.'

The old man scratched his head while Emmett sat and stared at him with sinking heart. He had known that there was something wrong with his feelings and his thoughts. When he was thinking it never seemed to him to be worshipful and elevating as the thoughts of St Thomas Aquinas, according to the Christian Brothers. Rather he arranged ideas around in his head, and most of these ideas were about how he would like people to change. The old priest in Dranmore said he must love them as they were.

'Ye better give up the idea of priesthood if ye go on thinkin' like that! Those little blacks ye want to convert, now do ye suppose they're saints? Do'ye suppose they'll raise shining, honest faces to ye? Pure as the driven snow? Never be plagued or enchanted by the dirtiest or most exciting thoughts, depending on which side ye're on? De'ye suppose they don't fornicate in Africa? Or cheat? Or steal? Or murder? O'course they do, an' they'll break yer heart and yer faith if ye don't love them *because* of it, not in spite of it. Understand? Otherwise, Emmett, me boyo, it's an unrealistic dream ye have an' ye'd best give it up.' His voice was testy.

'What must I do, Father?'

'Love God's children, Emmett. Love them as they are.'

'How can I do that, Father?'

'Do ye love the Lord yer God?'

'Oh, yes, Father.' The old priest was surprised by the fervour in the boy's voice. He really did love the Lord his God.

'Well then, see the face of God in all mankind. Without exception.'

That meant Uncle Joe, Emmett thought. Uncle Joe, drunk and disgusting. 'I'll try, Father. I'll try.'

'Then go in peace, boy.'

Chapter Forty-Two

The men sat in Drat Regan's talking to Barney Boland and savouring a pint. Joe had passed out in the snug and Gabriel had finished telling them about Mourna's love affair with the Count.

'Bejasus, a German! I don't know! I'm not at all sure about it, Gabriel,' Tom said doubtfully.

'Well, *you're* not marrying him,' Gabriel said with asperity.

'You've hardly laid eyes on the man. What do you know about him anyhow?'

'Nothing. Nothing. I just thought ... a German!'

'It's him being a Count that worries me,' Gabriel said. 'I'm not at all sure I'll enjoy having one of them in the family.'

Barney laughed. 'Will ye listen to yerselves?' He boomed his big belly laugh. 'By "one of them" you separate him from yourself. Aren't all men the same, for God's sake? We're all flesh an' blood. We bleed, we get colds, we get sick, we laugh, we fall in love. We're all the same underneath, God's sake.'

That helped Gabriel. 'The man's right,' he said. 'Provincial, we sound. Insular.'

'Have you ever tasted anything so perfect as a plum?' Barney asked out of the blue, smacking his lips. 'A ripe purple plum? I had one today, an' I'll tell you, boys, I near died of joy.'

'Will ye listen to the man? It doesn't take much!'

'It's a miracle, so it is. The mouthwatering flesh, soft and sweet, the skin a mite bitter but flavourful. Divine!'

'You're daft, man. Who the hell cares about plums?' Tom cried.

'Ah, but I do. They're perfection. It gets me every time.'

'Another drop of the weavel juice. A short this time, I think.'

'Yer friend ever in his right mind?' a local asked, coming out of the snug where Joe had lain his head on the table in the slops of beer.

'Ah sure, God love him, he's three sheets,' Barney said.

'Clutters up our pub like garbage,' a red-faced individual announced.

'Ah, now, lave him be. Sure, he's harming no one.'

'Michael Morgan, how many times have I given you the shoulder an' you not much better than he is now?' Barney sounded indignant, 'Ye know what they say: God loves fools and drunks. Won't do to upset yer neighbour, now will it?'

Barney winked at the man and turned back to the others. Behind the bar miniature bottles of Drambuie, Grand Marnier, Paddy, Jameson's, Cork Gin and Teacher's stood in little rows, neat as pins and never opened. Barney said there wasn't a decent mouthful in any of them. The Smithwick's and Guinness handles were wet with foam and constant use. There was a sign over the bar that said, 'God created Whiskey to keep the Irish from Ruling the World!'

'Sure aren't we more intelligent than any other nation in the world, Gabriel? Let's drink to Erin,' he cried, raising his glass.

'Sure. *Erin go Bragh!*'

'Did ye know,' Tom said, licking his lips free of foam then tossing off a short, 'did ye know that Hadji Bey Turkish Delight is made in Cork? Eh? Did ye know that?'

The men fell about laughing and thumping the table with fists at the humour of it.

285

' 'Tis true,' Tom cried. ' 'Tis true.'

Then Barney told them about America, about fishing there. 'Everything's so big,' he said. 'There's marlin off the coast of Florida big as whales. Out there in a catamaran, one of those on the end of your line, ye feel like the English king!'

'G'w'an!'

'No, 'tis true. Catching marlin is better than most anything.'

'Better than salmon?' Gabriel asked. There was nothing he liked better than a bit of fly-fishing and sport with a fine leaping salmon.

'Ah, now, that's another thing entirely. Dunno I wouldn't rate that higher even!' Barney said with relish. The trouble with Barney, he seemed to enjoy most things he did.

'Why don't ye stay there, Barney?' Tom asked, and Barney squinted up at him.

'Ireland has a tenacious umbilical cord, Tom,' he said. 'Ah, no. When all's said and done ye can't beat Ireland. Ah, no. I'll eventually settle down here and get myself a nice woman. Eventually. Eventually.'

'What sort of woman you lookin' for?' Ben glanced at Gabriel, the same thought in both their minds.

Barney thought, rubbed his chin, took a draught and said, 'It's easier for me to tell you what I *don't* want. I don't want some young whippersnapper, no matter how curvaceous, who'll keep me up all night dancin' in the tennis club, tryin' to teach me be-bop and jive. No, sir. I *don't* want a razzle-dazzler who'd hate Dranmore an' want me to move to the city an' paint the town red. I *don't* want a sex-pot who'll demand her conjugal rights every blessed night an' exhaust me. I'm a man who enjoys all the pleasures life has to offer, but at my age in moderation. Everything in moderation.'

Ben blushed and Tom looked incredulous but Gabriel nodded his head.

'I don't want to start a family. I don't like babies. Kids are okay, but I draw the line at babies. Squalling little things. I'm too set in my ways. I need a nice, intelligent and pretty, mature woman with a sense of humour who'd fit in with my life as it is.'

'God'n you'll be lucky!' Tom said. 'I would have thought, though, you'd fancy a bit of firm young flesh?'

'We're not all like you, Tom,' Ben said slyly, and Tom glared at him but didn't reply.

Barney shook his head emphatically. 'No,' he said. 'I would not.'

'Well then, I might have an idea,' Ben said.

'Now, none of that. Not on your Nellie. I'll have no matchmaking here, thank you. Better men than you have tried and failed. As I say, I'll do it in my own good time. In my own good time. Now drink up, lads, it's time for another.'

Chapter Forty-Three

They were sitting in the lounge in the afternoon; Kurt, Mourna and Colista. All day the sun had shone and they had remained in the shade, under the trees, sipping lemonade and fanning themselves, unlike the families cavorting joyously like seals on the beach below. Kurt and Mourna had played mixed doubles against Colista and Eddie. Eddie was irritated that they could not find Iain. Colista complained that she hardly ever saw her son.

'I think he is being excessively silly,' Eddie said. 'We pay all this money to provide a salubrious background and he chooses instead to hang around with the rabble down on the beach.'

Mourna blushed. She hated conflict and she was their guest. Kurt saw her predicament.

'I don't think they are, as you say, rabble,' he remarked mildly. 'And the young always like to be one of a crowd. Perhaps Iain finds us stuffy.'

Eddie took himself off grouchily and Kurt and the two women went into the lounge.

'There are no children up here,' Mourna said, thinking about Kurt's remark.

'No. Children are frowned on at the Grand, unless they're exceptionally well behaved.' Colista pursed her red lips, sought a waiter's attention and ordered tea.

'Maggie Moran wouldn't fit in then,' Mourna laughed, and Colista shuddered delicately.

'God forbid.' She opened her bag. 'Damn, I've left my cigarettes up in my room.'

'Permit me. I'll get them for you.' Kurt rose with his usual courtesy.

'I think Eddie's in the room. He'll find them for you.'

The two women watched as he crossed the lounge. The quartet were playing 'You Were Meant for Me', and there was a steady buzz of conversation and the clink of china and cutlery as guests nibbled on sandwiches and sipped tea.

'You like him?' Colista took a gold cigarette-case from her bag and chose one.

'You had them all the … ' Mourna spluttered. Her aunt laughed. She lit the cigarette with a neat little gold lighter.

'You're naïve, Mourna,' she laughed softly. 'I wanted a word with you. Whatever you do, whatever they tell you, I *don't* want you to marry Iain.' She plucked at the padded seat, puffing on the cigarette. She seemed nervous, Mourna thought, but said nothing.

'You like Kurt?'

'Yes, Auntie Colista. Very much.'

'Good, Mourna. Very good.' Colista looked relieved. She stared out into the middle distance where an old gentleman in a Panama hat, flannels, a dark blue shirt with a spotted scarf knotted at his throat, and a navy blazer, was fussing about the sun coming in through the window he was sitting at. An attentive waiter in a white jacket drew the rose pink curtain and the man hit him on the thigh with his stick.

'Damn you, move the bloody *chair*, man. Turn it *around*, you fool,' he commanded. The waiter remained unperturbed. At least, if he was upset he didn't show it.

'People conceal things,' Colista said. 'We are all actors.' She looked at Mourna. 'Colonel Renshaw,' she said, nodding towards the irate old man. 'If the sun wasn't blazing he'd blame the staff here for the bad weather. Now, because it's shining on him, he's angry with them. It's old age,' she sighed. 'Never a tranquil time, no matter what they say.' She leaned forward. 'Well, dear, has he asked you? Can we make the announcement soon?'

'Oh, well, there's no hurry, Auntie Colista, is there? I mean … '

'Yes, there is, if only you knew … Oh, child, I'm trying to save us all from disaster.'

Mourna looked at her in astonishment. Her aunt's face was pale. She looked abstracted.

'What do you mean, Auntie?' Mourna was confused. 'I don't understand.'

'How would you? How could you? Oh, don't expect an explanation, I'm not sure I even understand myself. I may be wrong … '

'About what, Auntie?'

'About … ' She caught sight of Eddie and Kurt getting out of the lift in the foyer and stubbed out her cigarette, popped the gold case and lighter into her bag and snapped it shut, smoothed her skirt and patted her hair,

289

'I'd be happy if you and Kurt announced your engagement here, Mourna. When you make up your mind, of course. But strike while the iron is hot.' She leaned over towards her niece so that their faces almost touched. 'I would love to give a surprise party for you. Only don't tell Eddie. It will be our little secret.' She patted Mourna's hand. 'Has he proposed to you yet?'

Mourna nodded and a look of relief crossed Colista's face. 'Well then, if you like him … '

'Love?' Mourna interpolated.

'That will come later,' Colista said briskly. 'You know how modern I am, Mourna, but the old-fashioned way is best. You marry someone because they are your own class, because they fit in, because you have to live their life-style. If you are comfortable together then all will be well. Take my word for it.'

Mourna thought of her mother and father. She looked at Kurt crossing the lounge. So tall, so handsome, so distinguished. Yes, she could happily spend the rest of her life with him. She had gone over it a million times and the answer always came out the same. But she would not be rushed, no matter how Auntie Colista tried to hurry her. She wondered why her aunt was so anxious for her to commit herself. She supposed the Count was a spectacular catch and Auntie Colista was afraid that if she left her decision until they got back to Dublin she might lose him to another. Well, it was better that happened before rather than after.

Mourna was predisposed to do what was expected of her. She wanted to please. But there was a core of wisdom in her that would never allow her to marry a man she did not deeply care for and she wanted to be sure.

She was not 'in love' in the popular interpretation of the emotion. She had never felt that hectic tidal-wave she had so often read about. Kurt did not make her heart beat fast, did not give her the urge to burst into poetry or song, and as for dying without him, that was not how she felt at all. What she felt was, happiness to be with him, peace in his company and harmony with him. She liked him, admired him and felt safe with him. He could give her the things she yearned for, the security she needed, both emotional and financial, for Mourna thought the latter was important. She liked his physical appearance and she felt a warm glow when he kissed her.

All her life she had needed order. She wanted – no, it was essential – that she have a gracious background, the availability of comfort and amenities that some struggling young professional or business man could not possibly provide.

If she married Kurt she would have all the things she most needed. It was nice to know everyone else would be pleased as well. She bit her lip in concentration, looked up and saw him smiling at her. His smile was reassuring and loving and he took her hand in his. She smiled back at him, making up her mind.

She decided she'd tell Kurt tonight that she would marry him. They could announce their engagement on their last Saturday when her father and mother were there. How pleased her mother would be. Her father would have his doubts but they would soon be allayed and he would be happy to see his beloved Mourna cossetted in luxury. Kurt would help the family too. She would, she realized, prefer that her mother and father had some much-needed backing from her husband than from Uncle Eddie. She smiled calmly to herself. Oh, the bliss of everything decided, taken care of. She would look forward to her future with serenity and joy.

Only thing, her Uncle Eddie would not be pleased. He wanted her to marry Iain. Well, Uncle Eddie would for once in his life not have his own way. She could not rid herself of a niggly little feeling that there was something going on that eluded her, that she did not understand.

Some game unfamiliar to her that people were playing in the Grand that summer in Dranmore.

Chapter Forty-Four

On the Friday Banan arrived. Molly went to the station in the car to collect him. Ardel felt sick.

Banan came to see him almost as soon as he dropped his cases in his room.

'Where's the money?'

'That's long gone.' Ardel tried to sound nonchalant.

The room was full of cigarette smoke. Ardel spent days and nights smoking endlessly. Roac said going in there was like going down a mine and Ardel asked him how'd he know what a mine was like.

Banan's eyes glittered. 'You'll pay it back,' he said. 'You'll have to.'

'How?' Ardel asked helplessly.

'You're a shit, Ardel O'Shea, an eejit, a fuckin' eejit!' Banan shouted in exasperation. 'I warned you. I told you not to be foolish, not to get any ideas. I *told* you.'

'Well, an what can I do now? It's all gone.'

'Ye'll get it or they'll kill ye.'

'Ah, don't be daft, Banan. Sure, where'll I get it from?'

But he knew his cousin wasn't joking.

'It wasn't *my* money,' Banan said. 'It was theirs.' He turned on Ardel savagely. 'I warned you.'

'Shut up in there,' Emer yelled. 'Yer disturbin' me.'

Banan looked in the direction the voice had come from. He stared at the wall, a pulse beating in his forehead.

'This is a farce!' he hissed. 'A fuckin' farce.'

'Can't they let me pay it off gradually?' Ardel suggested.

'Are you mad? They're *here*, man, here. It's only me's restraining them.'

'Well, you didn't do a great job there,' Ardel said sarcastically. 'Beat me up, they did, your gorillas. Think they'd be satisfied, wouldn't you – nearly killing me?'

'Well, they won't be satisfied until they get their money,' Banan said decisively. 'So do something about it. I don't know how much longer I can hold them.'

Banan left. He was in a foul mood and kept away from the others. He had lost face. His relation had messed up and respect had gone. He was treated now with suspicion, his position suddenly shaky.

He was worried, nervous, because they gave him the impression that he was blamed too, that in some way he was accountable for his cousin's irresponsibility.

He had persuaded them that Ardel had not informed on Billy Macken and they had believed him because the police said so too. He told them that there had not been time. Ardel had not left the van once he had picked up the fugitive. Ardel didn't know who or what was in the van when he drove away from the men in Drimnagh. He had had neither the knowledge nor the opportunity to inform.

' 'Tis well for you, Banan O'Rourke, that you're the son of Sean O'Rourke and therefore unassailable,' they told him, just as if he were some tuppeny-halfpenny novice and under suspicion. 'But if we find you've sullied your dead father's name, you'll be for the high jump.' When he'd reached the door they'd called after him, 'Get the money.'

He'd no way of doing that unless he went to his step-father and he'd die before he'd do that. He wouldn't ask Tom Moran for sixpence never mind the money owing; they could garotte him, disembowel him, shoot him. He'd rather that than be under an obligation to such a man.

Ardel would have to get it. It was his debt to pay, his burden. Banan wandered about outside Kincora, an alien, uncomfortable in strange surroundings, and turned up his jacket collar from habit even though the sun was scorching and Mrs Flanagan's geraniums drooped in the heat.

Emer had heard the whole conversation between Banan and Ardel. She had come up to the house to get a sun-dress because the front of her chest had turned a little pink, according to Brigid, and she did not want to get burned before the competition.

'Sure, who minds a bit of sunburn?' Uncle Tom had said. 'Isn't it what a holiday is for? Oh, yer conceit will be yer downfall, Emer O'Shea.'

'An' mebbe it'll be her victory, Tom Moran,' Granny O'Shea retorted. She enjoyed scoring off Tom and she held court on the beach under a huge striped umbrella in an ancient bathing suit that covered her old bones, rebuking when necessary as befit her age and position.

Emer went into Ardel's room now without knocking.

'Get out, Emer. I want to be alone,' he said ungraciously.

'Listen, Ardel, I figure you're in big trouble. 'Tisn't alone you'll be but dead.' She could see that for all her brother's bluster he was frightened.

'Yes, if you must know. They're going to kill me, is all. Big trouble? More like catastrophe!'

'An' it's money?' she asked gently.

'More'n you believe. So much I can't actually *say* it out loud.'

'I don't wanna know,' she said firmly. 'But you can have all my savings. I've got five pounds.'

Ardel smiled faintly at her. 'Ah, thank you, Emer, but it's not near enough.'

'You owe more'n five pounds?' she asked in disbelief.

Ardel nodded, then said, 'What're you an' Brigid up to? I've nuthin' to do but sit here, an' I must say you two have been actin' *weird*!'

294

Emer gripped his knee in a fever of anxiety. 'Oh God, don't tell Mam or Da! Oh, please don't, Ardel. I'll do anything you say, only don't spoil it.'

He looked at her, amused at her vehemence. 'What are you up to?' he repeated.

'Well, if you *promise*. If you swear ... '

'I promise, brat! I swear.'

Her eyes searched his, then satisfied she said, 'Okay. Okay. I've entered the Miss Dranmore Beauty Contest, Ardel, and ... '

He burst out laughing. He hooted, rolled up on the bed, then screamed with pain.

'Jesus, my ribs hurt! Oh God! Oh Jasus! Don't crease me up like that an' me a sick man. Oh God, Oh God!'

She stood up, face flaming. 'You are going to be very surprised, Ardel. Very, very surprised. I'm going to be a big star some day and then I'll pay whatever bills you want me to. I'll be able to afford it then.'

A thought struck her.

'Why don't you ask Uncle Eddie? He's got bags of it an' he's nice, y'know, easy to talk to. An' all he could say is no. You've got nothing to lose.'

Uncle Eddie! He hadn't thought to ask him. He had been so full of self-pity that he hadn't really looked for a solution. Of course, Emer was right. It was the answer to his dilemma and the worst Eddie Benson could do was say no. But he might say yes. There was that hope.

Ardel had been asked to the Grand on Saturday to the party up there with Mourna, Briana, and Mam and Da. Laughlin had been asked too but had refused the invitation. Said something about going to Sneadhact, though why he wanted to go there was a mystery. Ardel had not been able to make up his mind whether to attend or not and his mam and da had mixed feelings about it as well.

'He might get set upon on the way up the hill,' Oonagh had been fearful, but Gabriel was more confident.

'They'll not attack with outsiders present. Don't be ridiculous, Mother.'

Well, he would go, and when he got there he'd ask Uncle Eddie if he could lend him the money. It was nothing to Eddie Benson and he'd pay him back. Make an arrangement. So much per week. Relief flooded him. He felt as if he had been carrying a huge burden that was suddenly lifted.

He hugged his sister. 'Thanks, Emer, thanks,' he cried.

' 'S all right,' she said, cheeks flushed. 'Yer welcome any time.'

Chapter Forty-Five

Laughlin asked at the desk for Mr Hector Breen. The receptionist bade him wait in the lounge with the curved brocade love-seats. He felt he was the focus of all eyes as he obeyed the receptionist and walked awkwardly to a small table near the entrance. He had not the courage to go further.

He had spruced himself up for the occasion, put on his cricket blazer, his best striped cotton shirt and his flannels. Nevertheless, he felt like a country bumpkin in this place and kept crossing and uncrossing his legs as he sat and waited for Hector.

What am I doing here? he wondered. Hector has probably forgotten about me. Oh God, I made a terrible mistake.

The lounge was almost deserted and full of light, the wall to wall windows revealing the panoramic view of the headland and the sea beyond. There were birds on the skyline, riding the breeze with graceful abandon, and Laughlin sat and stared out of the windows until his eyes watered.

Hector had probably not meant his invitation seriously. Being an actor, in the limelight, he probably issued casual invitations to lots of people who knew he didn't mean them, and certainly didn't show up at his hotel expecting to be entertained. Hector was, even now, he thought, thinking up an excuse to get out of having to go down and meet with this thick native who was so unsophisticated that he couldn't see the difference between common courtesy and a serious invitation.

Laughlin nearly got up and ran out of the lounge. The only thing that kept him pinned to his chair was his reluctance to make that terrible journey across the vast expanse to the exit.

'Hello, dear boy, how nice to see you.' Laughlin looked up into the handsome smiling face. It was Hector, standing between him and the light, a dark shape above him. He jumped to his feet, but Hector pressed him down again, pushing his shoulder with one hand, beckoning a passing waiter with the other.

'No, don't get up, old fellow. Tea. That's what we want, tea.' He glanced at Laughlin. 'Or would you prefer a drink?'

The waiter was looking at him, one eyebrow raised. 'Tea,' he said. 'Please. Tea would be fine.'

'Terrific. Tea for two then.' And Hector sat down beside Laughlin and took out a cigarette case and offered it. 'Smoke?'

Laughlin shook his head, feeling gauche. 'No, thank you. I don't.'

'Wise man. It plays havoc with my breathing. I keep trying to give it up but it's difficult. I'm very weak-willed.'

He smiled. In the fierce light of the room Laughlin

297

could see he was wearing make-up. It was an almost imperceptible film of matt colour over his face that gave him a film-star look. His eyes were a startling blue and he was, Laughlin thought, the most glamorous person he had ever seen. It made him feel very grown-up, just being with Hector.

He lit a cigarette, looking up under his eyebrows with a quizzical glance, 'The old voice, you know, is very important to an actor. Yet I play ducks and drakes with it. Tempting fate. How's the holiday?'

Laughlin shrugged. 'Boring.' he replied. 'I'd much rather hear about you. About the show. It must be so exciting being an actor.'

Hector smiled at him, an intimate smile that made him blush, then he patted Laughlin's knee which caused him to jump just as the waiter arrived with a huge silver tray laden with sandwiches, cakes, teapots, cups, saucers, milk and sugar.

Hector gave the waiter a cold glance, then said, 'Put it there, Sean, please.'

'Yes, sir.' There was a tiny hint of disrespect in the waiter's voice but he put the tray down on the table and moved it closer to Hector and Laughlin.

'Is that all, sir?' the waiter asked. Again the almost imperceptible coldness.

'Yes, thank you, Sean. That will be all.' Hector's tone was crisp and he waved his hand in dismissal.

'Now, Laughlin, how do you like your tea? Black, with lemon, or with milk and sugar? You see, I don't know yet so do tell me.'

He made it easy. Within minutes Laughlin had told him everything of note in his life. Even about Ardel. Hector shuddered but he was smiling.

'Oh, help! I wouldn't like to have those people after me. Sounds like *Richard III*. You said you went to Belvedere? That's my Alma Mater.'

298

'Yes ... well, no. I'm going there in September. Next term.'

'Oh?'

'Yes. Well, you see, I am ... was, at the Christian Brothers until, well, there was this Brother Nathan and he, well, did things ... Father is taking me away.'

Hector was watching him, sympathy in his eyes, 'Ah! I see.'

'That's why I'm going to Belvedere.'

'Oh dear, Laughlin. That was an unfortunate introduction to sex, wasn't it?'

'What do you mean?'

Laughlin felt a stirring of excitement within him, a feeling that something he had never expressed before could be revealed and that he was going to find out a secret, that a missing piece of a jigsaw was about to fall into place.

Hector shrugged. 'I simply mean that sex should be the culmination of love felt by a man for a woman.' He paused, his blue eyes on Laughlin. 'Or a man for a man.'

'A man?' It was there, the concept that had been near the edge of his consciousness, something he knew, yet did not know.

'Yes,' Hector said softly. 'Men love each other, Laughlin. Sexually, I mean.'

There it was, in place, the knowledge acknowledged. He let out a breath he had been holding for a long time.

'Aaah!'

'Some men, Laughlin, are born that way. They cannot help it. It is the way they were made. You must not feel guilty if that is your nature.'

'I think it is. But you knew, Hector, didn't you? You knew.'

Hector nodded. 'Yes, I guessed,' he said. 'And I've spoken to you about it, perhaps too soon in our friendship, because I'm afraid for you. People will try to make you feel

299

guilty about your nature. Don't let them. You must not let them spoil your life. They'll tell you it's unnatural. What is natural? I think it is what you know is right for you.'

Laughlin nodded. He felt calm and peaceful for the first time since Brother Nathan had interfered with him and he had felt disgust and horror, but also a curious excitement. The dilemma had been resolved, the questions answered.

'Yes,' he said. 'There was a bit of me,' he looked at Hector, 'a *tiny* bit that, well, not liked it exactly, Brother Nathan I mean, but … '

'It didn't repulse you as it would if you were … '

'Normal,' Laughlin interpolated, but Hector shook his head.

'The one thing we know about nature, Laughlin, is that little in it is "normal". There is an infinite variety in nature as there is in human beings. Don't type-cast yourself. Or others. Let people be themselves, with all their grubby and noble predilections. Ah, if we could only learn to be less critical of each other, what a wonderful world this would be.'

'Now,' he turned to Laughlin, 'when you've finished tea you can walk me around the headland to the crossroads. Then you can have a good think on the way back.'

'Will I see you again?'

'Don't see why not.'

'Tomorrow?'

'Tomorrow's matinee. What about the next day? Here? Same time? Good. Well, come on.'

'Let me pay.' Laughlin fumbled in his blazer pocket, knowing full well there was nothing there.

'Nonsense. I'm working, you're not. As a matter of principle, in the theatre, we never ask someone out of work to pay. It's against the rules.'

He smiled and Laughlin felt his heart lift. He followed Hector's slim figure out into the sun. The brilliant dazzle that blinded them prevented him from noticing his Uncle

300

Eddie arriving back from the golf course with a bunch of friends. But his Uncle Eddie saw him.

Chapter Forty-Six

On that Sunday they went to Mass in the little church on the hill. The family took up four rows. Briana wasn't there and neither was Ardel.

'We can't risk it,' Oonagh said in reference to him.

Granny O'Shea, between Emer and Emmett, was mumbling sibilantly 'Veh-veh-veh-veh-veh' on an inward breath, and 'Veh-veh-veh-veh-veh' on an outward one.

'What's she sayin'?' Brigid beside Emer asked.

'She's prayin',' Emer replied tartly. 'It's the way she does it. It don't make sense.'

Dot and Ben and the crocodile sat in front of Oonagh and the O'Sheas. Maggie Moran had wriggled out and stood in the centre aisle just below the altar and every time the priest said, '*In nomine patris et filius et spiritus sanctus, Amen,*' she raised the front of her skirt over her head and flashed a stretch of sunburned skin and her frilly pants.

'It's not modest. You should stop her,' Oonagh whispered to Dot.

'Ah, sure, she's only little,' was the sanguine reply.

'Maggie may learn, eventually, but Dot, never!' Gabriel whispered to his wife. 'Give up, pet. It's no use.'

There were three stained-glass windows in the little church and the sun shining through them splashed the congregation with shafts of blue and red and green. Little motes hung lazily in the golden beams. Emer came back down the aisle from communion, hands pressed together under her chin, eyes upturned, a sanctimonious expression on her face.

'She thinks she's Saint Bernadette,' Dot whispered.

'Hypocrite!' Emmett hissed when he saw her. But Emer paid no attention. Gabriel had his head bowed, thinking of Oonagh.

She was trying to tell him something, working up to it. He had been aware of it, without knowing he was, for some time now, ever since they arrived in Dranmore, and perhaps even before. He could not imagine what it was, but, looking at her, Gabriel saw her face intent in prayer, bombarding Heaven with requests, and he knew that the something was important. He made up his mind to give her every opportunity to unburden herself.

Emmett looked at the old priest, remembering their conversation last night after confession. 'You're not having fun here, Emmett, are you?' the old priest had asked the boy.

'Well, I'd rather be in the church than on the beach,' he'd answered, pat.

'Why?' The old priest had peered through the grille and Emmett could see his eyes glittering in the dark. He was thrown by the question.

'What do you mean, Father?'

'Why would you rather be in the church than having fun on the beach?'

'Because God is here. Present in the Blessed Sacrament.'

'Oh, and He's not on the beach? God is everywhere, my son.'

Once more Emmett was disconcerted. 'But the Presence of God in the Sacrament … '

'Stop mouthing doctrine! Listen, God made the world. You understand that?'

'Yes, Father.'

'What do you think he made the world for?'

Emmett was by now totally confused. In Religious Knowledge, in school, you answered the questions from the Catechism, no ifs, buts or maybes. The old priest was decidedly off, Emmett thought.

'I suppose, Father, so's we could live in it.'

'A place for us to live, right?'

'Yes, Father.'

'And, in your considered opinion, did He make a good job of it?'

Was the old priest making fun of him? 'Yes, He did, Father.'

'Good. Now, who made the church? Eh?' Too late Emmet saw the trap.

'Some people … men … but they made it for God.'

'Just answer the questions. Right. We have established that God made the world. The trees. The sea. The flowers. The rivers. The grass. Waterfalls, lagoons, woods and forests. Right? Men built the cathedrals, the churches, the monasteries, nunneries, etc, etc. Who did the better job?'

'Well, God, of course.'

'Why do you say "of course".'

'Because He is God. God is Perfect.'

'Emmett, Emmett, listen. Think. Answer not as you think you should, but really, truthfully, with reason. Would you prefer to have been responsible for creating the world or the churches?'

'The world, Father.'

'Fine. So God has something to be proud of? His work pleases you?'

'Yes, Father.'

'Good. Then why do you think it's better to be in a man-made building and spurn God's creation? For the beach, after all, *is* God's creation?'

'I don't know, Father.'

'Emmett, I want you to go away and think. Think of the artistry that went into the making of a rose, say, or a tree.

Just one. Those Monterey pines below Kincora, for example. A man could spend a lifetime trying to produce a single thing half as perfect, quarter as perfect. God spreads His handiwork lavishly across the globe, boy, an' you spurn it. You'd rather be in a man-made edifice of dubious artistry, in out of His sun, because you can't find Him out there in His creation?'

'But the Church is where God lives,' Emmett said defensively.

'The *world* is where God lives. The world is the house of God. The church is there to remind us of that, it is a place to go and express our gratitude. to renew our faith, thank our Father in Heaven, acknowledge His mastery. No, Emmett, a church is not a place to *live*.'

'But priests ... '

'Priests care for these temporary dwelling places of the Lord, Emmett, and men decorate them, sometimes wonderfully like in Florence and Rome, but never as opulently, never as perfectly, as God decorated His world. Priests do God's work. They pass on a message, that's all. Do you know what that message is?'

'To keep His Commandments so's you go to Heaven and not to Hell.'

'Oh, no, my boy. Oh, no. Christ came on earth to teach us to love one another. Just that. And He meant *everyone*. Can you tell me one sin anyone could commit if they did just that? Loved everyone? No, of course not. You cannot steal from those you love. You cannot be angry. You cannot kill or be jealous. That's the trick – to try to love everyone. The way to God's heart is to live in His world and love His people. To see the face of God in all His creatures.'

Love Uncle Joe? Love that drunken sot? Emmett cringed. Oh, he could do almost anything, love almost anyone, but not that!

'Can I be a priest if there's one person I ... I ... loathe?' he whispered.

'That person has the face of God. So that means you loathe God,' the priest said, and Emmett's heart sank. That was a terrible thought.

'But he's disgusting. A drunk.'

> ' "I sought my God,
> My God I could not see.
> I sought my soul,
> My soul eluded me.
> I sought my brother
> And I found all three." '

Ah, Emmett, he maybe needs more help than most.'

'Yes, Father. Isn't there any other way?'

'I'm afraid not my boy.'

'Then what must I do?'

'I think you already know.'

Uncle Joe was not in the church that Sunday and Emmett was relieved. He could not imagine Jesus with Uncle Joe's face. It would be a sacrilege. Yet what the old priest said was certainly accurate, if unpalatable. Jesus had made it quite clear that the thing He wanted most was that mankind should love each other. Emmett had thought that loving holiness and sacred places was enough, but apparently it was not.

He'd have to force himself to love his uncle. He'd try to wean him away from alcohol, lead him on to a sober and holy path. How could he manage that? He did not know at present, could not begin to imagine.

But he'd try.

'Dear Lord, help me to help my Uncle Joe. Help me to change his evil ways. Help me to bring him nearer to You. Amen.' He crossed himself piously and bent his head.

Chapter Forty-Seven

They went to the play in Sneadhact in several pony-and-traps that Mrs Flanagan gathered from the highways and byways around Dranmore, she being on good terms with the jarveys. Molly and Tom, however, took their car filled with the young people.

The journey was lively, the cousins calling to each other from the traps and the car, laughing over nothing at all. Mena hung out of the Ford yelling at Des who shrank back and became almost totally immersed in the rug. Tom followed the traps at a snail's pace. The ponies could hear the engine behind them and their ears went back and they rolled their eyes and the jarveys complained to each other about the nuisance and the danger motor vehicles were to mankind and how much better off the world would be without them.

'As if a horse and cart isn't fast enough for anythin',' Cally O'Malley shouted to Ignatius Houlihan.

'An invention of the divil,' Ignatius shouted back.

And John Joe Delaney shook his grizzled head and muttered that the world had gone mad, what with aero-machines and nasty smelly ingins clutterin' up God's apple-fresh creation.

Their clients were not listening to them. The men were making ribald jokes and the women shushed them, the whole party in great form except for Tom and Molly who did not exchange a single word.

The moon hung low and stars studded a heavy blue velvet sky that draped the horizon in mystery.

The performance was outside in the open air. There was at Sneadhact a natural amphitheatre, or perhaps the remains of a Druidic circle; huge prehistoric stones, ten foot high, backed by trees. The actors played their main scenes within the semi-circle which was lit by artificial lights and arc-lamps. The whole scene was magical and mysterious and the audience, sitting on hard benches, forgot their discomfort and were enchanted by the world the actors skilfully drew them into.

The party from the Grand had their own chairs, comfortable padded seats with arms and cushions, brought by the staff from the hotel. Eddie Benson put Kurt beside his wife and Mourna and Iain together. He had been very firm about the placing and Mourna and Iain had made no fuss, Mourna glancing occasionally across at Kurt, and Iain smiling every few minutes at Briana, sitting beside her mother on a bench.

The story held them all in thrall. A world of fairies and goblins, love and mistaken identity, of wicked tricks of comedy, unfolded in moonlight.

When Oberon said: 'Ill-met by moonlight, proud Titania,' a scarf of pearl grey cloud moved across the face of the real moon which hung just above the oak tree, and Emer shivered.

The beauty of the place and the language, the superb acting, the marvellous story, the enchantment of the evening, transported Laughlin into another world, a world of mirthful merriment, of impish pranks and wondrous beauty. A world where anything was possible. A world where love triumphed but people were human and weak, imperfect and vulnerable.

Hector was brilliant as the confused Lysander, running in and out of the wood, but the whole cast was perfect. Diarmuid McDiarmuid, a handsome yet strangely

307

menacing Oberon, reminded Oonagh of Eddie and his Titania was equally passionate and amoral, a godless fairy queen intent on mischief. The costumes seemed to be made of shards of gossamer, such light draperies that Dot wondered aloud if the actors didn't catch colds. Bottom was uproarious, hilariously comic, reducing them to helpless laughter. The whole performance was an unqualified success.

In the interval, much to Eddie's chagrin, Iain went into the woods with Briana, and Mourna and Kurt could be seen talking under an ancient oak.

'You are like the play, Mourna,' he said to her. 'Enchanted. You are like the sleeping beauty waiting to be awakened.'

'You think I am asleep then?' she asked, smiling.

'Oh, yes,' he said. 'Yes.'

'Will you wake me?' she enquired shyly.

'If you will let me.'

'You'd think he'd have cottoned on by now, Bri, wouldn't you?' Iain whispered to Briana, and they sat together for the next scene and saw that Colista had changed places with Mourna. Briana giggled as the kettle and the tuckets clashed, announcing Bottom's arrival.

'Who?' she whispered back.

'Father, who else?'

Briana had realized how much Iain's father liked to get his own way, and his determination to separate them frightened her more than she liked to admit.

'Oh, we'll wear him down, like you said,' she murmured in his ear. She glanced over at her uncle and saw he was not looking at the performance but staring at Mourna and Kurt.

Iain squeezed her hand. 'Mother's on our side, though,' he said.

'Is she?' Briana sounded doubtful.

Someone said, 'Shush!' and they lapsed into silence.

In the next interval Eddie came swiftly over and asked Iain to get some champagne from his car.

'How's school, Briana?' he asked her, watching her intently, lids half-veiled over his eyes.

'Fine. It's my last year, Uncle Eddie,' she replied.

'Well, well, and what do you plan to do when you leave?' His voice implied something exciting was lying in wait for her. Far away from Iain. She wanted to say, 'Marry your son, it's all I'll ever want to do.' But she said nothing, staring at him till he shifted his gaze and looked elsewhere.

'If you were as beautiful as your sister now, the decision would not be too difficult,' he said lightly.

'Iain thinks I'm prettier!' she was stung to reply, and grimaced in annoyance at her impulsive retort.

'Well, that just goes to show how ignorant and impressionable he is,' Eddie said, and she could hear the cruelty underneath the light tone of his voice. 'He can be very muddled and immature, my son,' Eddie continued, 'I think you should bear that in mind, Briana.'

Iain returned at that moment, glancing apprehensively at Briana whose face was flushed and whose eyes shone with anger and unshed tears.

'Bring it to your mother,' Eddie instructed, not looking at Iain. 'Briana and I are talking.'

'Here, Father. Take it. Mother is beckoning *you*,' Iain said, and firmly thrust the bottle into his father's hands. 'Whatever you were saying to Briana will have to wait.' And he took her arm and pulled her away, leaving Eddie helplessly holding the champagne bottle, a savage expression on his face.

He cursed and looked to where his wife stood and, as Iain had said, saw she was waving him over. Containing his irritation, he carried the wine past the O'Sheas and the Morans to Colista, Mourna and Kurt.

'You must speak to your son, dear,' he said, thumbing the cork ferociously. 'He has just been extremely rude.'

309

'Really?' Colista cocked her head. 'And I pride myself on how polite he is.'

Was she laughing at him? Her tone was amused. He shivered in anger. He would not forgive her easily for that. In the complicated game they played she would recognize her punishment when it came, disguised as quite something else.

'Mourna, come and see the woods,' he said, taking his niece's arm, but Colista forestalled him,

'Kurt has already offered, dear,' she said, and drew his arm away, taking it between her hands, locking her fingers over his upper arm possessively. 'Now you and I will sit here quietly, as befits the older folk, and drink some champagne and talk about the play, how very beautifully it is done. Do you suppose, my dear, that the lovers' eyes will be opened to who they really love? Or not? Will they sort it all out so that each of them gets the right companion?'

'Oh, I'm sure they do, Colista. It's a play after all. It is not supposed to be real life.'

Chapter Forty-Eight

'You were very brave,' Briana said, under his lips, as he kissed her again and again. The trees met above them, branches intertwined. There was a damp smell of moss and age-old roots and they could hear, from the clearing, the mediaeval music played by members of the company in costume who had weaved in and out of the play. It set a plaintive mood, the melancholy notes of the flute hanging on the still warm air in the dense copse like an echo.

'I'm fed up, Bri.' Iain lifted his face from hers. 'And I'm not going to wait much longer. Father gets worse and worse. My love for you grows and grows. I've made up my mind, Briana, we're going away.'

'What? What do you mean?'

'Darling, he's *never* going to come around. I thought at first we'd wear him down, being nice, you know, but it's not working. So I want to take you away from here, take you to Scotland, Gretna Green, and marry you.'

'Oh, Iain, if that's what you think.' She smiled at him, then a thought struck her and her hands flew to her cheeks.

'But it's Protestant! It'll *kill* Mam.'

'We'll let her know it's only really pro tem. We'll get married in any church she likes, full regalia, in the Pro Cathedral if she so desires, when the deed is done and we come back.' He looked at her tenderly. 'Only, I'm afraid, Bri.'

'Of what?' She looked at him in the green shadow of the wood. She loved every line of his face, every bone of his body. They desired each other so feverishly and she knew this was another reason he wanted to run away. They could not keep away from each other much longer. Each day it got more and more difficult. She loved him and she would do whatever he wanted, whenever he wanted.

'That father'll succeed in separating us. He has the habit of getting his own way. He always wins. He does not take defeat kindly. I'm scared of losing you.'

'He'd have to kill me, Iain, you know that.'

'Anyhow, we won't take the risk of him succeeding. We'll run away. I've quite decided. Mother says Mourna'll get engaged to Kurt next weekend, the end of the holiday. She'll give a party for them on Saturday,' Iain told her.

'Oh, gosh! I'm so happy for Mourna.'

'Yes, Bri, that's all very well, but we've got to think of ourselves.' She nodded. He held her very close, their

311

bodies fitting together snugly, curve to curve, not passionately now for they were too intent on their arrangements, but comfortably and tenderly.

'So what is the plan?' she asked, confident of his ability to look after them.

'Well, we'll do it *then*. When the party is in full swing. We'll slip away. No one will notice. They'll be too busy and excited to check up on us. Even if they do, there's nothing they can do about it. They won't even notice next day. For ages.' Iain was persuading himself as much as her. 'It will be all right.'

'And we'll leave a note explaining?' She wanted to be sure her parents would be spared unnecessary anxiety and uncertainty.

He nodded, frowning, thinking up the wording.

'Yes. We'll say we've gone to England to get married. That we want to have a family wedding on our return in, let's say, a month. That we'll phone and let them know we are okay. That we love each other, and them, but we've thought it all out and decided this is the best way.' He looked down at her upturned face. 'And we know what we are doing,' he finished swiftly. 'How's that sound?'

She wrapped her arms around his waist. 'Oh, good. So good,' she said.

'Then no one can separate us,' he whispered. 'Ever.' He thought of something. 'Bri?'

'Yes?'

'I may be cut off. Father may chuck me out.'

'We've been through this before, Iain. We'll manage, you'll see. We can get work easy. If not here, then in England.'

'You sure you don't mind? Things might be rough.'

'We've never had it easy, Iain,' she said softly. 'Not our family. So I won't miss what I never had.'

'I forget that sometimes,' he said. 'Only I always envied your family. You seemed so happy together. So much a part of something good.'

'We quarrel all the time,' Briana said.

'I don't mean that. I've always been alone. No one to quarrel with. Mother pulling me this way, Father that. To me your family looked great.'

'We'll have a family, Iain. I'll give you the kind of home you want. If you're with me I can do anything,' she added in a whisper, and he caught his breath at the passionate and deeply felt avowal.

'We'll make it, you and I,' he said.

At that moment the gong sounded through the woods to summon them back for the last act of the play, and hand in hand they joined the others.

Chapter Forty-Nine

Laughlin did not leave his seat during the whole evening. He was bemused, transported to another world. In a daze he sat, oblivious of his family, of people milling about during the intervals, unaware of Emer taunting with: 'Will ye look at him! Janey, he's got the daftest face on him.'

Ideas and thoughts so exotic, so exciting, ran around his head. There seemed to him no past, no future, only these moments under the gigantic dappled moon, the multitudinous stars, the deluge of seductive words that held him in thrall. And, above all, Hector, Lysander in his Greek tunic, an alien god yet warmly familiar. Hector's voice drowning him in a cataract of poetry, words to taste and savour:

' "To-morrow night, when Phoebe doth behold

> Her silvery visage in the watery glass
> Decking with liquid pearl the bladed grass … '

The lines he said, the way he said them, leaning out towards the audience, taking them into his confidence, his blue eyes bright as stars, made Laughlin shiver and kept him immobile in his seat.

He wanted to talk to Hector about those words, the poetry, share this tremendous discovery. He had 'learned' Shakespeare in school but he had never heard it spoken before by people who could make the words sing. The soaring voice of Diarmuid McDiarmuid sent tingles down his spine at the breathtaking beauty of his speeches. From,

> ' … and heard a mermaid on a dolphin's back
> Uttering such dulcet and harmonious breath
> That the rude sea grew civil at their song,
> And certain stars shot madly from their spheres
> To hear the sea-maid's music.'

to:

> 'With this field-dew consecrate,
> Every fairy take his gate.'

Laughlin listened, his faculties alert to every nuance, every singing sound, his thirsty soul satisfied.

As the moon seemed to recede, flooding the dark sky with silver, Kurt took Mourna's hand in his and saw her eyes widen and reassure him, nodding her head to the question in his eyes. Briana and Iain were also holding hands, not looking at each other, their problem sorted and solved. They were observed with an amused smile by Colista while Eddie stared unmoving at Mourna, and Emer and Brigid whispered under the fairy lights, giggling secretively, and Molly and Tom sat cold as strangers, and Mena pinched Des's thigh, and he, in a terrible quandary, was torn between lust and shame and sat, knees clenched, eyes wide, seeing nothing, absorbed only in what was happening in the general area of his groin, and Rita sat beside Oonagh and Gabriel and thought how simple things must have been when time was young and the huge pain of economy had not yet twisted the guts of the world, and Laughlin did not move a muscle, even when the actors took their bows and the artificial lights had gone out and left the stars and moon in full possession of the sky and the voices of his mother and father called him to the trap.

Only when Emer plucked his sleeve and shook him did he come to himself, as if from a long dream.

'C'mon. Mam is tired and Da wants to get home. C'mon, Laughlin. You enchanted or somethin'?'

Chapter Fifty

The next morning Gabriel met Rita in the boreen. She was walking slowly towards the harbour and he fell into step beside her.

'Not with the others on the beach, Rita?' he inquired.

'No,' she replied. 'Can't stand all the questions. Or the sympathy.' She wore a smart frock, a white crêpe with blue forget-me-nots printed all over it. It crossed softly over her breasts, and with it she wore medium-heeled blue sling-back shoes. She looked, Gabriel thought, surprisingly pretty.

'I bought it on the way back,' she said, seeing his glance, understanding its relevance. 'With my last bobs,' she said defiantly. 'I cleaned myself out, Gabriel, so I did, spent every bloody penny, and I don't feel guilty.'

'Then why are you justifying yourself to me?' he asked.

'You always do it, Rita. You don't owe me an explanation.'

'When you are indebted to people, you explain everything,' she said.

'Yerra, you shouldn't.'

'Why're you not on the beach?' she asked.

'Oh, I will be,' he replied. 'But I'm getting the paper below. I always get the newspaper of a morning. Those philistines, Tom and Ben, are content to remain in ignorance, but not me. I like to keep my finger on the pulse.' He grinned at her.

'Well, I'll leave you here. I want to take a walk over the headland.'

'Now why would you want to do that? In this heat?'

'I'm quite cool, Gabriel, and I'd rather be by myself this morning. I'll mull over that wonderful production we saw last night.'

They had stopped walking and were standing together at the cross-roads. The world seemed deserted here, there wasn't a soul about. The laughter of the youngsters far below them on the beach sounded faint and faraway, their voices blown by the breeze in the other direction or out over the sea.

Rita drew circles on the sandy ground with the toe of her sling-backs.

'You know, you look wonderfully pretty this morning, Rita,' Gabriel said.

'Why, thank you, Gabriel.' She squinted at him, her eyes dazzled by the sun. 'I used to be, you know. Thought pretty, I mean.' She laughed ruefully. 'A woman can't be beautiful and desperately tense, the last cancels the first.'

'Well, this morning you look a treat.'

'I'm not tense any more,' she said. Her dress blew against her legs. Her ankles were no longer swollen. They looked slim in the sling-backs.

'How'd that happen?' Gabriel asked.

'I just gave up.' She shrugged. 'I suppose, in a way, I

snapped. In that place … '

'Lisdoonvarna?'

She nodded. 'Yes. It was awful, Gabriel. Those men! Women to them are … like animals. They'd treat you very well, like they'd treat their best dog; with kindliness and firmness, not tolerating disobedience, refusing to believe that women *must* use their imaginations, have aspirations, and … Oh, I'm a stroppy lady, Gabriel.' She grinned at him.

'I know, Rita.'

'I thought then, what the hell! I'm not solving anything with this worry, this tension. I'm simply immobilizing myself. What can they do to me? Break my bones? Maybe, but if they *really* want their money's worth that would seem a waste of time and counter-productive. No. I was allowing fear to consume me and I decided to get brave, get my courage back, get my nerve back, Gabriel, and live again. The hell with it!'

He burst out laughing and she joined him, throwing back her head, looking more girlish than he could ever remember seeing her.

'Keep me company down to the harbour?' he asked her.

'Well … ' She looked at him, surprised.

'Ye'll come with me first before ye go anywhere else,' he cried gleefully, grabbing her arm. 'An' that's an order.'

'Where, Gabriel? Where are we going?'

'Just a wee bit wide of the harbour. See that little shop?'

'Yes,' she said, smiling and shading her eyes with her gloved hand. 'It's cute. Ever so pretty.'

'What's in it is even cuter,' he retorted, and she looked at him suspiciously.

'Gabriel, what is this? You playing some kind of joke?'

'No joke, Rita. Please God, no joke.' And he pulled her along the road with him.

She saw the little white-washed cottage, thatched, immaculately groomed, window-boxes full of bright

317

geraniums in front of each sparkling window. She thought, it takes a woman's touch to keep it like that. No man could have such delicacy. She saw the paper-shop beside the cottage. There were racks of newspapers and magazines in the doorway and the shop window was full of jars of sweets sweating in the sun.

'Wait here,' Gabriel commanded, and stood her in front of the window. With a pang of nostalgia for younger happier days she stared at the sweets, remembering treats, savouring sticky glutinous lumps of sugary substances: bull's eyes, barley sugar sticks, licorice in long black twists, wine gums, gob-stoppers, toffees and chocolate. Had she once really found bliss sucking a mouthful of such tooth-decaying, cloying, sticky goo?

Yes. Once. A long, long time ago.

She became aware of a face peering at her through the window, behind the jars of sweets. At first it was shadowy then it hove into focus: curly pepper-and-salt hair and two bright eyes looking out at her from within.

She liked the face, it made her want to laugh. Such twinkling eyes buried in laugh lines. A smiling face, a jolly face, someone who would laugh a lot, ride lightly over adversity and surmount misfortune. She couldn't help but smile back.

The face disappeared and she was looking again at the rows of jars and wondering if she had imagined it.

Then Gabriel was at her side, saying, 'I'd like you to meet a friend, Rita. Barney Boland, my sister-in-law, Rita.'

It was the face in the window materialized here in the sunlight, a big bear of a smiling man, looking at her shyly, examining her discreetly. She was glad she'd worn the pretty dress.

'Hear ye went to the Shakespeare last night,' Barney Boland was saying to Gabriel, glancing at her every now and then. His handshake had been firm and warm. 'Pleased to meet you, ma'm. Isn't it a treat?'

Gabriel nodded. ' 'Twas a grand evening,' he said.

'Here's your paper.' Barney handed Gabriel the *Irish Times*. 'Man'd die without his paper,' he remarked to Rita, still smiling.

'Well, Gabriel, I'm off around the bay. See you later.' She turned and walked away from the men, a lilt in her hips.

'Nice woman,' Barney Boland said.

'Aye. She is that,' was Gabriel's reply.

Chapter Fifty-One

Everyone had left the beach at four o'clock the following day. Sun-dazed, red turning brown by now, ready for a rest before tea, they did not hog the sun as much as they had in the days when they arrived, white, hungry for golden rays and the well-being a day at the beach gave them. Cranky children fell on beds in their sun-dresses. Adults also.

It had turned unseasonably chilly that day and Oonagh shivered as she mounted the steep steps to the house. Her forehead was damp and felt strangely cold; she didn't think it was caused by the sea.

She felt very odd, shaky and peculiar. She was sweating and her sun-dress was sticking to her, yet she did not feel hot. She wished Gabriel was with her but he had gone down to have a chat with his friend Barney Boland. She had told him she didn't feel too good.

'You've had a tough time, love. Ardel's beating up shocked you more than you realized. Go down to the

319

beach and have a nice rest and a swim and you'll feel better. I'll catch up with you around tea-time.'

She had done as he suggested only she didn't feel better. If anything she felt worse. Dry-mouthed, she went inside and drank a glass of water from the bathroom tap. It was cold and tasted fresh and sweet and she drank it greedily.

She could hear voices coming from the other houses. Everyone was inside now, sleeping or getting ready for tea, coating themselves in lotion, washing the sand out of their hair.

She pulled her dress over her head, feeling dizzy, and went to steady herself. Standing in her bare feet she shook her head, then her attention was caught by a stain on the dress she had just removed. The dress was white seersucker with red checks which must have been why no one noticed the stain.

It was a blood-stain.

She looked down. Her pants were stained too and she could feel a pressure in her, a too-familiar feeling, building and building, pushing down inside her, an inexorable tide. It overcame her and her knees started to shake. She stood, pale and frightened in the bathroom, watching her blood drip on the tiled floor. It was happening now, but not as it had happened before. This was no waking in the night, or calling out in the day, a certainty of the rightness within her, excited about the coming of a precious and warmly awaited new child into their lives. This was her blood, a cold and angry feeling in her very bones, and this time was not right. She'd make an exhibition of herself. The relations, children around, the teenagers, would be shocked. Their holiday would be spoiled by embarrassment and fear. And concern. To be concerned and worried was a burden she did not want to dump on their fragile shoulders.

The spotting had turned to a stream and she looked at the blood running down her leg and whispered, 'Don't let anyone come in, dear God.' Then, 'Holy Mother of God, help me.'

She stood helpless in the little bathroom, not knowing what to do. Then, in the silence, she heard the thunder of the sea. It came to her, the answer to her prayer, and suddenly she knew what to do.

She pulled her stained sun-dress back on and left the house unnoticed. She went down to the pounding sea, down to the rocks. She felt as secure and solid as they were and suddenly very strong. The sea crashed to the shore, then whispered to her that everything would be all right.

Yet a chill of fear ran through her. The sea had called her here and the sea was cruel. From the house it had looked calm, tranquil, a frill of white foam here and there on its blue skirts, fluffing in the breeze. But in the cooler air it had roughened up, and down here, beside the rocks, it tumbled high, growling angrily, and the lacy foam was a booming cataract.

It was her time and the elemental sea knew it. There was no reprieve now. She took off her clothes slowly, painfully, folding them, leaving them in a neat pile. Her poor body, she thought, how old it was, how it sagged. Yet Gabriel loved it, worshipped it. 'It's yours, Mother, it is *you*. It's the real you. All we've been through, the kids, the struggle, the work, the love, it is all there. This is your body, my love, and it is a map of our life together. My most precious map.'

Tears came into her eyes at the thought of his tenderness. She stood naked, only her miraculous medal on a chain hung down on her tanned and puckered chest. She took a deep breath and moved towards a rock a little way out. The sea was calmer there. The waves gurgled around it and sucked back out with a sound like water down a sink. There was no one at all around except, bobbing on the horizon, the black bathing cap of a long distance swimmer, the white flesh of his arms as they cleaved the water. She blessed herself as if she was going for a swim, then she made her way over the rocks. She nearly slipped on some black seaweed but regained her balance and continued until she reached the rock she had her eye on.

Just below the flat surface, a couple of inches down, there was a pool, then another rock and another pool. She stopped at the first one. The water was up to her knees. She saw the blood from her legs lift and rise in the water, then a wave broke and the blood disappeared. She felt hot now, feverish, and the water cooled her. The sea was very cold when she stepped down into the pool. The water here was up to her waist. This one would do. A wave broke over the pool and nearly knocked her over.

She sat down abruptly on the rock behind her and let the next wave slide over her body and recede, sucking at her legs, growling darkly at her ankles. She was gasping now, trying to control her breathing, not succeeding. She looked at the rock behind her. A ledge stuck out and she gripped it tightly. She moved to see if she felt secure, then satisfied she opened her legs and prayed.

'Dear Mother of God, Mary most holy, help me dear Mother in this hour of my need.'

She could feel the pain bearing down. It was strange how the timing was right, the water ebbing and flowing in unison with her spasms. The water was refreshing, cool, cleansing.

She went with the familiar contractions. Her body knew what to do now and did it automatically. Only it was tired, very tired. No energy left. In the last tremendous heaving contractions, she cried to the sea and her face was wet with tears. The cold sea remained indifferent.

'Mary Mother of God, take it. Take care of the little unfinished thing,' she wept.

It would be all right in the clean bosom of the sea, Oonagh thought. She was exhausted and weak. Her grip on the rock loosened. The sea became rougher, crying out, singing under the whip of a sudden wind. It lashed her tired body, sucking at it, embracing it, possessing it. She tried to hang on but the rock slipped from her grasp. She was worn out.

The sea's rhythm, the waves breaking over her, whispered to her to let go, to relax and follow. Slip away into peace. The peaceful bosom of the sea was so soothing, a benediction. She felt slack, tired. All she wanted to do was sleep. Her hands were washed back over her head and she felt herself gradually losing consciousness and a wonderful warm darkness overwhelm her.

Chapter Fifty-Two

Gabriel saw the blood in the bathroom and felt a moment's irritation. Then immediately he realized none of the girls would ever leave a mess like this. Oonagh would kill them.

Oonagh! Jesus, Oonagh! He knew now suddenly what she had been trying to tell him, what was wrong with her. And he knew it was her blood, knew it for certain. He felt suddenly very frightened. He followed the stains and saw they led down the path to the sea.

He became light-headed. Oh, Mother of God, no!

Heart pounding, terrified to look, he ran down the steps, following the trail she'd left. He ran to the rocks, slipping and sliding over them in his hurry. Raising his eyes, he saw her at once and guessed – no, *knew* all. He scrambled over the rocks, cutting his ankles and feet in his clumsy rush to get to her.

The life-force in her was stronger than the lure of the sea and her own weakness. She struggled to reach him, but the waves were sucking her greedily out to sea.

He fell on his knees, his teeth chattering, clawing his way to her. He was gibbering prayers, making wild promises to God, if only he could reach her. He saw her begin to slide from the pool. If the sea pulled her out she'd be lost forever. Outside, the water churned and boiled in ceaseless motion that bespoke dangerous undercurrents.

Then one arm was caught, trapped in a crevice. It slipped behind her head and stretched out to him as if to reach him.

For a long moment he failed to catch it. He strained every muscle, stretching, his breath rasping through his nostrils. Then, miraculously, he gripped it. He felt the sea try to drag her away from him, sucking greedily at his wife's cold fingers. He held on firmly with both hands, held on cruelly, falling on his face, crushing her flesh in a vice-like grip, to hold her, to keep her. Then suddenly the tussle was over, the sea relinquished its hold and he had won.

He dragged her out, that dear naked body, his love, his life, and held her to him, shivering and weeping. He carried her back over the rocks, sure-footed now with this precious burden, then laid her on the sand and took off his shirt and wrapped it around her.

She was breathing. She was alive. Still weeping, he picked her up and carried her home.

Chapter Fifty-Three

Mena flicked her painted nails under the chin of Art McEvoy, the leader of the local bike boys. Des's attentions had begun to annoy her and so she had returned to her flirtation with the gang on the sea-wall. Des had been sniffing around her like a mongrel on heat and once or twice in the last few days she had allowed him to touch her breasts and put his hand up her knickers. He got overexcited however and his fumbling irritated her and she wanted to be shot of him. The lads on the sea-wall seemed infinitely more sophisticated and therefore desirable to her.

She wriggled her bottom each time she passed them and got whistled at as she strolled by.

'Hot stuff!' Art said between his teeth. He held the lit end of the cigarette facing his palm, his fingers curled over it. It glowed in there like a night-light when he took a drag on it. She walked slowly past the line up. There were six of them including Art. The sun shone down and the boys sweated in their jackets, the Brylcreem on their hair glistening almost as hotly as their eyes. She sauntered up and down, looking them over, her red shoulderstrap gliding down over her upper arm like a cut.

She got to Art and touched his chest with her finger. He nodded and she strolled away, an invitation in her eyes. He followed.

There was an ancient Martello tower, neglected,

moss-covered and ivied, and she went into the musty-smelling interior confident of her power. But when she turned and saw Art blocking the light from the door her self-assurance deserted her.

She had not meant to have him follow her here, into this small enclosed space. It had been like a game to her and now she was faced with the reality of a strange and powerful male, an unknown quantity. She, who liked to be in charge, was now vulnerable.

She shivered, fiddled with the top buttons of her dress, then let her hands fall as Art moved in the doorway.

'Well?' he broke the silence. 'Aren't you goin' te take them off?'

'What?' She was startled.

'Yer clothes, dumb-bell.'

'Oh! Yes.'

She did not want to lose face. She had played the Jezebel and he was calling her bluff. She couldn't plead innocence now.

She opened the buttons, one by one, reluctantly, then let her dress fall back over her shoulders and on to the ground. She noticed it was dirty, cluttered with sweet-papers, cigarette packets and all sorts of filth. A bluebottle buzzed, was quiet, then began to buzz again.

'What you doing?' she asked nervously.

He was undoing the belt of his trousers.

'Gettin' these off. Can't fuck trussed up in these.'

Her blood froze. The obscenity frightened her in its crudity. She felt suddenly threatened. She had played around with men, always daintily, always on her own terms, and she had never actually looked at a naked man. She felt hysteria rise in her and knew she had bitten off more than she could chew. She knew she had to get out of there. She knew too the only way to do it.

'Come on,' he said, unbuttoning his flies.

She laughed.

She started on a giggle, then got louder, then simply laughed. There was hysteria in her mirth but he did not hear it. He only heard her laugh. He did not know what she was laughing at, but it humiliated him. He wanted her to stop. Suppose his mates heard her? All desire left him. He wanted out.

'Shut your mouth, you silly bitch!' he commanded, but she continued. 'Bugger you!' he hissed at her, but still she continued. 'Tart!' he threw at her contemptuously. 'Whore!' he cried, rebuttoning himself into his trousers, and he spat at her, full in the face. Then he was gone.

She stayed there a long time, until she was cold and the light was fading. She felt defeated and humiliated. Worst of all she felt she had deserved what had happened to her. She thought: I asked for his contempt and I got it. It would never happen to Briana or Mourna.

It was dark when she left and there was no sign of the bicycle gang. She was glad the holiday was nearly over. She was glad she would soon return to her home territory.

Chapter Fifty-Four

As Emmett walked down the boreen he saw Mena coming from the Martello tower. He let her get ahead, not wanting to talk to her at the moment. She would ask him where he had been, and when he said he had been to church she would make fun of him and he didn't feel he could stand that right now. Things were not too good between him and the old P.P. The old cleric kept repeating himself about the love of your fellow man, only when he went on about it now his voice had a distinct edge to it, and tonight he had accused Emmett of trying his patience.

'Oh, you're a thorn in my side, my boy,' he had said, sighing. 'A thorn in my side.'

There were people coming out of the pub ahead of him so once more he stopped and waited. He hated drunks and didn't like pubs and he thought it might be better if he waited until the boozers dispersed. He listened to their slurred farewells, until all the sounds had faded away, and then he continued his walk home, unseeing. He did not notice the silver shining moon or the stars that scattered the sky. Nor did he see the tossing trees nor feel the slight wind that shook them and cooled the land after the scorching day.

But he did see ahead of him suddenly, rounding a corner, the leaping shadows of men, and as he walked on he heard the voice of violence, the growl of the mob. It upset him, and he thought of the old Parish Priest and his love of peace and kindness and knew this was the sound of the devil.

A crowd had followed Joe from the pub. A group of about ten men had come out after him for he was alone, no Tom or Gabriel to keep him company home, to protect him. They were picking on him because he was weak and seemed to them to have more than they.

'Fuckin' tourists, comin' down here, money to burn,' they yelled at him, certain that anyone who could afford the train fare to Dranmore was a wealthy man.

Emmett came closer, staying near the ditch, keeping out of the moonlight, fearfully hiding. The shadows leaped. They seemed grotesque and elongated in the silvery light. There were five of them now. The rest, the taunters, were gone, melting away one by one, either ashamed or finished with the bullying. The remaining men grouped around Joe. They held branches of trees they must have torn off as they converged on their victim. He was caught in their vortex, fuddled, uncertain. They hopped around him in a circle. Around and around they went, jeering, hitting him, now lightly but with growing savagery. Like boxers they danced, poking their branches at the stupefied man who staggered, ape-like, not able to get his bearings, unable to comprehend what was happening.

'Fuckin' drunk!'

'Never pay yer whack!'

'Mean bastard!'

'Filthy pig!'

'Piss in yer pants!'

The men taunted. The branches made a singing noise in the air, swishing at him, cutting him.

Blood had appeared on his cheek. A trail of blood. His eye was cut now and he was limping, bewildered, unable to understand.

Emmett watched. Moonlight bathed the scene in a calm and cooling light, silvering the world in pale beauty, indifferent to the leaping violence below. The men did not see the moon. Rabid, intent, the taste for blood growing into the need for sacrifice, they circled the drunken man, hurling insults at him, whipping him and their own hatred to a frenzy. Their anger crystalized into abhorrence of this pathetic, staggering figure reeling about in the night. The switches sang through the air, slashing his cheeks, cruelly cutting his back.

Their taunts were becoming manic now as the men were carried away on a tide of fury. Paralyzed beside the ditch, Emmett watched as the jeers became chanting and the voices fused into a ritualistic chorus.

'Fuckin' drunk! Fuckin' drunk! Fuckin' drunk!'

He watched their hate-filled faces, grotesque in the moonlight. Uncle Joe's face had never looked like that. He reminded Emmett of someone he had seen, someone familiar. Uncle Joe's face was turned to the sky, in agony and a kind of ecstacy, too, and he was praying. Not

329

begging. Not pleading for them to stop. Praying. Saying the Our Father. Then Emmett knew who he looked like and he shuddered. Uncle Joe's face was the same as Christ's on the crucifix on his wall. That was who he resembled.

The beating was in progress in earnest now, the blows delivered to the tempo of their chanting. Uncle Joe seemed to have sobered up a little. He looked pathetic, a spectacle of a man, staggering about in the circle. He did not try to escape the blows that rained on him and his eyes had a wild and frantic expression that held both acceptance and pain.

He suddenly saw Emmett by the ditch and looked at him, unable to formulate a cry for help. His face was criss-crossed with blood now and the chanting of the circling men became louder and faster. He was muttering again, Emmett realized, and wondered what it was he was whispering so fervently.

The chanting stopped. There was a sudden silence. Emmett heard an owl hoot, away somewhere, far away. The men stood still in their circle and Emmett wondered for a moment if it was all over. But there was no slackening of tension in their stance or attitude, there was rather a drawing in, a gathering of strength for some final horror that Emmett could not even imagine. He heard then what his uncle was saying. It was the *De Profundis*:

'Out of the depths I cry to Thee O Lord,
Lord hear my prayer … ' "

Emmett knew they were winding up to a climax, some awful blood-letting ritual that would annihilate Uncle Joe and appease their blood-lust. He couldn't let that happen. Suddenly, joyously, with an enormous flood of relief he saw evil personified in the circle of men, good in his alcoholic uncle, and knew he couldn't stand by and let him be destroyed.

330

He had been crouching. Now he stood and ran into the circle, breaking it, an alien intrusion shattering their rhythm and smashing their concentration.

'Leave him, for God's sake! Leave him be. He hasn't harmed you, has he? Leave him, in God's name.'

He wasn't frightened and the men looked dazed, as if they had been brought back from the edge of an abyss. Appalled, they dropped the branches stained with blood and, unable to face the boy, sloped away down the boreen, ashamed now of their blood-lust under his clear gaze.

Uncle Joe lay sobbing in the dirt, a sorry sight, pathetic and repulsive. Yet Emmett felt no contempt.

'You okay?' he asked, giving his uncle his hand.

'Ah, God, Emmett, thanks be to Jasus ye came along. They'da killed me so they would. Janey Mac, I thought I'd breathed my last. Here, boy, give me a hand. Get me home to Maisie is all I ask.'

He smelled of stale wine and booze and tobacco but the boy did not mind. He managed to get him to his feet. Joe leaned on him as they moved towards Kincora, relying on his support.

He was a dirty smelly old alcoholic, given to self-pity and promises he would not keep, but Emmett, feeling the man's bones beneath his hand, feeling the helpless dependence on his own young strength, knew a great rush of love.

'Hold on to me, Uncle Joe,' he said buoyantly, 'I'll have you home in no time. Never fear. Just hang on to me.'

Chapter Fifty-Five

Joe lay on his bed in his room. He could hear the lonely crying of the gulls and the shouts of the children asserting themselves on the beach, the screech of carefree voices raised in high-pitched laughter.

His skin crawled. His head felt hollow as if some demon had sucked his brains out.

'Maisie, are you there?'

'Yes, dear.' Her voice sounded tired. She came and sat by his bed.

'Why do you put up with me?' he asked.

'I guess I love you,' she replied sadly.

'It gives you no joy.'

'How can it?' she asked in a rare burst of honesty.

'I had a surprise tonight ... last night ... yesterday. Whenever I was out last.'

'What happened?' She was used to his never knowing how much time had elapsed, never knowing whether it was night or day, whether a day or a week or a month had passed.

'Young Emmett helped me.'

'Yes, I know.'

'I suppose you do. I never remember everything. Only bits. I have pieces in my head, never the whole picture.'

'I know.'

He cleared his throat. His mouth tasted sour and his tongue coated and rough.

'They were beating me.'

'Who, Joe?'

'Men from the pub, I think … I'm not certain.'

'What had you done?' It was curious, she reflected, that she felt sure it was her husband's fault, that he had deserved his treatment because he provoked it. Drunks were belligerent, they ask for trouble, they goad.

'I don't think I had done anything, Maisie. I just think they don't like us.'

Drunks also suffer from persecution mania.

'Why, Joe? Why should they dislike us?'

'They think we're rich. They think that tourists have a lot of money and they resent that. And the intrusion.'

'That's no excuse for beating you.'

His face was filmed over with cold sweat and straggling strands of hair were plastered unattractively to his forehead. He smiled at her, sadly realizing that he had stultified her growth. Living with him had limited her interests, to say the very least. She had not developed as the other women had in all sorts of ways. She never went to the cinema or theatre, her interest in fashion and art had long since dwindled, and she never now read a book or newspaper. So she had atrophied, and it was his fault entirely. He had become her *raison d'être*, or rather his drinking had. She was limited to anxiety over his condition and the monitoring of her responses to him. Her whole life revolved around that. Morning, noon and night, going to work, coming home from work. What condition would Joe be in? How best to deal with him? That was all she thought about, concerned herself with.

He felt tears prick his eyes; alcoholic tears, sentimental and self-pitying. He shook his head and thought he heard his brains rattle. He was pickling them, that's what he was doing. And his liver.

'Your back is badly cut,' she said as he tried to move, and winced. 'I bathed it in iodine. I thought you'd scream but

333

you didn't feel a thing.'

'That's what they say, don't they? "Feeling no pain".' He laughed hollowly.

He remembered patches of the night. He remembered being in the pub and seeing the ceiling hit him. It had suddenly descended upon him, swirling and twirling around overhead, then down, suddenly. He remembered his head being pulled up roughly in someone's fist, then falling back on the table. He remembered the shock of the air as he left the pub, the sound of someone singing 'Mother Macree'. He recalled the circle of faces, red faces, gargoyle faces, going around and around and around. The swish and sting of the branches on his back, the hatred in the eyes of the men. What had he done to deserve that? He was a nuisance, he knew, but that hatred was palpable, out of proportion to anything he had done. Did they always go by how you appeared? Surely he had not appeared that prosperous to them? What was it then, this desire to kill, to destroy, to draw blood?

He sighed. His head began to throb fiercely and thinking was too difficult. He looked at Maisie's anxious face above him. 'I would like to get some … ' he faltered to a stop. Was he really going to say it?

She waited, then said, 'What, dear?'

'It's difficult to say. You know how often I promise never to drink again? Swear on Bibles?'

She nodded, acceptance on her face.

'Well, I'm not going to do that now. But I would like to get some … to get some help.'

There, he'd got it out. Her heart stirred in hope. He had never said that before. He had never sounded so humble.

'I would like to try. Do you think that's possible?'

'Oh, yes, Joe. Yes. We can try.'

He smiled at the way she said 'we'.

She bathed his face. He did not ask for a drink as he usually did. She looked into his eyes and saw despair.

'Don't worry, love. If you *want* to, you can do it.'

'You'll help me?' he asked.

'I'll help you,' she promised. 'Oh, my darling, I'll help you.'

Chapter Fifty-Six

Rita sat in front of the little oval mirror in her room, making her face up with infinite care. She pencilled her eyebrows with feather strokes and gave her eyelashes meticulous individual attention, spitting on to the black cake, rubbing the tiny brush in the moistened mascara and smoothing the lashes upwards with careful sweeping motions. She rubbed a little colour on to her cheeks and flicked her powder-puff over the whole, then carefully painted her lips.

It was wonderful having a purpose. She could not remember applying make-up for a man since her courting days. She put on her new dress, humming to herself.

'Every penny, Rita, every penny you've got.'

But the dress had been worth it. What it did for her morale could not be measured in pounds, shillings and pence.

She would go down the hill in her sling-backs to buy a magazine. They would kill her feet on the way back, but it was worth it. Her ankles looked good in the sling-backs.

She did not think about what she was doing. She did not dare to. She simply knew it was a sunny day in Dranmore, the butterflies thick in the buddleia, the sun dancing on the blue, blue sea and shimmering in the blue, blue sky.

Bees droned and birds chirped incessantly and she felt like a teenager.

She had had a week off now, she had done no housework and she was rested. She was not going to think about tomorrows and tomorrows, she was going to enjoy herself. She had quit worrying, left her problems aside for the time being.

She stood outside Kincora, the handle of her empty white bag over her wrist. She turned her face to the soft breeze from the sea and she smiled. The sun was in her eyes on her way down the hill and she hoped they wouldn't water and her mascara wouldn't run after all the trouble she had taken.

She could smell the green smell of the grass and the sharp scent of the gorse bushes and the sweet perfume of lavender and honeysuckle. The palms of her hands were damp and the plastic handle stuck to her fingers, slippery in the heat. She could feel the soft material of her skirt flap against her bare legs and the sand from the boreen between her toes.

Barney's face lit up when he saw her. 'An' how's your good self this fine day?' he asked as she put the magazine on the counter, her last threepenny bit on top. Sheer extravagance!

'I'm grand,' she said. 'Just grand.'

'And don't you look it!' He handed her back her threepence. 'Have it on me. Now don't embarrass me by refusing, please.' He paused, cleared his throat. 'I can't close the shop right now,' he said, 'but I'd like to meet you at … '

Not at the Grand, she pleaded inwardly, not up there on the hill where she'd feel dowdy in spite of her new dress. Not up there with Colista and Eddie casting their glances over Barney Boland in his open-necked shirt and florid countenance. Not up there with manicured hands and dainty drinks and savage undertones. But where else?

He was staring at her, open admiration in his eyes, his request hanging on the air.

'Yes?' she said, smiling.

'I'd like to take you for a drink in Drat Regan's pub at lunchtime. If it wouldn't be beneath you, that is? If it's all right with you?'

'Yes. Oh, yes. I'd love to,' she cried. 'Yes, that would be lovely.'

'See you at twelve-thirty then?'

'You're on!' she laughed, and waving her hand left the shop.

'A woman with warmth,' Barney said with delight and chuckled to himself. 'Yes, a fine woman indeed.'

Chapter Fifty-Seven

They met as strangers, their enthusiasm off the boil, both shy and a little apprehensive. But they thawed gradually in the sunlight. They walked down the boreen to Drat Regan's in silence. Bees droned, the sound becoming suddenly aggressive then softening to a low hum. She dodged the nettles and he took her elbow in his large fist and steered her along beside him.

They sat in Drat Regan's snug, a shaft of sunlight between them. Redolent of beer and stale cigarette smoke, the small, beamed room, womb-like and welcoming, could not diminish the expectancy that snapped and crackled between Rita and Barney. She felt an amazing buoyancy in his presence. She trusted him, felt confident of his good intentions.

He was excited by what he saw. She seemed to him the personification of womanhood as he felt it should be; round and warm, middle-aged yet pretty, a rose in full voluptuous bloom. There was a vulnerability about her that touched him, a tension he very much wanted to ease.

'What'll you have?'

'A Paddy, please.'

He liked her smile, her direct blue gaze. He smiled back at her. 'I'll join ye in that,' he said, and went to the bar to order.

She stared at his broad shoulders and thought how reassuring his back was. Large enough to carry a load of troubles. I'd like him to be my man, she thought. I'd like very much for him to be my very own, to say to myself, 'This is my fella.'

There were a thousand motes dancing in the beam of sunlight. It fell on the table, spotlighting the grooves made by lighted cigarettes left at the edge to burn themselves out. She traced a ring on it with her index finger, deciding to borrow some nail-varnish from Dot and manicure her nails. Make her hands look pretty.

Barney returned and sat beside her. They sipped their drinks in silence, then both began to speak together.

'Sorry,' he said. 'You first.'

'I was just going to say that this is a lovely place to live.'

He nodded. 'It is that. But I go away in the winter.'

'Oh?'

'Didn't Gabriel tell you?'

She shook her head. 'He never mentioned you. That morning was the first time I heard your name.'

'Oh!'

'You sound … '

'I thought he was … '

She laughed. 'Well, maybe he was, but I didn't know anything about it.'

They were silent again for a moment, neither of them

338

knowing what to say yet full of questions.

'Where do you go in the winter?' she asked at last.

'What? Oh, Florida, California, the Bahamas. I like to sail.'

'So do I.'

He looked pleased. 'Do you?'

'Oh, yes. My husband … ' She glanced at him, stammering a little. 'He died.'

He nodded. 'Yes, I know. Gabriel said.'

'So he talked to you about me, but not to me about you?' she laughed, feeling more at ease, glad not to have to explain.

'I'm afraid so,' he laughed with her.

'Oh, well, I don't mind. No, we had a little sailing-boat in Bullock Harbour. It's not like sailing in those exotic places.'

'The fundamentals are the same,' he assured her, relishing the masterful feeling she was giving him.

'Tell me about America.'

'Would you want to move?' he queried doubtfully.

'I'd want to do whatever my … partner and I figured was best for both of us,' she replied carefully.

They realized simultaneously that they were both of the same mind and that they hardly needed to finish their questions, so in tune were they with each other.

They looked at each other directly for the first time and he took her hand in his.

'Hello, Rita,' he said.

'Hello, Barney,' she whispered back.

Chapter Fifty-Eight

Sunny day followed sunny day. Mourna stayed up in the Grand. Ardel was moved again, this time to Brigid's room. Des bunked in with Roac and Brigid shared with Emer, which pleased both girls. Oonagh relaxed once more in the big front room, recharging her batteries, Molly said.

Molly missed her company on the beach. She and Tom moved separately as if in different worlds, together, yet totally out of tune.

Briana was hardly ever home, spending all her time with Iain. They looked a proper pair of beachcombers and stayed out by the sea, early morning to late at night, sailing or swimming, turning a gypsy brown.

Laughlin went for drives with his new friend, and talked and talked and talked.

Granny O'Shea's nose was a little out of joint for her old chum Emmett spent a lot of time now with his Uncle Joe. The unlikely friendship surprised everyone, and the sight of the boy sitting on a bench under one of the Monterey pines with his alcoholic uncle was both touching and odd.

'He'll become human yet,' Tom remarked, but Oonagh was worried.

Gabriel reassured her. 'He's all right, love. God has him in the hollow of His hand and he'll be all right. No, it's Ardel is the problem.'

But Ardel did not seem worried any more. He was looking forward to going up to the Grand for the dance.

340

Granny O'Shea complained, but that was her wont. 'It's confusing being here,' she said. 'I'm not sure where I am half the time. I wake up and I think, How'd I get here? Where is this place? It's not my home. Have I died? It's confusing, Gabriel, very confusing.'

'Well, Mother, if you're unhappy we'll let you stay at home next year.'

'No, no, no. Then I'd have given up. Don't you see?'

'I suppose so, pet.'

'Do you want to get rid of me, son? Is that it? Have I become a burden to you?'

'No, you're not, Mam, you know you're not.'

'Well, ye frighten me when ye talk like that. Leave me at home indeed!'

'Then we won't talk like that any more, dear.'

'I want Emmett. Where's Emmett?'

'He's with Joe, Mam.'

'That old soak! Watch out he doesn't lead Emmett into bad ways.'

'He won't do that, Mam.'

'What does he want with Emmett anyhow?'

'I don't know, Mother. I think Joe has cut out drinking.'

'Oh, he's done that before but it never lasts.'

'Well, there's always a first time, Mother.'

Gabriel's patience seemed inexhaustible and eventually she gave up and sat in the shade on the beach, listening to Maggie Moran's squeals and the laughter of the others, and remembered, peacefully. She recalled the dim and dusty past and things forgotten, scenes that drifted in and out of her mind like old lithographs, infinitely sweet. She saw the family around the tree at Christmas, and her brother singing carols in the snow. She was dancing with her sailor husband to the strains of 'Alice Blue Gown', and she was young and he was beautiful. Tears gathered in her eyes and she swallowed them down. If he saw them, Gabriel would worry. But her son was preoccupied with his wife.

341

For a few days after her ordeal Oonagh felt very weak. Her children and husband fussed over her but she was adamant over playing down her condition and told the girls it was her woman's time and the boys that she was a little off-colour. She promised Gabriel that as soon as they returned to Dublin she would see Dr Grey and have him check her, see she was all right. Gabriel told the rest of the family that Oonagh had a tummy upset. Mrs Flanagan didn't like that at all and Dot said it was peculiar.

'Ben is ever so finicky about food an' has a weak stomach an' he's had no trouble here.'

So Gabriel poured oil on troubled waters by saying she had probably picked it up in the Grand. Mrs Flanagan, somewhat mollified by this statement, looked after Oonagh whom she liked and brought her soup and appetizers.

The holiday was drawing to a close when Mourna announced her engagement. She phoned her mother in Kincora to tell her the news.

'We're officially engaged, Mummy. I've said yes to Kurt.'

'Oh, darling, I'm so happy. Are you sure?'

'Quite sure. I wanted you and Daddy to be the first to know.'

'Thank you, darling, I appreciate that. Have you told Colista and Eddie?'

'No. I wanted to tell you first. Auntie Colista keeps asking me. She's going to give a party for me on Saturday, she said, if I decide to announce it. You'll come?'

'Of course I will, my darling. I hope she hasn't hurried you? That the party isn't …?'

Mourna laughed warmly. 'Of course not, Mummy. I'll phone you. Come early on Saturday so we can talk. 'Bye.'

Gabriel was not as pleased with the news as Oonagh had hoped, but he was so gentle with her these days, so tender and kind, that there seemed to be no lengths to which he would not go to keep her happy. Therefore he hid from her his real misgivings.

He did not want to lose the daughter of his heart to a foreigner, a stranger who would take her far away from them. He knew he was being selfish and unreasonable but he could not help how he felt.

Oonagh got herself together for the party. She drew on whatever hidden resources of strength she had left and decked herself out in her grey moiré, and feeling a little weak but very, very proud, determined to enjoy the evening.

She and Gabriel went early to the Grand as Mourna had asked. She left Gabriel at the bar and went to her daughter's room and helped her to dress, as if for her wedding. They embraced, tears in Oonagh's eyes, tears of joy and triumph and tears for the heartbreak of the change it would mean, the loss.

Mourna wore her black lace that moulded itself so smoothly to her perfect body and Oonagh zipped it up.

Where did she come from, this beautiful daughter she loved so much? How was she fashioned, each cell, each muscle, each alignment of bone and, soft skin, the miraculous shading of colour? She marvelled all over again at her eldest's perfection. Could I have done it again? she wondered, and thought of the sad little half-human in the bosom of the sea. She shook her head and decided not to think about it any more tonight. Not tonight. Mourna's night.

Gabriel came to hurry them down. When he looked at Mourna a funny lump gathered in his throat and he stumbled over his words.

'I couldn't find the room. One hundred and sixty-nine, so many rooms. You don't think when you're downstairs that there could be so many.' Then, catching his wife's glance of inquiry, 'The guests are waiting.'

'Let them wait,' she replied to his vast surprise, then added, 'Come and look at your lovely daughter.'

He stared at her standing there, clouds of dark hair

touching her creamy shoulders, wide calm eyes like violets damp with dew. It was almost pain that twisted his heart and he opened his arms, this most undemonstrative of men, and she rushed into them.

'Daddy! Oh, Daddy!'

He knew she loved him and trusted him, but soon she would shift her allegiance to another man. It was right that she should, but it gave him a twinge of jealousy nevertheless.

'I'll always love you, Daddy,' she said as if in answer to his thoughts.

'Be happy,' he whispered. 'Be happy, pet.'

She looked at him with a calm and steady gaze, 'I will, Daddy. I will.'

It was a moment of glory for Oonagh, descending the wide staircase on her husband's arm, her daughter just ahead of them. Look at her and admire us, she wanted to cry. Our lives have not been in vain for she is our creation, someone to be very proud of.

Kurt was waiting at the bottom of the staircase with Ardel. He looked at Mourna with joyful eyes, a smile on his lips.

Why did Oonagh shiver when she looked at Eddie who stood at his other elbow? The feeling was shortlived and she found herself caught up in the general celebration.

Mourna shone that night. She looked like the evening star — alone, incandescent, lighting up a night sky. Even Kurt became unusually animated and seemed to respond ardently to her bright splendour. Only Eddie lacked his usual high spirits.

Colista was triumphant. She too glowed, an inner excitement simmering, a hectic flush on her face. She told Gabriel that she would arrange the wedding and he refused her offer very firmly.

'No. I'll give my own daughter her wedding, thank you, Colista,' he said with determination, ignoring Oonagh's signs to accept. She visualized a smart wedding reception in the grandeur of the Bensons' home and couldn't understand Gabriel's insistence on having it in Griffith Avenue.

The Grand looked splendid. They had risen to the occasion, as expected of a first-class hotel and decorated the ballroom in the couple's honour. Eddie, of course, had greased a lot of palms. Great baskets of flowers festooned every available surface and the air was scented by their perfume.

Their table was the most prominent and already prepared for them, a glorious flower arrangement of pink carnations and roses with white freesias in the centre and a huge pink marzipan heart on a silver stand with FOREVER LOVE spelled out on it.

'It's rather vulgar but well-intentioned,' Colista whispered to Oonagh. 'Oh, aren't you the proud woman, and now you have a Countess for a daughter.' Oonagh could only nod.

Kurt and Mourna were put together behind the heart and everyone toasted them in champagne. Oonagh was bursting with pride at her daughter's composure, her modest acceptance of the praise she received.

Eddie upset Gabriel by putting doubts into his head about his future son-in-law.

'I'm worried about the German,' he confided to a reluctant Gabriel. Eddie's eyes roamed the room, restlessly seeking focus.

'Oh? Why?' Gabriel was forking caviar into his mouth, thinking how overrated it was.

'His background. Colista says she's done a complete character check. But you know what women are. She wants to believe he's all right. I worry, Gabriel. I worry for Mourna.'

'Again, Eddie, why?'

'His age, for one thing. He says he wasn't a Nazi, but

then, they all deny it now, after the event. His age is right for him to have been one. In fact, I don't see how he could not have been.'

'A Nazi? I thought he left Germany before the war broke out?'

'He says he did. I don't know. It's best to be careful, don't you think?'

Gabriel nodded, disturbed by Eddie's inferences.

Colista, on his other side, claimed his attention, 'What has Eddie been saying to you about Kurt?'

'Well, he seems to think … '

'He's prejudiced, Gabriel. Pay no attention to him. Kurt will make Mourna a wonderful husband.'

Gabriel nodded. What he couldn't understand was the bone of contention between Eddie and Colista about the German. There seemed to be an underlying tussle going on that was incomprehensible to him. Perhaps they simply enjoyed conflict. He had read about such people who thrived in their marriage on a struggle for power. Perhaps Eddie and Colista were one of those couples.

Colista then upset Oonagh by leaning over and whispering, 'Tell Gabriel not to pay any attention to Eddie. He's talking such nonsense about Kurt.'

'What nonsense?'

'That he's a Nazi. He's not, you know. No matter what Eddie says.'

Afterwards, while the young people were dancing, Oonagh caught Colista and tried to further the conversation.

'Why does Eddie seem to dislike Kurt?' she asked.

Her sister shook her head.

'Prejudice. He hates the Germans. And the Jews. He particularly hates the Jews.'

'But Kurt is not a Jew.'

'His family were Jewish bankers. It's where their money comes from. Kurt's mother became a Catholic, which makes him a perfect husband for Mourna. Look at them together … aren't they divine? But Eddie says once a Jew always a Jew.' She glanced out into the ballroom. 'And Eddie hates Kurt because he is more powerful. He has more money, more influence, a title. And he is discreet about it. He doesn't throw his weight about like Eddie.' A worried frown creased her face. 'Get them married soon, Oonagh. Anyone who underestimates my husband is foolish.'

'Why did you start all this, Colista?' Oonagh asked her sister.

'I don't know, dear. It seemed a good idea at the time. It still does. Mourna, rich, happy, a Countess.'

'I think you did it to get at Eddie. If so, it is unpardonable.'

'Maybe you are right. I did it to get at my husband, to prevent a madness you know nothing of. Anyhow, what difference does it make? The net result is the same. A good marriage for your daughter.'

'You have no morals, Colista.'

'Oh, come now, dearest sister. You were pleased enough to push Mourna into his arms, and if I remember rightly his title had a lot to do with it. Don't start moralizing to me!'

Oonagh had turned pale. Her sister spoke lightly but there was truth in her words. Oonagh was wounded. Tired and weak from her ordeal, she had been getting by on adrenalin from her excitement and joy.

She wilted now under her sister's scrutiny. 'I'm sorry, I'm sure, Colista,' she said. 'And, yes, I'm really glad that Mourna is making such a good match. She needs security, and flowers in the atmosphere here. I don't think she would be very good fighting for a living out there in the real world.'

Colista nodded. 'A girl after my own heart.'

'But I'd never have her marry simply for financial and social security, believe me.'

Colista raised her fine eyebrows. 'Why not?' she asked.

347

'Why on earth not? Oh, people are so dishonest! As if there is anything wrong in doing that. I married Eddie for social position and financial security, Oonagh. They were his trump cards. He's good-looking, but so is Kurt. So were many of the beaus who courted me. But you remember – I was only interested if the man had position and money. Why lie? I see no reason to be ashamed of that. Eddie comes first, last, and is everything to me. He has given me everything I need.' She spread her hands. 'Everything. Do you think I would change places with anyone in the world? I have the money to do as I please, go where I please, and travel first class. I have been protected from all the little inconveniences of life.' She shook her head. 'Oh, Oonagh, that's a comfortable thing. That is a very pleasant thing. I value my position more than anything. It is what I chose and I will hold on to it till my dying day.'

Oonagh shivered. There was something feverish about her sister she found disturbing.

'And what do you have to do to keep it?' she asked.

'Keep Eddie happy,' Colista said. 'And that's worth fighting for. It is not much to have to do.'

'And are you fighting for that now, Colista?'

Her sister's eyes widened. 'Oh, yes,' she whispered.

Before Oonagh could ask her what she meant Gabriel returned from the bar. She took his arm gratefully and asked him to find a sofa in a quiet spot where she could rest. He was only too delighted to do as she asked.

They sat a little away from the ballroom and Gabriel ordered a brandy for himself and one for his wife.

'Are you all right, darling?' he asked her. They could hear the buzz of conversation from the dining room and the band playing 'One and Only You'.

'Yes, love,' she assured him. She smiled at him, thinking about what Colista had said, her angry tone when she talked. It was as if her sister was in some terrible battle, engaged in combat with forces unknown. It seemed very

348

tiring, as if she had to gird her loins and prepare to fight at the drop of a hat. What an exhausting time she must have.

Gently she touched her husband's face and smiled in answer to his tender look. She suddenly felt very sorry for Colista.

Ardel caught up with his uncle at the bar. Eddie's eyes were glittering dangerously, and if Ardel hadn't known better he would have thought his uncle was agitated. But Eddie Benson was always calm and sounded that way as he greeted Ardel, in spite of his expression.

'Can I have a word with you, Uncle Eddie?' Ardel said in an extremely polite voice.

'What is it?'

'Well, sir … it's sort of private.'

Eddie smiled, a charming smile, a smile that drew them together.

'When you call me sir I know it's important, Ardel! Now, what can I do for you? Sit you here, in this booth, and we'll have a word.' He laid his arm over Ardel's shoulder and drew him to the seat. 'But you'll have to hurry. This is Mourna's big night, after all.'

'Yes, Uncle Eddie.'

'I won't order us a drink, it might tempt us to settle.'

He held a thick-bottomed cut-glass tumbler, full of whiskey. 'Now, Ardel, what is it? Something to do with money? Something to do with those men that beat you up, eh? Do they want money?' He answered his own question. 'Yes. It must be money, that's why you came to me. And Banan, I'm told, has arrived in Dranmore, gracing this gentle seaside town with his surly presence.' He glanced at Ardel whose mouth hung open in astonishment. Eddie grinned. 'I didn't get to where I am today, Ardel, by being slow on the uptake. How much do you need?'

He took a deep breath. 'One hundred pounds, sir,' he said confidently. If he was going to borrow he might as well have a little over for himself.

'Right. I'll have it for you in the morning.' Eddie stood. Ardel couldn't believe it was all over. 'Come up here about ten o'clock in the morning. I'll be finished on the courts then. If I'm not here there'll be an envelope at reception for you. All right, Ardel? Now off you go and enjoy yourself.'

He thought he would faint with relief. He wanted to shout and sing. It had been so easy! He could pay the money back, get off the hook, and square himself with the world.

There was no doubt – his luck had changed.

Chapter Fifty-Nine

Mourna fitted well in his arms. His cheek was against hers and she could feel the soft hairs at his temple brush her face. Violins soughed romantically. The crooner sang:

'To each his own,
I find my own,
One and only you.'

She hummed along then smiled up at him and rested her head back on his shoulder. They didn't speak. They didn't have to. They were quiet together. It was one of the things Mourna liked about him, his peacefulness.

He drew his face away from hers. 'They talk here sometimes,' he said. 'In the hotel.'

'What about?' she asked. She could see he was troubled. She was very intuitive about him, sensing his feelings.

'About my nationality.' He took a deep breath. 'I'm not, and never have been, a Nazi.' He sounded unusually vehement. 'I want you to know that. Do you believe me, Mourna?'

'Of course,' she said, reassuring him with a glance. 'You have no need to ask me. I know you were not.'

It was simple for her. No one as kind and gentle as Kurt could possibly have been one of Hitler's thugs.

'Of course I believe you,' she said, and he sighed, relieved. He had heard them whisper, talk, words like Belsen, Buchenwald, Treblinka. He wondered who had started the rumours, then knew with certainty it was Eddie. But why? Kurt could not think of a reason. It was a terrible thing to do, for rumours, once started, were very hard to disprove.

Eddie Benson was a strange human being. So attractive, so rakishly handsome, yet underneath that careless charm there seethed an emotional turmoil. Kurt would never have chosen Eddie as a friend, but he liked Colista and she had introduced him to Mourna.

'I love you,' he said, and she smiled.

'I love you too,' she replied, and his hand tightened on hers.

'I want so much for you to be happy, Mourna.'

'I will be with you, Kurt,' she said firmly, and they glided effortlessly to the music.

The Wilmots arrived. Eddie welcomed them with his usual charm. 'Ah, how good to see you,' he cried, beckoning Gabriel. 'My brother-in-law is here with us. You two know each other, I believe?' A heavy wink. Mr Wilmot laughed and Gabriel joined in the joke.

'Delighted to see you, Mr O'Shea. My wife ... '

Gabriel had Oonagh on his arm and they seated themselves at the table and Mr Wilmot told Gabriel how glad he was that they had met and their two wives had become acquainted.

'Mr McLaglan is leaving, Mr O'Shea. I don't know if Mr

Benson has told you?'

'I didn't think it should come from me, Dave.' Eddie smiled at the little man and ordered champagne.

'About time, eh, Mr O'Shea? Poor old McLaglan was a falling-down case. Exhausted, he was. Reached his natural end in Barnet's.'

Gabriel nodded and remarked, 'Very nice man he was, too.'

'Very nice. Very nice. There I'd agree with you wholeheartedly, Mr O'Shea.' Dave Wilmot nodded and twisted his moustaches between his finger and thumb. 'Yes. A good man. Still, you'll not mind stepping into his shoes, eh, O'Shea?'

It meant the job was his and Gabriel looked at Oonagh with a delighted smile and pressed her arm.

'Ah, here's the happy couple,' Aileen Wilmot said, and Mourna and Kurt returned to the table.

'Look at you, Mourna O'Shea,' Mr Wilmot greeted her. 'As lovely as a film star. Sure, I've known you since you were in nappies, eh, O'Shea? Well, well, well, and this is the lucky man? We met before in Kilcrony. Daresay you can't recall, but my memory is sound as a bell, eh, O'Shea? Is it not?' Gabriel hastened to assure him, and he continued, 'Ah now, isn't this a great day for the family?'

It would do Barnet's no harm to have a connection with Count Von Mensil, Oonagh thought, as she smiled and nodded and exchanged gossip with Aileen Wilmot.

It was pleasant too, that Aileen Wilmot, used to looking down her nose a little at Oonagh O'Shea, now wanted to cultivate her friendship. After all, her daughter was marrying a Count and her husband would be the next General Manager of Barnet's.

Oonagh saw Mourna smile at her and she smiled gratefully back at her daughter.

Mourna had been right. In her calm and quiet way she was wise. Everything was going to be all right.

352

Chapter Sixty

Ardel looked around the foyer of the Grand. Music throbbed from the ballroom and he hummed 'I Saw You Last Night And Got That Oooold Feeling'. He felt elated, but not part of the glamorous throng that swirled about him. The black and white evening dress of the men complimented them, giving them an elegance they did not normally possess. He caught sight of himself in a long mirror and was amazed at how handsome he looked. But he was not impressed with himself, he had no time to admire, he did not consider that aspect of himself important.

He looked at the charming bouquets of colour the women made in their long dresses; taffeta and chiffon, shot-silk and satin. The jewels any one of them wore would keep him for a year.

He could see his mother and father with the Bensons at the largest table directly in front of the orchestra, the dance floor between. Colista was smoking and Mr and Mrs Wilmot were talking to Mourna and Kurt.

It's all very well for them, he thought, they had it easy, the Bensons.

The girls eyed him admiringly and hopefully as he drifted from room to room. They longed for the tall handsome boy to ask them to dance but he remained oblivious to their charms and smoked his cigarette, isolated and self-contained, leaning against a pillar in the ballroom.

It came to him slowly, the 'pock-pock' of balls. Like a terrier becoming alert he registered the lovely familiar sound, raising his head and turning his profile whence it came.

'Ah, God, he's lovely!' Dodo Fitzwilliam murmured as the band beat out the 'Harry Lime Theme'.

Her sister said, 'I'm goin' to ask him for the next dance, I don't care if it's a Ladies' Choice or not.'

But when they looked back to where he had been standing there was no one there. He had vanished.

~~~~~~

Colonel Renshaw saw him enter the billiard room. Ardel sort of sidled in, slipping around the arch, hugging the wall, the cigarette dangling from his lips, his thin wrists a half-inch below his cuffs.

'Oi! Oi! Here's a green one, old boy,' Renshaw said to Gerald Belcher, his old friend and comrade-in-arms. Survivors of two wars, they both came to the Grand each year and declared another war on the staff, driving them crazy with unreasonable demands and their bad temper and bloody-mindedness, which they felt they had earned the right freely to express. They went home having won the battle hands down.

They both hated the young. They particularly hated young men, and anything either of them could do to humiliate or embarrass boys between the ages of eighteen and thirty gave them cause for celebration.

'Green as a Granny Smith,' Gerald Belcher said gleefully. 'Like to join us, young fella?' he called to the boy standing leaning against the arch. The young man looked around as if he thought they were talking to someone behind him, then, as if surprised, pointed to himself.

'Me, sir?'

'Yes, you. Like to have a go?'

354

The young man flushed, looked flustered. 'But ... you're experts, gentlemen. I can see that. And I ... ' he shrugged deprecatingly, never actually saying he was inexperienced but nevertheless indicating it with every gesture. 'Are you sure you want to bother with the likes of me?'

The Colonel nodded, his face red with excited anticipation.

Ardel shrugged. 'Okay then,' he said, then thought a moment. 'Do you ... do you wager any money?' he asked tentatively, then laughed. 'Oh, no. 'Course you wouldn't. Old people don't gamble.'

He couldn't have said anything more calculated to force their hand.

Gerald Belcher caught the Colonel's eye and responded to the gleam there.

'Yes, young man. Of course.'

'I haven't any money on me,' the young man said diffidently. 'But my uncle is Eddie Benson and he'll stake me. He told me he'd pay all my expenses tonight.'

Just the right touch of eagerness and gaucherie. The Colonel and Belcher did their best to contain their glee. They hated Eddie Benson almost as much as they despised the young. He was everything they loathed; rich, powerful, aggressive, always demanding and getting priority treatment. He stuck in their craws.

Ardel calculated how long it would take him to win. Although billiards was a different game it was one he was expert at. He sub-divided, then quoted his price, stammering, showing a respectful confusion, and if they were surprised at the large amount they did not show it.

'Is that too much? Or is it too little, maybe?' Ardel sounded uncertain.

The Colonel wiped his large moustache with a spotted handkerchief, 'Oh, Good Lord, no!' he said gruffly. 'Well, come on, let's play.'

They smirked at each other, winking and nodding to Grundy, the old waiter who hated their guts. They knew he hated them and part of the pleasure was ordering him about knowing that fact.

'Grundy, get us drinks,' Belcher commanded, and the waiter ran fast to the bar, hustled the bartender there.

'Young lad playing bloody Renshaw and Belcher,' he said, and the bartender went into high speed.

'They'll take him to the cleaners, poor little tyke,' the barman said.

'Not sure about that.' Grundy put the glasses on the tray. 'Something about him ... We might just see those two old farts trounced.'

'Well hurry, Grundy, an' don't miss it,' the barman urged and he hurried back.

They were squaring up, Grundy saw. Young kid couldn't win. What did he know? The old guys played a mean game in Grundy's book. He gave them their drinks and stood to attention at the door. The Colonel insisted on it; if he relaxed or shifted his weight from foot to foot, the Colonel shouted him to attention again as if he were in the army. Grundy crossed his fingers and they began.

When Ardel made a good break they were not too dismayed. Nevertheless they could see he was not as green as they originally thought him. But when he potted the first red and positioned himself on the black they realized suddenly and sickeningly he was an expert and they had made jack-asses of themselves.

Grundy's heart rejoiced within him, watching as Ardel pulverized them, took them to the cleaners, beat them hollow.

They made a fuss about paying. After all, it was a large amount. One hundred pounds. Fifty pounds each. They had looked forward briefly to collecting the money from Eddie Benson. Now they had to fork out to this shaver because Grundy was there, a witness, his eyes bright and triumphant.

Ardel refused to accept a cheque. He remained adamant. 'I want it in cash,' he insisted, his eyes unblinking with that oh-so-innocent look he wore that was so misleading.

'I'll cash the cheques now for ye, gentlemen, at the bar. 'Twill be no trouble, no trouble at all. There's bound to be plenty of cash in the till tonight an' yer credit is good!'

Grundy was ecstatic. And he was as good as his word, telling the bartender, 'Trounced them, he did! Knocked the stuffing outa the old bastards, God bless him.'

The Colonel had to hand the cash over to Ardel and they thanked him for the game through clenched teeth. Only Ardel was smiling.

Chapter Sixty-One

At the other end of the seaside town that Saturday night, overlooking the harbour, the beat of boogie-woogie throbbed out over the dark sea, and laughter at the racy repartee of the comedian, Bob O'Brien was loud and raucous, the smoke of cigarettes and the conviviality engendered by booze and music all mingled together to create an atmosphere that was warm and welcoming. People settled down to enjoy the evening, drink as much as they could and have a good time.

They had erected a catwalk running from the small stage where the band played to the ladies' toilet at the other end near the entrance. The contestants had been told to leave their outdoor clothes in the toilet, and now Brigid was fiercely guarding Emer's raincoat, brought with her to Dranmore in case of bad weather.

Brigid settled on her seat, holding on to the coat tightly. Imagine losing your clothes. It seemed to her a tragedy. She was sitting on a bench brought in from outside. Someone had put it against the door of the ladies' so that only the contestants could get in and out.

'There's another ladies' upstairs or all the women here 'ud burst,' Brigid whispered to her cousin, and settled on Emer's raincoat with, as she put it to herself, the best view in the whole place.

The contestants were a mixed bunch. A girl from Harcourt Street in Dublin was as pretty as Mourna but she had an unyielding cow-like shape and thick ankles. A Clare girl, a redhead like Emer, had bags of confidence and was very pretty, but one of her front teeth was missing.

'They'll never notice if I don't smile,' she said to Emer *sotto voce*. 'Or if I just stretch my mouth with my lips like this.' She looked like Bela Lugosi when she did that but Emer didn't say a word. There was a girl from Tralee in a green swimsuit with masses of dark hair who posed serious competition, and another from Tipperary who didn't.

Emer was given a huge yellow disc which luckily matched her swimsuit and had the number fifteen printed on it. She was told to fix it to her costume. The pin went through the cotton wool padding she had filled the uplift-bra part of the costume with, but it looked lovely on the yellow bathing suit and as long as she kept steady and it didn't shift she was all right. Otherwise the bust moved independently of her body.

She looked sensational and she knew it. An eejity girl from Sligo with an amazing cleavage had pinned her disc right in the centre of her *décolletage* and no one told her she had defeated her own purpose.

When their numbers were called they had to walk out,

pose, walk down the catwalk, pose again, then turn and walk back and off. That's what Bob O'Brien had told them before the bar had opened, when they had arrived and stood around shivering, their coats over their costumes. Now the room was full of people, smoke and laughter, the clink of glasses and the buzz of conversation, and over it all, through the microphone, Bob O'Brien's raucous voice cracking them up with his terrible jokes. Emer had to admit that she felt a thrill of excitement such as she had never known. Bob O'Brien made them laugh, he really got the audience going, and once the girls started parading the adrenalin in the stuffy little room was pumping madly.

'Now here is number fifteen, and if I say so myself this little lady lives up to the tune,' Bob called out, and the band played 'A Pretty Girl Is Like A Melody'. Bob was dripping sweat, his evening shirt was soggy and tight-necked and looked as if it might choke him. It had been a good few years since he had been able to button his dinner jacket but the audience loved him. 'May I present, Miss Emer O'Shea from Dublin's Fair City!'

Emer stepped into the spotlight. She felt a flood of excitement flow through her and thought, This is where I belong. Hand on hip, knee a little bent, she posed, then walk, walk, walk, right hip *out* as left foot goes forward, left hip *out* as right foot goes forward. Stop! She looked over her shoulder *à la* Betty Grable in the pin-up pictures, nice touch, before she turned, then around, both hands on hips, pressing them, raising one shoulder, then strut, strut, strut, hips *out*, stop, turn and ... She was off, finished, and the audience were cheering, calling out, whistling. Wow! She wanted to go right back out there again, she had not had nearly enough.

She hurried down the side passage to Brigid.

'How'd I do?' Whispering in the dark in case the other girls heard.

'You were gorgeous!' Brigid hissed back. 'None of the

others did those little extra wiggles. None.'

'I might get chosen in the finals.'

'You're sure to, Emer. It's a dead cert.'

'Oh, you're prejudiced, Brigid.'

'Listen, Emer. They're calling out the finalists. Listen!'

'Number one, number five, number twelve, number thirteen … '

Oh God, Oh God, don't let him pass me. Emer shivered.

'Number fifteen, number nineteen and number twenty.'

'Fifteen. Whee!' Brigid jumped up and down. 'That's you, Emer. It's you.'

'You're padded, you are. I know,' number two jeered. She was the Clare girl who wasn't chosen, the girl with the front tooth missing. She hissed sibilantly at Emer through the gap and flounced away.

Emer kept her eyes on the stage.

'And now, for the last time, our lovely ladies, one by one.' Bob O'Brien sweated, swabbing his neck with a none too clean handkerchief.

Emer felt calm. Certain. She would win, she knew. She shifted in the wings, moving from one foot to the other, flexing her neck, her shoulders, tightening her hips. 'Number five.' Then the next, then the others, until it came to her turn. One of the band winked at her, she winked back. 'Number fifteen!'

Bob O'Brien thought she was nervous because she did not immediately appear as the other contestants had. They had all jumped on the stage as soon as their numbers were called. She didn't. Instinctively she knew better. She waited that extra moment, counted five slowly, then entered, to a huge cheer, walked to the tiny apron and stood, eyes bright, not looking at anyone yet looking at them all. She took even longer walking down the ramp this time. She did her Betty Grable again and got a cheer, then again too soon it was over.

She hurried down to Brigid who draped her coat over

360

her shoulders and squeezed her arm and told her she was the best.

She went back to the wings where the other girls stood, waiting and nervous. Emer looked at the dark-haired number ten, the Kerry girl, and knew she'd lost. The girl was so pretty, her hair had a life of its own and her eyes were bright as cornflowers.

There was a break for a song. 'Ireland's answer to Bing Crosby', a thick-set tenor in evening-dress, came out on stage from the other side, put one hand on his breast, the other outstretched as if he were begging, and sang through his nose. Anyone less like Bing would be hard to find. He sang 'Come Back to Sorrento' and got encores and cheers when he'd finished. People thumped their glasses on the tables and stamped their feet.

'It doesn't take much to keep them happy!' the Kerry girl whispered to Emer.

At last Bob O'Brien came out again on the stage and related a few interminable jokes which also got applauded.

'Janey, did they leave their brains at home?' the Kerry girl enquired.

'What brains they had were drowned in drink!' Emer answered through her teeth. Her stomach muscles were clenched and the back of her neck was fixed sideways towards the stage. She felt she was rooted to the spot and would never move again. For a brief fearful moment she wondered what on earth she was doing there.

'And now, the moment you've been waiting for, the winners, in reverse order. Girls, are you ready?'

'Oh, come on, come on,' Emer muttered.

'Well, THIRD, the splendid number THIRTEEN, unlucky for some but not for MISS DOREEN BYRNE from DUBLIN!'

It was the cow-shaped one. I don't believe it, Emer thought in disgust. Bathing Beauty! Jasus!

The girl was squeaking and squealing and kissing the others, who stared at her with implacable hostility, not

361

even pretending to be pleased at her success. She ran onstage, lumbering like an elephant, and got her sash which fit a little too snugly across her breasts.

'She was in Bob O'Brien's room all last night,' the Kerry girl whispered to Emer.

'What?' Emer was shocked. 'I don't believe it!'

The Kerry girl nodded, her hair falling about her face in a becoming frame of dark curls. 'Oh, yes, I promise you. I·was next door in Mrs Malley's. He's a breast man, so he is.'

Emer's mouth hung open at this information and she stood staring at the smiling Doreen Byrne who posed in her place on-stage, simpering and looking smug.

'And now, SECOND place, sweet ANNIE LAUGHLIN from TRALEE.'

The Kerry girl glared at Emer and the group of girls. 'I shoulda won!' she hissed. 'It's been fixed. I shoulda won.' And easing a synthetic smile on to her face, she walked on stage with her eyes full of tears of fury.

'And now, what you've all been waiting for: the Dranmore Beauty Queen for this year … '

Emer's throat was dry as dirt and she felt she was going to faint.

'Number FIFTEEN, also from Dublin's Fair City where the girls certainly are pretty, MISS EMER O'SHEA, our winner!'

She couldn't believe it. She heard Brigid yell, 'I told you, I told you,' and floated on to the apron in a euphoric trance. She was walking two inches off the ground, she moved like silk. Bob put the crown on her head. It was decorated with imitation stones, gaudy as the lights in the club house, but to her the Crown Jewels were not more beautiful.

She walked down the ramp, taking possession of it, full of confidence, tremendously excited. She was the fairest of them all! She knew it wasn't true. There was no vanity in

362

her triumph. She was aware that she could not hold a candle to Mourna and that even Briana was prettier. But she knew now that she had the ability to make people *believe* she was beautiful and that was more important. She could make an audience think she was the loveliest girl in the room. This was her triumph and this was her dream and tonight her dream came true.

The crowd cheered and she repeated her triumphal walk, blowing kisses, smiling radiantly, savouring each minute, while Brigid held her raincoat, clapping until her palms were red, crying over and over, 'I told you. I told you. I told you.'

Chapter Sixty-Two

The room was dark, the curtains pulled closed. Mourna did not turn on the light. She was used to undressing in the dark. Sharing a room with Briana had forced certain disciplines on them both that became automatic wherever she was. She often forgot that she could leave the light on, and that there was no one waiting for the bathroom. One thing she had decided: when she and Kurt married she'd get him to finance another bathroom for her mother.

She loved the privacy the hotel room afforded her and liked to spend time there. She always came up early to dress for dinner. Now, when Kurt kissed her goodnight outside the door, and said, 'I'll go for a little walk before bed. Sleep well, darling,' she returned his kiss with pleasure and, smiling at him, opened the door.

The cool dark interior greeted her and she sighed with

pleasure as she closed the door behind her. She put on her satin nightdress, a special bargain from Barnet's Oonagh had bought 'in case'. She liked to linger over undressing and sit, arms around her knees, when everyone else had gone to sleep, feeling a warm gratitude flood her. This is what it will be like when I'm married to Kurt, she thought, and opened her curtains, then threw open the window on the dark star-strewn night in Dranmore.

Last weekend. Last few nights here. It was sad that it was over, it had been such a wonderful time. But on the other hand she would soon be moving into this lovely privileged life forever.

She leaned against the balcony rail. She could hear the pounding of the sea and see the searching rays of the lighthouse rake the darkness of the restless water with a white and brilliant beam.

She drew in a breath. The air was cold and salty. She thought of Kurt and realized that, day by day, he grew more and more dear to her. A new life was beginning, an exciting life, and she looked forward to it with a shiver of delight and no apprehension. It would be a challenge she would enjoy, and she would be protected by power and cushioned by money with a strong man to care for her. It was what she wanted.

A cold breeze chased the curtains which billowed towards her, ghost-like in the dark. She wondered briefly what had caused the wind to stir them so roughly, then realized that someone had entered her room. She did not for a moment feel threatened or alarmed.

'Who's there?' she asked calmly, turning to look into the room. Silence.

She could hear the band downstairs playing 'You Were Never Lovelier', and someone breathing.

'Who is there?' she called, suddenly uneasy.

Silence. Then movement. A shadow unfurling in the darkness near the door. Fear overwhelmed her, an unfamiliar feeling.

'Who is it? Tell me or I'll scream.'

Nothing could happen to her here in the hotel, she thought. It was crowded. People about all the time.

'Don't do that.'

'Uncle Eddie? Oh, you frightened me. What are you doing here? Why didn't you tell me it was you?'

She was relieved. She did not like her uncle but she did not fear him either. He would not harm her.

She walked into the centre of the room, not realizing how graceful she looked in her satin *robe de chambre*, like an arum lily, her white skin glowing. She turned on her bedside lamp.

'Uncle Eddie, what is it? What do you want?' Her voice was cool and matter-of-fact, a middle-of-the-day voice.

'Come here,' he said softly.

She obeyed. Near him she could feel his masculinity as if it was another presence. He smelled of brandy and cigars and haircream. Once she had loved that smell, been reassured by it, now it was repulsive to her. Now it was Kurt's smell she responded to.

'Oh, Mourna, do you know how beautiful you are?'

His voice was thick and husky and involuntarily she stepped back from the underlying message there. He caught her arm, his grip quite fierce, as if to hurt her gave him pleasure.

'No woman has a right to look so desirable,' he said, his grip tightening.

'Don't do that, Uncle Eddie,' she said in a moderate and reasonable voice, hoping to keep things calm, not realizing that her very tranquillity was infuriating him.

'Come here.'

He pulled her into his arms and she cried out in protest.

'What are you doing?' Alarmed, opening her mouth to scream.

'Everything else I have but not you. So cool. So remote.

365

Bitch!'

He threw her on the bed with a jerk of his wrist, cutting off her voice with the swift movement, and put his hand over her mouth.

She was too amazed to bite it, violent reaction was not in her nature and confusion and fear immobilized her. In that brief moment, when decisive action might have helped her, she did nothing.

'If you scream I'll see your father never gets his promotion.' He said it in a matter-of-fact tone, almost casually, and took his hand away. 'You'll be a good girl now, Mourna, then the German can have you. Otherwise I'll ruin your father and every member of your family. You know I can do that, don't you?'

She lay inert on the bed, staring at him wide-eyed.

'Anyhow, no one will hear you.'

She knew he was right on both counts. She pulled herself up, trying to make sense of the situation.

'Please stop this, Uncle Eddie.' She struggled to stand but he shoved her back roughly.

'One word from me, Mourna, will bring your whole family down. Did you know that Wilmot asked me would it be a good idea to give your father the job in Barnet's? Did you know Ardel is mixed up with the IRA? Did you know that Laughlin is having an affair with a homosexual actor staying in this hotel, and he could go to prison for that? One word from me and he'll be in Mountjoy. Did you know Briana is seducing my son? Did you know that Emmett ... '

'Stop, stop stop!' she screamed and he hit her, deliberately, coldly. She fell back, freezing in panic, losing her voice. She could hear the band playing 'Ballin' the Jack'.

'First you put your two knees close up tight,
    You sway 'em to the left and you sway 'em to the right ... '

She wished she was down there. She wished they'd stop playing. 'Please don't spoil everything,' she begged.

'Don't you see, my dear, that's exactly what I want to do?'

'Please, please, please,' she moaned, but softly, not to anger him, trembling now uncontrollably, terror gripping her.

To no avail. His hands were suddenly everywhere, violating her, outraging her modesty. She struggled and cried out, but he hit her again and she whimpered, almost out of her mind as he began to defile her, doing things to her she had never known could be done.

She wanted to cover herself, cloak herself in darkness, but he held her ruthlessly spotlit. She, who had never been treated with anything but gentleness, was suddenly subjected to savage violence, a brutality that made her gasp in pain and humiliation. She, who knew nothing of obscenity, was obscenely abused, belittled as a human being, her dignity stripped from her, her maidenhood abruptly and bloodily terminated, her body used as a receptacle of hatred.

A flood of darkness enveloped her, but he forced her back again and again, hitting her face with a controlled anger as he destroyed her. His actions made a mockery of the strains of romantic music that floated through the window.

'You're breaking my heart cause you're leaving,
You've fallen for somebody new ... '

The pure temple so tenderly guarded, so gently cared for, was desecrated by a terrible loathing, an appalling desire to humiliate and destroy.

She heard then, vaguely in her nightmare, from another world, a world she had left forever:

'Goodnight, sweetheart,
I'll see you tomorrow,

367

Goodnight, sweetheart,
Sleep well, banish sorrow ... '

At last it was over. 'Goodnight, Sweetheart' signified the end. People would be going to bed now. They would be in the corridors outside. So it had to be over.

He stood over her, looking at the soiled mess he had made of her. 'I didn't do this,' he said, coldly, fiercely. 'Kurt did. If you value your family, just say "Kurt". Do you hear me? Nod if you do or I'll ... '

She nodded.

'Say "Kurt", remember. It's all you've got to say. Just that. Kurt.' He went out onto the balcony and took deep breaths to calm himself. Then he left her with semen sprayed over her face, blood everywhere, her body ripped, bruised and beaten, its joyful innocence lost forever.

And when they found her she whispered: 'Kurt.'

Chapter Sixty-Three

'We're going the day after tomorrow, Hector. I've come to say goodbye.'

Laughlin stood in the dark room, a smaller edition of Mourna's one storey down.

'God, what time is it?' Hector groped for his watch, turning on his bedside light.

'You said to come and say goodbye.' Laughlin was near tears. He had not expected to feel like this and was both embarrassed and angry with himself.

'You'll be leaving?' Hector sounded foggy.

'Yes, Hector.'

'So're we. We're going too, old chap.'

'Really? Are you? I hadn't realized … '

'Oh, yes. Our run here is over.'

'Where're you going?'

'We're going to Cork after here. The Opera House. Then Liverpool.' He saw Laughlin's bleak face. 'We'll see each other in Dublin.'

'Will that be a long time?'

' 'Fraid so. Don't worry, old chap, you'll survive.'

'I expect so.'

Hector had lit a cigarette. He glanced at the boy staring awkwardly down at him.

'Don't take it so hard. There will be others, you know.'

'Others?'

'Yes. To love.'

Laughlin drew in a breath sharply, then relaxed. 'But not you,' he said, amazed at his courage. They had never spoken to each other in such terms, never been more than casual in both speech and gesture.

'I'll only ever love you.' Laughlin brought it out in a rush.

He thought Hector might laugh but the actor's face was serious. 'You'll fall for a pretty Irish girl, long floating hair and black eyes,' Hector kidded, and Laughlin shook his head.

'No. It feels wrong. I hate the thought of it even. No.'

'Listen, Laughlin, don't let them mess up your life. Remember the way *you* feel is too important. We've all only got one life to lead. It is not a rehearsal. Homosexuality … '

Laughlin drew in his breath again with a note of outrage at the word applied to himself.

'There now, I've said it. The forbidden word. Homosexuality, dear boy, is *not* something you grow out of, despite popular belief.'

'You mean, Brother Nathan is one?'

369

'Probably. Though he most likely doesn't know. He is ignorant, poor man, and thinks he's evil incarnate. He's drawn that way naturally, the way your cousin Iain Benson is to your sister, and Mourna is to her German.'

'And he was attracted to me because I'm … I'm … '

Hector nodded. 'Very likely. It's not something we can hide from each other.'

'You mean, you can see people, not obvious people, and you know?'

'Ninety per cent of the time. You see, Laughlin, it is natural, that is why it cannot be wrong. Promiscuity is wrong, no matter who does it with who. But love between whoever is okay. That's what I believe, anyhow.'

He looked at Laughlin with amused eyes. 'I cannot believe that God, who made me this way, expects me to deny myself love and the most natural of pleasures, or feel I should force myself to do something repugnant to me. I just don't believe it. Or if He could do that, then He's not worth knowing.' Hector's voice was bitter and he stubbed out the cigarette, smashing it in the ashtray.

'My brother Emmett always says that whatever happens to you has a reason, a meaning,' Laughlin said. 'I thought Brother Nathan proved him wrong. I could see no object in it. But perhaps it was meant to happen. So that I should know.'

'Perhaps.' Hector looked at him speculatively. 'But, you know, it's not going to be easy, I'm afraid. You'll be humiliated. You'll be made fun of. You will not have an easy time. And then there's the law. You have to be very careful. Only I think it is better to know what you are, and not be afraid of it, than live a lie, and, like poor Brother Nathan, think you are some kind of monster and that no one else in the world has the feelings you have.'

Laughlin nodded. 'I'm glad I know. At least now I won't hate myself.' He looked up. 'But I'll miss you. I'll really miss you.'

'We'll see each other, Laughlin. Just take it easy and don't let them get to you.'

Laughlin nodded, then awkwardly put out his hand. Hector shook it, then got out of bed as Laughlin reached the door. He went over to the boy and put a hand on his shoulder and turned him around, then hugged him. It was a bear-like kind of embrace and Laughlin hugged him back, then opened the door and left.

Chapter Sixty-Four

Gabriel went down each morning to collect the paper from Barney Boland's shop at the harbour. On the morning after the ball he arrived back, fuming. He marched into the dining room, surprising everyone by his vehemence.

'Look at that, Oonagh!' he said, slapping the *Irish Independent* down on the breakfast-table.

'Shush, Gabriel!' She glanced at it, uninterested.

'There's no point shushing me,' he said. Oonagh looked up and saw that he was angry. Gabriel rarely got angry. 'Everyone in Ireland with eyes will see my daughter, nearly naked, splashed on the front page of a national daily.'

His hand was shaking, Oonagh saw, and looked with more interest, though still bewildered, at the large photograph of a bathing-beauty with a dauntingly low *décolletage*, hair flying as if caught in a breeze, standing legs apart on tall slim heels, head back, teeth flashing, hand on provocative hip. Emer! Oonagh couldn't believe her eyes.

'Emer! Emer, what have you been up to?'

371

'Yipee! It's me! Oh, Mam, Mam, it's me! On the *front page!*'

'Yes. Half naked! Oh, my girl, just wait till I get you home! Don't think you've heard the last of this!

'Everyone will see!' Oonagh continued. 'Everyone up at the Grand will know *my* daughter, *my* daughter, goes in for tawdry beauty competitions!'

'Don't talk rot, Oonagh,' Granny O'Shea exclaimed, grabbing the paper. 'No one at the Grand knows your name. You're not famous, are you? Though Emer seems to be. It's lovely, Emer. Lovely. You look a total treat there. First prize no less! I'll bet you're proud.'

'And I'll go on from there, Granny, just you wait. I'm headed for great things.'

'You'll go nowhere, my girl. Daughter of mine on the front page with no clothes!' Gabriel sank down.

'Eddie and Colista will know up at the Grand,' Oonagh cried.

'Oh, they're not going to spread it around, Oonagh, for God's sake.' Granny O'Shea shook her head. 'They're not going to say, "She's my niece, Emer O'Shea." And it'd need Raymond Chandler to link up Emer O'Shea and Eddie Benson, for God's sake.' She shook her head again. 'I don't know why you're taking on so. Anyone else'd be bursting with pride. Turning into a snob like your wife, Gabriel. Never thought I'd live to see the day!'

'Shut up, Mother, and let me think. It has nothing to do with snobbery, only decency.'

'Oh, yes! So you say. But what's to be ashamed of, I ask you?'

'Listen to me, Emer … ' Gabriel began, but his daughter had fled, leaving a hiatus behind her.

'And this isn't only local,' he sighed. 'The whole of Dublin'll read about it.'

'Holy Mother!' Emmett grabbed the paper from his father. 'You mean all the boys at school … '

'And the whole neighbourhood, and the staff at Barnet's, and ... ' Gabriel was working himself up into a fine lather.

'The doctor, the lawyer, the Indian Chief,' Granny O'Shea snapped. 'They'll all say Gabriel O'Shea's daughter won a beauty contest in Dranmore. Isn't that grand? I wish I had, in my youth. It must be great to be chosen. Janey, you're a bunch of half-baked eejits, so you are. Should be thanking God it's won a beauty contest she has, and not got herself into trouble wi' some fella. Don't know when you're lucky, so you don't.'

'Mother, keep quiet, will you?' Gabriel pleaded, then lapsed into silence.

'Perhaps they won't see,' Oonagh whispered.

'Even if they do, it won't make any difference,' Granny O'Shea interrupted.

'She's right,' Molly said. She was the first of the others to speak. 'It's really not that important, Oonagh, Gabriel. Really.'

'And if it is,' Granny O'Shea continued to badger, 'if it put that stuck-up Count off our Mourna, then he's not worthy of her. And if it puts Mr Wilmot off promoting you, Gabriel, then the promotion is not worth having. Goodness, man, have you forgotten everything I taught you?'

Gabriel sighed. 'I suppose you're right. I suppose I'm coming the Victorian father here. All right. Anyhow, it's a bit late now to be angry. There's sweet nothing I can do about it.'

'That's better,' Granny O'Shea eyed Oonagh. 'That's more like my son. She's a little cracker is Emer.'

They forgot all about Emer and her beauty contest very shortly for they got a phone call from the Grand that was to shatter their lives and made her escapade seem trivial indeed.

Chapter Sixty-Five

She obeyed him without rhyme or reason. When they found her exactly as he had left her, legs spread apart, nightdress torn, blood and semen-stained, that was all she said:

'Kurt.'

The maid heard it clearly, and the housekeeper, who had responded to the maid's request for assistance as she couldn't gain entry to the room, heard it also, clearly:

'Kurt.'

Word spread rapidly though the hotel tried hard to hush it all up. This kind of publicity was bad for them.

Eddie and Colista were breakfasting in the sunny dining room. The fountain was playing, its cascade rainbow-dazzling with lights picked up from the sun. The sea danced in the distance and everything sparkled. Eddie was peeling an orange and Colista was drinking black coffee and smoking her first cigarette.

A waiter came to their table and told them that Miss Mourna O'Shea was ill and could they see to her?

Eddie said, 'You go darling. She'll need a woman.' He avoided his wife's eyes and continued peeling his orange.

Colista was appalled by what she saw. Shaken to the core, soliciting the help of the maids and the housekeeper, forgetting everything else, she set about bathing and tending her niece.

The girl was in deep shock and it was obvious to the

three women that she had been raped.

Colista's face was stained with tears she had not even been aware she cried, and the women spoke in whispers as if they were tending the dead, as indeed the girl on the bed might have been, so still and cold and lifeless was she.

'Thank God her mother didn't see her like this,' Colista said to the scared little maid. And to the housekeeper, 'Will you get the doctor, please? She'll have to see a doctor.'

They bathed her tenderly, put a fresh nightdress on her, a plain cotton one. The satin was the only glamorous one she'd had and in the simple white lace-trimmed garment, cleaned and tucked up in bed, she looked very virginal and young, almost childish. Too young to have undergone the terrible experience she had been subjected to.

'Ah, dear God, this is a tragedy,' Colista said.

'An' she looked so beautiful last night,' the little maid cried. They all wept as they tidied the room and tended her. To see so perfect a being broken and bleeding was a pity and a shame, and the women grieved.

'I've telephoned the doctor. They deserve to die, who done this,' the housekeeper whispered. 'An' she said his name: Kurt.'

Colista stopped and looked up, aghast at the news, 'Oh no, it couldn't be!' she cried.

'That's what she said, isn't it, Milly?'

The little maid nodded emphatically. 'Oh, yes, mum. I heard her.'

'That's the German gentleman, isn't it?' the housekeeper asked. Her tones suggested that it would be a foreigner. No Irishman would do this.

'No! No, I don't believe it,' Colista insisted.

'Yes, mum, it was,' the little maid cried. 'I heard her. She said "Kurt", quite distinctly.'

'Sure, you wouldn't put it past a German,' the

housekeeper said, bustling about now. 'Tortured people, they did, in them concentration camps.'

'Count Von Mensil wouldn't have done this,' Colista insisted, and the housekeeper's mouth tightened into a line.

'That's what they all said. After the war.'

'An' that's what *she* said. An' why would she tell us wrong?' The little maid glared at Colista. 'I don't tell lies,' she cried angrily.

There was a terrible thought deep, deep in Colista's mind, that she pushed firmly further down.

The doctor came and sent the staff away and they couldn't wait to pass on the news.

Eddie Benson called Kurt on the phone and advised him to leave the hotel.

'But I haven't done anything,' the German cried. 'I must see her.'

Distressed and not a little bewildered by the attitude of the staff and guests in the Grand, he made his way from the lounge, where he had been reading the morning paper, to Mourna's room. Reactions to him, on his way there, ranged from open hostility to icy disdain laced with disgust. The staff seemed to be fearful of him. Totally baffled, he met Eddie at the lift and asked him exactly what had happened.

'Mourna's been raped, apparently.'

'Ah God, no!' He thought of the sleeping beauty. He thought of her radiant innocence and shuddered, then looked at Eddie. 'Why would anyone think that I ... '

'She said your name, old man,' Eddie told him.

'But I didn't do it. I *couldn't*! I love her. She is a precious person. Oh, heavens, Eddie, do they really believe ...?'

Eddie nodded and a couple passed them by, the woman drawing her skirt away and looking at Kurt with loathing, the man tut-tutting through his teeth.

'Perhaps she was calling for me?' Kurt said. 'She was asking ... '

'Perhaps, but that's not what people think. Don't you see,

old man, you've got to get away until it's cleared up and Mourna can tell us what happened. Otherwise, you'll be lynched.'

'But I didn't do it,' Kurt said again, his control snapping. He went purposefully to Mourna's room. He didn't know which one it was and had to ask.

'You should be castrated,' the outraged housekeeper shrilled at him, backing away from him as if he was a wild beast. She was taking blankets to Mourna who remained icy cold.

Kurt followed her, banging at the door when she slammed it in his face. But the doctor wouldn't let him in and sent him away.

'Someone will have to call my sister,' Colista whispered, white-lipped. The thought of Oonagh appalled her. Mourna's mother would be devastated and Gabriel would break his heart at the atrocity. Still, it had to be done, so Colista telephoned Kincora, all the time remaining fiercely helpful but closed-minded. She had made up her mind what she was going to think and that was that.

Oonagh thought the call was about the front-page picture of Emer. It took a long time for Colista to get her to understand that Mourna was ill.

'My God, my God, what is it? What's happened to her? Oh, Jesus, Mary and Joseph, what's happened to my little girl?'

'Just come up here, Oonagh, and bring Gabriel,' Colista insisted.

'It's serious then? Oh my God, it's serious!'

'I'm afraid so, Oonagh. Hurry.'

Oonagh arrived, white-faced, with Gabriel, and the doctor had another patient on his hands. She collapsed when she saw her daughter and they told her what had happened. Shock and grief, added to her own failing strength since her miscarriage, caused a seizure and she was briefly out of her mind, her poor wits addled. It was only her daughter's need of her strength that drew her back. That and an injection the doctor administered.

Gabriel stood in the room banging his head against the wall in a terrible rhythmic motion. He was weeping and wringing his hands. 'Like a washerwoman,' the housekeeper whispered to Milly. He wouldn't look at Mourna, and Oonagh at last went to him and told him they had both better husband their strength in order to help her.

The doctor suggested that it might be better for Mourna if she spent a few days at the local hospital where she could be supervised and her progress monitored.

'I don't like the look of her at all,' he said, shaking his head. 'She's not responding to anything. She's sunk deep in shock, and I would like to get her out of this room.'

'Will she be all right though, doctor?' Oonagh asked. Colista, looking at her, thought her sister looked very old.

'I don't know, Mrs O'Shea. I wish I did. Whoever did this deserves to be horse-whipped. I'd do it myself if I was younger. The trouble is that it is very difficult to bring charges in Ireland. The judges here seem to think it's not a serious offence. God damn it, they should see the results of rape like we do and perhaps then they'd change their minds.'

'Gabriel, Gabriel.' Oonagh went to her husband. 'They want to take her to the hospital.'

He nodded dumbly. His eyes were glazed and his mouth trembled.

'It will take her out of this atmosphere,' the doctor said. 'I don't want her to come to in the place where it happened, if you see what I mean.'

'No. You're right, doctor, you must do whatever you think best.'

The housekeeper rang for an ambulance and Mourna, on a stretcher, left the hotel by the back entrance, accompanied by her mother and father and the doctor. The occupants of the Grand turned their attention to

378

gossiping about the loathsome thing that had happened in their midst, and their venom on Count Kurt Von Mensil.

He too was in shock. He could not understand people's behaviour. No one would listen to reason. His denials fell on deaf ears. In fact, no one listened to him. He had been prejudged. It was enough that the beautiful young woman who had so won the hearts of everyone in the hotel, guests and staff alike, had said 'Kurt' for him to be accused and condemned out of hand.

The waiters would not serve him. They simply ignored him, almost hissing as they passed him by. When he went to his room he found it had not been done. He put his hands to his head and stood holding it for almost half an hour, feeling the pain of his loss, the pain of knowing there was no way he could help, nothing he could do, knowing the fruitlessness of staying yet reluctant to leave so ignominiously when he was innocent.

Then he packed, rang for a porter and when, after a rather long time no one came, brought the cases down to the foyer himself.

A maid met him in the corridor and as he tried to pass her she deliberately stood in front of him and spat at him, her spittle hitting him full in the face.

He wanted to cry out. He wanted to weep and shout and declare his innocence, but his face remained stoic, almost cold. He was glad enough to see Eddie at the desk holding a piece of paper in his hand.

'I've paid it, old man. Save you the embarrassment. You can reimburse me whenever convenient.'

'No. Let me now. I don't want to be under an obligation. I'll give you a cheque.'

'Better not, Kurt. The natives are restless.'

Eddie looked about him and Kurt could not help noticing groups of fashionably dressed guests standing whispering heatedly and staring at him. They sounded like angry bees and their faces expressed fury and righteous indignation, disgust and contempt. There was no mistaking the climate of opinion and the Count had to agree that Eddie was right. He took the receipt from him and strode out through the crowded foyer, a case in each hand.

A cheerful taxi driver took him to the hospital and was the first person that day, with the possible exception of Eddie, who treated him with any degree of civility. When they reached the hospital he asked the driver to wait for him there.

In a cold corridor he saw Oonagh and Gabriel, and as he approached them realized he had made a terrible mistake. Wordlessly, Oonagh got to her feet, an expression of terrible grief on her face. She was holding a handbag and came towards him, hitting out at him, beating her fists at him, moaning and crying like an animal. She struck out at him, her face bleached and agonized.

'Get out of here,' Gabriel rasped at him, his eyes black pools of hate. 'Get out quickly before I kill you.'

Suddenly the corridor was full of nurses and nuns and hospital staff. He was propelled away from the O'Sheas and escorted firmly to the entrance.

So he got the taxi to take him to the station. There he saw Briana O'Shea and Iain Benson sitting together on a bench on the platform. He did not wonder what they were doing there, he was too preoccupied with his own terrible position. He ducked into the waiting room in order to avoid them. If anyone saw me they would indeed think I was guilty, he thought to himself. When the train came into the station he waited until the last moment then ran, a case in each hand, and threw himself into a carriage. He sat there, muttering to himself, tears spilling down his face, so that people stared at the tall, blond, foreign-looking gentleman and thought he was funny in the head.

Chapter Sixty-Six

In all the upheaval it was not until lunchtime that anyone noticed Iain's disappearance and then only because his mother went to his room to talk to him about Mourna. She found a note on his dressing-table.

Colista told Eddie when he came to the bedroom at twelve-thirty to change for lunch.

'I have just seen Ardel in reception picking up an envelope I left for him,' he said. 'He doesn't seem to know about his sister yet.'

'How should he?' Colista said, and her voice was expressionless. 'She has just been taken to the hospital. Poor Oonagh hasn't had time to let anyone else know.'

He turned. 'The hospital? But is she that bad? I thought ... '

'You thought what, Eddie dear? What would you know about it?'

He shrugged. 'I thought it was rape,' he said. 'I did not think that would need hospitalization.'

'I'll ignore that remark,' Colista said icily. 'Oh, Jesus, Eddie, don't you know what it is like for a woman?' Then, without waiting for a reply, she took up the note that she had brought back to their room and held in her hand, reading it over and over.

'Iain, our son, has run away to Dublin with Briana O'Shea,' she informed him.

She was not prepared for his outburst. 'Good God! That

little snake! Don't you realize, woman, that the only train from Dranmore to Dublin leaves at one o'clock? I'll just have time to stop the pair of them, and I'll give them hell, you'll see. I'll make them sorry they were born.'

'Don't be ridiculous, Eddie,' she began, but he had gone, running out of the bedroom before Colista could stop him.

~~~~~~

Briana and Iain were sitting dozing on a bench on the station platform. Their cases were at their feet. She rested her head on his shoulder and he had his arm around her. They were very sleepy, not having been to bed the previous night. They had come down to the station in the wee small hours, unaware that they could not get a train until one o'clock that day. Knowing nothing of Mourna's tragedy, they waited patiently for the train to arrive.

Eddie came roaring on to the platform, his fury out of all proportion to the situation, and yelled at them to pick up their cases and get in the car at once.

Daunted by his father's unusual display of passion, Iain took Briana's hand and got into the Bentley.

'Don't worry, dearest,' he whispered to her.

'What did you say?' Eddie shouted, backing the car violently, tyres screaming under his rage.

'I told Bri not to worry,' Iain said, squeezing her hand.

'Well, I wouldn't bank on that, Briana O'Shea,' he said tersely. 'Not at all, I wouldn't.'

Iain squeezed her hand again and Briana felt his strong unworried strength pass into her, giving her encouragement.

They were at the hotel in minutes.

'Up to the room,' Eddie ordered, and marched them through the foyer and up the staircase, down the corridor, throwing open the door of the room without knocking.

Colista sat in front of her dressing-table mirror, Iain's

note in her hand. She turned slowly, forestalling Eddie, holding her hand up and cutting off his babble about not permitting such disobedience in his family and Briana being a slut.

'Don't shout like that, dear,' she said. 'You don't accomplish anything.' She looked at him squarely, staring at him with cold eyes. He had never seen her look like that before, and he thought for a moment he might be imagining her expression. But no, those eyes were like stones.

'When you think about it, my dear,' she said, 'you'll come to see, as I do, that Iain's marrying Briana is not such a bad idea. In fact, it is a very good thing.'

He stared at her in astonishment. That she should flout his wishes so flagrantly was unbelievable. They had played games, each of them getting their own way, but this was different. When it came to the point and he laid down the law, she always gave way to him.

Then, gazing at her, he realized something terrible. She *knew*. From what female instinct she had guessed the truth he could not know, but she knew about him and Mourna. She silently told him so.

'We'll give you a lovely wedding, dear, if your father is agreeable. We've always wanted to keep Bensons in the family and Briana is, after all, family. Dear, dear child, don't look so scared. It is going to be all right. You don't have to run away, need they, Eddie?'

He shook his head. He could not speak. He felt cold and old, jaded and burnt up, foul and aged. An old man with only loathing in his heart. His obsession gone, the victory in truth a defeat.

He left the room hearing a shout of delight from his son, a burst of laughter from Briana, and the sound of his wife's congratulations as they, no doubt, embraced each other in his absence. She would tell them about Mourna soon, but would let them have their moment of celebration first.

It suddenly occurred to him that she might talk about

383

him to the other members of the family. His knees went weak at the thought. He could not bear the humiliation of that. The horror of it would kill him. Then he recovered himself. She would not betray him. She would protect him, she would never let the outside world know of his guilt. She valued her position and she had too much to lose. But, he realized grimly, he would be made to pay, and pay dearly.

He walked down the corridor, teeth bared, head back, poison in his soul, and knew there was no earthly way to rid himself of his agony.

Chapter Sixty-Seven

Maggie sat between Ben and Dot on the sea-wall. Looking directly down the sheer rock-face gave her the weirdest feeling of vertigo which she loved. Her stomach *left* her. It will fall right out, she thought, and her knees went weak.

She did not normally listen to the boring conversation of her parents. She thought all adults were kill-joys, spoilers of fun, and her natural enemies. Textures were there to be explored yet grown-ups took a fiendish delight in stopping you doing just that. What was snow for if not to roll in? What was sand for if not to throw? And stones? And paint? Why was paint kept in one room? And what would happen if you painted a field red and another field blue? And why weren't you allowed to find out?

Below her on the wet sand great swatches of seaweed lay, their pods just waiting to be popped, and the twisted snarls of driftwood were waiting to be played with. Yet

here she was, stuck on the wall, the bicycle boys angry that
their position was usurped, and all there was for her to do
was scare herself.

'He was terrible … a terrible man … a Nazi,' her mother
was saying. 'What he did to Mourna – a beast he was, a
beast! Deserves to be whipped!'

'Well, the Grand showed great common sense not letting
him stay,' her father said.

'They showed him the door an' no mistake.'

'Serves him right. Still, it's awful to think he got off
without being punished. I'd lock him up. Throw away the
key.'

'Yes, well, Oonagh'd never allow poor Mourna to go to
court.'

'No. You can't let a thing like this become public. It
would destroy Mourna. Follow her for life. No, best to let
it die.'

'And Gabriel all worked up about Emer's picture in the
paper.'

'Yes. It seems so innocuous in comparison, doesn't it?'

They were quiet for moments and Maggie watched a
bird of prey soar, something wriggling in its mouth.

'Sure, who wants to stay in the Grand anyhow?' Dot said.
'Things like that happening there. We're far better off in
Kincora.'

'Sure, didn't I say that all along? Servants nosing about
among your things and hovering so you can't even scratch
your head.'

'And it was Saturday night, then? After dinner he did
that to Mourna?'

'Yes. They put it at just after midnight. Twelve o'clock.
He attacked her then, doctor says.'

'He couldn't!' Maggie said firmly. She was tired of
listening to their silly conversation and she had heard that
about the German and hadn't she seen him with her own
eyes?

'What, darlin'?'

'The German. He couldn't have attacked Mourna. He was on the beach. I saw him.'

'What were you doing? Don't talk nonsense, pet, you were in bed.'

She almost let them think she was imagining things. She knew she might get into trouble and for a moment was tempted to let the whole thing drop. Adults were so unexpected in their reactions. But she enjoyed her power, knowing something they didn't, and she wanted to prove them wrong. They weren't always right, no matter what they said.

'No, I wasn't. I was here.'

They glared at her, and realizing that they might in fact be terribly angry, Maggie squirmed backwards off the wall and tried to run away but her father grabbed her by the elastic in her knickers.

'No, no, hold on a minute, Maggie. What do you mean, the German was here?'

'Well, he was. I saw him. I saw him. Down *there*!' She pointed down and tried once more to wriggle out of her father's grasp.

'No, my lady, you don't get away till you tell me everything.'

'Be gentle with her, Ben. She's fragile,' Dot said, and for once her husband looked astonished.

'Fragile?' he said incredulously.

Dot pursed her lips out stubbornly. 'Little girls!' she stated enigmatically. 'Anyhow, you'll get more out of her if she's not frightened.'

Ben could not imagine the red-faced Maggie ever really being frightened. However, he adopted a kindlier tone and pulled the child back up on his lap.

'What did you see, dear? We're not angry with you.'

'I saw the German down there when the band played "Goodnight, Sweetheart". Emer said that's the last dance of the evening. She said that's what it was called. It came from the Grand.'

'Ah, so that's who you were with, Emer O'Shea? I might have known.'

'I *love* Emer O'Shea. She's going to be a film star, so she is. She was comin' back from a competition she was in. You know, the one Uncle Gabriel got mad about.'

'She never misses anything, does Maggie,' Ben said to his wife proudly, but Dot shushed him and asked Maggie to go on.

'He was down there. You couldn't mistake his goldy hair.'

'Did you see anything else, Maggie?'

'Yeah! I saw Uncle Eddie.'

'Where?' Dot's face was flushed, a hectic red staining her cheeks as possibilities, questions and answers flashed through her mind.

'On Mourna's balcony. Breathin' *in*.' She drew her breath in sharply in imitation. 'Breathin' *out*.'

'What do you mean?'

'In an' out, like a doctor tells you.'

'But how did you know it was Mourna's room?'

'Hers is the only one with a balcony.' She pointed up to the Grand. They could see the room clearly, the curtain blowing. Someone was airing the room, the window was open. And outside it, because it was over the entrance, a tiny wrought iron balcony curved outwards gracefully.

'The one below has a balcony.'

'Yes. A *wide* balcony. Stretches three windows.' Maggie opened her arms wide, and pointed. 'The room Mourna was in had one little cute one, like Rapunzel's, only one window wide.'

It was true what Maggie said. Beneath the tiny one-windowed balcony a far wider and deeper equivalent curved out over the entrance to the hotel.

Ben's eyes met Dot's above the child's head, sharply excited. 'That would mean ... ' he muttered.

387

'But how do you know that that was Mourna's room?'

Maggie was getting impatient. If they could not understand simple facts they were stupid. It was typical! She squirmed and wriggled, desperate suddenly to get off the wall and go down to the beach. She saw Emer and Brigid far below her and longed to join them.

'Mourna waved to me every evening from there, so she did. You'da seen you'da looked. Waved at us an' we comin' up from the beach. Can I go now? Can I? Can I?'

'Yes, I remember. I noticed she waved, but thought nothiing of it ... Just one thing, Maggie. You sure of this?'

'Course I am. Course,' she said with certainty. 'You ask Emer you don't believe me.'

'That means ... ' Ben whispered.

Dot nodded. 'Oh, yes! I see what it means, all right. I see very well what it means.'

Ben stared at his wife's triumphant face. She looked as if she had scored some wonderful victory.

'Can I go *now*? Can I go *now*?' Maggie's voice was spiralling upwards and she slipped down from her father's knee and fled down to Brigid and Emer.

'What are you going to do?' Ben asked, staring at his wife's rapt expression.

'I'm going to make Eddie Benson pay, that's what I'm going to do, Ben lamb. Joe is going to get treatment. Even if he doesn't respond, he's going to be given an apartment, him and Maisie. A nice one. No more caravan.'

'Have you gone potty, Dot?'

'No, Ben. I'm telling you what's going to happen. Mary, Clare, Tina, Angela, Roger, little Dec, Maggie and Jamie are set up for life. They'll be looked after from now on.'

'But, Dot, that would be blackmail.'

'Yes, I know,' she continued. 'You are going to rise, slowly but surely, in the Department.' She closed one eye and looked out to sea. 'No,' she said, 'change that to quickly. You are going to rise quickly in the Department.

388

To Senior Executive, or whatever it is called. Important, that is what you'll be. Important.'

'Don't talk daft, Dot,' Ben said, but a gleam had come into his eye and he looked at his wife in admiration.

'Oh, it will all happen, you'll see,' she continued with certainty, 'Gabriel will get the promotion in Barnet's. And Rita'll have some money. Enough so she doesn't have to worry. It's nice for a girl to have a little money of her own. Lots of other things will be provided by that benevolent man Eddie Benson.' She smiled. 'He'll wish to God he'd remembered our appointment for morning coffee!' She took her husband's hand in hers. 'He didn't really appreciate the sweater, Ben. Not really. He didn't even try to show enthusiasm when I gave it to him. I know it wasn't Maurice O'Brien or *haute couture*, I know that, but he could have pretended. Oh, he'll regret his attitude to me and you, Ben, just you wait and see.'

Dot thought of Oonagh and Gabriel up in the hospital, waiting beside a white bed that contained the shell of their beautiful daughter. Her heart filled up and tears splashed her cheeks.

'She'll never be beautiful again,' she said sadly.

'Who, love?'

'Mourna O'Shea. Her time has gone. Fled, never to be recaptured.'

The sea looked navy blue below them, heaving and moving, restless in its constant tossing. The sun hung overhead, spraying a dazzling sheen that blinded.

'Do you really think so?' Ben asked. Dot nodded emphatically.

'I know so. Her beauty was ephemeral. It depended on happiness and tranquillity and innocence. He pulled the plug on all that, our fine brother-in-law.'

'Oh, we're not sure of that, Dotty.'

'*I am*. You may not be, but I am. It's what he wanted to do from the beginning, that party at Oonagh's, and what Eddie wants, Eddie gets.'

'Did he realize the bill to be paid?' Ben inquired. Dot shook her head.

'No. He's never looked at a bill in his life. He never counts the cost. Never had to. But now he will and it'll destroy him, the reckoning. And I don't mean financially, Ben. Not money, though he'll hate that too. But he'll never be able to play the big-shot again. No, our Eddie's hoist himself with his own petard.'

She looked down to the beach where Mary was collecting the crocodile.

'Look at her, will ye?' She smiled at Ben beside her on the wall. Her eldest had her skirt tucked into her knickers. Her corkscrew curls blew every which way and she was twisting and turning, trying to pluck little hands from their clamouring grip on her. 'Proper little mother. Thank God she's not beautiful.'

'Oh, I don't know. Our Mary can look lovely.'

'I know that, Ben. Think I'm blind? No, I meant outstanding. Different, a head-turner. She's not that. Our Mary'll make someone a grand wife.'

'That's the truth, Dot lamb, it is so.'

'Ah, we've a lot to be grateful for, you and I.' She beamed at him tenderly. 'Dear old Benny,' she cooed.

'Dearest, darling Dot.'

Chapter Sixty-Eight

They had had a few lunches together. They had walked the length of the beach in the moonlight. They had held hands in the Candlelight Room of the Kilmore Hotel near Waterford. And they had talked, and talked, and talked. They had come to relish each other's company, enjoy each other's honesty.

'We're too old to lie to each other, Barney,' Rita said. 'Anyhow we'd know. I'd know at once if you deceived me. I'm not an eejit and neither are you. So what'd be the point?'

Barney smiled at her, his crinkly smile that she had grown so fond of.

'Still, there are some things we have to get clear,' she said to him.

'Yeah, fire ahead. There'll be no secrets between us, Rita girl.'

Her heart was pounding. She was terrified that he might leave the table. Desert her. Go out of the life that he had filled so completely since they had met. But she knew they had to be frank with each other. She had to risk all to gain all.

'I want a husband for security,' she said in a rush.

'Sure, there's nothin' like security. What's wrong with that? A woman your age ... well, she'd be a fool if she didn't.'

He always surprised her, always took her breath away,

always made her feel she was a fool to worry, always gave her that comfortable feeling she had reached home.

'Would ye be grateful?' he asked. 'If I took you out of it. The squalor? The worry?'

'Oh, God, yes.' The reply was spontaneous and warm.

He sighed happily. 'Gratitude is one of the most underestimated feelings,' he said.

She leaned towards him, oblivious of others staring at them. 'I want ... ' there was yearning in her voice ' ... I *need* you to be kind.'

He exploded with laughter and she couldn't help but join him. 'Kind?' he said eventually. 'Kind? I invented the word. I'll even give up my trips to Florida if you want me to.'

'Oh no,' she replied quickly, 'I'd love to come with you. You could go out fishing and I could lie by the pool.'

She saw the picture in her mind. It was like something out of the movies, and this was her, Rita Maguire, talking about it as if it might actually happen.

'It will happen,' Barney Boland, her lovely knight in shining armour said, reading her unspoken thoughts. 'It will happen. At the end of this holiday we'll go, you and I, take the children with us, fly out to Florida for another holiday. They'd love that. We'll be married by then. Then we'll come back here to live. You can bank on it, Rita. You can bank on it.'

She couldn't suppress her emotions. She leaned over and kissed him. They looked at each other, bright-eyed.

'It's all too good to be true,' she said. 'I pinch myself every so often to see I'm not dreaming.'

'It's no dream, Rita love. You've gotten out of the habit of enjoying yourself. I'm here to see you start having fun again. You've had it tough. You've had it very tough. Well, not any more if I can help it. I'll look after you and the kids from now on, never fear.'

She couldn't credit her luck. She tried to believe him,

392

she knew he meant every word, yet still she had her moments of fear, of projection. It was going to take time to lose her apprehension, the habit of worry. But little by little she was improving. Little by little it was getting better, and her smile was more often on her face than off. Everything seemed brighter to her, everything seemed more exciting. He was healing her.

The children adored him. Without a moment's hesitation Brigid and Des fell for his bluff, good-natured jollity. He liked everyone so he was easy to like. He did not criticize, he did not try to change them, or her. He accepted them as they were and made them feel good to be that way.

He had come into her life and changed it. She wept in bed from sheer joy and thanked God for sending Barney Boland to her. Tiredness fled, self-pity disappeared. She woke up bright and expectant, eager for the day, the sunlight, and Barney.

Chapter Sixty-Nine

That morning in Kincora Molly went to tell Mrs Flanagan that Oonagh and Gabriel would not be there for lunch. She was worried about Mourna; reports were garbled and she wanted to get to the hospital to give what support she could to her grief-stricken sister-in-law.

Mrs Flanagan was not in her kitchen but Tom was. He had a terrified Aggie against the wall and was squeezing her breasts. Molly stared in disgust.

'Let that child go,' she instructed coolly.

Tom bounced back as if he'd been scalded. 'Oh, Moll ... it was ... it was ... '

'It was the last straw, Tom, that's what it was,' she said with icy calm.

'Now, Moll, don't rush to hasty conclusions. You don't understand ... ' Tom said frantically.

'I understand only too well, Tom.' The little maid had fled.

'No, Moll, listen.' He was desperate. 'It's not what you think, I promise it's not. I love you, Moll.'

'You love the pool hall. The house. The security, Tom, that's what you love. Not me. The cushy position is what you love.'

'No. No, you're wrong. So wrong.'

He knew as he spoke that he told the truth. He loved his wife. It was just that he could never resist a pretty girl, or trying his chances either.

'Oh, shut up, Tom,' she said with contempt. 'Cut out the phoney protests. Let it drop.'

He followed her out into the sunshine, still protesting.

'I'm taking the car, Tom, up to the hospital. Mourna, your niece, has been raped.'

He was shocked and for a moment couldn't take the news in. 'What? Mourna? What are you talking about?'

'News came through while you were busy in the kitchen that Mourna is very ill. I'm going to the hospital to be with Oonagh and Gabriel.'

'I'll go with you. I'll ... '

'No, Tom. You're not going anywhere with me. I want you out of here when I get back. Out of my life forever.'

'What, Moll? What are you ...?'

'You heard me, Tom. Don't be here when I get back.'

His mouth fell open and his eyes popped, looked as if they'd fall out.

'Wha—?'

'I'm sick of it, Tom. Sick of it all. It's over.'

'But this was the first time, I swear it!'

'Don't swear, Tom. You must think me a fool or something. I'm fed up with your little Hot Chicken waitresses, fed up with *you*, if it comes to that. I don't even *like* you any more.'

'Going to condemn a man for one little slip, one little mistake … '

But she had gone and he was left staring at the exhaust smoke, alone and bewildered, protesting his innocence to the sea and the sky.

Chapter Seventy

Molly drove up the hill without looking back. She drove past the Grand, stuck her two fingers in the air, and drove right on by to the hospital. She found Oonagh and Gabriel in a peaceful antiseptic-smelling room, sitting beside their daughter's bed. Molly put her arm over Oonagh's shoulder.

'You'll have to take a break, Oonagh dear,' she said. 'You've been here a long time. I'm sorry I did not come sooner.'

'I'll stay as long as it takes her to get better,' Oonagh said dully.

'How is she?'

Gabriel looked up at her. 'The same. She's deep in shock.'

'What did the doctors say?'

'They say it'll take time.'

There were tears staining his cheeks and they began to flow again, a sob breaking from his chest, hurting him. He looked old, Molly thought, very old. It was the tragedy, Molly thought, the two of them, unable to understand, holding each other's hands, holding on to each other, looking tired and grey and worn out.

Mourna lay like the sleeping beauty, a beautiful corpse-like effigy. There was no glimmer of her warm and loving personality, no sign of animation. She looked waxen, and lying there under the white sheet, spiritless, as if life had left her.

'I think,' Molly said suddenly, 'You should take her home.'

Gabriel and Oonagh looked up at her. Hope appeared in Oonagh's eyes.

'Oh, could we, do you think?'

'I'm sure you could. As long as she has medical supervision. And her own doctor in Dublin can attend her. He knows her.'

It had not occurred to Oonagh that they had any choice in the matter. She obeyed doctors as if they were oracles handing down orders. Their authority was unquestionable. Mourna was here and the doctors would send her home when they thought fit. They were simply waiting.

'I'll ask,' Molly said, and left the room.

They sat there, hand in hand, watching. Now and again Gabriel or Oonagh said something to their child but there was no acknowledgement. Now and again Gabriel sniffed and Oonagh moaned sadly.

Molly returned. 'You can take her. I've spoken to Dr Samuels. He'll talk to you. He is quite willing. Said it might be a very good thing.'

'Really, Molly?'

'Yes, Oonagh. You see, I think, and they agree, she'd be better at home. In her own room, surrounded by her own things.'

396

'Yes. Oh, yes.' Molly saw Oonagh was weeping now. Her tears flowed. She blew her nose with a wringing wet handkerchief. Her face became blotched and Gabriel hung on to her, crying too.

'Oh God, I could kill that man,' Molly muttered. 'Bloody German.'

'We'll go home?' Oonagh begged Gabriel, sobbing.

'Yes, pet. We'll go home.'

'I've chucked Tom out,' Molly said. Oonagh looked at her a glimmer of interest in her swollen eyes.

'Yes. Caught him with Dymphna, then Aggie. So I told him to get lost.'

'Do you mean it, Molly?' Gabriel looked at her keenly. 'After all, he is your husband.'

'Oh? And I should put up with it, is that it? Like poor Mourna here? In this bloody male society ... Oh, I'm sorry, Gabriel. I didn't mean that.'

'It's all right, Moll. We're all under a strain. I know Tom is weak but he loves you, I'm sure he does.'

'Well, Gabriel, that's not good enough. He's a skirt-chasing weak little bastard!' Molly said bitterly. 'And I'm worth more'.

Oonagh glanced at Mourna's still frame as if she was afraid the news would affect her unconscious daughter.

'Shush, Moll. Think of Mourna.'

'A few bits of news might bring her back,' Molly said.

Gabriel patted his wife's hand. 'Oh dear, oh dear!' Oonagh gave a shuddering sigh and wiped her face with her saturated hankie. Molly took it from her and felt in her pocket.

'Here. Here's a fresh one,' she said, and Oonagh took it without noticing and blew her nose again.

'I'm sending Laughlin, Emmett and Emer up to town in Ardel's care,' Molly said.

'Ardel?' Oonagh looked startled. She had forgotten all their other problems in the shadow of this terrible event.

397

'Yes. He's all right. He's sorted his problem.'

'What was his problem, Molly?' Gabriel asked.

She sighed. 'It was Banan. He owed Banan and the Organization.'

'He did what?' Gabriel looked at her, aghast. 'Is there no end to the shocks I'm getting this day?'

'Oh, don't fret yourself, Gabriel. It's all been dealt with. I've felt it was partly my fault, but I think Ardel's learned his lesson. These weeks shut in have changed his view of life entirely.'

'But what did he *do*?'

'He did a job for Banan.' Molly shook her head. 'Banan's a lost cause. He'll follow in his father's footsteps right or wrong and end up like his father, dead. He can't help himself and there's no talking to him. Ardel did this job, taking Billy Macken to Dun Laoghaire. He was paid for it. Well, you know what happened then. Billy Macken was picked up. They'd have shot Ardel … '

Oonagh cried, 'Oh, no, no, *no*!' And Molly continued, 'Hush, Oonagh love, they'd not hurt Banan's cousin.'

'They harmed him enough on the train,' Gabriel said bitterly.

Oonagh was crying, 'Oh no! Oh no! Oh no!' her hand on her heart, and Gabriel took it in his own and patted it.

'Now calm down, Mother,' he said soothingly, shooting warning glances at Molly. 'She's had enough shocks, God help us, Moll, and she's not well either.'

Molly's eyes widened. 'She was pregnant,' he told his sister-in-law. 'She lost the baby.'

Molly pulled a chair over and sat down on Oonagh's other side. 'Oh, God help you, love. God'n you've had enough shocks to kill a saint.'

She put her arms around her sister-in-law and rubbed her cheek against Oonagh's forehead. 'There now, darlin'. We'll look after you. We will take care of you. We'll get you back to Dublin an' your own home.'

'I'd like that, Molly.' Oonagh sobbed. 'But about Ardel?'

'Now, I told ye, don't worry. See, they roughed him up because they wanted their money back. They don't think he's an informer. All they want is the money.'

She saw the piteously anxious expression on Oonagh's face and embraced her again. 'It's all right, dear, I keep telling you.'

'How could it be? Ardel has no money,' Gabriel said.

'Ardel came to me. I'm not short, you know that. He told me about Banan and I gave him cash. Banan told me Ardel gave it to him this morning. I told Ardel not to tell Banan I gave it to him. So, it is all fixed up. Ardel promised never to do anything like that again. It's all settled.'

'I'm glad you think so, Molly! I don't like my children being mixed up in illegal organisations. And I don't like them going to anybody else when they're in trouble. Ardel's got to learn that everything cannot be fixed that easily.'

'Gabriel. Oh, Gabriel,' Oonagh sighed, 'don't let's quibble now. You can speak to Ardel when we're home … when we're home.' She ached to be there in her house in Griffith Avenue. She ached for familiar things around her. She had an irrational belief that when they went back there everything, including Mourna, would revert to the way they were before they left for Dranmore.

Molly thought, oh, Banan, Banan, you're your father's son. You'll break my heart some day just as poor Mourna, through no fault of her own, has broken Oonagh's.

'Now listen,' she said to Oonagh, 'I'm sending Ardel in charge of your lot and Mena and Roac, up to Dublin on the train. Mrs Flanagan has been wonderful, but her next guests will be arriving and she needs to air out the rooms and prepare them.'

'Of course she does.' Oonagh looked a little relieved. Getting ready to leave gave her hope.

'Now, don't start worrying about Mrs Flanagan,' Molly said, 'I just want to brief you about the arrangements. Dot and Ben will, of course, return by train. They'll keep an eye on our kids. They sent their apologies and will be in to see you later. They have gone up to the hotel.' She frowned. 'Though what they wanted to see Eddie Benson about I can't imagine. Some hairbrained idea of Dot's, I suppose. You know her!'

'Yes. I'm just as glad. I don't think I could face her at this moment,' Oonagh said.

'I thought she wasn't on speaking terms with Eddie?' Gabriel asked. He could hear himself talk, hear the words emerging from his mouth, but felt himself not present, apart from everything. He shook his head. It hurt where he had banged it against the wall.

'Yes, I thought so too. But you should have seen her. She was full of herself. "I want to speak to Mr Benson," she said to me, and you should have seen her eyes, Gabriel, she looked as if she had won a prize. Anyhow, that's where she is and I've delivered her message.'

'I should send a message to the Bensons to thank them … to thank them for the party,' Oonagh suddenly said, then shuddered, a terrible trembling shaking her body, and Molly held her as tightly as she could and went on talking in a calm voice.

'You can do that later, my dear. Everyone understands. We must concentrate on Mourna,' she soothed her. 'Eddie and Colista are driving back. They are taking Briana and Iain. You know about them?'

Gabriel nodded. 'Apparently they have given their blessing to Bri and Iain. But I don't know … ' He hesitated. 'I don't know. Everything is happening so fast.'

'Didn't you know all about it really, before you came? That Briana and Iain were in love?' Molly asked. 'Just as I knew about Tom. We should be more honest about things, shouldn't we? But as you yourself said, Gabriel, don't let's think about that now. Just let's concentrate on Mourna.'

'Well, Briana is radiant,' Oonagh said. 'She was so upset when she saw Mourna today, but she had this aura about her, like Mourna used … ' Once more the trembling shook her from head to foot and Molly tightened her hold.

'Rita is scandalizing the whole place by moving in with Barney Boland, without the blessing of the priest,' she told them.

Gabriel smiled for the first time, 'Ah, that's grand. Isn't it, love?'

But Oonagh wasn't listening. She was holding her daughter's hand against her cheek, bathing it in her tears.

'What about the kids?'

'Brigid and Des? They think they've died and gone to heaven,' Molly laughed. 'They are going to stay here in Dranmore, at the seaside, and spend their vacations in Florida. In the United States of America, for God's sake!'

She laughed, a big happy belly laugh, and Oonagh saw Mourna's eyes flicker.

'Look, look, she stirred when Molly laughed.'

'Laugh again, Molly. Laugh!'

'I can't. Not just like that.'

'Try. Oh, try.'

'I'm trying to tell you that I'll take you both and Mourna back home in my car.'

'Oh, that's very kind of you, Molly.'

'Not at all.'

'Only laugh, Molly, laugh!'

'But what about Tom?' Gabriel asked.

'Tom can walk!' Molly said, and laughed, but this time it was tinged with pain and Mourna did not react.

'A lot has happened,' she said. 'You lost the babby, Ardel was beaten up. Poor Mourna … '

'But Bri is happy. Rita too.'

'And guess what I saw?' Molly brightened. 'On the sand, this morning, early?'

'What?' Gabriel asked.

'The tide was out and some girl had drawn a huge heart, the dimensions of a house, enormous, on the damp sand. In the heart, in huge letters ... you couldn't read from down on the beach, you had to read from up on the wall above ... '

'Well, what? What was written?'

'I LOVE YOU LAUGHLIN AND I'M NOT ASHAMED TO SAY IT. It was signed H. Does he know a Helen or a Hetty? Who do you suppose it was?'

Gabriel smiled. 'They're all growing up.'

'It's been a very strange holiday,' Molly said.

'It's been a nightmare,' Oonagh whispered. She still held her daughter's hand tightly in hers.

'For Rita it's been the realization of a dream. A happy ending,' Molly remarked.

'And for Briana and Iain,' Gabriel added.

'Eddie and Colista had a cushy time as usual,' Molly mused. 'Everyone doing their bidding. Running around, having everything their own way. I wonder what Dot wanted with them?'

'Yes, it's odd.'

'Is Joe all right?' Oonagh asked.

'Yes. Maisie is with him. He's been dry for a few days now. But Maisie will look after him. She always does.'

'My mother?' Gabriel enquired.

'She's with Emmett. He's another who's cheered up a lot. The holiday did him good.'

'Yes. He's taken a fancy to Joe, oddly enough. They go for walks together, would you believe?'

'I'm not sure that's a good thing,' Oonagh said, lips pursed.

'Oh, he'll do the boy no harm and it'll help Emmett a bit with the realities of life, get his head out of the clouds.' Molly stood. 'Well, I'll talk to the nurse and see about leaving. See about getting you home.'

402

Griffith Avenue. The house would welcome them, Oonagh thought. She'd have so much to do, she wouldn't have to sit, just sit, watching her beloved daughter like a corpse in this terrible hospital cot. She could tend her and feed her and bring her back to warm life. Get her to smile again. Get her to forget.

She fingered her miraculous medal. Please Mary, Mother of God, help her, she prayed, eyes closed. She could feel the tears squeeze under her eyelids and run down her cheeks. How many tears had she shed? A million? Two million? Mother's tears. The overwhelming desire to suffer for one's child. Remove the pain, O Lord, and give it to me. I'll take it. I am strong. She's only a babe. Such a short time from the infant at my breast.

Emmett said there was a purpose to everything. If so, what could be the purpose in this wanton destruction of her most precious child? She did not know, could not imagine. But she would have to believe, have to have faith.

Chapter Seventy-One

Gabriel opened the door to Dot's nervous knock. Instead of her usual twitter she remained silent, then went to Oonagh and put her arm around her sister-in-law's shoulders in silent sympathy.

Then Molly came back. 'It will be all right, Oonagh love,' she said, and when she saw Dot, 'You mustn't ... ' Then stopped as Dot, still patting Oonagh, hit them with the bombshell.

'I'm so sorry about this. It is a tragedy, Oonagh love.'

She took a breath. 'But it wasn't Kurt.'

'What?' Gabriel looked at her in disbelief. 'But … '

'No,' Dot was adamant, 'it wasn't him. Maggie saw him, on the beach. She said they were playing "Goodnight, Sweetheart". That's always the last dance. And the doctor said twelve, it happened.'

Oonagh shook her head. They had made up their minds about Kurt. 'No,' she said. 'No, it *was* him. Mourna said so. She said his name. Maggie must have been wrong.'

'It wasn't only Maggie who saw him. It was Emer and Brigid. They were coming back from the Beauty Contest.'

'Mourna *could* have been calling for him,' Molly said.

They all remained silent, rearranging their thoughts.

'Then who …?' Gabriel looked around, perplexed. 'Jesus, who?'

'We don't know, Gabriel,' Dot said hastily. 'Maybe we'll never know. You don't want this to become public, do you? Mourna would never survive that. Everywhere she went, people whispering, "That's the girl who was raped." No, leave it, Gabriel. All we know, it wasn't Kurt.'

'Yes, leave it, Gabriel,' Oonagh wept. 'Just leave it.'

'It wasn't the German,' he whispered. 'It's hard to take it in.' He shook his head. We need someone to blame, he thought. I need someone to hate.

'If she was calling for him … if when she called his name she was asking for him, maybe it would help if she saw him?' Molly suggested.

Gabriel looked doubtful. 'It's hard to stop thinking of him as a villain, but I suppose … '

'We could write to him. Let him know.' Oonagh looked up. 'We'll have to apologise,' she said. 'He was treated disgracefully, if he was innocent. *I* treated him disgracefully.'

'Shamefully. If he was innocent,' Gabriel said. 'He was done a terrible injury.'

'Well, he *is* innocent,' Dot said. 'Ask Emer or Brigid.'

'Maybe we should telephone him when we get back to Dublin?' Gabriel said.

'But he's here!' Molly cried. 'I thought you knew.'

They all looked at her. 'I saw him. He's in the waiting room. He's been there almost from the beginning. The nurse said he'd got off the train and come here and he wasn't going to budge until he could see Mourna. I asked her to evict him, throw him out, but she said she couldn't. I'll get him, if that's okay?'

The German came quietly into the room. He didn't look at anyone except Mourna. He went directly to the bed, knelt beside her, opposite Oonagh, and took her hand in his. There were tears on his cheeks and he looked exhausted.

'I couldn't leave her,' he whispered. 'Oh Mourna, Mourna, sweet sleeping beauty.' He laid his face beside hers and kissed her cheek. 'I'll take care of you, my love,' he said. 'Listen, *leibling*, I love you. Hear me? I love you.'

There was a little gasp as Mourna turned her face towards his, only fractionally, an imperceptible movement, a stirring. The flutter of her eyelashes was only a butterfly's breath and her fingers tightened, a tiny tremor in the hands that held them so tenderly. Oonagh's hands. Kurt's hands. But they all felt those things. They saw those things.

Hope was born in the room. Mourna would never recover completely, Oonagh knew that. She had been brutally damaged, but perhaps this man could help to heal her. Perhaps. Perhaps. Oonagh could only hope and pray.

She smiled across the bed at him. 'We will take her home,' she said.

'I will come every day.'

She sighed. They would all go home. Life had to continue. It had to be lived, badly or well. It happened to you and you could not escape it. Except in death. She shivered. At least she had not lost any of them. They loved

405

her and they were alive, her children. At least she was here to care for Mourna who needed her and this stranger across her bed. They would grow close because of his love for her daughter.

And she had Gabriel at her side. Her rock, her shield, her refuge, her strength.

She took a deep steady breath. They would go home to Griffith Avenue, and the holiday in Dranmore would finally be over.

THE GREEN YEARS

Genevieve Lyons

In the lush, idyllic countryside of County Wicklow, two friends share their childhood years . . .

Aisling, rich and beautiful, looks forward to a charmed life. But disappointment and tragedy are to shadow her as her career as an actress is shattered and love eludes her.

Camilla, improverished but fiercely proud, learns early to expect nothing for free and it is in Dublin that she finally finds the success and fame for which she has fought for so long.

As Aisling's life deteriorates into the self-destruction of alcoholism it is Camilla who stands by her, who reminds her of the precious green years of their youth and who shows her how to realise those far-off dreams of happiness and love.

From the beauty of Ireland and the quiet charm of Tuscany to the sensuality of South America, *The Green Years* is the passionate, vivid story of two women and the friendship that shapes their lives.

FICTION

DARK ROSALEEN

Genevieve Lyons

She was a gypsy woman, as wild as she was beautiful.
They called her Rosaleen. Dark Rosaleen – after
Ireland . . .

Some might say their love had been destined. He came to
the old ruins one pale-gold day, drawn there by the
sweetness of her song. He came and he stayed. But he was
Creagh Jeffries, aristocrat and son of Ireland, and he
could not stay for long – could love no woman as much
as he loved his country and its cause. Not even her, Dark
Rosaleen, the mother of his child. But the legacy of their
love would set into motion a chain of events that would
change both their worlds forever.

From the opulence of Usher Castle to the slums of
Dublin, from the lush countryside of Wicklow to the
dazzling decadence of Paris in the 1860s, here is a story
peopled with unforgettable characters, filled with life and
love. Here is a story that only Ireland could have
inspired.

'Engaging' *Irish Times*

FICTION

☐	The Palucci Vendetta	Genevieve Lyons	£4.99
☐	Zara	Genevieve Lyons	£4.50
☐	The Green Years	Genevieve Lyons	£3.50
☐	Slievelea	Genevieve Lyons	£3.99
☐	Dark Rosaleen	Genevieve Lyons	£3.50

Warner Books now offers an exciting range of quality titles by both established and new authors. All of the books in this series are available from:

Little, Brown and Company (UK) Limited,
P.O. Box 11,
Falmouth,
Cornwall TR10 9EN.

Alternatively you may fax your order to the above address. Fax No. 0326 376423.

Payments can be made as follows: cheque, postal order (payable to Little, Brown and Company) or by credit cards, Visa/Access. Do not send cash or currency. UK customers and B.F.P.O. please allow £1.00 for postage and packing for the first book, plus 50p for the second book, plus 30p for each additional book up to a maximum charge of £3.00 (7 books plus).

Overseas customers including Ireland, please allow £2.00 for the first book plus £1.00 for the second book, plus 50p for each additional book.

NAME (Block Letters) ....

....

ADDRESS ....

....

....

☐ I enclose my remittance for _____

☐ I wish to pay by Access/Visa Card

Number ⬚⬚⬚⬚⬚⬚⬚⬚⬚⬚⬚⬚⬚⬚⬚⬚⬚⬚

Card Expiry Date ⬚⬚⬚⬚